# An Inessential Liaison

## FRANCES TALBOT

HOPPING HARE BOOKS

Sur les champs sur l'horizon
Sur les ailes des oiseaux
Et sur le moulin des ombres
J'écris ton nom

[On the fields on the horizon
On the wings of birds
And on the mill of shadows
I write your name]

From *Liberté*, by Paul Eluard, *Poésie et verité 1942* [recueil clandestin]; *Au rendez-vous allemand* [1945, Les Editions de Minuit])

# Contents

For more information, contact: frances.t@hoppingharebooks.com.

First published in Great Britain in 2022 by Hopping Hare Books

ISBN 978-1-7390971-0-3 (paperback)

ISBN 978-1-7390971-1-0 (ebook)

www.frances.talbot.co.uk/www.hopping hare books.com

# CHAPTER ONE

## March 1943

'THE APPLES ARE NOT free, *monsieur*.'

Who did he think he was? Maybe he viewed himself as a conquering hero whose very presence here automatically entitled him to such bad manners?

Élodie had watched the two German soldiers make their way through the ever-dwindling weekly market at Sainte-Honorine-des-Anges, whose village square was dominated at one end by an ancient grey-stone church with massive oak doors. One of the men was medium height, silver-haired, distinguished; the other was taller, fair, younger. Both wore impeccable field-grey uniforms, and their highly polished boots and peaked caps marked them out as officers. The usual lively mid-morning chatter had died away as they progressed and, despite the thin spring sunshine dappling the leaves of the lime trees that lined the Place de la Mairie, the biting wind that whipped down the road was laced with mounting unease.

The men had stopped at a few stalls before reaching her own, where the older of the pair, ignoring her, had picked up an apple and taken a bite. His steel-grey eyes never wavered from her face as, seemingly mystified by her accent, he spoke to the younger man in accented French.

'What does she say?'

Élodie was gratified to see that his subordinate looked embarrassed. He avoided her cool regard and converted her words into German.

'Tell her she has a sharp tongue in that pretty head, and she'd do well to think before she speaks.'

Élodie pursed her lips at the return translation. Hateful man. Worse: arrogant pig. She glared back at him, wrinkling her nose at the strong waft of cologne that crossed the gap between them.

The officer spoke again, his anger barely controlled. 'Name?'

'Duchamp. Élodie.'

'Address?'

Élodie gave no answer, running a hand through her dark curls, which were full of knots as usual.

'*Address*!'

'Les Coquelets blancs, rue d'Argentan. And you are?'

In the ensuing silence, Madame Leroy, who had been choosing fruit when the officers stopped at the stall, now stood as if turned to stone. Élodie sighed loudly.

'I am *Major* Wolff. I suggest you remember that.' His tone was icy. He flung the apple down and ground it under his heel.

Immediately, a dog shot out from under the next stall and began to devour the crushed, sweet-smelling fruit. Élodie tensed as the Major stepped forward. If he mistreated the dog, she would not hold back, but to her astonishment the German bent down and extended a hand. She crossed her arms. This would be interesting. Blaireau, so named because his coat resembled that of a badger, didn't take kindly to strangers. Totally against his legendary nature, the dog allowed the Major to stroke his head and then rewarded him by licking his hand. Miserable traitor. Without a backward glance the Major straightened up and strode off towards the top of the square. She stared after him in disbelief.

The Lieutenant moved into her line of vision, fished in his pocket and held out a handful of coins. Élodie took one. His hands were not those of a soldier or workman—the skin was soft and the nails well shaped. She managed a clipped 'Thank you, monsieur' and handed him an apple. 'You've paid for two.'

When he reacted with an amused smile, she looked at him properly for the first time. Her first thought was that he was typically Aryan. A cliché really, with his morning-blue eyes and mid-blond hair, but that smile lit his entire face. She struggled to resist the undeniable: he was remarkably good-looking. *Au diable tout ça*—she would not admit it.

She observed the hostile glances from other stallholders. She tossed her head and smoothed her flower-sprigged apron to calm herself.

'You speak good French, monsieur.'

'My grandparents live in Alsace. I spent my childhood there.'

Élodie nodded. 'And you are...?' She pointed to the insignia on his uniform.

'Leutnant Rudolf Hoffmann, Mamselle.'

It was time to get rid of him. Handsome or not, he was a German officer.

'Well, *Leutnant* 'Offmann, I thank you for paying your fellow officer's debts.'

Some instinct distracted her attention. She looked across the road and her heart sank as she registered the unmistakeable lanky figure of Serge Martin leaning idly against the church wall, smoking. When he caught her eye, he stubbed out his cigarette on the stonework and pocketed the butt, then spat contemptuously and headed in their direction. She was immediately on alert. Surely he wouldn't cause trouble?

She looked back at the Lieutenant, who was apparently in no hurry to leave.

'Was there anything else?'

He shook his head.

Serge came to a halt, his eyes still on Élodie, then reached across the German and picked up an apple. The Lieutenant raised his eyebrows but said nothing.

'You're not going to charge an old friend, I'm sure?' Serge was clearly aping the incident with Major Wolff.

Élodie clicked her tongue in exasperation. Why was he always so damned objectionable?

She stuck an open palm in his direction. 'I'm not a charity worker.'

'Really? I thought you'd do anything for a good cause, *chérie*, specially your own.'

His tone was scornful as he bounced the apple from one hand to the other.

'There's no need for rudeness to this young lady.' The Lieutenant's annoyance was clear in the wash of pink that tinged his cheeks.

Serge looked him up and down. 'Well, you wouldn't really know if she was a lady or not, would you? Or maybe you're hoping to find out?' He let his words trail, threw a few coins onto the stall, and sauntered away.

The Lieutenant took two steps after him but halted when Élodie said quietly, 'Let him go. Please.'

He inclined his head, adjusted his cap, and walked away with an easy, athletic gait to join the Major, who was waiting further up the square tapping his gloves on his thigh impatiently.

Old Guillaume leant over from the neighbouring stall. 'Don't play with fire, Élodie, or you're bound to get burnt.'

Élodie stuck out her chin and gave him a tight smile before realising she still had Mme Leroy's string bag. She stashed it under the trestle—she could always drop it off later. Its owner had typically scuttled away the minute the senior officer left. The Major had moved on and was now, she noticed, at the top of the square talking to the café owner Marc, instantly recognisable in his long white apron. A shiver ran through her as the German lifted a hand and pointed her out. After a moment, she dismissed her unease as Mme Leroy waddled back into view and reclaimed her shopping.

Taking a pan and brush from the trailer, Élodie skirted the stall to clear up the remaining slippery apple fragments that were turning brown. Two dark eyes were watching her from under Guillaume's stall. 'Traitor', she hissed. In response Blaireau gave a low growl and bared his teeth.

She was relieved when the last customers dwindled away. The scornful looks in her direction after the incident with the German officers had been unrelenting, though fortunately she'd managed to avoid further unwanted criticism from Guillaume. She'd known him all her life, and though he was kind he was also quick to scold. After packing what was left into the home-made bike trailer, whose once cheerful red paint had long since faded, she cleaned the stall and slid into her shabby wool jacket, grateful for the warm fabric on a chilly spring day.

When a hand squeezed her shoulder she froze, before whirling round to see her brother's puzzled face.

'Something wrong, Él?'

'Oh, Félix, *c'est toi*! No. All well.' She pulled him into a cocooning hug, instantaneously reassured by his comforting warmth. Despite the four years between them, they were like peas in a pod with their dark curly hair and slim build, though Félix had inherited his father's rich nut-brown eyes and Élodie her mother's elegant grey-green ones.

'You're not going to tell me about it then?'

He knew her too well. Denial was useless, so subterfuge it would have to be.

'Just Serge making mischief.' She gave him a version of the truth that was close enough, omitting her spat with the Major.

'Serge is a damned idiot', Félix retorted. 'Always skating on the verge of trouble. One day he'll get us all...' He stopped mid-sentence.

'All what?' His sister knew him equally well.

'No matter. D'you need a hand here?'

Élodie shook her head. 'I'm ready to go. But if you came by bike, we could ride home together?'

Félix indicated the café, its blue-and-white awning flapping in the breeze, and prepared to wheel his sister's bicycle to where his own stood propped against the wall. Élodie groaned inwardly as Guillaume shuffled over. Bypassing her, he clapped Félix on the shoulder and shook his hand. Despite his age, Guillaume's gnarled fingers grasped the younger man's hand in a grip so firm that her brother's skin whitened.

'It's good to see you, *mon garçon*. How are you?'

'I'm well, thanks. And you?'

'Mustn't grumble, though I could wish your sister had half your common sense.'

Élodie watched the old man warily. What else might he say? Félix gave her a teasing smile, laughed affectionately and put a protective arm around her.

'She's too grown up to change now, I fancy.'

The old man grunted. 'That's what I'm afraid of.' He shuffled back to his stall and whistled for Blaireau to follow him as he collected his bags and crossed to the path towards the river.

Élodie hurried Félix up the square, avoiding eye contact with the few remaining stallholders. Marc was still outside the café, rearranging chairs that had been scattered across the pavement and pushing them back under the tables with a metallic clatter. His wiry frame moved nimbly, like a boxer dodging an opponent. He acknowledged them both with a nod and a smile. Élodie raised a hand in reply and debated whether to ask him what the Major had said, but thought better of it. No need to arouse Félix's curiosity. She took a deep, appreciative sniff of the warm, inviting coffee aroma that filtered through the open café door. Doubtless the real thing was still available for the Germans.

As they made their way home along the familiar country lanes, Élodie noted that the banks were covered with primroses, glowing buttery yellow in the mild warmth of early afternoon, their heads bowing to the stiff breeze. She reflected that away from the villages and towns it was possible to believe life would one day be simpler and even happy again.

She thought about how she and Félix, born and raised on the family farm, had grown into a life of mostly hard work and little free time, customary though this was for all farming families. But that was before, in 1940, the German troops had arrived and imposed a whole raft of new rules that Élodie was inclined to disobey. She was only too aware that, among her list of failings, she had always rebelled against authority. So why should the French put the clocks forward to suit the occupiers? This might make things simpler for the Germans, but it certainly didn't suit the farming schedule. Or market-day mornings.

She remembered the day the mayor had told them at a hastily convened village meeting that Sainte-Honorine fell within what the occupiers called a strategic military zone, which encompassed a large area from Saint-Lô and Caen to the north, to Falaise and Argentan further south. Well, suddenly their quiet village was becoming entangled. And now her own feathers had been ruffled by that major today.

Their slow, pedalling peace was broken by the harsh snarl of engines approaching from behind. Two German motorcycles roared past and slewed sideways, blocking the road. Two magpies on the verge abandoned whatever carrion they had been pecking at and flapped into the air, their beaks red with bloody flesh as they screeched their shrill alarm call.

Élodie and Félix came to a stop.

One of the Germans dismounted and strutted towards them, hand outspread.

'Papers.'

Élodie grimaced. Now what? Wasn't there half an hour's respite to be had? They handed over their documents, which received annoyingly close scrutiny.

'You are going where?'

They glanced at each other. Félix replied. 'Home.'

'From?'

'The weekly market.' Élodie couldn't keep the irritation out of her voice, which elicited a scowl from her brother and a pursed mouth from the fleshy German, whose bulbous lips made her shudder.

'In the box?' He indicated the bicycle trailer.

'Unsold produce.' Two could play at this monosyllabic game.

The soldier's stare was flinty as he marched past her. He lifted the box, roughly examined the contents, then upended it.

Élodie gave a yell as the apples rolled across the road and the few remaining eggs smashed on the packed earth. Félix managed to grab her before she could attack the soldier, who sidestepped smartly and put his hand on his holster.

'Look what he's done. Such a waste!' She was struggling and furious.

'Leave it, Él. Not worth it.'

Félix loosened his grip, but only temporarily, as she immediately fought to free herself again.

The soldier had by now levelled his pistol at her.

'Enough!' Félix pushed her to the roadside and held her firm. She knew that tone. He'd used it when she misbehaved as a small child, and it had always been her limit. Her body slackened a little against his chest.

The sound of an oncoming vehicle averted further discussion. The soldier returned to his motorbike and he and his companion pulled over to the side of the road. As the car swept alongside, Élodie recognised Major Wolff in the passenger seat. The hot metal of the engine gave off a rhythmic ticking as the car idled. The Major wound down the window and the two soldiers snapped to attention. He barked what was obviously an order because they mounted their bikes and roared off. Turning in his seat, he gave Élodie a long hard stare of appraisal from head to foot, at which she squirmed imperceptibly. He touched the rim of his cap, giving her a stiff nod of acknowledgement, spoke to the driver and the car sped away. *Salopard*. She was sure he'd engineered the document check because of the market incident, and from the upward curl of his lips he clearly considered it highly amusing.

Félix let her go and she bent to pick up the discarded box. Even the few undamaged apples were visibly bruised from being hurled onto the road. She set the box back into the trailer, not looking at her brother.

'Now do you want to tell me the whole story?'

She pulled a face and kicked one of the apples towards the verge.

'I suppose that was one of the two officers you met today.'

'Mmm.'

'And I suppose you upset him somehow?'

She explained briefly, this time leaving out any mention of the Lieutenant. Félix shook his head and sighed, before ruffling her unruly hair.

'You're even more likely to cause a riot than Serge is. It's not worth calling attention to yourself or provoking them, Él. You can't win. And you won't.'

'One day. One day we'll kick their backsides.' She gave a perfect *bras d'honneur* in the direction of the now departed car.

'Oh, Él', Félix's stuttering laughter broke the tension. 'We're never going to make a lady of you, are we?"

She stuck her tongue out at him. 'Did I ever pretend to be one?' She picked up the apple she'd kicked and lobbed it at him. He ducked expertly.

'And you can't throw either.' Félix mounted his bike, pedalling away fast as she ran at him.

She followed him as speedily as she could, hampered by the unwieldy trailer but laughing now. Thank God for Félix. What would she do without him?

# CHAPTER TWO

## *April 1943*

FÉLIX SET OFF AT 11 p.m. The rest of the family were already in bed, so there had been no awkward questions to answer. Fortuitously the threatened thunderstorms had not materialised, and the banks of high cloud presented no landing obstacle. He knew the only reason for a landing tonight, rather than a drop, was to pick up an agent whose presence had become a focus for the Germans in Argentan. Nonetheless, they were also to gain a radio operator who was expected to be on the incoming flight.

Thierry was bound to have arrived in advance to place the torches for the flare path. An almost full moon was visible, the norm for such clandestine operations, but he pitied the pilot, who, it was said, would be relying on map and compass. He reached the crossroads in a little under ten minutes. A dark figure slipped out of the shadows and fell into step with him. He was glad it was Michel, the local mechanic and his oldest friend, who had volunteered tonight. He was as dependable as Thierry, knew the area like the back of his hand, and his list of local contacts was legendary. He was also powerful and harefooted. How, after a recent failed mission, he had single-handedly deflected their German pursuers before vanishing at speed down some dark alley, Félix would never fathom.

They exchanged few words en route. Both were aware of the likely dangers and were high on nervous tension. When they reached the field, Félix gave a low whistle and they waited, pressed against the hedge, for Thierry's answering signal. All was quiet apart from the snuffling of some invisible animal on the far side of the lane. Félix clamped his arms across his chest, his old dark hunting jacket no longer a match for the cool, insistent breeze. A double whistle, low and throaty, preceded the lumbering figure of Thierry, short and broad and immediately recognisable.

'Who else is with us?' Félix asked.

'Serge and Lisette.' Félix scowled. Not the answer he was hoping for. The two Martins were the least reliable in the group. Thierry was watching him closely, so he limited himself to a resigned shrug. Not his call tonight—his tough luck this time.

A few minutes later the rumble of an engine grew louder. Thierry gave and received the agreed Morse signal, Serge quickly turned on the flashlights and the pair of them retreated. The Lysander, indistinct thanks to its black-painted undercarriage, flew in low and slow scarcely above hedge height, taxied after landing and circled to the right of the two furthest lamps. The aircraft bumped to a halt on the tussocky grass, facing the way it had come. All five figures ran to the plane as the door opened. A tall man ducked as he exited, then climbed down the fixed ladder and turned to his fellow passenger, who wore coveralls and a headscarf. He took the briefcase-sized bag handed down to him and steadied her as she jumped the last few feet. He held out his hand to Thierry. 'I'm Doug. And this is Clémence.' The young woman was struggling out of her cumbersome overalls, revealing a dark jumper and slacks beneath, as Félix reached out to take the bag from Doug.

'I'll take that, thanks', she said in impeccable French, neatly retrieving the case and giving him a half-smile.

Félix noted her candid blue eyes and the wisps of blonde hair that escaped her scarf. Another time, another place, he thought briefly, she would have been exactly his type. He ran his hand across his chin and was conscious that a day's stubble gave him the appearance of a vagabond.

Doug was talking quietly with Thierry and a dark-clad figure, obviously the departing agent, who had slid out of the shadows to join them. The English crewman climbed back into the plane and handed down three heavy boxes. 'That's most of what you asked for. They aim to send the rest next time there's a drop.' The last item was a battered cardboard suitcase, which the girl allowed Félix to take. Thierry eyed Clémence and then him with one eyebrow raised, a look of amusement lighting his normally unfathomable, broken-nosed countenance. He followed this with an almost imperceptible nod in the direction of Lisette. Félix turned and saw the hostile glare at Clémence that was bestowed on him in turn. He sighed. This was exactly why the Martins were more trouble than they were worth. He put down the case and stacked the boxes with Michel.

The pilot leant out of the cockpit and tapped his watch. Doug raised a hand to the assembled group and clambered back on board behind his new passenger. The aircraft been on the ground less than five minutes. The engine roared, the tail lifted, and the Lysander picked up speed and took off, clearing the hedge by about ten feet.

'*Vite!*' Thierry recaptured their attention. 'Time to go in case the Boche are alert tonight.'

The group hefted the three boxes and followed Thierry to the copse at the eastern end of the field, where they stashed them under a thick covering of fallen branches for retrieval later. A cloying odour of damp earth and decay rose and spread as they rearranged the woodpile. Clémence still had a tight grip on the smaller bag and followed Félix, who had retrieved her suitcase, towards the truck that Thierry had parked behind the hedge some distance from the field gate.

Clémence stopped short of the vehicle and pointed at the roof of the cab, on which were bolted three cylinders. 'What on earth—?'

Félix followed her gaze. 'Runs on gas. A little modification by our mechanic and the local blacksmith.' He omitted to identify Michel and Thierry by name.

Thierry climbed into the driver's seat. He motioned for Clémence to sit beside him and Lisette followed her. The other three men stowed the flashlights as they jumped onto the cargo bed and sat down with their backs to the cab. Félix strained to follow the conversation he could hear through the open window.

'It's too dangerous to take you into town now. There's too much risk of a German patrol. Félix will stay with you overnight somewhere safe.'

Lisette frowned and glared at him. 'He doesn't need to. I could do that.'

'No need. It's all arranged.'

Lisette threw herself against the seat back with a petulant 'Pfft!' and crossed her arms. 'Well, I don't think it's right.'

'That's enough. My decision.'

Thierry forestalled further conversation by starting the engine. The truck bucked as he drove it slowly to the gateway, hesitated before turning left and headed back in the direction from which they'd come.

As anticipated, there was no traffic and the earlier clusters of cloud had cleared completely. Thierry drove without headlights on the moonlit lanes, turning right after approximately two miles onto a grassy track that led to an old barn, its wood silvered by age. He eased the truck through a broad semi-circle and stopped beside a battered zinc water trough. Félix heard Lisette start to speak in a whiny voice that was silenced by a swift rebuke from Thierry. He watched as she flounced sulkily out of the truck to change places with Clémence.

Félix retrieved the cases, plus a box Thierry had indicated earlier, and set them down by the heavy barn doors. He undid the padlock with a key he retrieved from under the trough, picked up the box and motioned for Clémence to follow him inside with the cases she was already clutching. Unfortunately there was no other exit, but the rarely visited building was so secluded that it was considered safe enough. With the doors closed behind them, he orientated himself with a quick sweep of torchlight. Crossing to a bench, he lit a couple of candle stumps that were set on saucers. They cast only a dim, flickering light. The barn was stacked with bales of tarpaulin-covered hay that filled most of the interior and would provide some insulation against the night-time chill. There was a strong smell of dried grass mingled with the fusty odour of an unaired room. From outside, the sound of the truck grew fainter as it rumbled off up the track. Félix indicated a pair of battered old chairs beside a small, rough wooden table.

'Welcome to the Hotel Ritz.'

She laughed softly, and as her face reflected the candle-glow the purple smudges of tiredness beneath her eyes were visible. He had no idea what time her journey had started but he guessed it had been a long day of preparation and stress. He inspected the contents of the box Thierry had provided

'Let's eat. You look as if you're about ready to get some sleep.'

'I'm not even sure I'm hungry, I'm so tired.'

Félix set out bread, cheese, pâté and two plates. A bottle of wine followed, and one chipped enamel cup.

'Sorry, looks as if the Ritz is out of glasses.'

'No problem. It all goes down the same way.'

She smiled and Félix registered again how stunningly attractive she was. Business, not pleasure tonight, he told himself. He poured wine into the cup and passed it to her, his hand touching hers as he did so.

'You're ice cold!

She shook her head. 'No, just tired. I'm always that way when I'm tired—or hungry. Or both. But the smell of the cheese and pâté is reviving me.'

Félix pushed one of the plates closer. 'Help yourself.' He watched as she surveyed the food carefully. She frowned and looked up, her blue eyes soft in the flickering light.

'Is there a knife in that box by any chance?'

As Félix checked, the sound of a vehicle drew closer, its tyres rasping on the stony track. He was on his feet in a flash and reached the door in three strides, pulling a pistol from his jacket on the way. He indicated for Clémence to move behind the hay bales to her right. It was too late to blow out the candles as footsteps approached the door.

Félix braced himself against the door jamb, then heard Thierry's distinctive low double whistle. He opened the door cautiously until he could see that Thierry was alone. He appeared to be carrying a crate. Félix whistled in return and opened the door just enough to let him in.

'It's OK', Félix called quietly as Thierry dumped the crate on a bench inside the door. When Clémence joined them, Félix was surprised to see that she too had a pistol in her hand.

She shrugged. 'Backup.' She paused, adding as the two men glanced at each other, 'I *am* trained to use it.'

Thierry unpacked a sizeable enamel bowl, a threadbare towel, a facecloth and a small, cream-coloured bar of soap. He squinted at Clémence, clearly embarrassed, as he finally took out a large flagon of water.

'When I got home my wife said we couldn't expect a young lady not to wash before bedtime. So I brought these.'

As Clémence thanked him effusively, Félix could see even in the feeble light that Thierry's face was reddening. He clapped his friend on the back.

'Quite right too. And well done, Yvette. Some wine before you leave?'

Thierry shook his head and made for the door. 'I'll be back in the morning with the bikes. Around seven-thirty. If it gets to eight-fifteen, don't wait any longer. It's only twenty minutes' walk across the fields.'

After he'd gone, Clémence picked up the cup and drank. To Félix's amusement, she made a face as the rough wine flowed into her mouth. She offered him the cup. It was an intimate gesture, he thought, between two strangers. Nevertheless, he took a swig from the chipped side and wiped his hand across his face as the liquid trickled down his chin.

After they'd eaten, Félix retrieved blankets and pillows from a chest. They felt damp, but they'd have to do. He indicated the washing things.

'I'll go outside. Is fifteen minutes enough?'

Clémence's expression relaxed. He made the excuse that he wanted to smoke anyway—a clearly hazardous activity in a hay-filled barn, he explained unnecessarily—and slipped out into the inky darkness. Somewhere close by a tawny owl was hooting and he could hear the throbbing of a distant engine, but otherwise all was quiet. Even though the barn was two hundred feet from the road behind a dense stand of trees, he slowly circumnavigated the wooden building and arrived back at the doors, which faced a wooded valley, before lighting a cigarette and inhaling deeply. As he leant against the rough woodwork and exhaled, the distinctive aroma of Gauloise Caporal filled the air, and he watched the smoke float away on the light breeze. He took his time, reflecting on the evening's events. After a few minutes more, he gave a firm pinch to the butt and put it back in the packet before ruffling the soil with his boot to scatter the fallen ash.

Tapping softly on the door he waited till Clémence appeared, fully dressed once more. She smelt of a soft perfume that Félix didn't recognise but which was at once earthy and floral, and distractingly sensual. He stepped past her and headed swiftly for the hay bales.

# CHAPTER THREE

## *April 1943*

ÉLODIE STRETCHED AND TURNED over. Through the gap in her flimsy bedroom curtains a faint glimmer of pale apricot was visible as the dawn determinedly nudged the night aside. She groaned: time to get up. She pushed the blankets away and shivered. It might be spring, but the room felt glacial and she was glad of her long-sleeved winter nightdress. She picked up the pink-flowered porcelain jug from the dresser and ran downstairs for warm water. Cold was bearable in the summer, but not on a freezing April morning.

The gloom of the kitchen was bathed in gold by the slanting rays of the rising sun, but the room was as silent as a tomb. Where was her mother? Élodie sighed in sympathy as she spotted the aproned figure already outside in the vegetable plot pulling up leeks and adding them to a pile of kale, doubtless for the midday meal. It was bitter even in the house, and she massaged her own cold-blanched fingers as she watched her mother's breath steaming in the freezing outdoor air.

Not for the first time, Élodie wondered whether her mother ever regretted abandoning her livelihood as a seamstress to marry a farmer. If she did, she never said so, but doing the occasional sewing job for Madame Lagrange up at the Manoir must be a poor substitute for making pretty dresses. Élodie shivered again and hurried back upstairs with the jug, warming her free hand on the hot porcelain. She decanted the water into the matching bowl, washed and rubbed herself dry without further ado.

Back in the kitchen, she found her mother had already cleaned and sliced the leeks and was chopping the potatoes she'd fetched from the shed. Élodie picked up a handful of the kale and made a face. Her mother smacked her hand gently.

'What was once food only for the animals has to satisfy us now, my child.'

Élodie shrugged. She'd grown used to the odd things that supplemented their diet these days. Speaking of which, the strange, sweet tobacco-smoke aroma coming from the stove told her that her mother had made a pot of chicory coffee. She wrinkled her nose and poured them each a small bowlful.

'Where's Félix? I didn't hear him come in last night.'

Rose frowned and paused before sliding the chopped potatoes into the cast-iron casserole that stood on the kitchen table. 'I've no idea. He said he might not be home but wouldn't tell me where he was going.'

'Perhaps he's found a beautiful girl, Maman?' Teasing her mother usually elicited a tight-lipped smile, and today was no exception.

Rose put down the chopping board. 'Have you any idea what he's up to, *chérie*? He's becoming more and more uncommunicative. He thinks I can't see through him when he's so evasive, but it means he's doing something he knows I won't like.'

Élodie shook her head. 'Nothing he's told me about, no, but don't worry, we're all aware he can be an expert *baratineur* when he wants to—a real smooth-talker.'

She reached across and squeezed her mother's hand. Rose gave her a taut smile.

'Well, if he does tell you anything, you'll let me know?'

Élodie nodded, not wanting to say something she might later regret. She leapt up from her chair as the hall clock struck seven.

'I'm late today. I must see to the hens.'

Outside, Élodie pulled her old jacket tightly around her and rubbed her arms to warm herself. She smiled to see frosted cowslips on the bank, bravely defying the chill, and looked up as she heard the sibilant shriek of a swift. High above, six of them scythed through the clear air on swept-back, silent wings. At last, two welcome signs of spring. The sudden whine of engines from the main road dispelled her good humour in a flash. An early German patrol, no doubt, destroying the morning peace. She wrenched open the bolts to the enclosure in exasperation and sucked the knuckle she snagged, sidestepping as the chickens bustled out competitively onto the dewy grass. In the henhouse, the noise from the road was almost inaudible. She picked up the first basket and concentrated on collecting the large white eggs. Her father was right about one thing: the black-and-white Gournay chickens were prolific layers.

Once the hens were fed and watered, she picked up the two full baskets and sauntered back to the house. Her father appeared from the direction of the mist-shrouded lower fields as she reached the yard.

'You're late this morning. And your brother's nowhere to be found.'

Élodie laughed. 'Oh Papa, stop being such a grouch!'

Henri glared at her. 'What d'you expect? The whole bloody place is overrun by the Boche.'

As if in confirmation, the sound of an approaching engine grew louder on the driveway. Henri waited only long enough to see that it was clearly a German vehicle before stomping off into the house. Élodie followed him, unwilling to deal with whoever was about to delay their impending breakfast.

Rose turned from the stove as the two of them entered the kitchen. 'Did I hear a car?' A peremptory knock made her jump. She frowned at her husband and daughter and headed for the door.

'*Guten Morgen, Madame.*'

Henri stamped into the scullery, slamming the door behind him.

Élodie's skin prickled. She recognised at once that the voice belonged to Major Wolff. He followed her mother into the kitchen and immediately his eyes were on her, devouring her with unnerving prurience.

'Ah yes, this is your daughter?' Before Rose could answer, he added, 'We've already met.'

Élodie sensed her mother's confusion. 'At the market, Maman.' She turned to the officer, who was miraculously capable of speaking French today. 'Good morning, Major. To what do we owe the honour of your visit?' His tight-lipped expression told Élodie that her sarcasm was not lost on him. Serve him right for disturbing them. The major turned to her mother.

'We shall require three dozen eggs per week to be delivered to the Manoir, Madame. I assume you can comply with this request?'

Rose's irked expression reflected that she was not being presented with a choice. 'I think we could manage that, Major.'

Wolff was again watching Élodie, who jutted her chin out and returned his stare unblinkingly.

'*Wie die Mutter, so die Tochter*', he muttered.

Rose frowned. '*Pardon?*'

He ignored this. 'Very well, Madame, then let us say every Friday. And in that case your children will be permitted to keep their bicycles if they register them. Otherwise, they will be requisitioned.'

Without waiting for an answer, he bowed his head fractionally, turned on his heel and left.

Élodie shook her head as her mother, open-mouthed, waited for her to speak. 'Don't worry, Maman, he's just an exceptionally rude man.'

'But what did he say in German?'

Élodie's laugh was contemptuous. 'I would guess it was "Like mother, like daughter".'

'But how does he know about your bicycles?'

'Pfft, too long a story Maman.'

Rose still looked perplexed, but instead of explaining further Élodie wrenched open the scullery door. 'You can come out now, Papa. He's gone.'

Henri appeared in the doorway. 'What did the *sale Boche* want?'

'Eggs, Papa. For his officers I assume. I doubt he could eat three dozen a week by himself.'

Henri swore. 'Free of charge, I suppose?'

'But of course, Papa. He certainly didn't offer to pay for them if that's what you mean.'

'Enough!'

Henri and Élodie stared at Rose in surprise. She rarely even raised her voice.

'We have no choice, so we will do what we have to do, and there's an end to it.'

'But not with good grace, Maman.' Élodie winked at her father. 'We could always poison the eggs.'

Rose's withering look was not unexpected. Henri eased himself into his usual chair at the head of the table as his wife poured a bowl of the chicory coffee for him. 'Is there any bread?'

'It's stale, but with plum jam it'll be edible.'

Henri grunted. 'That'll do fine.' He furrowed his brows as Rose prepared it for him, then dipped it into his coffee and ate slowly, apparently deep in thought.

Élodie supposed he was thinking about the Germans, but eventually he said, still frowning, 'And where *is* Félix this morning?'

She spread her hands wide. 'No idea, Papa. Nor has Maman.'

'Well, he knows I needed his help today and now it'll be down to me, as usual', he growled. 'Your brother needs to roll up his sleeves and get on with things.'

Élodie knew better than to answer back. How many times had she heard that well-worn refrain? It was obviously one of those days when her father was going to be ill-humoured, doubtless as result of Major Wolff's visit. Instead, she grabbed her coat and said, 'I'm going down to see if there's bread available today. I'll be back well before lunchtime.' She flicked her eyes to her father, who was finishing his coffee. 'Maybe I'll meet Félix on the way.'

Henri pushed himself up from the table without comment and pulled on his field boots, unhooked his jacket from the pegs in the hall, headed for the door and disappeared.

Rose kissed her daughter's cheek and gathered up the crockery. 'Don't forget the coupons, and if you do see Félix, you'd better warn him what mood his father's in. And please, call in to the pharmacy and see how Hélène is.'

Élodie opened her mouth to refuse but stopped short at the distressed look on her mother's face and forced a smile. She had no wish to see her older sister, who was apparently convinced she had gone up in the world since marrying the local pharmacist, but neither did she want to further upset their mother.

Élodie back-pedalled to admire a bank studded with tiny violets, which were the perfect foil for the lush lime green of the new leaves unfurling on the trees above. She sighed, remembering how Hélène had scolded her for picking road-side flowers when she was a toddler. Six months ago, she'd asked her sister why she no longer brought Lucie to visit her grandmother and an almighty row had ensued. They hadn't spoken since, so she could only guess what her reception might be at the pharmacy.

The sun was warm on her back, but even as she suppressed memories of her sister the major's visit to the farm kept resurfacing. Why had he come himself? Why not send the lieutenant or another junior officer? It unsettled her even more that she couldn't come up with a reasonable explanation.

Outside the bakery a queue had already formed. She joined the chattering women, who were shuffling forward like trained tortoises. As she greeted her old teacher, Mamselle Bonnaire, who was a little way up the line and as usual dressed in sombre black, the woman directly in front of Élodie swung round. Madame Martin looked as if she'd sucked on raw rhubarb. Élodie attempted a bright smile.

'Bonjour, Madame.'

'Hmm, Élodie Duchamp. Been making eyes at the Boche, I hear.'

Élodie wondered if she'd heard correctly. She frowned. 'Madame?'

'Serge told me how you'd made a spectacle of yourself in the market the other day.' She sniffed. 'You'll soon get yourself a bad reputation if you keep that up, I can tell you.'

The queue became silent as half a dozen pairs of eyes watched the simmering exchange. Mamselle Bonnaire tutted and shook her head. Élodie could feel her own temper rising, but this was not the time for a scene.

'I think your son is mistaken, Madame. If Serge is referring to the two German officers who stopped at my stall, they were soon on their way—and I gave them no encouragement.'

The older woman raised one eyebrow and sniffed again but didn't reply. She turned her back on Élodie and the rest of the women resumed their conversations on realising there was no credible gossip to savour.

There were three loaves left when she finally got to the counter. Mathilde Brodeur, still shy at sixteen, had become a regular fixture at the boulangerie, but was so flustered today that she dropped the bread twice. Élodie concluded she too had been the victim of Mme Martin's sharp tongue for some reason. As the girl looked close to tears, Élodie simply asked if she was well. Mathilde nodded, her long blonde hair falling across her face.

'And your sister Mireille?'

Mathilde managed a fleeting smile. 'Still pining after Félix of course, but otherwise well, thank you.'

Élodie shrugged her shoulders. 'Not my brother's keeper, I'm afraid!' They both laughed at the hopelessness of that situation and Élodie picked up the precious loaf. '*Merci et à bientôt*, Mathilde.'

There was still a queue, now even longer, as she left the shop. Envious eyes followed the loaf as she passed those still waiting. A wave of guilt engulfed her at the knowledge that, unless more bread had been baked, they were going to be disappointed. Several small, solemn children stood clutching their mothers' hands and she was tempted to divide the bread between the hungry families and go home empty-handed. But, she reasoned, her parents had a right to bread too, even though as food producers they still ate better than most. Or, at least, thus far.

She crossed the square and reluctantly pushed open the door of the pharmacy. As luck would have it, it was her brother-in-law Guy who stood behind the counter. He came out to greet her, kissing her affectionately on both cheeks.

'*Salut*, Élodie. We haven't seen you for ages.' His smile was broad and genuine.

'No, well, um, you know how it is—it's a busy time on the farm.' Élodie was fond of him and had no wish to upset him.

She acknowledged too that he doted on Hélène and their daughter. He was slim and studious, looking the more so because of his metal-rimmed spectacles, an educated man who was well qualified and treated everyone with equal courtesy.

'You are well?'

'As you see', he said.

'And Hélène?' She hesitated before adding, 'Is she here?'

'She's well, thank you, but she's taken Lucie down to the river to see the ducks. You could find her there.'

Élodie made the excuse that she must get home before her father arrived for his midday meal. 'But please tell her that Maman was asking after her and hopes she will bring Lucie to visit one day soon.'

Guy sighed. 'I'll try, Élodie, but you know how it is. It isn't that...' His words trailed away. Élodie patted his arm in reassurance.

'Don't worry, Guy. Families are all the same.'

He reached back to the shelf behind him. 'Do take something for your mother. What would she like? The stock's very limited, but I have some perfumed soap hidden here somewhere.'

Élodie beamed at him. 'Thank you, she would love that.'

Guy solemnly wrapped the small pink bar in a square of brown paper and tied it with a length of string that he fished out of a drawer. 'With our love', he said.

If only Hélène were as agreeable. Élodie thanked him again and left. There was no longer anyone outside the boulangerie, so they'd almost certainly been sent away disappointed. Damn the Boche. Since they had requisitioned a regular bread supply, the villagers had gone without. She knew, too, that supplies of most food were low in the towns, whose inhabitants now travelled to the countryside regularly at weekends in search of anything edible to augment their meagre diet.

As she collected her bicycle, a woman and small child were walking up the path from the river. Without waiting to confirm whether it was Hélène, she pushed her foot down and peddled away. After the unexpected arrival of the major this morning, she'd had quite enough irritation for one day.

# CHAPTER FOUR

## April 1943

FÉLIX WOKE EARLY, HAVING slept only fitfully. It was hard to tell in the windowless barn what time it was, but he could see a streak of pale daylight beneath the door. He looked across at Clémence, who appeared to be sound asleep, one hand hanging down below the dark-wool blanket, exposing the pale, creamy skin of her slim wrist and long fingers. She stirred almost immediately, and her eyes fluttered open. She looked startled to see Félix watching her and sat up quickly.

'Good morning. I hope I wasn't snoring?'

Félix was impressed that she'd spoken in French from the moment she woke. 'Not at all. I was glad to see you'd been able to get some rest.' He thumped the hay bale beneath him. 'Not exactly deluxe beds, are they?'

'I think I could have slept on a concrete floor last night.' She ran her hands through her hair and picked out a few strands of hay. Félix reached out and extracted a stalk she'd missed, inhaling the perfume that still lingered on her. Her eyes looked directly into his and a thrill of pleasure rocked him as she smiled again. He was aware of being unwashed and unshaven, and was suddenly lost for words. He cleared his throat.

'I'm sorry, I think there's only stale bread for breakfast.' He checked in the box Thierry had given them. 'Bless Yvette, she's put a pot of jam in here. Unfortunately, we've no coffee.'

As he spoke, the rumbling of tyres on the track outside grew louder. Fairly sure it would be his friend, Félix nonetheless took no chances, collecting his pistol as he headed for the door. A reassuring double whistle was followed by a tap on the wooden planking. Félix opened the door slowly, the ancient hinges creaking alarmingly, and was greeted by Thierry's gap-toothed grin.

'*Bonjour, vous deux.* I came early. Yvette said you would need coffee to wake you up—and she sent clean cups!'

'Your wife is a wonder, you lucky bugger. She thinks of everything.' Félix ushered him inside, where Clémence was already clearing the table of debris from the previous evening. The three of them sat and drank the coffee, Thierry perched on an upended hay bale while Félix and Clémence shared the bread and jam. Félix was amused to see Clémence looking on with distaste when a blob of jam slid off his bread as he dunked it in the coffee, spreading a greasy film across the surface.

Thierry slapped his palm on the table. 'OK, my friends, time to be going before the Boche move their fat arses.' He stole a quick sideways look at Clémence. 'Sorry for my language.'

'Couldn't have put it better myself.' She gave Thierry a dazzling smile and was rewarded with a warm grin.

They folded the blankets and stowed them with the pillows in the wooden trunk, which Félix pushed behind the hay bales out of sight. Clémence had packed everything else. As the men carried out the box and crate, she made a final check, stooping to pick up a knife lying half-hidden under a hay bale.

Félix returned for her radio and suitcase while, outside, Thierry was unloading two old bicycles from the flatbed. Félix lashed the suitcase onto the carrier of the nearest one with a length of thick twine, checking it was secure. As Clémence handed him the radio case he paused, hand in mid-air, as Thierry frowned and rubbed his chin.

'If you get stopped... Clémence, it would be safer to let me take that and deliver it to your base.'

She appeared doubtful. 'It's supposed never to leave my sight when I'm out.' She looked from one to the other. 'But what you say makes sense.' The two men were unaware of the strict rules of her training, accustomed to using only gut sense and practicality for guidance.

Thierry stowed the small case deep under his seat in the truck. He solemnly shook hands with Clémence, whose slim fingers disappeared in his bear-like grip, slapped Félix on the shoulder and climbed into the cab.

'I'll go straight into town and drop this off. Félix, I'll see you later.' With a quick wave, he disappeared up the track and was gone. The piercing squawk of a jay from somewhere near the main road signalled his progress and then there was silence.

Félix mounted one bike and Clémence followed suit on the other, struggling with the height of the crossbar.

'You have your papers?'

'In my coat.' She tapped the pocket to be sure.

'OK good. *On y va*! If we're stopped, let me do the talking, in case they ask where we're going and where we've come from.'

The morning air was still fresh as they pedalled eastwards under a pale blue sky streaked with gold, and a glance at his watch confirmed to Félix that it was not yet eight-thirty. The roads were quiet until the first buildings on the edge of town came into view. A convoy of German vehicles approached. Félix held his breath, but they didn't stop and a quick check over his shoulder confirmed they were already out of sight. He exhaled and waited till Clémence was level with him, then indicated that they should pull over to the verge.

'We're only a few minutes away now. Your room's above a draper's. You can come and go through the shop, which won't draw attention, but there's also an exit into a back alley in case of trouble. When we arrive I'll slow down—but if I don't stop it's because it's not safe. You're clear on your story?'

Clémence nodded and for the first time Félix detected an air of vulnerability about her. He couldn't guess how she must feel. Her French was mother-tongue level, though a tad too correct to his ears and her accent wouldn't pass for local, but she'd been set down in an occupied zone totally unfamiliar to her, except perhaps from maps. He snapped his attention back to their surroundings. This was neither the time nor the place to lose concentration. He checked the road and set off again. They passed several more German patrols, but none displayed any interest. Félix began to relax marginally.

They turned off the main road into a side-street that was claustrophobically confined. Félix registered that the pavements were eerily deserted, save for a few passers-by walking briskly with faces firmly averted. What the hell was going on? He quickly spotted two German motorcycles parked fifty yards ahead. *Merde.* Surely this couldn't go wrong so soon? As Clémence pulled alongside him the soldiers dismounted, motioned them to stop and strutted purposefully towards them.

'Papers.' The soldier who demanded the documents somehow looked familiar to Félix: the tunic straining at the waist and the pudgy lips sparked a memory. *Ah yes, got him.* He examined the papers Félix had handed over, then scowled at him.

'I know this name. I have seen you before. Where?' The man's French was poor but the menacing undertone in his voice was clear.

Félix heard Thierry's mantra in his head: always tell the truth unless it's impossible. 'It was a couple of weeks ago near Sainte-Honorine. I was with my sister.'

The soldier stared at Clémence. 'This is not your sister. I remember your sister. She has no manners.'

Félix ignored the comment. 'No, this is my cousin.'

The soldier's eyes narrowed. 'Really? No resemblance.'

No, Félix thought, you don't know the half of it. 'None at all, regrettably. My aunt got the good looks in her family, which her daughter inherited.'

The soldier looked stumped by the rapid-fire French, held out his hand again and Clémence gave him her documents. Without looking up, he said, 'And why are you here?'

Félix indicated the case on his bike carrier. 'To buy a railway ticket. My cousin is going to visit her grandmother in Argentan.'

The German raised a hand to silence him and turned to Clémence. 'You can speak for yourself, I assume?'

'But of course, Sergeant.' Clémence smiled prettily.

The fat lips contracted. Félix was sure the soldier was a corporal, but he hoped Clémence's smile was working its charm.

The soldier re-examined Clémence's documents. He turned them over and back and looked up, tapping them on his free hand as he spoke.

'Your papers are very clean. They look new.'

'Not at all. I simply take care of them.'

The soldier's eyes scrutinised her for a full thirty seconds before he inspected the papers again. He held them up to the light and handed them to his comrade, raising his eyebrows. The other soldier, thin and with a rat-like edginess, wiped his free hand across his nose, studied the documents carefully and handed them back with a shake of his head.

The bulging lips tightened again as the man cleared his throat. He thrust the documents at Clémence. 'Very well, on your way.'

As Félix re-mounted his machine, a fat hand crushed his fingers onto the handlebars. 'But I know you now, and I shall remember.'

Félix was tempted to say that he wouldn't forget the soldier's face in a hurry either but, following Clémence's lead, he limited himself to 'Yes, Sergeant'. Why they'd caught the soldiers' attention he couldn't fathom. Maybe it was simply a question of being in the wrong place at the wrong time, but now Clémence had come to the enemy's notice before she'd even had a chance to settle in. He frowned in disbelief at their bad luck. He took a deep breath as the soldier and his companion mounted their machines and shot off in the direction of the station with a roar that echoed in the narrow street.

'*Tant pis*, Félix. No harm done, thankfully. What happened with your sister?'

'I'll tell you another time. Come on, let's get going.'

Félix hoped they weren't planning to check that he and Clémence were indeed in town to buy a railway ticket. Perhaps he was worrying for no good reason, but something didn't seem right. The station was only two streets away. Within minutes they could make a circular detour and check that the motorcycles weren't parked there.

He didn't share his misgivings with Clémence, who followed close behind keeping up the same pace. The station yard was almost deserted, with no sign of the two soldiers or their machines, so Félix rode on hoping he remembered the way to the draper's shop from this direction. By the time they arrived the small street was busy, which was probably an advantage. Coming to a halt, he indicated to Clémence the tapering alley alongside the shop, where they leaned the pushbikes against the railings that protected the rear entrance. Félix headed back up the passageway with Clémence's case. Seeing nothing amiss when he reached the road, he motioned for her to follow.

A bell tinkled as he opened the shop door, and a bird-like woman looked up from behind the counter. 'Ah, bonjour Monsieur Duchamp.' He inhaled the pleasing smell of fresh fabric as she put down a bolt of cloth and came across to join them. 'And this is?'

'Bonjour, Madame Tailler. This is Clémence Aubert.'

The two women shook hands. Clémence spoke formally. *'Enchanté de faire votre connaissance, madame.'*

Mme Tailler reached under the counter and handed a key to Félix.

'You know the way, Félix. I'll stay here in the shop.' She smiled at Clémence. 'We shall talk later. In the meantime please come and go as you wish, including the kitchen. The key opens the back door and the shop door.'

Félix hoped Thierry had managed to deliver the radio earlier. 'Has Monsieur Gosse...'.

Madame Tailler reassured him that yes, Thierry had delivered a package earlier, which he'd put in Clémence's room. Félix thanked her and led Clémence through a door set into the shelving. The small hallway beyond was dominated by an uncarpeted flight of stairs rising directly in front of them. To the right, a tiled passage led to a sparsely furnished but pristine-looking kitchen.

Félix climbed the steep stairway with the suitcase and Clémence followed. She gave a quiet laugh and Félix turned to see what had amused her.

'I don't need to worry about keeping fit if I'm going up and down these regularly.'

'No, sorry about that, but it's a good location and, besides, Madame Tailler is a hundred per cent trustworthy.'

Félix hesitated on the upper landing, took the short corridor on the left and headed for the far end. He looked up and checked the boarded square in the ceiling, pointing out that the attic was accessible via a retractable ladder should the need arise. Clémence looked at him, her expression fleetingly apprehensive. He opened the door of her room and ushered her in ahead of him.

The walls of the small room were papered with a pattern of blowsy Delft-blue flowers, much faded, and a china pitcher and bowl stood on a dark-wood chest below a foxed, gilt-framed mirror. The single bed bore fresh white sheets and an enormous blush-pink satin quilt, and a serviceable rug lay on the floor of polished boards. The only other furniture was a small square table and an upright chair, pushed beneath the window that overlooked the side alley.

Clémence smiled approvingly and put her suitcase on the bed. 'I shall be fine here. Of course, I shall need alternative sites for radio transmissions. I'm told the Germans have become expert at tracing them all too quickly.'

Félix had heard a few hair-raising stories but had never worked with a radio operator, so could only guess at the dangers she would live with daily. There was a sudden awkward silence.

'I should leave you to unpack. As I'm your contact, we must set up signals and regular meeting times now you're here, so I'll be back tomorrow, probably late afternoon. Does that sound reasonable?'

'Of course.' She walked with him to the door. 'Thank you for all your help, and for taking care of me.'

Félix's smile was business-like. *'De rien, et à demain*—I'll see you tomorrow.' As he clattered back down the stairs, he heard a faint click as the door closed.

# CHAPTER FIVE

## May–August 1943

ÉLODIE ARRIVED EARLY AND set out the market stall with eggs, goats' milk and cheese, plus the artichokes her mother had harvested the evening before, and by mid-morning the dozen or so stalls that were occupied were doing good trade in the warm sunshine. Élodie was nevertheless fidgety and distracted, checking the comings and goings constantly. As she served Mme Leroy, her thoughts kept sliding back treacherously to the blue-eyed German Lieutenant. She struggled to stifle a deep sense of disappointment that he hadn't reappeared.

Ten minutes later she looked up and her stomach lurched as Rudi Hoffmann approached the stall.

'No apples today?'

His broad smile left her tongue-tied and exasperated with herself in equal measure. She ignored Guillaume, who cleared his throat forcibly. She found her voice. 'Those were the last we'd overwintered. You might like my mother's goat's cheese though.'

He made a face. 'Not to my taste, but I will take some artichokes.'

The Lieutenant again seemed in no hurry to leave and began asking about her family and their farm. When the two other customers who were now waiting began to shuffle restlessly, he apologised and paid for the vegetables.

He took a step then stopped. 'I gather you have agreed to bring eggs to the Manoir now? I assume by bicycle?'

Élodie snorted. 'If "agree" includes no choice, then yes.'

With an apologetic shrug, he moved closer and said so quietly that she had to strain to hear, 'I would be happy to collect them myself to save you the journey. I know where the farm is. I'll be there at three on Friday afternoon.'

Before Élodie could reply he touched his cap and was gone. She groaned to herself. Maybe not such a good idea, and yet she savoured the tantalising thoughts that crept into her head at the prospect of being alone with him.

Rudi arrived at the farm punctually at three. Élodie had made sure she was busy with the hens, out of sight of the house. Hearing the approaching motorbike, she pulled out of her pocket a tiny round mirror and a stub of lipstick and applied a firm slick of rose pink to her lips. She held the mirror at arm's length. Far too obvious. She had no intention of looking like one of the *tapineuses* who solicited the German soldiers in Flers. A quick swipe across her mouth with the back of her hand removed the excess colour. As she straightened up, the bike pulled onto the verge. When the machine grew silent the Lieutenant kicked the metal stand into place, swung one well-muscled leg over the saddle and took off his cap, resting it on the pillion seat.

Élodie's insides twisted into a knot as he flicked back his hair and strode towards her, seeming relaxed today. She wrestled with the warm sensations that flooded her and forced herself to regain her composure.

'Good afternoon, Lieutenant.'

'*Bonjour, Mamselle*. Won't you call me Rudi?'

His smile was utterly disconcerting and Élodie opened her mouth, then shut it again. Telling herself not to mimic a cod-fish, she turned away and picked up the eggs she had packed earlier.

'These are what you've come for, aren't they, Lieut— ... Rudi?' She savoured the unfamiliar name, assuming it to be her pronunciation that made his eyes crinkle in amusement.

He took the trays, and a surge of chagrin ran through her when he immediately strode over to secure them onto the motorbike carrier. She had obviously been expecting too much. He replaced his cap before returning his attention to her.

'I'm sorry to be so rushed today, Élodie. I may call you that?'

She nodded and at last managed a smile.

'Would the same time be suitable next week?'

Élodie was unused to such correctness. 'Yes, of course. That'll be fine, Rudi.' This time she used his name more boldly. He spotted the pink slick across her hand and frowned. She hastily pulled down her sleeve, self-conscious at the percep-tive smile that spread as his eyes lingered on her rose-tinged mouth. But there was no mistaking the clear sensuality in his expression as he took his leave.

As the bike roared off, she inhaled the lingering masculine scent. A week suddenly seemed a long time to wait.

On the following Friday, after lunch with her parents, she slipped upstairs and fingered the few frocks she possessed, but rejected the idea of changing into one of them. Her mother was far too astute for any excuse she might proffer. She slammed the wardrobe door in frustration and settled for a clean pair of dungarees, adding her favourite lavender shirt and a purple cotton handkerchief that was big enough to knot at her neck. She stood in front of the shabby cheval mirror and sighed. Cinching a brown leather belt round the dungarees to emphasise her narrow waist, she cocked her head on one side and pouted at her reflection.

At five to three she stood outside the grassy enclosure, rubbing at the goosebumps on her arms raised by the brisk breeze. Rudi arrived as before, almost exactly on the hour, and this time he lingered for fifteen minutes. Élodie relaxed a little as he led the conversation.

'You have always lived here?'

'Yes, always.' She explained how many generations of Duchamps had farmed the land, and how the original acreage had been divided and re-divided as sons came into their inheritance. 'And you? Do you live in a town or the country?'

'In Dresden. My father changed his job when my sister and I were young.'

'And you like it there?'

Rudi made a face. 'It's where Geneviève and I finished school, and it's a fine city, but I much preferred spending time with my grandparents on their farm in Alsace, where we too originally lived.' He hesitated. 'Of course, when *Opa* moved there from across the Rhine in Freiburg it was part of Germany.'

Élodie noted his rueful, almost embarrassed smile when she retorted, 'And then belonged to France. And now...'.

'Well, as for now... Let us not speak of it.'

Élodie shrugged. 'Where were you before you came to Normandy?'

Rudi shook his head. 'In Russia. On the Eastern Front. But, please, no questions about that.' He balled his fists. 'I'm sorry, but I saw things—saw people do things, and on both sides—that were inhuman, and inexcusable.'

Élodie watched as his expression changed, his eyes haunted and faraway. Without a second thought she took his hands in hers, lifted them to her face and kissed them, as she might have done with Félix if he were upset. He snapped back into the present, his startled blue eyes focusing on her face. Had she shocked him? She let his hands drop but didn't speak, aware that she was blushing. She was almost relieved to see Rudi glance at his watch.

'You probably need to leave now?'

Rudi's weekly visits lengthened, and each time she was more flustered as three o'clock approached. They talked in the sunshine or stood under the nearby apple trees, discussing their childhoods, their families, the weather. But after that first time, not the war. Never the war.

On the fourth occasion Rudi bent and picked two tiny late-flowering violets, tucking them behind Élodie's ear. 'They bring out the colour in your eyes.' His hand brushed her face.

Élodie could feel her cheeks colouring up. How unlike the local boys she'd been at school with, farmers' sons who treated cows and girls much the same, thinking a smack on the rump was flattering. To be fair, most weren't entirely crass—and many were kind-hearted—but they lacked the slightest finesse. Though they all remained her friends, she had never viewed any as a potential lover.

As she looked up, Rudi's face was inches from her own. He leant in and kissed her, and though her head urged protest, her body said otherwise. All too soon, or so it seemed, Rudi drew back, a hand on either side of her face.

'I'm sorry, I've wanted to do that since the moment I met you.'

Élodie could feel the warm blush that spread again across her cheeks under his fingers. For answer, she put her arms around his waist and stood on tiptoes to return the kiss. For a long moment they stood entwined, the war far distant.

A grating sound from the direction of the gate startled them back to the present. Élodie shot away like an arrow from a bow, spinning round to determine the cause. Was it a trick of the light, or had a figure disappeared behind the hedge?

Rudi had hung his cap on an apple tree and now retrieved it. He gave a wry smile. 'I hope I haven't caused trouble for you.'

'To hell with whoever it was. I'm tired of being judged—.' Élodie stopped herself.

'Judged for what?'

'Oh, you know, talking to you in the market and so on.'

A gap as big as a trench suddenly yawned between them.

'Are you saying you don't want me to come here again?'

Élodie shook her head. '*No*, no. I'm not saying any such thing.'

Élodie wrestled ceaselessly with her conscience and her emotions. She tossed and turned in bed at night, thumping the pillow in despair at her wakefulness. She stared at her sleep-deprived face in the bathroom mirror in the mornings, and did her daily chores like a restless will-o'-the-wisp, her feelings torn between Rudi and everything else she had ever known or experienced. She had never felt this way about any man, yet now she did, that man wore an enemy uniform. Was she attracted to him simply because he was the unknown, the unencountered, the exotic even? She'd never met a man with such corn-blond hair, such mesmerising blue eyes. And yet, no. It was everything compelling beyond his outward appearance: his sharp intelligence, a warm sense of humour, the roiling inner conflict between a sense of duty and an unwavering moral compass set against the injustices of the regime he found himself entrenched in by accident of birth.

Over two months their compulsion grew stronger, their restraint weaker. They began to frequent the barn behind the henhouse as their urge for each other became almost irresistible. The first time Rudi eased down the straps on her dungarees and began to unbutton her blouse, Élodie clutched at the material, her Catholic upbringing rearing like a barrier.

Rudi stepped back and held up his hands. 'I won't do anything you don't want. If I've gone too far, I'm sorry, but you surely know how I feel by now?'

Élodie nodded, letting her blouse hang loose from her shoulders. She stared at the ground, rubbing the edge of one thumbnail with the other. 'I've never, it's just that I've never...' She looked up shyly, expecting him to be laughing at her, a *péquenaude* in deepest Normandy.

He pulled her tight against him, whispering so quietly that it was hard to catch his words. 'I hope I will never do anything to hurt or embarrass you, *Schatzi*. I love you for everything you are, and I want to love you in every way, but only when it's right for you.'

Élodie nodded, feeling the heat radiating from him as their intimacy aroused him. Could she let go and surrender to this foreigner who had inexplicably invaded her heart despite his despised grey uniform? She was only too aware that her own body was winning out over her head, yet still she held back—for now.

Several times in the following weeks they barely stopped short of crossing that unspoken line, Élodie almost inevitably the one to draw back.

On a hot Friday in August, Élodie had made her decision, aware that her very existence now revolved around him. She drew him into the cool interior of the barn, folded her arms round his neck and kissed him fiercely. She felt his immediate resistance, felt his hands grip her shoulders and push her away.

'What's wrong? Why not now? I thought it was what you wanted?'

Rudi ran his hands through his hair. As ever, a blond lock escaped and hung like a comma over his left eyebrow. He peered towards the closed door. 'Yes, you know I do.'

Élodie heard the exasperation in his voice but pressed the point. She put her hands on her hips and challenged him. 'Well then?'

'Élodie, not here, not now. This is not how I want it to be between us.'

She raised an eyebrow and glowered towards the hay. 'So, what alternative palace have you in mind?'

To her intense annoyance, Rudi threw back his head and laughed. Was he making fun of her now? She crossed her arms, unsmiling. Rudi tilted her chin upwards. 'Don't let's fight.'

She touched the smooth wool of his tunic. 'So what do you suggest?'

'I'm due a free half-day next week. You could meet me in Argentan?'

She frowned. 'Because...?'

'Oh, I know somewhere there.'

'Somewhere German officers take their whores?' As soon as the words were out of her mouth, she regretted her habitual outspokenness. Rudi dropped his hand from her face.

'Is that what you think of me?' His voice was controlled but taut as a watch spring. 'What you honestly think of me?'

Élodie shook her head. 'No, of course not. I'm sorry.' She bit her lip.

'If you mean that, maybe you know someone you could be visiting in Argentan, *Liebchen*, so that you could get away? If you need an excuse, that is.'

Élodie hesitated, burying her head in his chest, her cheek against the warm fabric. 'I do have an old school friend I've almost lost touch with, so I suppose...'

'*Prima*. Let me see what I can do. Could we say Wednesday?' He moved his left arm and peered over her shoulder at his well-weathered military-issue watch. 'But now I have to go.' Before she could protest, he kissed her and stepped away. 'No, I mean it, I have to go. I'll find a way to confirm tomorrow.' He stroked her hair, straightened his tunic, reached the door in four long strides and was gone. The chickens cackled at the disturbance, and lapsed back into their habitual clucking.

Élodie sniffed the air, drawing in the lingering trace of his strangely seductive cologne before it faded. She wrapped her arms around herself and sighed, seeing only his warm smile and burning blue eyes. Bloody war.

That evening, while her father was still in the barn, Élodie set out the cutlery on the old pine table, her back to her mother who was at the stove.

'Maman, you remember Agnès who was in my class at school?'

She turned as her mother looked up. 'That girl with big ideas who couldn't wait to move to Argentan?'

'Yes, that's her. Are you being a bit harsh?'

Her mother laid the wooden spoon across the stockpot. 'No. And why are you mentioning her now?'

'Oh, I ran into another school friend in the market, and she told me Agnès would like to meet up again.' She added four glasses to the table.

'And?'

'Well, I thought maybe one day next week.'

Rose folded her arms, but before she could answer Henri appeared at the back door, kicking the step to dislodge the dirt from his field boots.

'What's happening one day next week?'

'Élodie says some girl she was at school with has a burning desire to see her next week in Argentan.'

Élodie bridled. 'Maman, that's not fair!' She shot Henri her best effort at a winning smile. 'You remember Agnès, Papa?'

Henri grunted. 'A *garce*, as I recall. Complete trollop. But, Rose, let the girl go and have some fun for a change.'

Rose raised an eyebrow and shrugged. 'If that's what she wants.' Giving Élodie no chance to speak, she added, 'But don't forget it's market day next Tuesday, *ma fille*. And not too much "fun".'

Élodie fiddled with the place settings. She smiled again at her father. 'I was thinking next Wednesday?'

'You'll need to be back for the chickens in the evening.' Henri trudged off to wash before supper.

Rose dumped the heavy stewpot on the table. 'Anything else you'd like to say about this Agnès girl?'

Élodie shook her head. Her mother was plainly sceptical. Why, she wasn't sure; best to leave it at that and change the subject. She regarded the four place settings. 'Did I need to lay a place for Félix?' Her brother was away as much as at home these days.

Rose shrugged again. 'I've no idea. I'll leave enough for him, if and when he arrives. It'll keep warm on the stove.'

On the following Wednesday, Élodie rode her bike to the station in Flers. She had chosen her sky-blue dress, the most serviceable of the three she owned, and had stuffed her only pair of court shoes into her bag before leaving home in her hideous but practical everyday lace-ups. As she joined the queue in the booking hall, she cursed under her breath. Lisette Martin, Serge's gossip of a sister, was standing at the wood-framed ticket window. Élodie stepped squarely behind the man in front of her, glad of his reassuring height and bulk, and wished she'd brought a scarf to cover her hair. By the time it was her turn, Lisette was nowhere to be seen. Élodie lingered in the furthest corner of the waiting room until Lisette's unmistakeable flirtatious figure strolled down the platform. Two German soldiers watching the passengers gave her the once-over as she passed, her high heels clacking, one smiling as he made some comment. Lisette smiled back coquettishly, tossing her dark hair.

The train was late, but only by ten minutes. It whooshed and hissed as it steamed into view. Élodie slipped into the nearest carriage as Lisette boarded the train further along the platform but, as she did so, the two soldiers were wandering back, checking each compartment before climbing into her own.

'*Guten Tag, Fraülein.*' The soldier who had spoken to Lisette smiled broadly at Élodie, who ensured her return smile was cool. The two men stood while she settled into the window seat and then sat opposite her. Both wore perfectly pressed uniforms, the buttons polished to a shine, as were their black leather boots. Élodie pinched her nose as the cloying odour of warm shoe polish drifted across the aisle.

With a jolt and clouds of smoke, the train began to move. The soldier spoke again in poor, halting French: '*Go you to Argentan?*'

Élodie nodded. '*Ah bah oui, Monsieur.*' She rattled off that she was going to visit her aunt who was ill, immediately doubting the wisdom of telling him such a stupid lie.

He turned to his companion, who shook his head. He raised his hands, palms spread wide. 'Sorry, I do not understand.' He said something in German. Élodie mirrored his gesture to put a stop to any further conversation. She studied the fields beyond the window, the growing crops beaten down in places. Tiny rivulets of rain hurried the smuts down the glass as a sudden shower began.

As the train pulled into Argentan, Élodie gathered up her bag and straightened her skirt. One of the soldiers stood smartly when the carriage came to a halt, stepped down onto the platform and held up a hand to her. She hesitated, then gripped his glove as lightly as possible as she negotiated the steep step. She smiled crisply and thanked him. He released her fingers as his companion joined them. 'We can help in any way?'

Élodie shook her head. 'Thank you, but no. Someone is meeting me outside the station.' His puzzled look suggested he hadn't understood but he stepped back and stood stiffly to attention. She forced herself to walk slowly towards the exit, conscious that Lisette must now be somewhere behind her. Spotting a sign for the toilets she hurried in, changed her shoes, and waited five minutes before emerging. There was no sign of the two soldiers from the train, although an ominous figure loitered by the street exit, probably Gestapo. To her profound relief, he appeared uninterested and she followed the last stragglers out to the pavement, wrapping her jacket tighter against the miserable weather.

She looked to right and left, then across the street. Rudi was standing on the opposite corner. To her annoyance, Lisette was chatting to him animatedly. Looking up, he saw Élodie and smiled. As Lisette turned to look over her shoulder, Élodie shook her head at him and ducked back into the station, noting with relief that the Gestapo officer had moved to talk to an SNCF official by the ticket barrier. It took another five minutes of watching through the grimy window before Rudi was able to extract himself from Lisette's attentions. Élodie's eyes followed as Lisette wandered into a nearby shop. Damn the girl. And damn it that she worked at the Manoir.

Élodie smiled to herself as Rudi folded his jacket carefully on the back of a chair before undoing the top button of his shirt. How different he looked without that uniform. Both younger and more vulnerable. For a moment she wavered. It was madness to be here in this room, now, in the middle of a war that had set them on opposing sides, wasn't it? He took off his socks and trousers. Before she had time for further doubts, Rudi picked her up and lifted her tenderly onto the sagging bed, whose threadbare sheets were at least clean and vaguely white. She pulled her dress over her head and closed her eyes, suddenly shy. All thoughts of the boy vanished as the man tenderly expressed his feelings for her, which she returned, diffidently at first, and soon with a matching passion.

Later, lying in the curve of his arms as he slept peacefully beside her, his chest rising and falling, Élodie studied his face. His features were boyish and untroubled in repose, his pale lashes twitching slowly. Whatever became of them both, the fulfilment of those earlier hours would remain imprinted on her memory. She returned to the image of him folding his jacket, seeing in her mind's eye a young, solemn boy obeying his mother's exhortations to be tidy.

Somewhere outside, a church clock struck four. The drone of heavy aircraft—whether Allied or German she couldn't tell—rattled the window glass and startled her out of her reverie. Élodie clambered off the bed, bending to pick up her discarded garments from the floor. As she retrieved her underwear and straightened up, she banged into the battered cheval mirror that stood beside the wardrobe. In the silvery reflection she saw Rudi sitting up in bed, a broad smile on his face. She grabbed her frock to cover herself and spun to face him.

'You were asleep a moment ago.'

He laughed. 'Well, I'm certainly not now. And why are you clasping your clothes like that. An hour ago...' He left the sentence unfinished as Élodie, suddenly feeling exposed in her nakedness, fussed with her frock. He patted the bed.

'Come and sit with me.'

She shook her head. 'I can't. I said I'd be home to see to the chickens and I won't, even if there's a train waiting in the station.' Her father would be furious that she'd broken her promise, especially as her mother would step to her defence and deal with everything herself, though would be sure to express her displeasure later in no uncertain terms.

Rudi ambled over, totally at ease with his own naked state. 'I'm sorry. I'm sure I could get a car to take you home.'

'No!' Élodie was conscious that her voice had risen an octave. 'No, that is definitely not a good idea. I'll deal with it when I get there.' She tried to hide a sudden whirl of disorientation. What was she doing here? Why had she agreed to this?

*She had slept with the enemy.*

'I must go.' She dressed, snatched up her bag and headed for the door. Rudi followed.

'When will I see you again?'

Élodie sighed. 'I don't know. I shouldn't be here.'

'Why?'

'Because ... because', she heard her own voice, small and low now, as she faced him. 'Because they will say I've become "a mattress for the Boche".'

Rudi looked as if he'd been stung. His lips were pressed together, his back ramrod straight.

As she waited for him to answer, the clock outside chimed the quarter hour.

When he finally spoke, his voice was gentle, displaying no anger. 'That's a pity. I'm sorry you feel that way, because you must know I love you. Now more than ever.'

His hurt expression was tearing Élodie apart. But the grey uniform on the chair behind him was an irrefutable reminder of what he represented. Her mind was so conflicted she was sure her head would burst.

She scrubbed crossly at her face as tears formed. 'Don't you see?'

'See what?'

Her words came out in a rush. 'Don't you understand, that's the whole damn problem: how can I love you too?'

'*Liebchen*, you just showed me that you do. Or are you telling me I've got that wrong?' He stroked her cheek and gave the smile that never failed to melt her resolve. She could feel her lips quivering as she tried to smile back.

'That's better, *Schatzi*. Come, I'll walk you to the station.'

'No. Absolutely not. What we have is private, and it has to stay that way—you must realise that?'

Rudi sighed and kissed her forehead. 'Then I have to let you go. But I'll see you soon, I promise.'

Élodie opened the door and peered both ways along the corridor. She saw no one familiar as she descended the stairs. The clerk looked up from the desk and she tensed as his suspicious eyes followed her, serpent-like, across the exposed reception area. She held her breath, waiting to be challenged, but when she reached the door and risked a glance, he had returned his attention to the papers in front of him.

Halfway back to the station Élodie was conscious of a commotion somewhere ahead. A dozen or so approaching people rushed past her, eyes down. A sudden loud shout of '*Halt!*' alarmed her. She still couldn't see what was causing the ruckus as she reached a bend in the road but froze abruptly at the sight of two German soldiers, pistols raised and pointed at two male figures heading for a side alley across the road from where she stood.

The command was repeated. '*Halt! Hände hoch.*' The men kept running as the loud crack of pistol fire rang out and reverberated in the winding street. One of the men swerved and dinked towards Élodie and the other turned sharply in the opposite direction. As more shots were fired, she was suddenly seized and propelled into a shop doorway, shielded by the size of whoever had grabbed her. She caught a glimpse of one of the targets, who was now fleeing down the alley opposite. He looked uncannily like Michel. She gasped—surely not? Further shouting and another shot filled her with fear. She hadn't even looked at the other man. Where was Félix today? She pushed against the greatcoat that was enveloping her and recognised Rudi's soothing smell. She looked up into his concerned face.

'Why are you here? Did you follow me?'

'Why in God's name didn't you move? I thought for a moment you would be shot.' He enveloped her in his arms and held her close.

'I'm OK. Really, I'm fine.' She knew she was trembling, but also that she was unhurt.

Running feet stopped behind Rudi. It was one of the soldiers who had been firing, a pistol still in his hand.

He stood to attention when he registered Rudi's rank. '*Entschuldigung, Herr Leutnant.* Did you see where that Résistant went?' He looked from Rudi to Élodie, then insolently back at Élodie, eyeing her from head to foot.

Rudi frowned at the soldier's brazenness. 'No, I did not. And you need to be more careful when there are civilians around. What's your name and unit?'

Élodie watched the exchange in consternation. Several people were now staring at the three of them. The last thing she wanted was this kind of exposure, but currently she was trapped. From beneath her lashes, she focused on a young woman standing with her arms folded and a resentful scowl on her face. Please let it not be—yet it was, of all people it had to be, didn't it? Lisette, of course, who gave her a sly smirk and swept off towards the station. Élodie closed her eyes in despair and sighed. When she opened them, the soldier had gone and Rudi was staring at her, his back once more to the street.

'Just someone I didn't want to see. Too late now. I must go.' She laid an open palm on his tunic. He covered it with his own warm hand and squeezed her fingers.

'I get it. But please be careful, for your sake and mine.' Élodie kissed the back of his hand, ducked under his left arm, which still rested on the shop window frame, and set off again.

Within twenty yards, her way was blocked by a small crowd gathered around something she couldn't see. Terrified at what it might be, she wriggled her way through the onlookers. A man lay on the pavement, face down and motionless, his arms flung out in front of him. He looked young, though his face was half-hidden by dark, curly hair. Blood was trickling in a steady flow across the pavement, and one of the soldiers stood guard over him, pistol at the ready.

Élodie's voice was reluctant to work. She swallowed and managed to say to the man closest to her, 'Is he...?'

The man inspected her incuriously. 'Dead? Yes. He didn't stand a chance.'

Élodie's head swam. She willed herself to look at the motionless shape on the ground. Heart pounding, she realised the man was too short and too heavily built to be Félix. As relief flooded through her, she felt a stab of remorse: this was someone's son, probably also some girl's boyfriend or lover. She eased back through the hushed spectators and quickened her pace as soon as she was out of sight.

The station was crawling with troops but Élodie ignored them, intent on avoiding Lisette. There was a train leaving for Flers in five minutes. On the platform Élodie remained uneasily behind a shabbily dressed couple until she caught sight of a pair of crazily high heels twenty yards ahead. She slowed her pace and waited till Lisette boarded halfway down the train. The nearest carriage was already overfull, so she made her way into the next compartment where one seat remained. Now she only had to avoid the wretched girl when they reached Flers.

Still thinking about the events in Argentan the previous day, Élodie took the loaf from Mathilde and paid. She turned as the door opened and her heart sank as the matriarch of the Martin family strode up to the counter, her flowered overall visible beneath her shabby, shapeless coat. She tensed automatically.

'Bonjour, Mme Martin.' She smiled brightly, or hoped she was giving that impression.

At first there was no reply. Élodie watched the older woman for some reaction. She didn't have to wait long.

'I have nothing to say to those who provide a bed for the Boche.'

Out of the corner of her eye Élodie saw Mathilde's head drop. She had a naturally pale complexion, but a rosy flush flooded her cheeks. One of life's innocents, Élodie was sure. Doubtless utterly embarrassed by such rudeness.

'I assume, Madame, that you are talking to me?'

'I'm talking to whoever my comment applies to.'

Élodie stuffed the bread into her bag.

'I would be careful who you accuse, Madame. And of what.'

'Indeed? I dare say I can add collaboration into the mix.'

Mme Martin's unjust words hit home. Élodie could feel anger erupting. Doubtless this was all the result of Lisette's spite. It was better to leave than let the situation get further out of hand. She couldn't resist one riposte, however.

'I wish you a good day at the rumour mill, Madame.'

To her great satisfaction, as she reached the door and looked over her shoulder to say 'Au revoir' to Mathilde, Mme Martin's mouth gaped open speechlessly.

Élodie checked her watch as she measured out the chicken feed. She frowned: Rudi was late today. Had he had second thoughts? Five minutes later she heard the sound of a truck braking on the lane outside and smoothed her tangled hair. It was odd that he should not be on his motorbike. Before she reached the door of the barn it creaked open. She took a step back as Major Wolff ducked his head and entered, brushing his jacket with a gloved hand. Élodie's smile froze.

'Good afternoon, Mamselle. You look surprised to see me.'

Élodie retreated as he stepped confidently towards her. She struggled to control rising apprehension. 'Good afternoon, *Herr Major*. I thought it would be Leutnant Hoffmann, as usual. Have you come for the eggs?'

Wolff moved closer. 'Yes, I said I was passing this way. Leutnant Hoffmann speaks so well of you that I decided I should get to know you better. Perhaps I have misjudged you.' His comments were as rapidly toxic as liquid poison.

Élodie could feel her heart thumping. 'Did you bring the empty tray from last week, *Herr Major*?'

His smile broadened but the vulpine steel-grey eyes remained icy. 'No. Hoffmann can do so next time. You seem nervous Élodie. That is your name, yes?'

Élodie quickly picked up the eggs she'd collected earlier, and held out the tray, placing it firmly between them.

'There's no rush.' His eyes traversed her figure, pausing at breasts and hips. Élodie squirmed as if her clothes already lay on the floor. He took the tray from her and set it down. 'Come', he said, grabbing her arm and pushing her towards the stacked hay. As Élodie began to protest, he gripped her other arm and pulled her close. She smelled warm leather as he cupped her chin in his gloved hand. 'You know, you are a most attractive young woman.'

Before she could reply, he bent his head to kiss her. The clean, sharp aftershave he wore was strangely arousing. The very thought disgusted her. Why was he doing this? Because he considered he had the right, she supposed. In a sudden flash she knew. In his arrogance he did have the right, assumed it—the invader, the occupier. She struggled to free herself but was imprisoned in his powerful grip.

Wolff moved his mouth close to her ear. 'Oh, but you taste good.'

Élodie wrenched her head back. '*Herr Major*, I am no more free for the taking than the apples I sell in the market.' She batted his hand away, furious with him, and equally furious with herself—for letting herself be cornered.

Wolff grabbed a clump of her wild curls and twisted it at the base of her skull, tightening his grip as he did so.'

As Élodie debated the consequences of kneeing him hard in the groin, the barn door hit the wall with a loud crash. Wolff's reaction was trigger fast. With her hair still grasped in his left hand, his right flew to the unbuckled holster on his hip.

A yard inside the door, Félix stood with a shotgun pointed at Wolff's chest. 'Let my sister go. Now.' Élodie gasped as Wolff drew his pistol. He held the Luger to her temple.

'I suggest you lower that weapon, you arrogant *Scheißkerl*, and reconsider who you're threatening. Don't think I won't shoot. After all, you're giving me the perfect defence.' His lip curled in scorn. Élodie's alarm turned to anger. How sure of himself he was. So supreme in his authority. One day there would be a reckoning.

Wolff was speaking again. 'And why do you have that gun? All weapons were to be handed in long ago.'

'My father has a permit. He uses it to shoot rabbits to keep his family from starving.'

Élodie turned her head a fraction to look at her brother. His tone was like acid. She'd never heard Félix speak like that to anyone, but there was fear in his eyes as his gaze flicked between her and the Major.

Despite the danger of the weapon pressed against her temple, her greatest terror was for her brother.

She cleared her throat. '*Calme-toi*, Félix.' She was relieved to see Félix's forefinger rise subtly from the shotgun in acknowledgement.

The raucous sound of a loud motor stopping outside startled Élodie and set the hens cackling frenziedly as they scattered. Félix stood his ground but looked over his shoulder through the open door as Rudi stepped inside.

'*Gott im iHimmel* ... what's going on here?' His shocked face was pale, a tic twitching his left cheek. He addressed his question to Félix, who nodded at Wolff.

'I suggest you ask the Major.'

Rudi stared into the half-light of the barn, adjusting from the dazzle of the afternoon sunlight.

Wolff re-holstered his pistol. 'As you will see, Leutnant Hoffmann, this young idiot tried to threaten me, leaving me no option but to react accordingly.' He released his grip on Élodie and dusted down his jacket again. 'Why are you here, Hoffmann?'

Rudi looked from Félix to Élodie in disbelief. He addressed the Major. 'Obersturmbannführer Fuchs wants to speak to you urgently, Herr Major.'

Wolff nodded. 'I'll leave you to deal with this girl, since she seems overawed in my presence.' The Major stared at Élodie with apparent undisguised disdain. On his way to the door, he stopped in front of Félix and indicated the shotgun.

'I will take that. Your father will have to reconsider how to feed his family. Besides, there is no such thing as a permit for civilians, *das ist absoluter Scheiß*. Count yourself lucky that your foolishness has not ended in your arrest or a heavy fine for your father.'

Félix hesitated before handing over the weapon, then thrust it at the Major.

'I shall be watching you carefully, you young idiot. And don't forget I know where to find you.' He broke open the shotgun, tutted in fury when he registered that it wasn't loaded, and barged Félix out of his way as he made for the door.

Élodie kicked the stool that lay overturned beside her. 'I'll be fine now Félix, thank you.' She explained to Rudi, 'Félix is my brother'. Rudi held out a hand, which Félix ignored. 'Félix, please, for my sake.'

Félix eyed the outstretched hand scornfully and turned on his heel. He paused in the doorway. 'I'd suggest you don't let Pa see your friend hanging around here.' Before Élodie could reply, he was already striding towards the lane.

In the gloom of the barn, Rudi enveloped Élodie in his arms. 'What in the world was all that about, *Schatzi?*'

How should she explain what had just transpired? But, dammit, she had no reason to feel accountable for Wolff's inexcusable behaviour. 'Did you know he was coming here?' Her voice was unfairly accusing but she couldn't stop herself. She spat out her next words. 'He told me you "spoke so well of me". Does he know about us? How?'

'No, no he doesn't. But—.'

'But *what?*'

'He said you were a fine-looking girl, and he'd like—.'

Elodie bunched her fists and chittered with anger. She waited for him to continue, but he looked away before doing so.

'I think I shouldn't tell you what else he said.'

'Don't. Just don't. *Quel con.* I really thought... I wish I'd done him harm. But he's so strong, I couldn't stop him.'

'Thank God you didn't try. He wouldn't spare a woman any more than a man. You have to believe that. There's no argument when his mind's made up. Promise me you won't provoke him again.'

Élodie scowled. 'So now it's my fault?'

'Don't be ridiculous. Of course not. But he's a dangerous man with a short fuse.'

'I hear you.'

'But will you heed me? Do you promise?'

'Yes. Maybe. You are welcome here if I know you are coming. But from now on I'll deliver the eggs to the Manoir myself. I don't want him here again, ever.'

# CHAPTER SIX

## August 1943

FéLIX HOISTED HIS FISHING bag onto his shoulder and picked up his rod. The weather was in his favour, with only a few scattered clouds and no breeze. He was aching for the solitude of the riverbank after a morning working with his father, who seemed to be perpetually cantankerous these days. There was no pleasing the old grouch, however hard he might try.

When he arrived, he was relieved to be alone on his favourite stretch of the chalk stream. He could just see the small grey-stone bridge away to his right, and the crystal-clear water below him bubbled over stones and languidly swirling vegetation. After an hour and a half he'd caught three plump brown trout, which lay submerged in the keepnet, and as he landed a fourth he marvelled as always at the jewel-like colouring—olive-brown back, creamy-yellow belly and pale-ringed dark-red spots.

A flash of movement to his right caught his attention. Two German soldiers were ambling along the bank towards him, ostensibly relaxed. Off-duty maybe? He decided to ignore them unless challenged but kept them in sight as best he could without turning his head. The younger one approached him but the other hung back, scowling. Certain he would be asked to show his papers, Félix slipped the fish into the watery mesh and wiped his hands down his trousers with the wry realisation that he would now stink of fish and river weed. The soldier indicated the net.

'*Forelle*?' Then, enigmatically, in English, 'Trout?'

Félix nodded. '*Truite*, yes.'

The German held out a hand and pointed to himself with the other. 'Matthias. You?'

Félix hesitated. He registered with a degree of surprise that the open-faced young man before him couldn't be more than eighteen or nineteen. The soldier smiled, showing even, white teeth that highlighted his fresh, boyish features. Ash-blond hair spilled from the edges of his forage cap and almost white eyelashes lined wide-spaced blue-grey eyes. Félix shook the outstretched hand and gave his name—after all, the soldier could soon check.

Matthias pointed to himself again, then the rod, and raised his eyebrows.

With reluctance, Félix held out the rod. Was he going to lose both his gear and his catch?

'Merci.' The soldier held up his index finger.

Unsure of his motive or meaning, Félix nodded and stepped back, seeing the second soldier still standing with a sullen expression about twenty feet away, smoking and looking alternately up- and downstream. After a long, belligerent stare in their direction he seemed to lose interest, checked his watch, and lit another cigarette from the stub of the first.

Félix turned his back and watched as Matthias baited the hook and cast expertly. Within ten minutes he'd caught a fish, which he dispatched smartly with the wooden priest that Félix handed to him. Taking a clean, precisely pressed white handkerchief from his pocket he dropped to his knees, dangling the cloth in the water before squeezing out the excess.

Once the fish was deftly wrapped up, he fashioned a knot with the two spare corners.

He stood, smiled, and extended his hand again. '*Danke—merci.*'

Félix smiled back automatically, then let the smile fade. What the hell was he doing fraternising with a German soldier? But, he reasoned, without the damned war he would simply be a young fellow fisherman, and besides, no point in antagonising the Boche when he wanted to keep his profile low. He took the proffered hand and shook it.

'Perhaps again, one day?'

Félix shrugged, glancing at the other soldier who had remained at a distance, unsmiling and clearly ill at ease. Matthias re-joined his comrade, his catch dangling from one hand, and the two soldiers made for the bridge, the older man apparently grumbling—presumably in disapproval. When he'd watched them cross the bridge and disappear, Félix began dismantling the rod and packed away his own fish, shook the droplets of water from the net and set out for home. Despite the soldiers intruding on his peace, he felt far more relaxed and turned his mind to the upcoming night's task.

When he reached the farm, his mother, wearing her habitual faded-blue crossover apron, was in the vegetable garden picking *haricots verts*. Félix smiled and held up four fingers as she raised her eyebrows at the wicker creel in anticipation.

'I have things to do before supper, Maman, but I'll gut the fish for you and leave them in the kitchen. I should be home well before six.'

His mother looked puzzled. 'Where are you going now?'

Félix had hoped she wouldn't ask. 'I promised to pick up some stuff for Thierry. I'm seeing him and Michel this evening.' He kissed her cheek and held up the creel. 'Need to get these done now.'

'Make sure they're covered before you go. There are so many flies about.' Félix was amused to see that his mother had already returned her attention to the colander, doubtless assessing whether she yet had enough beans for the four of them.

Forty minutes later he stood outside the barn where he and Clémence had spent her first night in France. He reached under the old zinc tank and retrieved the key to the large padlock, which appeared to have rusted even more after the recent rain, but the lock was well oiled and yielded the moment he turned the key. After checking in all directions, he slipped inside and pulled the door only semi-shut behind him so that he could locate what he was looking for. It made a loud, graunching sound as he did so, and he noticed that one of the hinges was hanging loose so that the bottom edge of the corrugated iron door was catching on the ground. He made a mental note to look in the tractor barn at home for another hinge—not much point in securing the place with a padlock if the door could be ripped open from the side. After finding the trunk containing the bedding, he dragged it into the half-light and groped through the contents till his fingers hit a hard object wrapped in one of the pillowcases at the bottom of the box. He took it out, slid the slim tin into the inside pocket of his jacket and rearranged the bedding so that the box would shut.

As he replaced the padlock, he heard the growl of several heavy vehicles on the main road. He slid the key into its hiding place, retreated into the nearby trees and waited, alert to the engine noise that grew steadily louder and then remained constant before gradually fading into the distance. The barn was invisible from the road but the entrance to the track was clear. One day, Félix was certain, some inquisitive German patrol would investigate where the track led. Thankfully, not today.

That evening Félix ate with the family, an increasingly rare occurrence these days. His mother had cooked the fish and there were potatoes and the fresh beans she'd picked earlier, a meal that for once elicited an appreciative smile from his father. As the hall clock struck seven, Félix excused himself from the table.

Henri's good humour faded. 'Where are you off to now?'

'Thierry's invited me and Michel for a beer or two.'

Félix noted the look of scepticism from his father. 'I've still got that broken piece of fence to mend, Papa, then I'll be off.'

'But you'll be home later?' This question came from his mother, and Félix thought—not for the first time—how care-worn she appeared these days. He bent and kissed her fore-head.

'I might be late, Maman, but yes, I'll be home again tonight.' He watched his mother gauging Élodie's reaction. His sister, bless her, gave their mother a reassuring smile and jumped up.

'Come, Félix, I'll give you a hand. Leave the dishes, Maman, and I'll do them later.' Rose nodded as if in acquiescence, but Félix knew that by the time Élodie came in again the supper things would all be clean and stacked to dry—that had always been their mother's no-nonsense way.

Down at the bottom field, Félix deposited the two new fenceposts he'd been carrying. Between the old weathered broken posts lay a heap of barbed wire, which Félix unrolled with care after he had donned a pair of heavy gloves and warned his sister to be careful. Élodie swatted away a cloud of midges, gave him the mallet and he set to work.

She spoke as he struggled to remove the base of the nearest post. 'What are you actually doing tonight?'

Félix looked up in surprise. Clearly, he hadn't been convincing. 'You heard me tell *le paternel*.'

'I heard what you said. But I didn't believe you any more than he did.'

'Then I can only say, nothing you need to know about.'

He guessed correctly that this would parry further questions. Élodie gave him a pensive look and began passing him the thick metal staples to fix the wire. An hour later, task finished, they strolled back to the house. Félix carried the tools as Élodie dabbed at the blood on her hand from a wire cut, slipping her arm through his.

'You know I couldn't bear it if anything happened to you?'

Félix squeezed her arm firmly. 'Not planning to desert you yet, Él.'

Yvette answered the door almost before he'd knocked, apologising for the lingering reek of onions, and kissed him on both cheeks. '*Bonsoir, chéri*.' Félix had grown fond of Yvette. Small and well-rounded, she adored her husband and Félix knew the feelings were entirely mutual. As she smiled at him, dark eyes twinkling, he remembered how she had scooped Thierry up—almost literally—from a disastrous early love affair that had left him reeling, and had since supported him in everything he did. And now, though he was aware of her terror since she had wormed it out of Thierry that he was working with the Resistance, she supported the group without comment. She motioned for Félix to join the others in the front room.

'Michel's already here. I'll bring you a beer then leave you all to your work.'

Félix stopped in the doorway. 'Before I forget, Clémence asked me to be sure to thank you for your kindness when she arrived.'

Yvette gave him a mischievous smile. 'I might even get to meet her one day.'

Thierry and Michel looked up from a map as he entered.

'*Bonsoir, mes alliés.* Sorry I couldn't get here earlier.'

'No problem, *mon vieux.* You've heard the news?' Félix shook his head. Thierry indicated the nearest chair and pointed to the table, where Félix joined them. 'The Boche have surrendered in North Africa. The tide is turning.'

Félix thumped the table with his fist. 'Good news at last!'

Thierry's answering look was solemn. 'But it makes our work all the more vital now.'

Yvette had slipped silently into the room. She handed Félix his beer, her outwardly calm smile radiating to all three men. 'Thierry's got the bit between his teeth tonight. Make sure you keep each other safe.'

As she left, she squeezed her husband's shoulder. He snaked a strong arm round her waist and held her close. 'Don't fuss, *ma poule*, we know what we're doing.'

Yvette gazed at him pensively. 'I certainly hope you do.' She wriggled her way out of Thierry's grip and headed for the kitchen.

Thierry waited till the door shut before he spoke again. 'For tonight, I think it's better to go on foot. We can keep close to the verge and disappear into the woods if any Boche patrols are out. Agreed?'

Michel nodded his approval.

Félix grunted. 'For sure—I'd prefer not to get caught with a pocketful of detonators.'

Thierry's dry smile and solemn glance at Michel echoed his own feelings as they bent their heads to the map, their fingers tracing alternative backup routes home across the fields.

At half-past eleven Félix and Michel stood and eased tensed muscles when Thierry said it was time to go. The bridge over the railway line was a bare kilometre away, and within fifteen minutes they reached the bridge and crossed to the other side before clambering down the steep embankment to the track. The sky was overcast, making them almost invisible in their dark clothes and caps. They estimated from below the bridge where the charges should be placed and scrambled back up the grassy bank.

Félix stationed himself at the first bend in the road on lookout while Thierry and Michel surveyed the stonework. There was no safe way to place the explosives under the arch without a rope or a ladder to hand, so they had chosen an area at the foot of the wall where the charges could be buried level with the ground. The recent rain had softened the packed earth somewhat, but Félix reckoned his companions would be sweating by the time they'd finished digging.

Félix could see them from where he stood. He heard a faint rumble in the distance and soon picked out the pale glow of two sets of headlights advancing from the direction in which they'd come, giving a warning whistle just as Thierry straightened up and mopped his forehead. He indicated that two vehicles were approaching and would arrive in a matter of minutes. Thierry waved in acknowledgement and Félix stepped across the ditch behind him, crouching down in the trees. A minute later Thierry joined him.

'All done?'

Thierry shook his head. 'We've stamped down a light covering of earth, but we'll have to set the detonators once they've passed. Michel's cleaning up.'

As the sound of the approaching vehicles became clear, Michel looked up, clearly estimating the distance to the woods. Félix stood, shook his head and signalled desperately that he was out of time.

As two *Kübelwagen* appeared, each containing four grey-clad soldiers, Félix held his breath as his friend charged down the steep embankment and disappeared. The trucks drove past slowly and stopped by the bridge. Thierry grimaced as the soldiers climbed out of the trucks, but a remark by one of the drivers was greeted with answering laughter. The men proceeded to light cigarettes from one another before leaning on the parapet and chatting animatedly.

One of the soldiers crossed the bridge and peered over at the railway line below, dropping his cigarette end onto the track. He leant over further and shouted something inaudible. Félix gripped Thierry's arm as two more soldiers headed across the bridge, but almost immediately their comrade began to saunter back. He stopped halfway, stamped his left foot on the earth and kicked the stonework to the side of him. Félix heard a sharp intake of breath from Thierry. His own throat was dry, and he swallowed hard, stifling an urge to cough.

The German examined the sole of his boot and fumbled in his pocket, extracting what looked like a flick knife. After a few seconds he held up the offending stone he'd extracted, lobbed it over the parapet and parried a playful punch on the arm when he reached his nearest comrade. An agonising ten minutes later, with no checks made on the bridge, the soldiers finally got back in the trucks and drove on.

As Félix stood and stretched stiff limbs in the tension-filled silence, Thierry winced and rubbed his back with his fists, then shook his head and gave a quick grin. '*Putain*! How that Fritz who crossed the bridge didn't discover Michel or the explosives I shall never know.'

Félix remained puzzled. 'I don't understand what he was shouting about.'

'Whatever it was, luckily for us it wasn't Michel or the explosives.'

When he re-joined them, Michel—as so often—was silent. But Félix didn't miss the trembling hands his friend shoved firmly into his pockets.

Félix resumed watch, heart still thumping, as the others ran down the road and finished their work, placing the pencil detonators in the explosives. Although they'd initially opted to use the tin of No. 10 half-hour delay switches that he had retrieved from the barn, so as to be well clear before the explosion, they'd now agreed on the ten-minute delays Thierry had thought to bring with him. This, they reasoned, would allow less time for the patrol to return and possibly spot the disturbed earth. It would take Michel only seconds to crush the ends of the copper tubes in the detonators.

Félix was relieved when the three of them were finally jogging back in the direction of Thierry's house. As they reached the Flers crossroads, a thunderous whoomph and an echoing thump as the charges exploded shocked him to a stop. The others were already looking in the direction of the blast, Michel wide-eyed and Thierry sporting a satisfied grin, but the thick forest foliage was between them and the bridge—or, Félix hoped, whatever little was left of it.

What none of them had anticipated was two further German trucks careering towards them from the direction of Flers. As Thierry and Michel sprang into the ditch on the left, Félix flattened himself behind the nearest tree on the right. As soon as the trucks disappeared round the bend two hundred yards away, there was a screech of brakes followed by loud shouts.

Félix joined the others. 'They must have met that patrol on the way back. They'd obviously re-crossed the bridge before it blew. I'll head for home across the fields and through the forest and you two can split up on the way back to Thierry's. That way we've all got a good chance.'

The sound of revving engines halted further discussion. Félix nodded to the others and sprinted to the nearby field gate, hopped over and, crouching low, set off up the hill towards the woods he knew would give him cover all the way home. As he ran, a beam of light tracked slowly towards him. He jinked left and right as the light played across the damp grass, but as a second beam illuminated the open ground he was caught in the glare. He neither turned nor faltered as the shouts grew louder from behind and below. A quick glance upwards showed that he was close to the trees now. Ten seconds was all he needed. As two shots rang out, he threw himself onto the grass, his lungs bursting for breath, then wriggled on his belly until he was clear of the light before scrambling up and lurching on. As he melted into the trees, he cracked his head on a low-hanging branch. Swearing softly, Félix shook his head as blood streamed down his face. He ran on until his legs gave out beneath him and slumped down in a small clearing, where he lay gasping and dizzy from the head wound.

Élodie was woken by a sharp sound she couldn't place. There it was again, from outside the window. She slipped out of bed, and through the chink in the curtains made out a dark figure standing below with one hand poised to throw again. Who the hell was it at this time of night? It certainly wasn't Félix, who would have come straight into the house. She pushed the curtain aside as the upturned face was briefly lit by moonlight. Michel? Yes, it was Michel. She opened the window a fraction and indicated she would come down.

Something terrible must have happened to Félix. She knew it. She'd been sure he was up to something dangerous, but why wasn't Michel with him now? Hauling on her work dungarees and a dark jumper with clumsy hands, she dragged her hair back into an elastic band and crept downstairs, thankful that

her parents slept on the other side of the house. Almost unbe-
lievably, there was no sound from their room even when the
ancient stairs creaked.

She flew at Michel in the yard. 'Where's Félix?'

Michel winced at her sharpness. 'Sorry. I thought that was
his window. So he's not home?'

Élodie frowned. 'Wait here. I'll double-check but I'm sure
his door is still half-open.'

She returned to the yard shaking her head. 'Michel, you
have to tell me what happened.' She grabbed his jacket and
shook him.

'We ran into some trouble with the Boche, and—'

'Why? And who's "we"?'

Michel vacillated. 'I can't tell you that. It was our bad luck
there was one German patrol, let alone another on the way
back. Félix headed for home. He ran to the woods that come
out up there.' He pointed, as if half-hoping to see his friend
emerge from the slate-black dark of the forest. Élodie shook
him again.

'On the way back from where? Oh, just *go on*.'

'We—I—heard shots. We'd separated and gone our own
ways.' He paused. 'Élodie, that's about all I can say.'

Élodie rubbed her face. This was all inconceivable. She let
go of Michel.

'I've got a coat in the barn. We have to find him—for God's
sake, Michel, he could be up there injured—or even...' She
couldn't bring herself to think about the alternative, let alone
express it.

Michel nodded glumly and followed her lead.

Twenty minutes later they'd crested the ridge where the
woodland path split into two. Élodie hesitated, then whispered, 'You go left, that must be the direction he was coming
from, and I'll go right. I know this section, I used to play here
as a child.' Her voice caught and she cleared her throat. 'If
you don't find him on that path, come back and follow me on

this one. It won't take you long to reach the edge of the wood down there.' She pointed to the right. 'This part's much denser but I know it well. And Michel—if you meet any Germans, save yourself.' Michel looked dubious, but she put a finger on her own lips, then his. 'Just go. And good luck.'

A few minutes after they parted, Élodie came to an abrupt halt at the edge of a clearing. There was a faint rustling somewhere nearby, followed by an eerie silence, broken suddenly by the screech of an owl. She scoured the area, her eyes straining: was there a figure out in the open? Félix? As the moon slid out from the cloud, it illuminated her brother on his knees, bent double, blood dripping from a gash on his forehead.

Before she could move, a grey-clad figure burst from the trees to her left, pistol drawn, and as he entered the felled area his athletic gait was unmistakeable, his face suddenly clear in the moonlight. It was Rudi. He appeared to be alone, but instinct rooted her stock-still. She felt sick, and her heart was pounding so cacophonously in her ears she was sure it must be audible to the two men in the hush of the night.

The silence was broken by Rudi saying softly, '*Lieber Gott*! It's you. You are Élodie's brother, yes?'

Félix looked up and glared but remained silent. As he attempted to move, Rudi shook his head and gestured for him to stay still.

'If you'd been caught by my men, you'd be taken in or likely shot, and I should do the same. You do know that, don't you?'

Félix grunted.

Rudi hissed in obvious exasperation. 'Do you realise how stupid you've been? If it weren't for ... you understand this would be very different if I were not alone at this moment?'

Félix hunched his shoulders and Élodie was terrified he was about to lunge at Rudi, but he simply shook his head and blinked as blood ran down his forehead onto his left eyelid and trickled down his cheek.

Rudi checked over his left shoulder. 'My patrol is behind me. Luckily for you, they don't have the dogs tonight. I shall say I've searched this area and found nothing. And you need to disappear.' He pointed towards where Élodie was standing and cocked his head, frowning. He was surely staring straight at her. She slid, serpent-like, further behind the sheltering trees. After a moment he turned his attention back to Félix, who glowered then nodded in agreement.

Élodie's stomach flipped as she heard at least two voices behind Rudi, drawing frighteningly close. She looked back at the two figures as the moon vanished behind dense cloud and the clearing filled with shadow. Be quick, she begged mutely. Rudi backed off a few steps, turned and was gone, running towards the sound of someone stumbling and cursing profusely in German. She heard him shout '*Nichts*', hesitated for only a second, wiped her moist hands on her dungarees, and was at Félix's side as full moonlight reappeared. She must keep him quiet. She put her hand across his mouth and pressed hard as he began to speak, helping him to his feet and leading him into the thick undergrowth from which she had emerged. Some creature shambled away in the darkness, rustling the leaves as it went. Better to move, better to wait? Impossible to know which areas had already been searched. Her thudding heartbeat still filled her ears like a demented metronome as she pulled Félix further from the clearing and dragged him down into the bracken. The earth was dank and soggy, the ferns exuding a pungent, woody odour. She found a handkerchief in her pocket and passed it to him to stem the bleeding.

The worst of the danger was probably over, but Élodie fought to stifle the tremors that shook her. She bit her lip hard. Félix shuffled closer and enveloped her in a bear hug, as he had done so often to soothe her when she was small. The warmth of his tensed nearness and the signature olive-oil scent of *Savon de Marseille* calmed her a little as the rough wool of his jumper tickled her face. She hugged him tight, knowing it was a waiting game.

After what felt like an hour but was probably less than half of that, Élodie sat up slowly and listened. A vixen's blood-curdling shriek nearby made the hairs on her neck prickle but otherwise all was quiet. She checked on Félix as he began to rise. Time to go—that wound needed fixing. She stared intently into the pitch-dark forest before leading him back the way she had come, stopping frequently to check her bearings. Thank heaven for those childhood hours spent playing *cache-cache* among the gnarled old trees that now loomed dense and hostile in every direction. There was no sign of Michel and she had to hope that he was safe. At least she had heard no shots. When they reached the edge of the wood that rose steeply behind the farm, she put a restraining hand on Félix's arm and stopped again.

The scene below them was untroubled. The ancient farmhouse lay dark and peaceful beneath a three-quarter moon, intermittently in shadow as clouds scudded across the sky, chased by the strengthening wind. No lights showed and there was no sign of movement.

Élodie turned to Félix and kept her voice low. 'Was Rudi—was that soldier the only one to see your face at any time tonight?'

Félix returned her anxious look with a glare. 'Yes. And there's no point in pretending any longer—or not to me. It's as clear as day that you're in over your head with that man. I hope you're not sleeping with him? You must have lost your mind, Él.'

Before Élodie could protest, the sound of snapping twigs somewhere behind them spurred her to action. 'Stay low and head for the barn. You go left, I'll go right.' She held his arm till the next ribbon of cloud covered the moon. 'Move, now.'

They bent and crossed the hundred yards of open grassland, then scrambled over the stone wall. Élodie reached the barn at the same time as her brother, just as the wide earthen space of the farmyard was illuminated as glaringly as a circus tent. After ten minutes, the forest edge remained dark and silent. Élodie indicated the back door of the house to Félix and, as he began to move, she peered up the hill one last time then followed him.

In the gloom of the kitchen, Élodie checked that the curtains were well drawn and lit a partly melted candle. She half-filled a bowl with water, grabbed a bar of soap and fetched a clean cloth and disinfectant from the scullery. Félix sat at the table with his face in his hands, which were covered in dried mud.

'Take your hands away and don't touch that wound', she whispered. As he sat up straight she recoiled at the extent of the ragged skin tear, the blood now crusting at the edges. Félix was chalk pale. What had he got himself into? She shook her head and wrang out the cloth. There was no sound from above and she prayed their parents wouldn't wake, especially when Félix swore forcefully as the sharp, sweet-smelling disinfectant flooded the gash on his forehead. Élodie frowned. 'Sorry, but I must.' When she was satisfied that the deep, irregular cut was clean, she held the cloth in place to staunch the now clotting blood and made him wash his hands thoroughly.

'How did you do it?' She was still scrutinising his forehead.

'I think I caught it on a low branch as I ran into the wood. I don't think it was from a gunshot but was all so fast—I can't remember the sequence exactly.'

'You don't *think* it was gunshot? Oh God, Félix, what the hell have you been doing?'

The old clock in the hall ticked rhythmically as she stepped back to look at him fully.

Félix caught her hand. 'Nothing I can tell you about. And why were you up there in the woods tonight anyway?'

'Michel came to look for you, to see you'd got home safely.' Élodie noted Félix's deep scowl and caught his chin between her thumb and forefinger. 'Before you say any more, he wouldn't explain. But we had to find you, and just as well we did. And why, Félix, why do you appear to be risking your life. Is it worth it?'

Félix stared back at her. 'Don't ask me anything more, Él, because I don't want you implicated in any way.'

Élodie's eyes flashed in the candlelight. 'Don't be ridiculous Félix, I'm your sister, so of course I'm "implicated", as you put it.'

'But no more than you need be.' He reached for her wrists and held them firmly. She opened her mouth to speak but he shook his head to silence her, hauled himself upright and kissed her forehead. 'That's an end to it.' Her hair was even wilder than usual, despite the loop of elastic, and he deftly extracted bits of fern that had worked their way in as they lay in the forest earlier.

'By the way', Élodie persisted, 'Michel said there were three of you. Who else? Thierry, I suppose?'

Félix shook his head. 'What have I just said? No point in asking questions I'm not prepared to answer, Él. The fewer who know, the better, for everyone's sake.'

'But if you must be reckless, I could help. I'd like to do something that might make a difference, and I'd do anything you wanted. You know that.'

'And where would your relationship with that German fit into all this?' Félix's tone was stinging.

'Don't be so ridiculous, Félix. That's something else entirely. I could be useful. I could take messages... And you must admit, it's as well it *was* him who found you tonight.'

Félix gave her a warning look that she recognised: his next word would be 'Enough', the same as the day they'd been stopped by those bullying soldiers after the market. No point in pursuing the matter, or at least not now. She gathered up the bowl and cloth and hurled the soap into the sink.

The hall clock struck one. She fidgeted as Félix made a face at her petulance. 'Leave all this to me and go to bed.' He took the bowl from her, set it down again and before she could object, pushed her towards the stairs. 'You've done enough. I'll be up soon.'

She stood halfway up, gripping the banister as she watched him empty the water and swill the bowl clean. He looked up and shooed her on. There was nothing more to be done tonight—or more accurately this morning. She crept along the corridor to her room, exhaustion overwhelming her.

Within five minutes Felix's bedroom door creaked shut. Against all expectations, Élodie felt her eyelids closing. She fell into a dream-ridden sleep. At three o'clock she woke in a sweat, her pulse racing. Had she heard something? She listened attentively. No, the house was quiet. Her fists gripped the worn blanket as she fought off a vivid dream image of the clearing, in which Rudi advanced on Félix with his Luger and pulled the trigger at point-blank range, engulfing them both in a river of blood. Knowing it hadn't happened didn't lessen her terror that one day soon it would.

# CHAPTER SEVEN

## August 1943

ÉLODIE SLACKENED HER PACE as she reached the Manoir and dismounted as she passed the gatehouse. Something was odd today. She looked to left and right. There were no vehicles visible, no soldiers striding about with their guns. The gravel showed tyre tracks, but the lawns were neatly mown and the hedges had been clipped. Had the Germans been ordered to alternative lodgings? She stifled a sense of unease as she rested the bike against the hedge and untied the string holding the eggs on the carrier. She told herself not to be an idiot and headed for the servants' entrance. Before she had taken ten paces, she heard footsteps on the drive behind her and peered over her shoulder, registering a grey uniform and polished boots.

'*Guten Tag, Fräulein.*'

Élodie froze. The voice belonged to Major Wolff. Could she ignore him? She half-turned. He was now only yards from her. She composed her face into what she hoped was a neutral expression.

'*Bonjour, Herr Major.* It's a lovely day.'

He smiled that predatory smile which never reached his piercing, steely eyes. 'Can I help you?'

'Thank you, no. I'm only here to deliver the eggs.'

He caught her arm, and his grip was unyielding. 'Yes. That was my original agreement with your mother before Leutnant Hoffmann chose to override my instructions.'

Élodie frowned. It was uncanny how he had found out about Rudi's visits in the first place, and quite what his latest comment implied she wasn't sure.

The major began to move. 'Come with me. We shall go in the main entrance.'

'No, really...' Élodie tried to protest but he held her firmly and guided her up the front steps and into the cool dimness of the hall. The ancient Manoir, built of pale Caen stone, had been fashioned with small windows to let in a measure of light but conserve the maximum of heat. Élodie blinked as her eyes adjusted from sunlight to shade. The major maintained his hold on her.

'Put the eggs on the table there. I'll make sure the girl takes them to the kitchen.'

Élodie could feel her heart thumping. What was his game? And had his French always been this good, or had it improved out of all recognition? 'Is Lisette not here? Or Madame La-grange?'

'No, they have gone to Argentan. They won't be back before five o'clock at the earliest.'

'And your soldiers? There are always some of them here, no?' He ignored this question, evidently a habit of his.

'Relax, Mamselle. I shall entertain you myself.'

'There is no need, Herr Major. I have to be getting back.'

'Nonsense. Come.' He spat this out like an order, indicating the staircase.

'Why? And where are we going?' Élodie fought to snatch her arm away, but the major only tightened his grasp. He strode across the oak-panelled hall and up the stairs, not hesitating when she tripped. She managed to right herself and concentrated on keeping her footing. At the top, he turned sharp left and dragged her towards a door halfway down a dimly lit corridor. Turning the handle, he ushered her in. He closed and locked the door behind him.

Despite her suffocating fear, the random thought struck Élodie that the room seemed familiar. Then it came back to her. She'd been in it once before. Some years ago, after her mother had mended the faded tapestry curtains that still hung at the mullioned windows, she had helped re-hang them. A large four-poster bed stood squarely against the middle of the far wall.

'I don't understand...'. Élodie froze at his next words.

'There's nothing to understand. You are in my debt and now you will repay what you owe.'

Had she misheard him? Élodie bunched her fists and backed away. 'What *debt*? I owe you *nothing*!'

He let go of her arm, took off his boots and began to unbutton his tunic while Élodie watched in disbelief, looking for any way to escape. 'Do you like the bed, or you prefer to stand?' In two long paces he closed the gap between them and grabbed the fabric of her dress. 'You were in Argentan two days ago. Yes?'

Élodie half-nodded. 'What of it?'

'Leutnant Hoffmann was also in Argentan two days ago. A coincidence?'

Élodie stared at him. Who? How? And then she remembered Lisette.

'And you visited a hotel, yes?'

Élodie could feel her face growing pink. She stuck her chin out. 'That means nothing.'

The major smiled again, his expression chillingly resembling that of a ravenous wolf. Élodie expected him to lick his lips at any moment before moving to devour his prey, overtaken by the growing terror that that was exactly what she was. She tried to hide her fear—predators knew when their quarry was afraid—but could hear her heartbeat echoing madly in her ears and her breath expelling in short, ragged gasps.

Wolff pushed Élodie backwards until she hit the wall, banging her head so hard that she yelped.

'There's also that matter of your brother and the illegal shotgun.'

Élodie struggled to free herself but was no match for his bruising strength.

'We shall make a truce. I shall not punish the Leutnant for a liaison he knows has been forbidden, and I shall overlook the matter of your brother. And in return you will do as I wish.'

Before Élodie could protest further, he grabbed her hair with one hand, yanked up the hem of her dress with the other and fondled her bare thigh. She could smell cigar smoke on his breath, and what else? Alcohol? At this time of day? Brandy, at a guess, and doubtless from Madame Lagrange's cellar. Overlying both was the tang of the same seductive cologne he'd worn that day in the barn. Today it was unbearable. Élodie felt sick and her ears were ringing as if she were about to faint, but she clenched her jaw and stared past his left shoulder as he freed her briefly and dropped his remaining clothing. She stood rigidly and swallowed hard when her underwear ripped as he tore it away.

'Do you like it rough, Élodie?'

She flinched as he used her name, feeling doubly violated before he'd even begun what he intended. She raised her eyes to focus on his face, fighting to show no emotion, determined not to display willing surrender, which it certainly wasn't.

'You could struggle if you wish. For me that would be a pleasure.' His voice was as soft as a cat's purr, and Élodie fought back a wave of nausea. Pleasure? She gritted her teeth and remained as still as her trembling legs allowed.

As he thrust into her, slamming her back against the wall again, she cried out, realising too late that her reaction aroused him further. Biting the inside of her lip so hard that she tasted blood, she clenched her fists behind her back in the certain conviction that he would kill her if she tried to fight.

She felt him convulse as he climaxed and prayed only for it to be over. His hot, sweat-covered shirt had soaked her dress and she winced as he withdrew.

His voice was hoarse as he whispered, 'You are a beautiful girl, with a body that says, "Take me, I'm yours"'. At this she snapped, raising her hands and beating her fists against his chest, but he was faster, grabbing her throat and her right breast so hard that she could neither breathe nor bear to struggle.

'I love that you are a demon, a real *Hitzkopf.* You excite me so. But I will let you go, and you will behave yourself.'

He released his grip slowly. Élodie stood unblinking, motionless as a shop-window mannequin. As he dropped his hands and stepped away, she whipped back one hand and slapped his face so hard that the marks of her fingers left red weals on his cheek. She braced herself, expecting a retaliatory blow, but he merely rubbed his cheek before reaching for his discarded garments, laughing in apparent amusement. Élodie looked down at her own stained, dishevelled clothing and did her best to regain some shred of decency, stooping to pick up her torn underwear.

She began to edge round him on legs that threatened to crumple like cotton wool and he made no move to stop her but, as she walked away, he spoke softly. 'I will see you at the same time next week.'

Élodie spun to face him, in shock. 'You will *not.*'

A slow smile spread across his authoritative face. 'Did you think once is enough to offset your debt? You are wrong. Same day, same time next week.'

As Élodie crossed the room, a silver-framed photograph on the chest by the door caught her attention. A handsome blonde-haired woman and two small, formally dressed, fair-haired boys smiled out at her. She looked at the picture and back at the major, sensing he was still watching her. His smile was full of pride. 'My wife and sons. They are fine boys, are they not?'

Élodie grasped the handle, fumbling to turn the key, and opened the door. Resisting the urge to slam it behind her, she pulled it slowly until she heard a soft clunk as the mechanism engaged. She leant against the corridor wall, shuddering, put her fist to her mouth and bit hard to counteract a scream that was roaring up from somewhere deep inside. The sense of revulsion was crushing. How could he? And effectively to have taken her in front of his family. She ached from head to toe, but that was physical. It was her mind that howled in silent protest. She was aware too that she smelt of sex, that unmistakeable odour which she'd only recently learnt should celebrate an act of love. She crept along the corridor, angrily wiping tears from her face, and went down the stairs, her legs still unsteady. The front door squealed in protest as she opened it. She stared into the courtyard, the vast space remaining cavernously empty in the sunshine, the day as tranquil as when she'd arrived. She picked up her bicycle, clambered onto the saddle, then pedalled away without looking back.

When she reached the forest above the farm, she veered off onto the well-trodden track the deer had made over the years and bumped her way slowly through the trees, where sunlight dappled the earthen forest floor. She stopped when the farmhouse came into view, threw her bike against a tree, and slid down into a foetal position. Putting her head in her hands, she tried to suppress the images that were whirling in her brain. She shuddered. The horror of the whole encounter. The major's apparent sadistic delight in hurting her.

His cologne. His hot breath. His sweaty exertions. Her vulnerability. That was almost the worst. Yes, she was a woman, but she'd always stood up for herself. And on the odd occasion when she couldn't, Félix had always been there to defend her. She put her hands out in front of her, aware that they were shaking like aspen leaves and knowing exactly how a wounded animal must feel. She picked up a long twig and broke it into tiny pieces, hearing a satisfying snap with each repetition. She watched a beetle scurry away as one of the fragments landed on top of it.

There must surely be a way not to repeat the degradation? But a small voice shrieked at her insistently and subversively: submit to anything to protect those you love. She looked down at her family home, lying solid and serene in the dip below her, and at that moment her mother came out through the open farmhouse door and crossed the yard, then came to a sudden stop and peered up towards the forest as if some primordial maternal instinct had alerted her. Élodie shrank down. She wasn't ready to speak to another human yet, least of all her mother. Rose resumed her route towards the herb garden, and Élodie closed her eyes, snapping them open again as the vision of Wolff forcing himself on her replayed itself in an endless loop.

Half an hour later she tiptoed through the open farmhouse door and into the hall, feeling as tentative as the wild deer in the woods as she stopped to listen. She heard the rhythmic sound of chopping from the kitchen and crept across the hall to the staircase, avoiding those floorboards that always emitted a tell-tale creak. When she had almost reached the top of the stairs, her mother appeared in the kitchen doorway, a paring knife in one hand.

'Élodie, is that you?'

'Yes, Maman.'

Her mother looked up and frowned. 'You didn't think to let me know you were home? And what on earth has happened to your frock?'

Élodie clutched the stain-marked dress to her legs. 'I fell off my bike, Maman, that's all.'

As her mother moved to climb the stairs behind her, her frown replaced by a look of concern, Élodie hurried up the last few steps. 'Don't worry Maman, I'm going to have a bath to clean up and I'll be down soon. I won't use too much water.' She was sure her mother would smell the residue of the major's assault and ask too many questions, when all she wanted to do was to shut the whole incident out of her mind as quickly as possible.

Her mother frowned again, shook her head, and returned to the kitchen.

Élodie ran a few inches of water into the bathtub, peeled off the soiled dress, and snatched up a bar of soap. She cleansed herself repeatedly, then took a nailbrush and with great deliberation scoured her inner thighs until they turned an angry shade of pink. She sobbed quietly at the humiliating recollections that ran through her brain like a series of still images, now scrubbing at her hands and arms, trying to erase the sensation of the powerful hands that had roamed over every inch of her slim form and taken possession of it against her will.

Finally she stopped, too exhausted to continue, and clambered out of the water. After rubbing herself dry, willing the towel to complete the cleansing process, she picked up the dress and ripped it to shreds before bundling it up with her torn underwear. She looked in the mirror, staring at the pale, blotchy face that looked back at her, and gave her reflection a grim smile: the major certainly wouldn't have touched her if he could see her now. Taking a deep breath, she came to a decision. That man would not define her, change her into a scared rabbit. Whatever it took, she would survive. And somehow, one day, she hoped he would pay for what he'd done.

Dressed in her everyday work clothes, Élodie shot down the stairs and called out to her mother on the way to the door. 'I'm going to see to the chickens, Maman. I won't be long.' She picked up a box of matches from the hall table and added it to the bundle of torn strips in the deep pockets of her dungarees.

Élodie mechanically fed the hens and topped up their water, distracted fleetingly by their repetitive noises. It was too early to shut them up for the night when there were still so many hours of daylight left—she could do that after supper. Checking that no one was in view, she went to the back of the barn and dropped the rags from her pockets into a pile. By chance it hadn't been her best dress, the blue one that Rudi had liked… She stopped in her tracks. Rudi. Shutting her eyes, she was suddenly unable to think about him and saw only the major's well-pressed uniform, but the memory of Rudi's smile surfaced insistently, and with a deep sigh she forced herself to focus on the task at hand. She lit a match and dropped it onto the green cloth, which began to smoulder. The addition of a few dry twigs and another match did the trick, and small flames began to devour the material. It took only minutes until all that remained was a small heap of hot ashes. Grabbing a few handfuls of damp grass Élodie cooled the remains and scattered them with a stick. Now she only had two frocks, but who cared? She never wanted to think about the green one again.

On the following Thursday night, Élodie hardly slept. In the morning she couldn't eat, brushing off her mother's concern and insisting that she would be hungry later. In the henhouse she collected three dozen eggs, dropping and replacing several as she packed them, and performed all her morning tasks like an automaton, scarcely aware of what she was doing. At lunchtime she ate a small piece of stale bread topped with her mother's home-made goat's cheese, compelling herself to swallow each mouthful.

At quarter past two she set off for the Manoir. This time she wore dungarees and a faded shirt. Maybe that would discourage Major Wolff. Her legs were like lead and twice she stopped with the intention of turning back but, each time, Félix's face floated in front of her. She pedalled on with gut-wrenching reluctance.

When she reached the Manoir, to her intense relief Mme Lagrange's old car was parked in the drive. The sleek and stylish Delahaye still looked immaculate, even though its maroon-and-cream paintwork was spattered with mud. Élodie remembered their father describing it to a wide-eyed Félix when he was about twelve, in those days a gangly boy with a mop of curls who had jiggled with delight at the idea of such luxury. She unpacked the eggs and walked round to the kitchen entrance, where Lisette was standing on the gravel flirting outrageously with one of the German soldiers. She registered Élodie's presence and waved a hand.

'You can put those in the kitchen.'

'And *bonjour* to you, Lisette.' Élodie wasn't surprised, yet how dare she behave like that? The German soldier acknowledged her with a nod, scarcely seeing her, his mind clearly focused on Lisette's charms.

In the gloom of the kitchen, Élodie put the egg container on the table. As she did so, the inner door opened and Mme Lagrange stepped in. 'Élodie, my dear, how nice to see you.' Her eyes skimmed the room. 'Have you seen Lisette?'

Before Élodie could answer Lisette scurried in, obviously having heard her employer's voice.

'Ah there you are, Lisette. Would you bring tea to the drawing room, please? And Élodie, you will join us?'

Élodie tried to refuse, feeling awkward in her work clothes and uneasy about who 'us' meant, but the older woman was insistent, brushing aside her protests and ushering her through the door and up the short flight of stairs to the hall. Mme Lagrange indicated the open doorway opposite and motioned for Élodie to go in, where she stopped short. The man on the sofa jumped to his feet as the two women entered.

'Major Wolff, I doubt if you've met young Élodie?'

He bowed his head and held out his hand as Mme Lagrange encouraged her forward. Élodie shook his hand, his soft grasp as abhorrent as an unwanted caress, and waited for him to speak.

'No, Madame, I haven't had the pleasure. I think maybe Leutnant Hoffmann has made the young lady's acquaintance in the market.'

Élodie was dumbstruck at the fluid lie. And he'd used that word 'pleasure' again. She withdrew her hand and wiped it surreptitiously on her trouser leg, feeling herself blush as Mme Lagrange stared at her with a puzzled expression.

'Ah yes, Leutnant Hoffmann—what a pleasant young man. Élodie, do join the major.'

Élodie sat as far away from Wolff as she could. As Mme Lagrange began to speak, Lisette arrived and clattered the tea tray onto the low, elegant table that stood on a threadbare Aubusson rug.

'Perhaps you would pour the tea, Lisette.'

Lisette did so with ill-disguised displeasure, glaring at Élodie as she thrust a delicate porcelain cup and saucer at her. As soon as she had finished her task, she swept out of the room. Mme Lagrange discreetly ignored the girl's behaviour and asked after Élodie's mother, before looking towards the major.

'Élodie's mother is a talented seamstress. She's done invaluable work for me over the years.'

'Is this a talent her daughter shares?' Wolff addressed this remark to Élodie.

'No, Herr Major. Not at all, I'm afraid.'

He smiled benignly. 'Doubtless you have other talents.'

Élodie struggled not to spit out her tea, or choke on it, but managed to maintain her composure while Madame Lagrange kept up the conversation. After twenty minutes, Élodie made her excuses and stood to leave.

Madame Lagrange stood up politely. 'Do remember me to your mother, my dear. I'll see you out.'

Wolff was already on his feet. 'Let me do so, madame. It's the least I can do.'

Mme Lagrange afforded him what Élodie perceived as a warm smile. Could she actually *like* the repellent man? The major put a hand under Élodie's elbow and guided her into the hall. Élodie turned towards the kitchen stairs but was led to the front entrance. Mme Lagrange appeared in the drawing room doorway and raised a hand in farewell as the major opened the heavy door.

He insisted on walking down the front steps with her, still within earshot of Mme Lagrange. 'I'm sorry your visit was so short, *Mamselle*. I hope to see you again soon.'

Élodie could scarcely believe his suave posturing, but apparently it came easily to him. The charm. The falsehoods. The subterfuge. He put a hand on her shoulder and spoke almost inaudibly. 'Same time, same place next week. I shall ensure we are alone. And perhaps you won't be looking like a ragamuffin, even though I somehow find that disturbingly sexy.'

A week later, Élodie again cycled to the Manoir. She repeated to herself endlessly that if this was what it took to keep her family safe, she had no other option. As she cycled under the archway at the gatehouse, her heart sank and her feet felt heavy on the pedals. She'd hoped Mme Lagrange would not have gone out, but the drive and lawn sprawled wide and teasingly silent.

A sudden movement by the front door brought her to a halt, and her stomach tightened as Major Wolff strolled down the steps, a sardonic smile on his face. By the time she'd dismounted and untied the egg tray from the carrier, he was at her side. He looked her up and down with a half-smile, his eyebrows raised in amusement at her plain short-sleeved blouse and dowdy flowered skirt. He twitched the fabric between his thumb and forefinger, stood back for a moment, then took her arm and guided her towards the front door.

'How nice to see you, Élodie. I had a feeling you wouldn't be here today.'

She hated that he used her name in that casual way. She heard her voice, so brittle it might snap, as she replied, 'Did I have any choice?'.

'Oh, but we all have choices, *Liebchen*. It's the consequences of *how* and *what* we choose that matter.' He smiled the vulpine smile again, and Élodie wanted so much to punch him that she had to bunch her free fist in her pocket to restrain herself. Instead, she adopted what she hoped was a neutral stare of complete indifference.

Wolff closed the front door behind them and then, as before, indicated that she should place the eggs on the side table. 'Come, all is quiet here. Everyone is out, so we can take our time for pleasure today.'

Élodie almost screamed at the word 'pleasure'—he clearly had a very different view of their encounters. She ignored his proffered arm and simply followed him dutifully across the hallway and up the broad-tread stairs. The sooner the nightmare was over, the sooner she could leave. When they entered his room, her eyes focused immediately on the chest of drawers, on which his wife and sons still beamed out of the photograph in its silver frame.

Today Wolff was different. Today he was infinitely more alarming, because he seemed determined to be endearing, like a cherished lover. Élodie felt only numbness—at least when it had been a violent act forced upon her, she had known she was powerless, that she was overwhelmed. Today it was as if he assumed she longed to be in his arms as he slowly took off his clothes, unbuttoned her blouse and kissed her shoulder, the strength of his usual cologne making her want to gag. He was muttering in German as if in a trance as he guided her down onto the bed. An image of Rudi floated into her mind as the foreign words continued. Tears coursed across her cheeks and into her hair as she lay and blocked all thoughts of him from her mind. She tensed as the major became ever more intimate, unable to react as he apparently wished her to, even for the sake of those she loved. Yet still she submitted as he lay on top of her and continued to whisper what she presumed were endearments. His movements were slow, languorous almost, and to her revulsion she felt her body responding to the stimulus. As he gave a final shudder and gasped, she whimpered in anguish at her own mortifying self-betrayal. He pulled away and lay on his back, his forehead beaded with sweat.

He leant over and spoke softly, his voice husky. 'If you would only reciprocate, *Liebchen*, we could make perfect love.'

Élodie sprang from the bed and grabbed her blouse. She briskly rubbed from her face the salty wetness of the tears she had shed, shrugged on the plain garment to cover her bare skin and snatched her underwear off the floor. She turned and looked at the major directly for the first time that day, her throat dry as she spoke. 'You must be out of your damned mind.'

She stepped into her now rumpled skirt and fastened the button at the waist, her fingers fumbling. After retrieving her shoes and slipping them on, she headed for the door. Beside the elegant tallboy she hesitated. She snatched up the photo frame, turned over the picture and slammed it face down onto the wood with a loud crash. Tinkling splinters of glass flew in all directions as Wolff rushed at her with an enraged bellow. He struck her once with a full backhander that caught the side of her face, then seized her as she fell and shoved her hard against the drawers. She stiffened, thinking he would hit her again, but he withdrew his hands and hissed '*Raus*—get out, *du Bitch*!'

He turned his back on her as she scrabbled at the door handle. The hinges protested as she pulled at the door with trembling hands, realising he hadn't even locked it this time. She watched as he turned over the frame and took out the photograph, which had been slit by the glass clear down the middle of his wife's face. Without looking up he said, 'If you ever come back here, you will soon wish you hadn't.'

Élodie fled down the stairs and outside. It had begun to rain, pelting her with big, stormy drops, and by the time she had reached the entrance gates she was already soaked. About a mile down the road, Mme Lagrange's Delahaye purred past from the opposite direction, its owner waving as she spied Élodie, who raised a hand and sped on. Had madame misled Wolff as to when she would return? What if... Élodie stopped the thought in its tracks. If Mme Lagrange had discovered her in the major's room—his bed... Roiling anger warmed the cool raindrops running down her face, and she pedalled as if the Devil himself were stalking her. Half a mile further on she stopped by the roadside and was sick. She wiped her face with a handful of wet grass and stared back down the road the way she'd come, obsessed with the notion that Wolff might take it into his head to follow her.

Two days later Élodie wandered up the path from the hen-house, concentrating on the warmth of the sun on her face and pleased that the hens were laying well. It was only with supreme concentration that she had begun to stifle the memories of the ordeal she had been subjected to at the Manoir. The full egg basket hung heavily over her right arm, and she steadied it with her left hand as she came to an abrupt stop in the farmyard. Parked outside the kitchen entrance was a German staff car. Major Wolff's, she was sure, and fear mixed with alarm filled her, causing her knees to buckle briefly as she contemplated what had brought him here. A uniformed soldier stood with his back to her, leaning against the driver's door, smoking a cigarette and watching the cat stalking birds.

Her father came out of the house scowling. He spotted her immediately, shook his head, and gestured for her to go away as the soldier's attention was drawn to the sound of his footsteps on the gravel. Élodie slipped down the side of the house unnoticed and in through the open scullery door, set the basket down on the wooden worktop beside the cracked white sink, and crept along the passage towards the kitchen.

She could hear two voices. She moved as close as she dared while remaining unseen, hearing Major Wolff's insistent voice say, 'Then where *is* he, madame?'

Her mother sounded angry. 'I've already told you, Major, I have no idea. He is twenty-five years of age and no longer has to tell me where he's going or when he'll be back.'

'Well, when he does come back, tell him he is to report to me at the Manoir immediately.'

Her mother's tone was patient but firm. 'I've no idea when that will be, Major, but I will pass on your message when I next see him.'

Wolff cleared his throat. 'I can't impress on you enough, madame, that this is an extremely serious matter.'

'I understand that, Major. Now I'm sure you're very busy—I certainly am.'

After a short silence the major, sounding no less annoyed, said, 'Then good day, Madame Duchamp. Please ensure that I don't need to call again. Oh, and one last thing. We shan't be needing eggs from here anymore. But we do need meat. I shall send someone to collect six chickens each week.'

'But Major—'. Her mother's voice came to an abrupt halt as the outer door was slammed.

Élodie heard the car's motor start, the sound of its tyres in the yard growing fainter as it pulled away. She peeped into the kitchen and saw her mother staring after the departing vehicle.

'What was that all about, Maman?'

Rose turned at the sound of her daughter's voice, her face red with anger. 'Pfft, that insufferable major says he wants to talk to Félix urgently. He said something about a shotgun.'

'What?' Élodie was alarmed. Was his visit, rather, the vindictive consequence of her outburst at the Manoir the other day? It had been madness to act as she did, but she told herself for the dozenth time that Wolff had left her no choice, and she knew deep down she'd do the same again in a heartbeat. Or, despite his comment about the gun, could he possibly suspect Félix's involvement in the destruction of the bridge?

'Who knows what goes through that odious man's mind? And as for requisitioning our chickens...' Rose's voice was still angry but Élodie heard the softening in her voice as she looked at her youngest child. 'Your brother may think I'm stupid but I'm not. I know that Félix is doing something dangerous. I'm afraid he's being reckless.' She caught Élodie's hand. 'Has he said anything to you?'

Élodie shook her head. No way was she going to tell her mother the little she knew or had pieced together so far. Nor

did she want to tell a direct lie—her own mind was in enough
turmoil already without trying to remember untruths.

# CHAPTER EIGHT

## *August 1943*

FÉLIX CHECKED HIS WATCH for the second time as he approached the draper's shop. He was still earlier than they had agreed, but with luck Clémence would be there anyway. He walked on to the next corner, where he bought a pack of increasingly scarce Gauloise Caporal from the *tabac*. He also picked up a newspaper, feigning intense interest in the cover story as he surveyed the street outside. He satisfied himself that there was no sign of any uniformed Germans, folded the paper under his arm as he left the shop, and returned the way he had come.

The shop bell's distinctive trill signalled his arrival, and Mme Tailler looked up from the counter where she was measuring out a length of cloth. The sole customer, a black-clad elderly woman whom Félix didn't recognise, eyed him suspiciously. Men rarely bought fabric on their own, he supposed.

He nodded to them both. 'Bonjour, mesdames.'

He watched as Mme Tailler assessed the situation in short order. 'Bonjour, monsieur. You're here to collect your mother's order? I'll be with you in a minute.'

Félix wordlessly blessed her astuteness as the old woman lost interest in him and struck up an inconsequential conversation with the shop owner while the cloth was cut and packed, then asked to look at threads to match the colour. Mme Tailler shot Félix a philosophical look as she fetched a box of yarn and waited while the woman dithered and deliberated, appearing unable to make up her mind. He was suddenly aware of a shadow cast on the bare boards of the sunlit floor and stepped speedily behind a tall gondola stacked with curtain material before risking a look outside. As he fingered the nearest bolt of fabric, he was startled to see the fat-mouthed German corporal standing in the doorway peering into the shop.

Mme Tailler's voice broke the tension. 'That's exactly the material your mother chose.' Her head inclined towards the old woman, who was watching the soldier attentively but suddenly fixed her rheumy gaze on Félix for a long moment, her mouth compressed.

Mme Tailler spoke again, holding up a cotton reel. 'The mid-green thread I think, madame.'

The old woman transferred her attention and nodded her agreement, concluded her purchase and shuffled towards the door. She stopped close beside Félix, shook his arm with a blue-veined, shaky hand and mumbled quaveringly, 'Take care, *jeune homme*, they're everywhere'. Félix peered back through the door. He was relieved to see that the soldier had moved on and was questioning a middle-aged man fifty yards away across the street. He looked into her ashen, age-lined face and noted the milkiness in her eyes. He patted her lace-gloved hand and smiled as a potent waft of lavender reached his nose. 'I'm sure they are. *Bonne journée*, madame.'

He opened the door for her and stood to one side out of sight as the bell sounded. The soldier was now barracking the agitated man whose papers he was examining. The old woman stood and watched the argument for a minute or so before turning in the opposite direction and hobbling away with her bundle, leaning heavily on her walking stick.

Félix raised his eyebrows at Mme Tailler. 'What was all that about?'

Mme Tailler refolded the material that was spread across the counter. 'She lost both her husband and son during the last war, and has since had a bit of a reputation as a mischief-maker. I wasn't sure what her reaction would be when you walked in. Though I do know that she hates the Germans more than she suspects strangers. And her son would have been about your age when he died.'

Félix grimaced. '*La pauvre*. So many families devastated in the Great War, and now it's happening all over again.'

'And no end in sight either, more's the pity. But you didn't come here to chat to me, Félix. Clémence came in from shopping about ten minutes ago. Go on up. I know she'll be pleased to see you.'

When Félix knocked on the door that had become so familiar to him, it was opened almost immediately. He suppressed a spontaneous smile when Clémence appeared. She looked stunning in a simple flowered dress that flattered her wide-set cornflower-blue eyes. He registered her solemn expression with a sense of dread and frowned.

'Clémence—what is it? Has something happened?'

She sighed. 'You could say that. Oh, I'm sorry—how rude of me. Do come in Félix.'

As he shut the door, she said quietly, 'I've been recalled.'

'What?' Félix spun round. 'To England? Why?'

'Reliable information has come in from another group that the Germans have wind of a radio operator in this area. The latest message says they're closing in, and it's only a matter of time.'

Félix longed to take her in his arms, beg her not to go, but he couldn't. Her survival was paramount. With tremendous self-control he maintained the gap between them. He looked

past her towards the window and chose his next words carefully, his voice brittle. 'I understand, of course. I'm sorry you
have to go. We've worked well together, wouldn't you say?'

He could hardly bear the thought that he was losing this
half-English girl. A solitary tear trickled down her cheek and
she brushed it away, but not before he had seen it. He took
two fateful steps, knowing it was foolish even as he did so, and
opened his arms. Without wavering, Clémence flung herself
into his arms and clung to him as sinuously as an ivy stem. He
breathed in her fresh scent, savoured her soft curves against
his own work-hardened form, and longed only to keep her
safe from the warring world outside.

All Félix's instincts told him this was not the moment to
express his feelings for her. Not now, not when she had no
choice but to leave. But if he didn't, and if she went without
knowing, how would he ever get her back? He knew as surely
as autumn follows summer that he wanted her in his life. But
he hadn't known whether she might want that too. He shifted
his weight slightly and leant back.

'Clémence—dammit, I still don't even know your real
name—I need to say something.'

She shook her head and put a slim forefinger to his lips. 'No,
you don't, Félix.'

He tensed. Had he misread her—almost made a fool of
himself?

Her smile said otherwise. 'You don't need to say a word. I
already know.'

She raised her face to his and any rational intentions deserted him. He kissed her long and hard, until they were both
trembling and breathless.

Félix knew this had gone far enough. Before he completely
lost control, he had to stop it right here. He let her go and
stepped back. 'I'm sorry, I shouldn't have done that. Forget it
ever happened.'

He accurately anticipated the hurt in Clémence's eyes. 'But I thought...'

'You maybe thought correctly, but you have to leave—and I have work to do.'

She frowned. 'I don't understand. I may never see you again, and...'

'Exactly.' Félix continued before she could say more, distancing himself with a tone he knew would sound abrupt. 'I'll need to make all the arrangements for your departure with Thierry as soon as it's confirmed. When will you know?'

Clémence stared at him, her incomprehension at his complete transformation written clearly on her face. 'They say either side of the next full moon.'

'So soon?' Félix was dismayed. 'But that means within the week!'

'I hope I can return when the danger's died down. If there are no further transmissions, they'll think I've moved on. And I've already been told the information we're providing is valuable.'

'That's good. And of course, it would be useful to know who we're working with if you do come back.' Félix checked his watch. 'I'm sorry, right now I have to go. When will you know the proposed date for your flight?'

Clémence fidgeted with the handkerchief she was holding. 'Tonight, they said. I have to transmit at 10 o'clock.'

'I'll come back tomorrow. Unless you'd like me to come with you tonight?'

Clémence shook her head, resolute now. 'I haven't quite decided on the safest place to set up the radio yet, and it'll be a brief exchange. I don't want to lug the equipment too far, but I don't want to risk being detected either. I'll be out and back very quickly.'

Félix accepted he might be more of an encumbrance than a help. Besides, he needed to warn Thierry that they were losing their radio operator. He hated behaving callously and leaving her like this, but someone had to be realistic for them both.

'OK, then I'll see you tomorrow around the same time.'

She didn't answer, simply nodded in acknowledgement, her expression stony. Félix shut the door and drew in a deep breath. Why was life such utter shit these days? He couldn't face Mme Tailler right now, so slipped out of the back exit into the alleyway.

Four nights later, Félix stood disconsolately in the moonlight with Thierry, listening for the sound of the Lysander's approach. They had set out the landing lights but, as usual, he would not switch them on until the aircraft's arrival was imminent. He peered up at the moon—two days past full, by his reckoning. Clémence was standing by the truck with Lisette, who for once appeared to be chatting animatedly. Félix had wanted to fetch Clémence himself, but Thierry was abnormally jittery and had insisted it would be much safer for her to leave Flers with another woman, especially as Félix had now had two run-ins with the fleshy German corporal.

Félix kept his eyes on Clémence as they waited. She was again wearing the ill-fitting dark coveralls she'd arrived in, her slender figure nonetheless distinct. He was aware Thierry was watching him but knew he wouldn't ask questions, even if he had probably made certain—wrong, as it so happened—assumptions. Within a few minutes, bang on schedule, the unmistakeable rumble of the Lizzie could be heard from the north. When Thierry indicated that the code had been exchanged, Félix mechanically flicked on the flashlights, all too aware of a thunderous ache in his belly and his soul.

As the plane landed and executed its usual tight turn, the two women joined them. Thierry anticipated the moment and directed a reluctant Lisette towards the plane with him. Clémence stood a foot in front of Félix, reached into her pocket, and placed something in his palm, closing his fingers over it.

She kept her voice low. '*Mon beau Félix, je t'aime de tout mon cœur.*'

'And I you, Clémence.' For one perfect moment, everything that remained unsaid flowed between them, a connection so ethereal that it vanished in an instant.

She kissed him on both cheeks and whispered, 'It's Giselle'. She put one slim hand on his cheek, turned and ran to the plane without looking back. He distractedly thrust whatever she had given him into his pocket.

The pilot taxied and took off, rising steadily, the Lizzie backlit by the bluish white of the almost full moon. As Félix watched the aircraft clear the copse of trees, Lisette floated into his line of vision, her face twisted in a curious mixture of contempt and jealousy. He turned away, angry at her reaction, angry at himself for not wishing Godspeed to Clémence as he'd wanted to—and at the recognition that, at their parting, she had been braver than he. A cavernous wave of desolation threatened to engulf him. His mind snapped to alert at the sound of a low whistle from Thierry, who cupped a hand to his ear and jabbed a thumb over his shoulder. Félix listened for a few seconds and heard the distant whine of several approaching engines. As Thierry collected the flares and canes, he picked up the only small box to have been delivered by the Lysander. They both followed Lisette, who was already running for the truck. Félix stowed the box on the flatbed and Thierry threw in the canes, handing him the three flashlights before securing the tailgate.

The two men leapt into the truck, one either side of Lisette. For once, Thierry had parked right inside the field gate. After a quick glance to the left that showed no visible oncoming lights, he floored the accelerator and the vehicle shot off, its wheels scrabbling for traction. About a mile down the road, Thierry looked in the mirror and grunted. Félix checked behind. One set of headlights was now in sight, at some distance but unmistakeably closing. Thierry wrenched the steering wheel, took a brutally sharp turn to the left, and Félix heard the loose container in the back slide across the boards and hit the wooden sidepiece with a thump. The truck's tyres squealed in protest. He hadn't asked what was in the box, and mentally prayed the contents were intact.

The vehicle slowed a little on the twisting country lane, but they continued without lights until the roadway was plunged into inky blackness by trees that formed a low overhanging arch that drooped perilously close above them. Félix wound the window down. He leant out with one of the flashlights and half-covered its beam with spread fingers, which gave enough light to drive by but was considerably less conspicuous than the vehicle's headlights. Thierry cursed and braked as a startled deer hurtled into the hedge about twenty feet in front of them, and snorted as Lisette said sarcastically, 'That would have fed us for a month'.

*Typical Lisette.* With the darkness of the wood now behind them, moonlight once more flooded the road and Félix extinguished the torch. He rummaged in his pocket and took out the small package he'd been given by Clémence—or should he now think of her as Giselle? He smiled to himself. Such a fitting name for a girl with the grace and form of a ballerina. Shielding the object with his hand, he took a quick look. It was a small silver robin with a tiny heart hung around its neck on a slim red ribbon. He closed his fist and returned it to his pocket, remembering how he had watched her receive a message one day, sitting with her head tilted to one side. He could still see her laughing, her head thrown back, when he told her she looked like an alert little bird. But now she was gone. To hell with this war. He hunched his shoulders, his fists clenching and unclenching in his lap.

'What's that you're hiding?' Lisette's sharp voice interrupted his regret-filled brooding. She'd been craning her neck to see what he'd been holding.

'Nothing you need concern yourself with, Lisette.' Félix didn't miss the grin on Thierry's face as he returned his attention to the road ahead.

Félix heard the commotion before he saw the cause. As he and Élodie entered the village square two days after Clémence's departure, six German soldiers had surrounded an old man and two of them were frog-marching him towards the back of a truck. The noise had drawn Père Bernard from the church. Félix heard Élodie's gasp as the priest tried to reason with the nearest soldier before being pushed roughly aside.

'*Merde*!' Félix caught his sister's arm. Her eyes were huge and fear filled. 'That's M. Abramson they have.'

'Your old teacher? But why?'

Félix's voice was strained. 'He's a Jew, Él.'

'But even so...'

The diminutive black-clad figure, yellow star unmistakeable on his coat sleeve, was unresisting. He stumbled on the cobbles and received a rough shove. Félix was outraged. He began to run, despite Élodie tugging at his sleeve, and yelled as he halted in front of the old man's captors, his arms spread wide. Two of the other soldiers immediately aimed their weapons at him.

'He's a teacher, for God's sake. Where are you taking him? What's he done?'

An officer stepped forward and faced Félix. He heard Élodie's startled cry at the same moment as he recognised the man in front of him. The Lieutenant. His sister's lover.

Rudi drew him aside and ordered the others to carry on. When they did so, he spoke quietly in French.

'Don't make a scene. You know I can't protect you.'

Félix was still fuming. 'That poor old man has done nothing, except to have the misfortune to be born Jewish.'

Rudi shook his head. 'Not so. Unhappily for him, copies of an underground leaflet were found in his house, which he had been distributing.'

Félix could scarcely believe it. 'So, what will happen to him?'

Rudi shrugged. 'He knows the penalty for acts of resistance. I will try and do what I can for him, but it won't be much.'

A mix of emotions crossed the Lieutenant's face. Félix was nonplussed to see shame in the German's eyes, the tic in his cheek, his jaw set rigid. Could he be genuine? Could Élodie have been right to look beyond the hated field grey? The blue eyes left Félix's face, alert to something behind him, before returning to focus on him once more.

'I'm sorry about this, but it's my only option.'

Félix had no idea what Rudi meant and was unprepared for the blow that caught him so hard that he staggered back and fell. He offered up silent thanks when he saw Père Bernard catch Élodie as she screamed and struggled to catapult towards him. He looked up at Rudi, who was ignoring his sister completely.

'What is going on here?' Major Wolff now stood over him, glaring down.

Rudi's authoritative answer took Félix by surprise, as did the fact that he spoke in French so that Félix could understand. 'I've dealt with the situation, Herr Major. A misunderstanding, basically.'

'Misunderstanding? With a member of this family? I doubt that. Have you arrested him?'

'That won't be necessary on this occasion, Herr Major.'

Wolff's face reddened, his eyes alight at the challenge to his authority. He surveyed the small crowd that had gathered. 'I will discuss this with you later, Leutnant Hoffmann. And you', he nudged Félix's back sharply with his knee, 'can expect no leniency if you cross my path again'.

The major returned to his car, giving them one last hard stare as his driver pulled away. Félix massaged his jaw and slowly got to his feet without taking the hand Rudi extended to help him up. He turned his back on the Lieutenant without a word and headed for his sister, who was still being safely restrained by Père Bernard.

Félix took Élodie from the priest's outstretched arms and held on to her as she watched the Lieutenant climb into the truck. Rudi sat bolt upright next to the driver and kept his eyes on the road as the vehicle wheeled in a semi-circle and drove past close to where they stood, the old man almost invisible in the back between the two hulking soldiers either side of him.

'Is there anything I can do?'

The priest's voice, solicitous though it was, startled Félix from his thoughts. 'Thank you, mon Père, but I think we'd best go home.' He fervently hoped the churchman believed his sister's concern was for him alone and not related to the lieutenant. He supported Élodie's weight in his arms and felt a surge of compassion at her dazed expression. Père Bernard nodded in agreement and stepped back, made the sign of the cross, and grasped his rosary beads as he headed for the church.

When they'd taken half a dozen steps, Élodie was shaking so hard that Félix sat her against the old stone horse trough on the edge of the square. She hadn't said another word, but he could see the inner struggle echoed on her face. He leant against her and stroked her hair, pushing it back from her forehead. She took a huge, shuddering breath and her eyes were vacant.

'Why, Félix? Why is this shitty war ruining our lives?'

'I wish I knew, Él.'

'But why did he have to hit you like that?'

'Él...' Félix cupped her face in his hands. 'Even I accept that he did it to try and protect me.'

Élodie choked. '*Protect you*! But he knocked you down.'

'Because that fucking loathsome major was about to pull rank on the situation, that's why.'

'Oh.' Élodie's reply was a murmur, her eyes still wide and unsure. She buried her head against his shoulder and hugged him fiercely. Her breathing gradually slowed to a steady rhythm. She sat back and managed a wan smile. 'Promise you'll be more careful, Félix—I think I should go mad if, if...'

Félix rubbed her cheek affectionately with his fist. 'I think we should see if Marc can give us some coffee, or what passes for that these days, with something stronger added.' He got up, hauled her to her feet and they set off up the road, which was now chillingly silent in the mid-afternoon haze.

The café was almost empty at this hour. Marc, who was another of Félix's old schoolfriends, delivered their coffee, which by sleight of hand he had fortified under the counter with a *digestif*. He sat to chat with them for a few minutes. By the time he left to serve two German soldiers who had positioned themselves a few tables away, Félix was pleased to see that the colour had returned to Élodie's cheeks, due in no small part to the brandy, he suspected. She turned to him, her expression troubled. She rested her chin on her upturned fists, her elbows on the edge of the table.

'It's going to get worse for all of us, isn't it?'

One of the Germans turned and stared at them as she spoke, though Félix was pretty sure he could neither hear nor understand at that distance.

'I'm very much afraid it is, Él. We're all going to have to be even more careful what we say, who we say it to...' He quickly checked her reaction, but she merely made a face and downed the last of her coffee. She got up from her chair briskly.

'Let's go, Félix.' She glared at the soldier who was again watching them steadily. 'I've had enough for today. I'd say you have too.'

Félix rubbed his bruised cheek and steered her to the exit. 'Given that we never got done what we set out to do, I'll come ahead of you tomorrow and mend the trestle table at least temporarily before you set up for the market.'

The German's eyes followed them fixedly and for a moment Félix steeled himself for another inspection of their papers. He breathed a sigh of relief as he shut the door behind them, the soldier's attention diverted by the arrival of Marc with their order.

To Élodie's surprise, when she reached the yard after cleaning out the henhouse that afternoon—a long overdue task that was today a welcome distraction—she saw a bicycle with a child carrier leaning against the wall outside the kitchen. It could surely only be Hélène? She sighed deeply, debating whether to retrace her steps and keep out of the way for another hour, but at that moment she heard a childish shriek of delight and Lucie ran out of the house with her hands held high, her hazel curls bobbing and green eyes sparkling. Élodie bent and gathered Lucie into her arms, turning in circles as the squirming toddler squealed with pleasure. She stopped sharply when she spotted her sister, who, eyes narrowed and arms folded, stood leaning against the kitchen doorpost. Not for the first time, Élodie reflected that the delightful child clearly took after her father. Moreover, Hélène resembled no other member of her family. Her thin face was framed by straight, mid-brown hair, which, however artfully arranged, could not hide the pinched features and sharp nose that together produced an expression of sour discontent.

'Do be careful not to drop her, Élodie.' As usual, Hélène's tone was shrill and critical.

Élodie set her niece down carefully onto her feet, irritation rising. 'Of course I won't drop her. Why would you even think that?'

'Because you're being impetuous and silly, the same as you always are, that's why.'

Their mother appeared behind Hélène. 'Come now girls, enough of harsh words. Élodie, we see little enough of your sister as it is. Let's enjoy her company while she's here.'

Élodie swallowed a tart rejoinder. 'Maybe Lucie would like to see the hens?'

Lucie, her blue eyes wide, joggled her mother's hand. 'Please, Maman, please may I?' Hélène huffed in disapproval, but Rose tapped her arm and nodded.

'Let her go, *chérie*, she so wants to.'

Hélène glared at Élodie. 'Then make sure she doesn't get dirty. That dress is clean on today.'

Élodie was relieved that her sister hadn't noticed the muddy mark she'd already transferred from her dungarees to the little girl's pale-pink frock when she'd picked her up and hugged her. Lucie grabbed her aunt's outstretched hand and skipped along happily at her side as they meandered slowly down the lane together.

Élodie caught sight of Rudi's motorbike beside the henhouse at the same time as Lucie spotted it. The child looked up at her hesitantly. Élodie smiled reassuringly, her brain whirring as she tried to think how to explain his presence, assuming he was in the barn. Why would he be here today? She groaned at the bad timing, realising that Lucie was still gauging her response.

She bent down. 'Stay here for a second, Lucie. OK?'

The child nodded solemnly but, before Élodie could move, the barn door opened and Rudi appeared, smiling with delight when he saw her. Lucie moved behind her, keeping a tight hold on her aunt's hand. Élodie put a finger to her lips. 'Lieu-tenant, what a surprise. This is my sister Hélène's daughter.' She hoped he would pick up on her hint. She needn't have worried.

He squatted as Lucie peeped timidly from behind Élodie's knees, and gave her a winning smile, which certainly melted Élodie's concern.

'Hello, *ma petite*. I'm called Rudi. What's your name?'

Lucie gave him a shy smile. 'My name is Lucie. But you're a German.'

Rudi chuckled. 'I am, yes. But I'm also a friend of your aunt.'

Lucie peered in puzzlement from Rudi to Élodie, who picked her up and held her close.

'Don't worry, *mon biquet*, the Lieutenant's a friend, as he says. Let's keep it as our secret though—just between you and me. No need to mention it to Maman, eh?'

Lucie was busy fiddling with Élodie's dungaree buckle, which she was trying to unfasten as Rudi spoke. 'I'm sorry if I've caused you a problem today, mamselle.' He winked at Élodie. 'I'll see you again soon, I'm sure.'

Élodie shot him a grateful look as he left, wondering what he had wanted but breathing a huge sigh of relief when Lucie asked no further questions. 'And now the hens, *chérie*?' The child wriggled to be put down, instantly distracted, and ran over to the metal fencing, cooing at the chickens that were pecking contentedly in their run.

An hour later, Hélène took her leave, promising to come again soon. Élodie doubted that. She uncrossed her fingers and silently praised Lucie, who had burbled on happily about the hens without once mentioning the German lieutenant. After a final wave to her niece, she followed her mother back indoors, a sense of exhaustion flooding over her.

Élodie and Félix pedalled into the village square the following morning to find that it was still eerily silent, with only three other stallholders already unpacking vegetables, haberdashery, and a few scrawny chickens onto the scrubbed tables. They greeted them all. She noticed the priest in his black robe appear from the direction of the presbytery. She waved across the square to him. He gave a nod of acknowledgement and smiled as he slipped into the church, the heavy door yielding to his weight.

Élodie longed for a few minutes' peace. Félix had already set to with hammer, nails, and twine, repairing the broken table leg with precision. It probably wouldn't take him much longer. She tapped him on the shoulder and pointed to herself, then the church, smiling at the bemused look on his face, but he simply nodded and returned to his task. She crossed the road and slipped into the sacred stillness of the imposing building, her nostrils twitching at the strong, peppery smell of incense that pervaded the huge space. She stopped in her tracks when she spied a lone figure sitting in the front pew, head bent. Could it really be Major Wolff? She felt resentment burning in her gut. What right did such a man have to class himself as a Christian, when he performed such execrable acts? Père Bernard appeared from behind the altar and stopped to speak to the grey-clad German, whose profile as he replied caused Élodie to take a step back—it was indeed the major.

The priest spotted Élodie standing half-hidden behind one of the enormous pillars that soared to the rafters, the fluted stone now darkened with age and chipped here and there, be it wilfully or carelessly. He hurried up the aisle as the major returned to his contemplations, and greeted her with quiet concern, seeming to be aware of her discomfiture in the presence of the officer. 'I hope you've recovered from the terrible upset yesterday, my child?'

Élodie glared past him at the major's back. She answered softly, anxious not to signal her presence to him. 'What else can I do, *mon Père*? We have no freedoms left and few opportunities for retaliation.'

Père Bernard's brows lowered. 'When did you last take confession, Élodie?'

She shuffled uncomfortably from one foot to the other. 'Well, I—um, I'm not exactly sure.'

The priest took her elbow. 'Come then, there's no time like the present.'

She accompanied him wearily to the confessional, keeping one eye on the major, who still had his back to them. As she slid into the dark confined space and sat in silence as the priest settled himself, her mind spun in circles. What on earth should she say? She began falteringly, with the ritual 'Forgive me Father, for I have sinned'. As she glossed over how long it had been since her last confession, the obvious answer shot into her brain. 'My sister came to visit us at home yesterday, and I realised that I don't like her. In fact, I dislike her intensely. I'm not sure what sin that is, but I'm definitely guilty of it.' She'd probably shocked the priest but had at least saved herself from having to juggle with any more devastatingly intimate revelations.

She left a few minutes later with a fistful of Hail Marys as her penance, escaping gratefully once Père Bernard had said 'Go in peace, my child' and she had answered formulaically, 'Thank you, Father'. She shivered and blinked as she emerged from the clerical coolness into the autumn sunshine. Looking to her right she saw that the major was standing in the shade against the wall of the building, apparently studying Félix keenly. She crossed the road and joined her brother.

'I suppose you know you're being watched?'

Félix had repaired the table leg and set out the produce for her. He grinned. 'Oh, I've seen him all right. But I've already served four customers too. What kept you so long?'

Élodie made a face. 'I got caught by Père Bernard, who twisted my arm to take confession.'

Her brother burst out laughing. 'Wish I'd been a fly on the wall!'

'Is the major still there?'

Félix checked without moving his head. 'Yes, but he seems to have lost interest, *Dieu merci*. If it's OK with you, I need to get going now before Papa blows a gasket.'

It was Élodie's turn to laugh. She gave him a hug. 'Thanks for all your help—and for being you, *mon ours*.'

'Always here for you, Él.' Félix picked up his bike and ruffled her hair. '*À plus tard*, if I survive Papa's wrath for being so late.'

He rode off at speed, but Élodie noted with alarm the car that eased out from behind the church and followed him. The driver wore a German uniform, and the passenger was unmistakeably Major Wolff.

# CHAPTER NINE

## September 1943

THREE DAYS LATER, FÉLIX was still bristling. He was restless and disconsolate, frustrated and furious at his inability to have helped the old teacher from whom he had learnt so much. He refused to dwell on what might have happened to the kind-hearted schoolmaster. And unless he could persuade Élodie to twist the lieutenant's arm for information, he supposed he might never know. He was also aware that Thierry was expecting details of another mission, which had already been delayed twice for reasons beyond their control. He longed for action—to do something positive—but was currently limited to his chores on the farm, which were seldom done to his father's satisfaction, it seemed.

He rose from the table and paced round the kitchen for the third time, aware that he was irritating Élodie, whose own fuse had been short lately. She took the last mouthful of her late breakfast, clattered her knife and fork onto her plate and scraped her chair back so hard that it toppled, landing on the flagstones with a loud crash.

'*Par pitié*, Félix, *tu me rends folle.*'

Félix slackened his pace to let her cross to the sink. 'Sorry, Él, too much on my mind.'

Élodie washed her plate and coffee bowl, her back to him as she scrubbed at the crockery. '*Mais alors*, haven't we all! But if there's anything I can do...'

'I know, I know. Thank you, but I need to pull myself together.' She looked over her shoulder as he drew in breath then thought better of it and shook his head. 'I've only about another half an hour's work to do for now, then I want to go and see Michel. I should be back before Papa reappears.'

His sister gave him a cheeky grin. 'Don't worry, I'll cover for you if not.'

He leant forward and tugged her wild curls. 'Thanks.' He could feel her watching him as he trotted off resolutely, determined to rid himself of his foul mood.

He found Michel at his workshop, his overalls as usual black with grease, the thick, treacly smell of which pervaded the cluttered room. He declined his friend's extended hand, even after it had been wiped vigorously on his grubby workwear. Somehow, being here amongst the chaos of metal junk always calmed him.

'Can I just finish this—have you the time to wait?' Michel indicated the car part he was working on, reaching across his workbench for the small component he needed.

'No problem.' Félix marvelled yet again at Michel's apparently instinctive ability to locate anything anywhere, whether here at work or out in the surrounding countryside. He could also carry on a conversation with ease while reassembling the most intricate engine parts or gearboxes. 'Any news from Thierry?'

'Yes, perfect timing on your part. He said he'd call in today on his way home for lunch, so any time now.'

Félix watched closely as the deft hands, now slick with oil, inserted the last screw, and adjusted it to a precise tension.

'What's that you're working on?'

Michel rubbed his hand across his nose, leaving a black, shiny smear. 'Part for one of the Boche cars that they managed to drive into a ditch. Thierry's been mending the leaf spring and he's coming to see if I've succeeded in putting this back together. Thank heavens I have, so that should keep them quiet.'

Félix's disapproving frown was not lost on his friend.

'Best cover possible, Félix. Think about it. Thierry and I mend their vehicles, so why would we be sabotaging them too?'

Félix was forced to agree, though it didn't sit well with him, and he'd heard several villagers muttering about the frequent German presence at the forge. It annoyed him greatly that it was too dangerous for any of them to defend Thierry. There had been enough spiteful letters sent to the Boche already, many of them, he'd been told, from back-stabbers only too keen to repay old grudges against their neighbours.

He was descending into pessimism again, he knew. Michel had set aside his tools and was leaning on the bench, eyebrows raised, waiting for him to reply. He gave himself a mental shake. 'Sorry. Yes, you're right. I—.'

Before he could continue, the door was flung open and Thierry's reassuring bulk filled the frame, a broad smile appearing when he saw the two of them.

'*Salut, les gars*! And I bring good news—we're on for tomorrow night.'

Félix felt his spirits rising. Action at last.

The following evening, heavy sheets of rain pelted down relentlessly. By the time Félix reached Thierry's house he was drenched, despite his heavy jacket. He took off the sodden garment when Yvette opened the door, and shook it before he went in. Yvette brushed off his apology for the water that pooled on the floor regardless. She disappeared into the kitchen and returned with a towel. Félix rubbed his dripping hair vigorously before dragging it into some semblance of tidiness, though not too successfully judging by Yvette's expression. He accepted gladly the glass of beer she had been holding in her other hand. She inclined her head towards the front room.

'The fire's lit in there. Go and get warm. I'll see you all before you leave, *mon chéri*, and I'll do my best to dry off your coat a bit by the kitchen range.'

Michel arrived within minutes, and Thierry gave a rundown of their task. Timing would be everything, as the message from London had specified rail transport on the line from Argentan, expected that night, of German equipment that they were asked to delay or disrupt for as long as possible.

Thierry shifted his thickset physique and settled back in his chair. 'The Boche have been active recently. Though if this deluge continues, it'll be to our advantage tonight.'

'*Mais quand même...*' Michel looked unhappy. 'It'll make shifting the bolts more difficult. Everything will slip and slide, and we'll need our wits about us.'

At midnight the rain was still thundering down on the deep-pitched roof. The three men grumbled, despite their thick jackets and caps, as they stepped out of the door into a howling gale that hurled fat drops of stinging water into their faces. They hunched like weary labourers habituated to their task, and made their way towards their target.

It was a forty-minute slog on foot to the railway embankment, which was on the far side of Flers, but Michel led them intuitively through the quietest streets and alleyways and they saw no German patrols. Félix glanced at his own watch when he saw Thierry anxiously checking the time. Thank God the train was not due—if it kept to the schedule they'd been given—for another twenty-five minutes.

Michel swung the canvas bag he'd been carrying off his back and emptied out the tools haphazardly. Félix couldn't suppress a smile. How his friend could work like that was beyond him. He chose a position halfway up the grassy slope, where he could see along the track but also keep an eye on the road above that ran parallel to the railway. Inevitably, removing the bolts from the rails involved a degree of noise, not least from Michel, who uttered a string of profanities as he caught a finger between two of the heavy lumps of metal when his grasp slipped, as he had predicted, due to the combination of thick grease and rainwater.

As his two friends sat back on their heels, task all but completed, Félix spotted the indistinct glow of a flashlight some way down the line. He watched for a couple of seconds. Yes, the light was moving, and in their direction. He swore softly. The others looked up at his hissed warning and stared in the direction of Félix's inclined head.

Thierry raised his eyebrows at Michel. '*Terminé?*'

Michel confirmed that they'd done all they needed to. The pair of them tidied up and Thierry flung the bolts they'd removed into the undergrowth that bordered the tracks. Michel packed away the tools and the two men began to climb the embankment to join Félix, who was already crouching at the side of the road. The earth on the incline was soft and slippery, and Thierry let out an involuntary yell as his feet slid and he landed heavily back on the trackside. Michel hurried down to help, and the two men clung to the tufts of wet grass as they again made their hazardous ascent. Félix could see that there were now three lights approaching, bobbing as their owners broke into a run. He leant forward and took Michel's outstretched hand. As soon as he was on a firm footing, the two of them grasped Thierry's jacket and dragged him onto level ground.

Sounds of guttural shouting were now clear and the torch-lights were closing in on their position.

Félix spoke quietly but urgently. 'Which way, Michel?'

Michel took one quick look at the approaching soldiers. 'Follow me.' He raced across the road, crouching so as not to offer a silhouette against the night sky, though it was highly unlikely that they were visible against the low, bruised-grey clouds and unending swirls of summer rain.

The three men ran across the wide stretch of open grass-land that bordered the road, but as they reached the edge of the sheltering woods a truck screeched to a halt on the road behind them and a dozen armed soldiers tumbled out, steady-ing their weapons as they landed. Félix could also hear shouts from somewhere nearby on the tracks. A blinding searchlight mounted on the top of the truck's cab swung in a wide arc and floodlit the area they'd just vacated. A quick adjustment of the beam highlighted the wet grass like broad daylight and showed up their footsteps as clearly as if they'd laid a paper trail. The three men had ducked down but with Michel in the lead they stood and bolted. Félix was sure they'd been spotted as they crashed onwards and several loud shots rang out from close by, thankfully missing their mark as they smacked into the surrounding trees.

Michel was as sure-footed as a gazelle. He slowed several times to allow the others to catch up. Thierry in particular was not built for speed. Félix was aware their pursuers were gaining on them and a quick check over his shoulder showed that the German flashlights were drawing closer. He speeded up. They needed to change tack, and fast. He caught Michel's arm and pointed behind them. Michel slowed his pace and frowned, looking from right to left. As Thierry joined them, panting heavily, Michel pointed to the left down a steep slope. Three more shots rang out as they swerved and fled in single file, and Félix could hear Thierry swearing repeatedly through clenched teeth. Michel chopped and changed direction several times. They appeared, at least temporarily, to have outwitted their followers. They plunged on regardless.

Félix stumbled on a tree root he hadn't seen. He righted himself as Thierry groaned and roared in discomfort behind him. His heavy-set friend's face was contorted in a rictus of pain, and he was grasping his right leg. Michel had retraced his steps and came to a stop beside him. At the same moment the two of them saw the blood dripping down Thierry's thigh. Michel grimaced at Félix. They took Thierry's weight with a supporting shoulder under each arm and linked hands behind his back for extra stability. Félix grunted as they made slow headway, Thierry hopping on his uninjured leg. Michel indicated that they should move into the thicker trees, which hampered progress but at least rendered them firmly beyond their trailing pursuers. They were soon forced to a halt by the magnitude of their effort, and propped Thierry's bulk on the mossy trunk of a fallen tree. Félix wiped the sweat from his forehead and heard Michel panting as deeply as he was himself.

'Thierry, *mon pote, t'es un grand gaillard—une vrai armoire à glace!*'

Thierry did his best to grin at Félix's description of him. 'Sure, yes, I'm a big guy, but you'll need to take that up with my Papa, who was also built like the proverbial brick shithouse!' He grimaced as he moved his right leg to get a better view of it. His trousers were now covered in blood.

Félix looked across at Michel and made a face. He bent and inserted a finger through the torn cloth. Thierry winced as the finger brushed the underlying wound, and nodded as Félix said, 'Definitely from one of those gunshots. We need to staunch the bleeding somehow.'

For answer, Michel pulled off his saturated coat, his jumper, and finally his shirt, which, with the aid of a penknife, he hacked into strips that he joined together firmly to fashion a rough tourniquet. He applied it above the wound, then bent and picked up a sturdy stick. He wound the loose ends of the fabric around it, twisted till the blood flow slowed, and knotted two more strips into place to secure the length of wood. He looked up at Félix. 'That should do it for now, but he needs a doctor. Could we get him to Dr Leblanc?'

Félix shook his head vehemently. '*Putain*! No way—not without him being handed over to the Gestapo. That old fool's far too friendly with the mayor. He and that bloody sadistic Major Wolff, I've been told they're *comme cul et chemise*!'

Michel looked shocked. '*T'es sûr*? I'd no idea they were in cahoots. What the hell are we going to do?'

'Get away from here for starters. I can't hear the Boche behind us since you led us on that tortuous zigzag, but you can be sure they haven't given up. How far are we from Ste-Honorine?'

Michel pulled on his jumper, now almost as wet as the coat that he eased on with a shudder over the sopping wool, and shoved the remains of his shirt into one of the cavernous pockets. He rubbed his chin as he checked his bearings. 'Ten, fifteen minutes or so? Well, at normal pace.'

'I have an idea—and it's the only obvious choice. We'll take him to the pharmacy. I'm sure Guy will help.'

'Guy? Ah, he's your brother-in-law of course. But Hélène?"

Félix snorted. 'Hélène? Leave her to me! Let's get going.'

They hauled Thierry upright again, flatly refusing his suggestion that they leave him there and let him take his chances. It took an agonising thirty-five minutes to reach their destination, with four stops for breath en route and constant checks to front and rear, but at last the crumbling old building that housed the pharmacy came into view. They stood deep in the shadows as a German truck roared down the street. When it was out of sight Félix indicated the narrow passageway that led to the rear of the premises opposite and they half-dragged Thierry across the road.

As he had already guessed, the back door was locked. He knocked circumspectly, aware of how the sound would carry in the stillness of the night. There was no response, though he'd hardly expected any that late at night. He studied the upper windows and hoped he'd made the right choice as he lobbed a handful of gravel upwards. It took a second attempt before the curtains parted and Guy's face appeared, pale in the faint moonlight that had at last emerged after the rain had petered out. Félix stepped back so that he was clearly visible. The curtains twitched shut and after a couple of minutes foot-steps could be heard approaching along the hallway inside. A key turned in the lock and Guy opened the door far enough to see out.

'Félix, what on earth...'

Félix stepped forward and spoke quietly. Guy looked over his shoulder, took Félix's arm, and hurried them in. He led them into the stock room where he made up the prescrip-tions, which providentially had reinforced shutters on the windows that also maintained the blackout. There was a strong smell that reminded Félix of hospitals, a strange brew of disinfectant and chemical compounds.

Guy snapped on the light and frowned at the blood staining Thierry's trousers. 'I'll have to cut his trouser leg to get a proper look. No point in asking how he did this I suppose?'

'Guy, better that you don't know. Please do whatever you have to. I'm—we're simply grateful for any help you can give.'

Guy grabbed one of two wooden chairs and indicated to Thierry that he should sit. He shifted the other to raise his patient's right leg level with his hip. Félix and Michel stood to either side as the scissors made slow work of the tough fabric. Guy inspected the wound and methodically swabbed the sur-rounding skin with iodine. He skilfully probed the entry hole, clearly visible against the red-brown liquid, and Thierry drew in a sharp breath as deft fingers made their assessment.

Guy withdrew his hands. 'Thankfully you have good strong muscles. The bullet's not lodged too deeply and I can feel it fairly easily. But it has to come out, my friend, and that'll be painful.'

He looked at Félix, who shrugged and asked, 'Can you give him anything to help ease the worst of it?'

Guy surveyed the shelf behind Thierry. 'I'll inject some local anaesthetic of course, but that's about all. *Chapeau bas* to whoever applied that tourniquet.'

Félix indicated Michel, who shuffled awkwardly, and returned his attention to Thierry. 'You're OK with all this?'

His broad-shouldered friend managed a grin. 'Anything to get that *putain* of a bullet out.'

Guy had gathered up everything he would need. He hesitated before he set to work, turning to Félix with a quizzical expression. 'I'd still be interested to know the source?' Félix had said all he was prepared to say. He was relieved that the pharmacist appeared to accept that no answer would be forthcoming. 'Well, anyway, thank God for the extra training I've undertaken, otherwise I wouldn't feel qualified to tackle this.'

Félix gave Thierry's shoulder a reassuring squeeze. 'Don't worry, *mon vieux*, you're in good hands.'

Guy donned surgical gloves, administered the injection, and set to work. Félix saw Michel blanch as the scalpel enlarged the wound sufficiently, but he was impressed by his brother-in-law's quiet competence as he located the bullet with a dexterous finger and slowly extracted the deformed lump of metal with a probe of some kind. He held it up to the light and frowned. Thierry, who had been holding his breath, exhaled lustily and proffered his profuse gratitude as Guy's slim, adroit fingers stitched the wound immaculately and placed a dressing.

Guy brushed off the thanks. 'You'll have to rest that leg as much as possible for about a week.' He looked from one man to the other as they exchanged glances. 'Do I gather that may be a problem?'

Félix was quick to reply. 'Nothing to concern you, thanks, Guy—you've done more than enough.'

Guy had been examining the bullet, his back to them. He turned slowly to Félix, his expression thoughtful. 'I know a bit about weaponry. Looks like a nine-millimetre Parabellum round to me, so fired from a German Luger I presume?' Félix endeavoured to give nothing away in his answering half-grin. Guy gave a grim smile and indicated Thierry's leg. 'I won't ask any questions, but I can draw my own conclusions. Don't let this sort of thing become a habit, but...' He paused, then seemed to make his mind up about something. 'If there were anything I could do, I'd always be willing to help.'

As he said this, Félix became aware of movement in the doorway. His sister's voice cut the bonhomie like a sabre thrust. 'Help with what, exactly?' She took one look at Thierry and rounded on her brother. 'Why are you always such a fool, Félix? Whatever you've been up to, my husband will not be helping you with anything else.'

Félix raised his hands defensively, but she continued. 'You're as ridiculous as Élodie—always getting involved in things that don't concern you. Leave Guy out of it, d'you hear?'

To Félix's astonishment, Guy's face flushed, and his mouth set in a stubborn line. He crossed the room to his wife, then spoke slowly and precisely. 'Hélène, may I suggest you go back upstairs and ensure Lucie has not been disturbed. We don't need her to see any of this. At her age she can't be trusted not to say the wrong thing to the wrong person.' Hélène opened her mouth to protest, but Guy put his hands on her shoulders and guided her unceremoniously towards the door.

As she left the room, she glared at Félix. 'I'm warning you, if anything happens to Guy, I will *never* forgive you.'

His sister's attitude reaffirmed to Félix exactly why she was the odd one out in the family. Yet the little pastiche he'd witnessed had overturned his previous assumption that she wore the bigger trousers in that relationship. He sighed and rubbed his hand across his forehead. 'Guy, I'm sorry for the trouble we've caused you, but I can't thank you enough. We'll go now. But, if I could check the coast is clear?'

'*De rien*, Félix, and of course—I'm glad to have been able to help.' He gathered up the instruments and dressing package as Michel helped Thierry to his feet.

Félix slipped back into the room. 'All quiet. Let's go.'

'Just a minute.' Guy had been rummaging in the far corner and produced a stout walking stick. 'This might help.'

Félix was the last to leave. He shook Guy's hand and thanked him again. As he was about to close the door behind him, Guy spoke again. 'Félix, I meant what I said. Any time.'

# Chapter Ten

## September 1943

Félix stood on the riverbank in silent concentration, fishing rod in hand, as he watched the line drift doggedly in the swirling current. He was sure there were trout in the fluttering weeds below the opposite bank. Sure enough, he saw a flash of olive brown flanked with silver as a fish snapped at the hook. He waited till he was as certain as he could be that it had taken the bait and began to play the line until the thrashing calmed, drawing the fish close enough to dip his landing net under it and bring it into the bank. He lifted the mesh clear of the water and extracted the fish. It was in perfect condition, its colours glistening in the dappled sunshine. This was proving to be an excellent season, as today's catch now numbered three perfect-sized specimens around ten to twelve inches in length and he had only been fishing for an hour and a half. He placed the trout into his keepnet and rebaited the hook.

It felt good to relax, however briefly. Searches and document checks had been stepped up since the railway sabotage earlier in the week. Fortuitously, the site of the disruption had led the Germans to concentrate their efforts on the other side of Flers. And, according to Thierry, their efforts had achieved at least partial success. Despite the German track-checkers almost having pinpointed their position as the three of them took to their heels in the downpour, the soldiers' attempts to alert the train driver were apparently too late to prevent the engine and first carriage hitting the loose rails and shuddering onto the trackside, where they ploughed a spectacular furrow before coming to a halt amid clouds of steam and screeching metal. The line had been mended and put back into action the following morning, but the delay had apparently made some vital difference, though what that was, Félix hadn't discovered.

As he cast the line, he saw movement to his right. He settled the rod comfortably in his hand and looked towards the bridge. The young German soldier, Matthias, was striding purposefully towards him, a broad smile on his face. Félix didn't hesitate this time to shake the outstretched hand and returned the smile with a genuine one of his own.

Félix proffered the rod and pointed along the bank as he did so. 'No companion today?'

Matthias laughed. 'No, he is *im Dorf*. He is, er, at the café. That is correct?'

Félix nodded. '*Tant mieux*—you can enjoy yourself.'

He stood back and watched, arms folded, as the soldier caught and landed two fish of his own. As before, Matthias dispatched them and placed them in a clean, dampened handkerchief before extracting a hessian bag from his pocket.

'I hoped you are here today. I am prepared, you notice?'

Félix smiled at the clumsy French, but admired the effort. 'Well done. I think you enjoy fishing?'

'Oh yes, I do so at home. There are *Forelle* in the brook.' The German was silent for a minute or two. Félix had to strain to hear when he spoke again. 'You know, I have a cousin in England. Before this *verdammter Krieg*, he is coming for holidays in Germany. He too is a fisherman.' He looked up at

Félix, his face solemn. 'But now I fear to meet him on the field of battle. You understand?'

'Of course.'

'If only there was not this war. I have family in Strasbourg too. Now they are in Germany but previously the city was in France.' Félix nodded repeatedly to indicate his understanding and noted the cautionary check Matthias made to right and left before he continued. 'I do not wish to fight the French—or the English, for that matter. This is the truth.'

Félix looked at the grey uniform and tried to untangle his thoughts. When all was said and done, this boy—for he was only a boy—wanted only to be at peace and at home. Instead of which, he found himself drafted into an army he didn't want to be part of, sent to a country whose language he struggled with, and expected to kill an enemy he didn't want to believe was his foe. What could he say?

'Thank you. I'm sorry you have to be here.'

A look of doubtful surprise crossed Matthias's face before he realised the words were sincere.

He smiled and handed back the rod. 'One day, after this war is over, I hope we meet again. I thank you also.'

Félix bent and picked up the neatly knotted handkerchief, which Matthias put into his hessian bag. He took his leave and set off along the bank, whistling a tune that Félix recognised as the popular German song *Lili Marlene*. The soldier clambered up onto the bridge and turned to wave, then headed in the direction of Marc's café.

After another half an hour, Félix packed up his kit, having caught no further fish. The sun had dipped behind the tall willow trees that lined the far bank, and the insects that had danced in the sunbeams had for now disappeared. The startling electric blue of a kingfisher caught his eye as he was preparing to leave, encouraging him to idle a few minutes longer to admire the small bird's plumage and darting movements.

On his way back to les Coquelets blancs, he remembered the supplies he'd promised to collect from the barn before the night's planned mission with Michel and Thierry. He hoped fervently they'd not included Serge in their plans, though four pairs of hands would, he admitted to himself, be useful.

# Chapter Eleven

## September 1943

Élodie couldn't shake off a sense of unease as she spread out on the stall the little produce she had to sell. There were few customers this morning so far and the general mood was subdued, matching the overcast sky. She looked up the square towards the café, where Marc was busy sweeping around the pavement tables and rearranging the chairs, the striped awning groaning in protest at the flurries of wind that gusted from the north and worried the fabric to and fro.

A sudden commotion to her left distracted her from Mme Leroy, who was complaining about the lack of almost everything she apparently needed. Two large *Panzergrau* trucks careered into the square and stopped with a squeal of brakes beside the church wall. Élodie felt her stomach tighten as a dozen German soldiers climbed out. Her alarm grew as she spied the signature flash of the Waffen-SS at their throats. They marched halfway up the square and began dispassionately seizing people, apparently at random, and all men. A heart-rending scream curdled Élodie's blood and she watched in horror as two of the soldiers dragged Marc down the road, his heavily pregnant wife the source of the wailing. Some of the shoppers had melted away; others stood rooted to the spot. Élodie counted the men who had been rounded up: nine.

As the group drew level with her, one of the SS men pointed at Guillaume. Élodie hurled herself sideways and stood in front of him. Two soldiers broke away and manhandled her forcibly out of their path.

She yelled as they grabbed Guillaume. 'Leave him alone—he's an old man.'

Guillaume appeared to be unresisting. '*Tais-toi*, Élodie. Better me than a youngster.'

As she surged forward again, an inimitable overpowering smell of cologne assaulted her nose and pain shot down her left arm as it was grabbed by a gloved hand. She knew without looking that it was Major Wolff. As one of the soldiers levelled his pistol at her, the major spoke sharply.

'Unless you want to join those men, I suggest you remain silent.'

She turned as he shook his head at the soldier and stepped closer to her. As he did so, a commotion drew their attention to the middle of the road, where Guillaume was now struggling with his captors. He looked over his shoulder and shouted to Élodie. 'Take Blaireau for me, *chérie*.'

Élodie's throat was completely choked, but she raised a hand to him and nodded, forcing her response. She turned to the major, who was looking at the dog lying warily under his master's abandoned stall.

She tore at the major's hand still gripping her arm. 'If you touch him, I will kill you.'

Wolff's laugh was harsh, mocking. 'I rather think you would—or at least you'd try. You need to learn some self-control, young woman, or you'll find yourself in even bigger trouble very soon. But the dog is safe. From me, at any rate.'

Élodie glared at him as he loosened his grip and strode away in the opposite direction from that taken by the patrol and their prisoners, who had disappeared behind the church. She bent and searched through Guillaume's bag for something to secure Blaireau. She knew he was never on a lead but was equally certain he wouldn't come with her willingly. As her hand located a ball of twine, a series of shots rang out. Blaireau emitted a high-pitched sorrowful whine and Élodie shivered. She fumbled with the thick string and fashioned a make-do slip lead, which she placed quickly over the dog's silky head.

She looked up as the heavy church door banged. Père Bernard ran in the direction from which the shots had come, black robes flapping like a crow in flight. Several minutes later he reappeared, his face ashen. A woman rushed up to him and spoke, but he shook his head. Élodie heard his response clearly. 'All of them.'

There were a few murmurs from those who remained gathered in the road, and Père Bernard beckoned them to follow him into the church. Élodie numbly packed away the remaining goods into one side of the trailer and lifted Blaireau gently into the other side, fastening the cord to the coupling on her bicycle, hindered by her shaking limbs. She cleared Guillaume's stall and set the bag beside the dog. As she passed the café, she saw Mme Leroy attempting to comfort Marc's wife, who was sobbing inconsolably.

She rode home slowly and systematically, constantly checking that Blaireau was still in the trailer, where he lay subdued and unmoving. She felt as if she were travelling through an alien land, her senses dulled by the freeze-frame images of the horrifying scenes she had witnessed. She was conscious only of her movement along the lanes, and the passing green landscape that seemed to swoop in to taunt her.

She turned into the farm gate and braked gradually, coming to a stop beside the kitchen door. It took two attempts to dismount, her leaden limbs refusing to obey their usual instincts.

She stumbled to the trailer where Blaireau remained motionless, ears down, his eyes following her every movement. She lifted him, unresisting, into her arms and staggered into the kitchen.

Her mother and Félix were at the table, relaxed and for once laughing at some shared moment. Élodie heard her mother's cry of alarm as she looked up at the sound of her daughter's dragging footsteps and, as if in slow motion, saw her clutch at Félix. Félix turned and leapt up in one fluid action, sending his chair onto the flagstones with a loud bang. In two paces he was by her side and held out his arms to take the dog, now alert and startled by the noise and movement. He set Blaireau down by the warmth of the stove and as he rose Élodie flew into his outstretched arms.

'What in God's name has happened, Él?'

Élodie heard the concern in her brother's voice but couldn't answer. She let him lead her to the table and dropped into a vacant chair as he leant and righted his own. She stared at the dog, then at her mother, and tried to force words out, but heard only a wail of gibberish leave her mouth.

Félix knelt in front of her and took her hands. 'Do we have any brandy, Maman?'

Her mother scarcely took her eyes off her as she reached into the back of the cupboard beside the stove, found what she was seeking and filled a small glass with Calvados, which she handed to Félix. Élodie looked down as the glass was put into her hands, but they shook so uncontrollably that half the sweet-smelling liquid splashed wastefully onto the floor. Firm fingers took the tumbler, which Félix lifted to her lips.

'Drink some, Él, there's a good girl.'

She took a large mouthful and swallowed, gasping at the fiery warmth of the spirit that hit her stomach like a punch. With a supreme effort, she focused on Félix and took a huge shuddering breath.

'I—Guillaume—the market...' She tried to steady her thin, wavering voice, balling her fists into her eyes to try and erase the jagged, uncontrollable sights of the last hour that swam through her vision. She felt her brother stroking her hair as she rocked back and forth. Another chair rasped on the stone floor as her mother pulled it across to sit beside her.

Finally, Élodie sensed her ragged gasps beginning to slow, no longer feeling as if her heart would burst through her chest wall. She took a deep breath and haltingly described the arrival of the SS soldiers in the market and the round-up of civilians. Félix swore, then motioned her to continue. When she got to the arrest of Guillaume, she stopped, devoid of words to describe the terrible outrage. Tears streamed down her face as she coughed and choked and shook her head, pointing at the dog. 'He asked me, Guillaume asked me...' She felt the strong hands of her mother and brother soothing her and let out a huge sigh.

Some while later, though she had no idea how much time had passed, only knowing there were no more tears left to shed, Félix stood and spoke.

'I have to find out what's going on, Maman. You'll stay with her?' Élodie could hear the controlled fury in his voice.

'How could I not, *mon fils*? You go—but promise me you won't ask too many questions and get yourself into trouble too.'

Félix bent and kissed his mother's cheek. 'I'll be back as soon as I can.'

The door slammed as he left, leaving the only audible sound the insistent ticking of the hall clock. Somehow, Élodie thought, its repetitive resonance was the most reassuring thing she could think of: it meant home, and family, and safety.

An hour and a half later, Félix returned, sober faced. Élodie was sitting where he had left her, and their mother was absent-mindedly preparing vegetables for the midday meal. The two women looked at him expectantly.

'Papa is coming into the yard—I'll tell you what little I've been able to find out when he joins us.'

Henri appeared in the doorway, frowning when he saw the three members of his family, silent and pale as ghosts, watching him remove his boots. He looked from one to another, then his eyes settled on Félix.

'What's happened? Will someone please tell me what the hell's going on?' No one spoke. 'I assume I'm not going to like what you have to say?' His attention was diverted by movement on the floor by the stove. 'And what's that dog doing here? It looks like Guillaume's Blaireau.'

Félix pulled out a chair from the table and saw his sister's red-rimmed eyes brimming with tears at the mention of Guillaume's name. 'Sit down, Papa.' His father's frown deepened.

'Why, exactly?'

'Henri, *please.*' Rose put a bowl of coffee on the table and motioned for him to sit, which he did with clear reluctance. She joined him at the table and put an arm round Élodie's shaking shoulders. Félix remained standing.

'Papa, there was an incident at the market this morning—.'

'What kind of an incident?' Henri growled, staring at his daughter. 'Were you involved? Has somebody hurt you?' Élodie shook her head.

Félix continued. 'Papa, you have to know that Guillaume is dead. As are nine other villagers.' Henri cursed, pummelled the table, and started to speak again, but Rose shook his arm and shushed him.

Félix cleared his throat. 'Last night when I went to meet Michel, I saw Mireille Brodeur's younger sister, Mathilde, talking to a young German soldier I'd met once when I was fishing.' Félix noted his father's hostile glare but carried on.

'Later, on my way back, I saw her arguing with Serge not far from her house. I couldn't hear what was being said, but she seemed to be in no danger, except doubtless from his acid tongue, which we've all experienced. I've been to find Michel, who told me he'd heard a German soldier was shot dead last night. Whether the two incidents are related, I've no idea, but Serge has some wild friends who wouldn't hesitate to ambush the Boche, I'm sure. As I cycled back through the square, a German patrol was putting up a notice outside the Mairie. I stopped to look—I've no idea what they said to me, but it certainly wasn't friendly.'

He saw that Élodie was watching him closely, her face drained porcelain white. 'And?'

Félix looked at each of them in turn before he spoke, then stared out through the open door. 'The notice said that in retribution for the killing of a German soldier last night, ten citizens have paid with their lives.' He hesitated before continuing. 'And that next time it will be fifty.'

Henri shot from his chair. '*Merde*—those murderous bastards!' He turned to his wife, his face darkening as she explained that Guillaume had asked Élodie to take the dog for him. He grunted. 'Félix, you'll have to come with me. We need to secure Guillaume's place before the news spreads too widely.'

'Why, Papa—is that necessary?' The two men turned at Élodie's question. 'Surely no one from the village would do any harm?'

Henri gave a harsh laugh. 'You're truly an innocent, my child. The place'll be ransacked in a flea's breath. For starters, the furniture would keep a fire going for a few days.'

'Then I'm coming too.'

'As you wish, though I don't know what for. Félix, we'll need the horse and cart. Let's get going. I'll meet you outside the barn.'

Élodie sprang up and followed her brother out of the house. He turned and halted her, holding her lightly by both arms. 'You don't have to do this, Él.'

He was reminded of their mother as her mouth set firm. 'But I do, Félix, it's the last thing ... I need to do this.'

When they reached Guillaume's neat cottage, a journey of only ten minutes, Henri checked the front door, which was as usual not locked. The grass outside was long and unkempt, but the house itself looked well cared for. He poked his head into the tiny porch as Élodie and Félix joined him. All three stepped in turn over a pair of muddy boots and went inside.

'It's all so tidy, Papa. I'm sure we're the first ones here.'

Henri nodded at his daughter and looked around. 'We should take any food before it goes off, and see if you can find whatever he feeds the dog.'

'We'll need to take his chickens too, or they'll soon starve.' This remark was addressed to Félix.

'And the cow?'

Henri scratched his head pensively. 'It'll be fine for now. One of us can come back and milk her later. She's still out in the field behind the house—I saw her as we arrived. We can think about bringing her over to our place tomorrow.'

Élodie spotted the old bag Guillaume had previously used for his market produce and set to work. She felt like weeping again when she saw how bare the larder was. No wonder Guillaume had grown so thin in the last year. On the middle shelf stood a jar of broken biscuit mix. She unscrewed the lid and sniffed, confirming from the savoury meaty smell that its contents were almost certainly for the dog. On the lower shelf under a wire cover was a lump of what appeared to be tripe. Élodie wrinkled her nose and fetched a page of the faded, out-of-date newspaper she'd spied on one of the chairs. She wrapped the offal, retrieved the jar of dog food, and put both on the table in the single main room. It housed a small kitchen space to the rear and a table and sitting area by the huge fireplace, its pale stone hearth blackened by smoke over the years. She surveyed the sparse furniture, and her attention was caught by the only untidy thing in the room: a pile of books that lay topsy-turvy next to the worn and threadbare armchair by the fireside. She picked up the top one, a well-thumbed copy of *Madame Bovary*, and saw that her father was standing with his back to her staring at a framed sepia photograph that stood on the mantelpiece.

'Papa...' She faltered, noticing her father's rigid stance as he took down the picture and gripped the photo frame, his knuckles whitening. 'Papa, do you think I might take this book?' She watched as Henri wiped his sleeve across his face before looking over his shoulder.

'What is it?'

He gave a half-smile when she told him, and she was astonished to see a tear trickle down his cheek. He turned away again, his voice gravelly. 'It was her favourite.'

'Tante Marie-Claude's?'

Henri nodded. He set the photo down methodically. 'I'm sure you don't know much about Guillaume's history, so let me tell you now.' He indicated the rough-hewn wooden table and Élodie sat across from him. 'Guillaume used to come here as a boy, after his father had left farming to become a corn merchant in Argentan—quite successfully, too, so Guillaume had a good education. The farm was run by his father's brother and wife in those days. He chose to spend his summers here helping out, and much to his father's disgust decided he preferred the farm to the life of a businessman. Tante Marie-Claude, as you knew her, was the local beauty. She was very popular, as you might imagine, and had all the local boys vying for her favours. But she was captivated by

Guillaume, the town boy who knew so much about the world beyond Sainte-Honorine. She'd had little learning, as was mostly the case with country girls in those days, but once they were married he introduced her to books. She always loved him to read to her.'

Élodie saw her father smile at a memory before he continued. 'You do know that Guillaume was like an uncle to me, and their son, two years younger than I was, became like a brother?'

'That was Léon, yes?' She hardly dared to mention the name that was, by unspoken understanding, never uttered at home.

'It was.' Henri got up and fetched the photograph, clearly composing himself with a huge effort. She peered at the sepia picture, which showed a smiling, much younger Guillaume with his wife and small son. 'When we were called up for the last war, I promised Marie-Claude that I'd look after him.'

Élodie waited hopefully as the silence lengthened. Her father had never spoken of what happened during his war. Would he now?

When he looked up from the faded image, he made no attempt to wipe away the moisture that had gathered in the corners of his eyes. Élodie reached out a tentative hand towards him, but he withdrew his fists and clasped the picture frame.

'We were put in the same regiment and fought alongside each other for over two years. We survived the battle of Verdun, amongst so many losses, and promptly found ourselves stationed against the Germans on the Chemin des Dames. In April 1917 the artillery was sent into attack—but the enemy knew we were coming.' He gave a harsh, bitter laugh. 'Our French troops were mown down like flies by the German machine guns. They were totally unsparing. Léon was blown up in front of me and I was covered not only in his blood, but—'

'Don't, Papa, you don't have to relive it all again.'

Henri heaved a huge sigh. 'You're right, of course, it doesn't ever make it go away, and it never will. But the worst of it was, it was left to me when I was sent home—because I'd been wounded too but survived—to tell his mother that I'd broken my promise to keep Léon safe.'

'But how could you have kept him safe? She will have known that you meant to, but surely—'

'That didn't matter. I'd said I would.' He looked at his daughter, his eyes misty and distant. 'We were young, Élodie, so very young. You have to understand that, like all young men, we thought we were invincible. Well, we certainly got that wrong. And Marie-Claude never completely recovered. Oh, she carried on like everyone else, and Guillaume was wonderful with her, but her heart was broken. He was their only child, you see. Your mother had a bright idea and asked her to look after Félix from time to time so that she could do some work for Madame Lagrange. Guillaume always said it was a lifesaver.'

'I didn't know any of that. But it explains why Guillaume was so fond of Félix.'

'You too, *ma fille*. He told me you were the granddaughter he never had. I hope one day, *chérie*, that you will marry well and be as happy as Guillaume and Marie-Claude were in those early days.'

Élodie's stomach turned to stone as Rudi's smiling face floated clear in her mind, his eyes tender, a lock of blond hair showing under his cap. He would never be what her father had in mind.

Further words were terminated by a sudden commotion outside, and Élodie heard Félix's voice, loud, angry. '*Va-t'en*—get lost you *pilleurs*.' She felt her stomach contract. Looters, already? The legs of her father's chair skidded on the uneven tiled floor as he jumped up and charged out. She followed him and stopped on the threshold. Two men she didn't recognise had taken to their heels across the lane and were running towards the Flers road.

Henri reached into the back of the cart and picked up the lengths of sturdy timber he'd brought with him. Félix had loaded Guillaume's six scrawny-looking chickens into a rusty wire cage he'd found in the shed and had already secured it on the cart. He now held a large hammer and a handful of sturdy clout nails.

'Get those things from the house, Élodie, and let's be gone from here. If you can secure the persiennes, so much the better. Oh, and take the book—Guillaume would have wanted you to have it.'

As she went indoors, she saw her father run his fingers along the top of the door frame and nod in satisfaction as he located the key, before shrugging at Félix. 'We can only do our best to secure the place, but it won't keep the determined out for long.'

Early that evening, Élodie milked Guillaume's cow in the byre beside the barn, where she had been tethered in a stall to settle her after the long slow walk from his cottage. After the sighting of the would-be looters, they had decided that leaving her transfer to the following day was too risky, and at least at les Coquelets blancs she would be well cared for. The gentle, long-lashed Normande, her white coat heavily speckled with brown, munched contentedly on the hay in the trough in front of her as Élodie finished her task. Her back ached from bending forward from the low stool and as she stood and massaged stiff muscles, Félix poked his head into the barn.

'Anything I can do, Él?'

'No thanks. Chickens next and then I'm done.'

'D'you want a hand with them?'

She shook her head. 'Thanks for asking but I need to keep busy. Are you out this evening?'

'Yes, 'fraid so. Michel and I need to talk to Thierry about Serge.'

'Because?'

Félix smiled but his expression remained unreadable and subdued. 'Usual answer these days—nothing I can tell you about.' She aimed the cloth she'd been wiping her fingers on in his direction. He caught it adroitly and handed it back to her as he passed her on his way out.

When she reached the hen run, Élodie was startled to see the motorbike that was parked half out of sight beside the lower barn, its engine still ticking as the hot metal cooled. A grey jacket lay folded on the seat. Instinctively she looked over her shoulder, then released a breath. Ridiculous. Why should either of her parents have left the house? She slipped quietly through the door and gasped as Rudi stepped forward into the half-light. Her heart skipped a beat as he cradled the hand that had flown to her mouth in surprise. His white shirt was unbuttoned at the neck, its brightness lighting his face in the shade of the barn.

'What are you doing here?' She tried to keep her voice steady.

'*Schatzi*, I had to come and check that you were OK. Major Wolff told me about the incident in the market—'

'*Incident*! The murder of ten innocent men, is that what you're referring to? And no, I'm certainly not OK.'

Rudi winced at her words, his jaw tight. He spread his hands. 'Élodie, what can I say?'

'Sorry? How sorry you are that your fellow countrymen are murderous brutes?'

Rudi turned away, sagging under the onslaught of her accusations. Élodie was suddenly overwhelmed by her own ferocity, her pulse racing and her gut in turmoil. But this man, this man with whom she had shared such gentle passion—was he not guilty too? Or was he, in his own way, as much of a victim as she was? For a moment she hesitated, then whispered his name questioningly. He looked down at her, his eyes bright with regret, and her question was answered. She opened her arms and hugged him so hard that she heard him exhale with a loud 'Ouf'. They stood as one, unspeaking, each gaining strength from the grip of the other.

Finally, Rudi spoke. '*Liebling*, I am so sorry, believe me.'

Nuzzled against his chest, Élodie's voice was, she knew indistinct. 'Guillaume told Papa that I was the granddaughter he never had. I didn't know...' She felt Rudi's arms tighten around her again.

'I understand, I really do, *Schatzi*. My grandparents mean the world to me, and if such a thing had happened to either of them...'

'Did you know the soldier who was shot?'

'Not well, but he was young—only eighteen or nineteen.'

'What was his name? Do you know?'

'His name was Matthias, I believe. Why do you ask?'

'Only because Félix wondered whether it could be a young soldier he'd met when he was fishing.' Élodie pulled back and looked up into his face. 'It does sound as if it was him—Félix said he was just a boy, not even a grown man. Will this hateful war never end?'

'Yes, one day of course, but God knows when.'

There was one more question Élodie had to ask. 'Where were you this morning?'

'When I saw the SS arrive, I volunteered to join those tasked with making enquiries where the shooting happened last night. Unsurprisingly, we learnt nothing.'

# CHAPTER TWELVE

## September 1943

FÉLIX SHIFTED UNEASILY IN his seat and cursed in exasperation. He glanced at Michel, who, though he hadn't commented, was frowning at Thierry just as Félix himself was.

One of them had to speak up, so he took the lead. 'Thierry, *mon pote*, you can hardly walk, even though the wound's healing well.'

'I can still drive.' Thierry's low growl was resistant, unyielding.

Michel shook his head and thumped the table. 'But that's not the point. *Sois réaliste!* If we're ambushed, spotted, caught in the act, and have to abandon the truck and make a run for it, you'll be a sitting duck for the Boche. You can't run yet. Just admit it.'

Thierry's usual affable demeanour had today deserted him. 'So, you're suggesting that even though this job is important, I'm not up to it? And therefore we abandon it, *hein*? Or ask Serge to make up the numbers while I sit at home and twiddle my thumbs?'

Félix ran a hand through his hair. '*Putain*, Thierry, it's not like you to be so obstinate. And Serge? *Hors question!* No. After that business with the Boche soldier, the further away from me Serge stays for the time being, the better I'll like it.' He saw that Michel was watching him keenly, head tilted questioningly. He sighed. 'And no, Michel, I have no proof it was Serge or his friends who killed him, but the odds are too high for it not to be them.'

Thierry's loud sniff irritated him. Dammit. Why did he have to explain himself? '*Ayez pitié!* He was just a boy—not even nineteen. Yes, I know he was a German, and God knows there are plenty of them hereabouts I could kill with my bare hands, but, if I'm right, his only crime, which got him killed, was to find young Mathilde attractive, for which none of us would blame him.'

'You have a better idea, Félix?'

As Michel posed his question and threw his hands wide, Félix sensed—as the tension strained taut as a cheese-wire—that it was time to make his suggestion. 'Ask Guy to drive and keep watch.' He hadn't quite expected the reaction his words received. Michel's mouth fell open in a perfect 'O' of surprise. Thierry looked equally stunned, before beginning to smile broadly as the idea sunk in.

'You think he would?'

'I know he will. He told me so the night he fixed your leg.'

Michel was clearly still doubtful. 'But he isn't officially part of the group. If only we hadn't lost Julien we wouldn't be shorthanded. If I hadn't swerved in the other direction that day in Argentan, I'm still sure I could have saved him, instead of which the youngest and last to join us paid with his life.'

Félix knew his friend would never cease to blame himself for what had happened, though the situation had been impossible. He spoke quietly but firmly.

'Michel, *mon brave*, there was nothing more you could have done. We know Julien was brave and willing, but he had that confidence of indestructability we all doubtless had at eighteen. And besides, you know full well it was almost certain you'd both have been shot if you hadn't tried to draw them away in your direction.'

Michel shook his head stubbornly. 'Drop it, Félix.' He took a deep swig of beer. 'And if we involve Guy further, what do we do about Hélène?'

Félix grinned. 'I certainly shan't tell her, if that's what you mean. But I also know now that Guy's his own man. He'll help, and willingly, when I explain the situation.'

The door squeaked as it was opened a head's-width. Yvette peered in and looked from one to the other of them. 'So serious, *les gars*! Are you nearly ready?'

Thierry winced as he half-rose, his expression abashed when he saw Félix's dry smile. 'Can you give us five minutes?'

Yvette motioned for him to sit again and disappeared with what Félix interpreted as a long-suffering smile. He hoped Thierry's short timescale meant that any further argument was over before it began. By good fortune, so it proved. Once they had all agreed, Félix assured the others he would go to the pharmacy the following day, hoping to avoid his sister by arriving early while she would still be busy with Lucie's breakfast.

The hot soup that Yvette had prepared was both nourishing and delicious. Thierry had replaced a loose horseshoe for one of his regular clients in exchange for a brace of pheasants, wisely not enquiring as to their provenance, and the meat from one of the birds had turned a mundane broth into steaming bowls of gamey flavour that now lined their stomachs with warmth and a fullness they rarely experienced these days.

Félix patted his stomach and grinned at Thierry. 'How I envy you your wife, you lucky blighter.' Thierry gave a delighted shrug in response, planting a kiss on Yvette's dimpled cheek.

Her eyes were twinkling as she leant across to Félix. 'There's apple pie too if you've room.'

It was well past curfew before Félix and Michel left, slipping out into the night from the darkened hallway. They were to meet again the following evening once Félix had spoken to Guy. The two parted almost immediately after a thorough check of the road in both directions. Being caught out after curfew was now out of the question. Each knew his way home from the forge without relying on the light from a cycle lamp.

When Félix reached the pharmacy the following morning, the shutters were still down. His watch confirmed that it was still five minutes till opening time. Noticing that there were only two women in the queue at the bakery, he tapped his pocket to make sure he had money with him and ran across the road to take his place behind them. At least he could save Élodie one task today. He breathed in the intense yeasty aroma of warm bread that reached his nostrils from the open door of the shop, and as his stomach rumbled he quickly swallowed the saliva that had flooded his mouth.

Mathilde greeted him shyly when he reached the counter. She looked out of sorts—not surprising considering she had been seen chatting with Matthias shortly before the young German had met his untimely end. Nevertheless, in Félix's opinion, she still exuded so much more appeal than her older sister in some unfathomable way, even though Mireille was generally considered the prettier of the two. It still irked several of his friends greatly that he had steadfastly ignored Mireille's obvious affection for him—and her consequent disdain for them. But, like her though Félix did, it was not in the way she clearly hoped. And of course, he'd since found

Clémence. His whole being ached for her as her face filled his mind, framed by her flowing blonde hair. If she didn't return...

He snapped his mind back to the slight figure in front of him, her smile still in place despite his silent preoccupation. When he checked behind him, he saw that there were now four customers waiting their turn. 'Sorry, Mathilde, I'm standing here daydreaming and you're getting busier by the minute.'

Félix watched half-absently as she passed him the bread and completed the transaction. He extracted a few coins from his pocket clumsily and juggled them with one hand. Mathilde took the right amount from him with a delicate touch. When she smiled again and raised her eyes to his own, he was dumbfounded—he'd never noticed before that, though less widespread, they were the same perfect cornflower blue as Clémence's. He stuttered his goodbye, trying to ignore her perplexed expression. There was absolutely no way he could offer her any explanation for his reaction, which he knew must have appeared odd to say the least.

Félix saw Serge's mother standing squatly at the end of the growing queue. He was more than keen to avoid her, as well as her son. He hurried back across the road as Guy unbolted the door of the pharmacy and followed his brother-in-law at speed into the cool interior of the shop.

Guy consented to Félix's request almost before the words were out of his mouth.

'I did say "any time", and I meant it. Tell me what you'll need me to do.'

He nodded several times as Félix fleshed out the plan, indicating his agreement with what was being suggested.

'No problem. It'll be Thierry's truck, yes?' He gave a half-suppressed laugh. 'I've driven one like that before, though never gas-powered, I confess.'

Félix saw movement in the shadows at the back of the shop. He put a warning hand on Guy's arm as Hélène appeared from the direction of the stock room. With no desire for another tongue-lashing from his sister, he winked at Guy before she could reach his side of the counter. 'Bonjour, Hélène. I'm in a rush, I'm afraid. I came to thank Guy again for his help the other night and to let him know that his patient's doing well.'

He heard Hélène starting to speak as he shot out of the door. He raised a hand in acknowledgement, righted the bike he'd leaned against the corner of the shop window and cycled away, the loaf under his arm as he rode along the lanes under a canopy of filtered green, intermittently blinded by the dazzling rays of sunlight that flashed between the sturdy tree trunks lining his route.

It hadn't taken long that evening for Thierry to give them all the details they needed. The mission was set for two days hence. Against Félix's better judgement, Thierry had insisted Serge should join them, given that they had firmly decided Guy's only involvement would be to drive the truck and keep watch. Michel assured Félix that he would supervise Serge and keep him at arm's length. If they had still had young Julien among them, Félix thought, things could have been different. He knew the fateful shooting in Argentan had shocked them all. Despite his initial evident immaturity, the boy had quickly become an invaluable asset, soon moving from running messages to being a fully competent member of the group. He had joined them as a known entity, of course, because his family had been neighbours of Thierry and Yvette since they had arrived at the forge. But for their first loss to be their youngest member was a particular blow. Since his death they had preferred to remain a small, tight-knit unit unless other trustworthy members could be enlisted. They all knew via other groups there was a growing awareness that German infiltrators were successfully presenting as entirely plausible

recruits and subsequently betraying whole Resistance net-
works, at great cost in both lives and information.

Guy had agreed to join them at the forge. Félix didn't ask
what excuse he'd made to Hélène but was simply glad to see
him there already when he arrived himself. Serge was the
last to join them, habitual cigarette dangling from his lips as
he rode in nonchalantly, knees bent almost at right angles to
the too-small, rusty cycle frame. Félix turned away as Serge
dismounted, intent on avoiding all unnecessary conversation.

Thierry was subdued but business-like as he ran through
the objectives for the last time. It had been drawn to the
Argentan group's attention that a train loaded with rein-
forcements of military hardware—both vehicles and armaments—was on its way to the German *Atlantikwall* coastal
defence line. In collaboration with local railway workers, an
attempt was to be made at Argentan to divert the train. However, German patrols and supervision had increased mas-
sively in response to heightened Resistance operations, with
crushing reprisals threatened for any acts of sabotage. Hence,
in view of the uncertainty, Thierry's group was tasked with
a back-up operation—a combination of track disruption and
explosive charges on the line abutting a thickly wooded area
near Briouze, east of Flers, where a trackside signal was located.

Before they left, Guy delved into the canvas bag he was carrying and extracted a pair of German military issue binoculars.
'I thought these might come in handy.'

Félix was astonished. 'Where on earth...?'

Guy gave a shamefaced grin. 'A German soldier came to me
looking for medication for a dose of the clap. I told him I'd

source it for him in return for a good pair of binoculars. Being that I'm such an avid birdwatcher, that is.'

Thierry's hearty guffaw answered for them all.

Guy passed the binoculars into Michel's eager hands as they went outside. Michel held up the field glasses and a low whistle escaped between his teeth.

'*Chapeau bas*, Guy—these are incredible.'

Each man tried them in turn, Félix last. He clapped his brother-in-law on the back. 'Good work, Guy. I never suspected you could be such a cunning devil.'

Guy looked pleased. 'The soldier boasted too that the Germans have developed some kind of night vision scope—all completely hush-hush so of course he shouldn't have been telling me—but apparently it's only available at the moment to a limited number of Panzer groups.'

The journey to their target was uneventful. Guy skilfully followed Michel's back-lane route and parked the truck a hundred yards back from the railway line, having executed a perfect about turn to face the way they had come. He jumped out along with the others and after a brief recce on foot in both directions chose his vantage point. Serge was to position the explosives and set the detonators as instructed by Michel, who had more experience in dismantling the track plate and bolts, in which he would be aided by Félix. Before they began, all three men checked that Guy was in their line of sight should he give any warning signal.

The whole exercise took only twenty minutes. Félix checked his watch. Another twenty minutes before the train arrived, if it had not been successfully re-routed, however temporarily. He swivelled at a sudden noise down the track that sounded like an owl. Guy's arms were raised and waving frantically. Félix lifted a hand in acknowledgement as Guy pointed down the road, indicating that two vehicles were approaching. The slight figure disappeared as it leapt into the roadside ditch. Félix stood and whistled to Serge, who grabbed something off the track and retreated into the undergrowth. Fortuitously this whole section of the line was bordered by thick vegetation, so Michel and Félix were able to follow suit from their own position. Félix prayed the truck was well enough hidden down the side road.

The heavy rumble of engines could be heard from some distance. Félix raised his head warily when he heard a squeal of brakes. Two large German personnel carriers had stopped not far from where Guy had taken refuge. No one got out, but, as on the group's previous foray, an operator switched on a powerful roof-mounted light. It arced slowly across the railway track, pausing twice before continuing. The vehicles moved on a hundred yards and stopped again, twenty metres short of Félix and Michel. As the stark light pierced the blackness, Félix spotted a bolt lying at the edge of the track that they'd overlooked in their haste. It was below the level of the beam. He inched forward and stretched out questing fingers, not daring to raise his head. He closed his hand over the greasy metal and retreated, grateful for Michel's hands tugging reassuringly on his ankles. As he immersed himself in the scratchy foliage, he sensed movement to his right. He held his breath as a German boot heel brushed his still extended arm and froze as a voice shouted directly above him.

'*Nichts hier zu sehen.*' The soldier strolled across to the track and kicked the rails. Félix felt Michel's grip tighten. A sharp metallic clack split the silence, but the rail didn't move. Félix could feel the sweat beading on his forehead as he inched back his hand, which was still clutching the stray bolt. The thud of footsteps retreating flooded him with relief, but neither man moved a millimetre until they heard the engines revving. Even so, Michel wriggled only sufficiently far to raise his black-smeared face fractionally, lest one or more of the soldiers had been left on guard. There was no sign of anyone, but the trucks had stopped again shortly beyond Serge's position. Félix watched Michel for his reaction as the track was illuminated once more. He'd heard the advice Serge had been given to place the plastic explosives on the inner side of the near track, and the outer side of the far one, where they would be hidden from any brief roadside inspection. To his immense satisfaction the arc light didn't hesitate in its trajectory, and Michel whispered that he could see no sign of Serge's work from where he lay.

The light snapped off unceremoniously, plunging the scene into darkness again. The two men waited till their vision adjusted and rose watchfully as the trucks moved off. Félix checked his watch anxiously. There was now a bare four minutes until the train was due. He shrugged his shoulders and made a face at Michel, who ran, keeping low, to help Serge crush the detonator fuses. It had been agreed that they would use short delays again, and Félix offered up a silent entreaty that they would function reliably, aware this was not always the case. Unsatisfactorily, it could only be a matter of shrewd guesswork anyway, as there was no way of knowing whether the train would steam into view, unhindered in its progress. He crossed his fingers in the hope that the obviously failed re-routing at Argentan had caused at least a fractional delay.

Félix checked his watch for the $n$th time and whistled to Michel, pointing beyond him. He punched the air in satisfaction. The upline signal had turned green—their work had not been in vain. He watched anxiously as the two men crouched on their heels to crush the copper tubes between their fingers, one on each side of the track. They thundered back, job done, and Félix joined them as they headed for the side road. Guy had returned from his lookout point, dripping foetid mud from the bottom of the waterlogged ditch. Félix hoped he'd be able to get his filthy gear off at home before he encountered Hélène.

The four men clambered into the truck. Michel directed Guy back to the forge down the narrow, pitch-dark isolated lanes, the four men crushed into the cab together, tense and silent. Thierry appeared from the house before the sound of the engine died, smiling once his eyes had counted all four heads. Serge was the first to leave, lighting a Gitane Maïs in a cupped hand as he went, the strong odour of the drifting smoke unmistakeable. Michel had volunteered to remain with Thierry for a mission debrief, leaving Félix to cycle home via the village with Guy to ensure he reached the pharmacy without incident. Yvette emerged before they left, insisting on Guy taking an old coat of Thierry's. She promised to clean and return his own without delay, holding the stinking garment at arm's length as she went indoors.

Before they parted company, standing in the shadows across the road from the old grey building in the village centre, Guy soberly shook Félix's hand, a self-conscious smile on his face.

'I hate to admit, Félix, but I enjoyed the adrenalin rush tonight. I so admire what you're all doing. I know not everyone does—Hélène being among them, I'm sorry to say —but someone has to take a stand.'

Félix squeezed his brother-in-law's arm. 'Thanks for your help tonight, Guy. It means a lot. To all of us.'

'I've said it already, but I'll say it again. I'm here any time you need a hand. It'll be a while yet before Thierry is fully fit, whatever he's telling you.'

Félix nodded in agreement. 'Thanks again. But we don't want to cause you any trouble with...'

The moonlight glinted on Guy's glasses, obscuring his eyes, but there was no mistaking his rueful smile. 'Hélène? Don't you worry about her, leave that problem to me.'

Félix grinned. 'You're a better man than I am, Guy!'

He watched as the slight figure stepped forward and observed the road in both directions, hunching his shoulders as he ran across to the blacked-out pharmacy. Guy raised a hand as he crept down the side passage and was then lost to view.

# CHAPTER THIRTEEN

## September 1943

'WHY DOES SHE INSIST on stirring up trouble wherever she goes?'

Élodie paused. She had entered the farmhouse via the scullery, so had seen no warning sign of her sister's presence. She supposed Hélène had cycled from the village and left her bike outside the kitchen or maybe the barn. But two visits within a few weeks—what had brought that about? Despite their mother's entreaties on the last occasion, she'd not expected to see Hélène for at least a few months—twice a year was more like the norm. She put down the items she'd been carrying and padded quietly towards the kitchen. It seemed obvious that the topic of conversation was herself, so she might as well face the music and get it over with.

'Hélène, what a nice surprise!'

Élodie was amused to see her sister jump at the sound of her voice. Hélène's stony expression when she turned in her direction satisfied Élodie that her sarcasm had hit home. She glanced at their mother, who raised her eyes heavenwards.

Hélène tutted sharply. 'I was just saying...'

'I heard what you were just saying. Who am I supposed to have been upsetting now?'

'The major who is living *chez* Mme Lagrange at the Manoir.'

'Oh, him.' Élodie was already annoyed by her sister's pompous attitude. 'I don't give a sh—' She saw her mother's eyes narrow. 'I have no interest in what that man thinks of me. Just so you know.'

'You see?' Hélène addressed her words to their mother. 'This is exactly what I was talking about. The Germans are a fact of life here now, and we have to live with them. I have to serve them in the pharmacy all the time. And the major is always extremely polite.'

'I'd have to say not in my experience, *chérie*, but I take your point. Why don't we all sit down and have some home-made elderberry cordial?'

Élodie smiled in gratitude as her mother crossed to the larder to find the bottle. Maman was trying to pour oil on troubled waters as usual, bless her. Hélène, typically, wasn't leaving it at that.

'I don't know what you've said or done, but the major told me that he thought you a "fine, spirited young woman"—apart from your rudeness, that is.'

Élodie bit back the yearning to tell her sister exactly what the major himself had, in fact, already done to her—and not once, but twice.

'How does the major even know we're related?' She watched Hélène carefully as she formulated her reply, which was sufficiently vague and thus uncharacteristic that she was sure it sheltered a lie.

'Oh, one day when he was in the pharmacy and there were no other customers, he asked me if I was born in Ste-Hon-orine.' Her smile was self-congratulatory. 'He said he thought my manners were more refined than he'd expect from a village resident.'

The absurdity of this statement caused Élodie to laugh out loud. 'Oh my, a class above the peasants, then? So you had to admit that, when all's said and done, you're a local farmer's daughter, is that it?'

Hélène, who had already sat down opposite her, jutted out her chin and leant across the table, jabbing her index finger with venom. 'You don't seem to understand that some of us have no option but to serve the Germans in our businesses. It wouldn't be so difficult if people like you—and worse still Félix, who's certainly old enough to know better—didn't continually behave like bad-mannered idiots.'

'That's quite enough from both of you.' Élodie heard her mother's warning tone and got up to fetch three glasses. The jug of cordial and a plate with a few home-made biscuits had arrived on the table and were set firmly between the two sisters. 'You're never going to agree about that man, but let's not allow him to tear this family apart.'

Hélène looked up at her mother from under her lashes. 'I'm sorry, Maman, I don't mean to upset you.'

Élodie counted to ten under her breath but didn't speak. Now Hélène was playing *sainte-nitouche*. How it dragged her back to her infant days, trailing along behind her sister who never courted trouble, while she herself never seemed to avoid it. Time to change the subject.

'You haven't brought Lucie today? That's a shame.' Doubtless it meant the purpose of Hélène's visit had been expressly to display her shortcomings to their mother.

'It's half-day closing today, so Guy has taken her to see his own mother in Flers.'

Élodie was relieved when, after half an hour's inconsequential gossip about the village, Hélène rose to leave. She hugged their mother, then proffered a cool cheek to Élodie, who knew a final barb would be launched in her direction.

'Do try and see past the end of your delicate little nose, *ma sœur*, and treat the Germans with courtesy. It would make life so much more pleasant for us all.'

*Pleasant?* Nothing related to that bloody major was pleasant. But a vision of Rudi, shirtless and carrying her gently to the bed in the Hotel Léopold, flashed unbidden into Élodie's mind. If only she were able to impart the shocking truth... Her hand flew to her mouth as a giggle escaped her. She gave Hélène a dutiful peck on the cheek and hung back as their mother accompanied her to the door.

'Do please pop into the pharmacy today and give this to Hélène for Lucie.'

Élodie looked up, marking her place in *Madame Bovary* with a finger. She knew she should hide her reluctance and took a calming deep breath before she replied.

'*Oui*, Maman. Of course, if you wish.'

Her mother gave her a long look. 'You'll never heal your differences if you won't even speak to your sister.'

Élodie finished her coffee in one gulp, grabbed a strip of paper from the table drawer and slipped it into her book. She leapt up from her chair to avoid further discussion and held out a hand for the small parcel. She was all too aware that her mother had unpicked her favourite cardigan to make a tiny one for Lucie from the precious wool.

'Lucie will love it, Maman.' She kissed her mother on the cheek. 'I'll be as quick as I can. I hope the bread queue isn't too long today.'

Surprisingly, perhaps because it was still very early, there were only four women standing outside the boulangerie—and none of them was Mme Martin. As she waited her turn, Mamselle Bonnaire arrived and greeted her warmly.

With a loaf tucked victoriously under her arm, Élodie crossed the road and headed for the pharmacy with the brown-paper parcel. She came to an abrupt halt as the shop door opened. Major Wolff spotted her unerringly as he emerged. The self-satisfied smile on his face vanished.

'*Guten Morgen, Fräulein.*'

His formal greeting was not lost on Élodie, who inclined her head coldly. He stepped in front of her, standing far too close for comfort. 'I've been having a most informative chat with your sister.'

Élodie's mind whirled. Exactly how had he originally found out she and Hélène were related? Hélène certainly wouldn't have volunteered the fact. She knew that from their recent conversation. And what did he mean by 'informative'? A niggle of alarm washed through her. Before she could answer, he spoke again.

'It is refreshing to discover that one member of your family has some manners. Of course, she's not as attractive as you, but then again, looks aren't everything, are they?'

'That wasn't the impression you gave me at the Manoir, *Herr Major.*' Élodie saw his jaw clench at her sarcasm.

'Don't try my patience, young woman, or the next time will be a very different experience.'

*Next time?* 'There won't be a next time. Ever.' Élodie spat out the words and tried to move, but she wasn't quick enough. The major grasped her arm so hard that she felt faint from the pain.

'There will be whatever I say there will be. And don't you forget it.' His face was inches from her own, and she recoiled at the smell of cigar smoke on his breath. Several villagers were watching curiously as they trudged past, taking care not to attract the major's attention.

Out of the corner of her eye she saw movement behind the major, outside the café door at the top of the square. Marc's widow was hanging on to the arm of a dark-haired man who was struggling to free himself. Élodie was horrified to see that it was Félix. If the major were to spot him, she couldn't even guess at the consequences. He had never reported to the major at the Manoir as ordered, of that she was sure. A quick count confirmed at least four other German soldiers in the square. She knew at once that it was her current contretemps with the major that was causing her brother's disregard for his own safety.

The major had relaxed his grip a fraction. Élodie wrenched her arm away and took a sidestep. Surely if Félix saw that she was free he would have the sense to disappear again?

'I have chores to do, *Herr Major*, and I'm sure you have better victims to pursue.'

Wolff stood with his arms folded as she turned away. His smug look and relaxed pose unnerved her, and she knew his eyes were following her as she walked with great deliberation into the pharmacy.

Guy was standing beside the counter, his pose watchful but uncertain. He was clearly aware of her encounter outside.

'Bonjour, Élodie. What was all that about?'

Élodie moved out of sight of the door and checked the café again. Its door hung open wide, but there was no sign of Félix. She relaxed her tensed shoulders. 'Sorry, Guy. Bonjour. The major's a *connard odieux* who won't leave our family alone.' His mouth twitched into an amused smile at her vulgar language. She perused the shop and frowned. 'But he said he'd just been talking to Hélène.'

'Yes, he probably was. I've just got back from delivering some medication and Hélène was here while I was out. Your friend the major was leaving when I arrived.'

'He's no friend of mine! But you didn't hear any of the conversation?'

Guy shook his head. 'No, why?'

Élodie tutted in exasperation. 'Pfft, don't worry—the major enjoys planting insinuations, that's all.'

'About what, exactly?'

*Dear Guy.* He looked so genuinely concerned. 'Honestly, nothing.' She put the creased parcel on the counter. 'This is from Maman. She's made a cardigan for Lucie. Please tell her that her *mémé* made it with love.'

'Of course. But you won't wait to see Hélène? She'll be back soon.'

'Another time. I should be getting back.'

Guy laughed. 'You girls. Always the same.'

There was no point in contradicting his remark. Élodie had no argument with Guy. She shrugged, smiled, and kissed him on both cheeks.

'Until the next time, Guy.'

She was relieved to see that the Germans had now all disappeared too. She set off for home, preoccupied by the major's remarks and the more so by his air of self-assuredness when she had first spotted him. What exactly could Hélène have told him?

# CHAPTER FOURTEEN

## October 1943

THE KNOCK AT THE open door made them all jump.

'*Bonjour. C'est moi, Michel.*'

Félix put out a hand to his mother to save her getting up. He stood up from the table, noting his father's raised eyebrows, and crossed the kitchen with a hunk of bread still in his hand, wondering why Michel was here in the middle of the day. When he reached the doorway, Michel backed off and motioned for him to follow. Félix frowned. Why the mystery? Once they were out of earshot of the house, Michel stopped.

'I've had a visit from Thierry. A plane's coming in tonight, bringing ammunition and, praise be, a radio operator.'

Could it be Clémence? Félix's ear-splitting grin earned him a playful clip on the chin from his friend, who had correctly interpreted his obvious delight.

'It might be her—we don't know yet. Could equally be a short, swarthy man who takes an instant dislike to you.'

Félix was forced to laugh at this suggestion.

As the sound of the approaching aircraft grew more distinct, Félix felt his spirits soaring in unison. Was he raising his hopes gratuitously? Thierry was standing looking skywards, a hand to his brow to shade the moonlight. Michel had elected to remain by the gate, in case any of the increasingly frequent German patrols put in an appearance. Félix moved towards the first of the landing lights as Thierry acknowledged the usual recognition code letter, and signalled for Lisette to switch on the other two. He saw that she was already watching him sulkily, a scowl on her face, but she did his bidding and they retreated as the Lizzie came in to land, low and slow as usual.

Once the plane had turned, ready for departure, the fuselage door opened. Félix stopped mid-stride, but the first figure to appear was that of Doug, whom they knew from previous flights. As if in slow motion, he handed out four boxes before jumping down himself. He turned and took two cases from the willowy figure who ducked through the opening and followed him down the ladder. As she scanned the faces around her on the field, her eyes met Félix's. With no further thought for protocol, he flew across the intervening space and flung his arms out, pulling her close, breathing in her glorious scent and burying his face in her hair, which this time was hanging free and not covered by a scarf.

Thierry's loud throat-clearing brought a silly grin to his face, and he looked round to see the astonished face of Doug, who was standing rooted to the spot with the documents Thierry had handed him, staring open-mouthed at the pastiche he was witnessing. His common sense restored, Félix heard Michel choking with laughter in the field gateway. Now self-conscious, he stepped back, ran his hands briskly down his sides and picked up one of the boxes.

Clémence retrieved her radio and suitcase and trotted alongside him to the truck, a brooding Lisette in her wake toting another of the boxes. Doug waved his goodbyes as he boarded the plane and Félix ran to help with the remaining containers and the landing torches. When the three men reached the vehicle, Lisette was standing with her back to the cab smoking, while Clémence was stowing her luggage inside. Félix made a face at Thierry, who gave him a knowing look and rolled his eyes.

After Thierry and Clémence had exchanged a few pleasantries, the journey to the barn was frostily silent, Lisette cramming herself against the truck door, thus positioning herself as far from the other girl as was feasible. This time she jumped out without comment when they arrived. Félix collected the two bags and Michel followed him with the food and washing paraphernalia again thoughtfully provided by Yvette. Clémence thanked Thierry, who gave her a quick grin and a wink as she pursed her lips at Lisette's firmly turned back. She crossed paths with Michel as he came out of the barn smiling broadly. Félix stood watching all this from the doorway, feeling as if the missing piece had been restored to the jigsaw of his life. When they stepped inside, Clémence pulled the door shut behind her and enfolded herself in his arms.

Despite her entreaties, Félix allowed himself only to revel in her presence, to smell her softly perfumed hair and to return her embrace. It took all his resolve to resist her persuasive lips and hands, and for a few minutes he succumbed. Finally, he held her at arm's length.

'I have no words to tell you how I feel at seeing you again.' She pushed hard against his hold. He shook his head, speaking fast as she opened her mouth to argue. 'But no, not tonight. Clémence, the day will come, and soon, but for tonight, just let me be with you and imagine what we shall share.'

Clémence gave no reply but helped him set out the food and wine—and this time two glasses—on the table, after he had wiped away the hay dust with his jacket. They sat opposite one another, their legs entwined beneath the table, their hands caressing as they shared the food and drink. Félix felt her touch like a series of tiny, exquisite physical shocks and the air between them sang with sexual tension. Gradually he saw her eyelids and limbs drooping as tiredness took over. He rose and found the bedding in the old box and made up two separate beds, refusing her offer of help. When he was done, he took both her hands in his and pressed his lips to them.

'I'm going outside to smoke while you—'. He waved his hand in the direction of the washing kit.

He had forgotten the sweet sound of her laughter. 'Félix, you don't need to.'

'Believe me, I do.'

He dodged her outstretched hands and slipped speedily through the barn door, drawing in deep breaths of cool night air. He saw that his fingers were trembling as he lit his cigarette ineptly, his mind full of Clémence and the anticipation of fulfilment on some not-too-distant day. His fingers rasped across his unshaven chin as he watched the smoke drifting away towards the trees. Maybe, just maybe they would all survive this war after all.

It had been arranged that Clémence would return to Mme Tailler. The dependable shopkeeper had never come under the slightest suspicion and had received few visits from the occupiers, apart from one or two soldiers looking for lace handkerchiefs with which to woo their French girlfriends. She had told Félix one of them said she reminded him of his *Mutti* at home, to which she initially took exception until she realised that in his eyes there was no greater compliment. Félix had laughed, then felt a pang of bitter sadness, thinking of young Matthias who would never again see his German mother or his English cousin.

On the following morning, Félix and Clémence cycled into Flers without incident on the bikes that had been stashed in the barn the previous day. Thierry had promised to collect the remains of what he had brought for them the previous evening, so they had simply tidied everything together, locked up and hidden the key in its usual place.

Mme Tailler and Clémence greeted each other like old friends. Félix hung back.

'I'll leave you to get settled—you know where everything is by now—and I'll come back tomorrow afternoon to see if there's anything you need.'

'You won't come up?'

Félix felt unaccountably embarrassed in the presence of the older woman, who was watching them with a charming but complicit smile hovering on her lips. He shook his head, repeated his promise to return the following day and took his leave.

Félix spent a restless night, his thoughts teeming. Holding Clémence in his arms again had cemented his all-consuming feelings for her, made him realise why the past months had been filled with a restless longing, a need for action, a sense of unfulfillment.

Perhaps providentially, his father needed his help in the fields for the whole morning, and the hard work absorbed his concentration. He ate his midday meal with the family, sensing Élodie was aware that something was different, that some crushing sense of melancholy had been lifted from him.

He caught her several times watching him with a puzzled frown, her head on one side, flashing an intermittent baffled smile in his direction.

After they had eaten, he excused himself and went up to wash and change. When he came down, his mother was busy in the kitchen but there was no sign of his sister. Good. Much as he loved her, this was not the moment for explanations. As he wheeled his bike out of the barn, Élodie sprang from the long shadow cast by the sun like a cat pouncing on its painstakingly stalked prey. He laughed as she jogged along beside him, pulling at his arm till he stopped.

'You know before you ask what I'm going to say.'

She purred and pleaded, but still he refused to divulge the reason for the change in his demeanour.

'When I'm ready to tell you, I will. That's a promise.'

She stamped her foot as he ruffled her hair, swung his leg over the crossbar, pushed down hard on the pedals and sped away.

Mme Tailler greeted him fondly. The shop was quiet, but she clearly sensed he was not in the mood for conversation.

'Clémence is in her room. She'll be so pleased you've come.'

Félix climbed the stairs with slow deliberation. He knew unswervingly what he wanted, but still this damned war hung between living for the moment and giving in to his desire, and an overbearing sense of responsibility to do whatever he had to do to see the fight for France through to the end.

He walked quietly along the corridor until he reached her room, where he raised his fist hesitantly before knocking. He heard no answering footsteps but suddenly the door opened and Clémence drew him inside, squeezing him so hard that he could feel her ribs rising and falling against his chest. He breathed in the soft smell of her, happy for a moment to hold her close. She stroked his back, whispered something too indistinct to comprehend and promptly let him go. She slipped past him and locked the door, took his hand and pulled him towards the bed, pushing aside the huge, yielding pink quilt.

Félix resisted still. He wanted her so much, ached for her, but was it right, when current circumstances decreed that even their continued existence was uncertain?

'Clémence, don't you think we should...' His sentence remained unfinished. She removed the clip from her hair, shaking it out into golden waves, pulled off her dress in one fluid movement and started to unbutton his shirt. He caressed her ivory skin, silky smooth under his touch, and felt her shiver as his movements intensified. When her soft hands moved down across his hips, he finally lost control.

They made love with an urgency that reflected the long wait for this day, but with the matching rhythm of seasoned lovers. Afterwards, as she lay across his chest, her blonde hair spread out in a pale, shining half-moon, Félix slumped drowsily, drowning in a deep contentment he'd begun to think he would never experience. He rhythmically brushed her hair away from her face, almost unable to believe she had given herself to him so completely. 'I love you so, Clémence. Say you won't forget me after this war ends.'

She looked up and gave him an impish smile, tapping his chin. 'Félix, you chump, d'you think I behave this way with every Tom, Dick and Pierre?'

He laughed and pulled her closer. 'I certainly hope not.'

'Well, I love you too, and there's no chance you can escape me now, war or no war.'

# CHAPTER FIFTEEN

## October 1943

'HELLO, *LIEBCHEN*.'

Élodie looked up in surprise at the sound of Rudi's voice, spilling a precious handful of the chicken feed she had been measuring out. '*Mince*, but you made me jump! I didn't hear you arrive.'

Rudi's smile was apologetic. 'That's because I left the bike down the road. As I was about to turn into the lane, a man passed me on a tractor. I thought from his expression that it might be your father, so I rode on then turned back. I know how he feels about the Germans, and I didn't want to cause you any problems.'

She straightened up from her task and dragged a hand through her tangled hair. She chose to ignore the comment about her father. 'What brings you here today anyway? It's Monday, isn't it?'

Rudi's smile widened. 'It is. But I came to tell you I can be free on Wednesday afternoon. We could meet in Argentan?'

Élodie stared at him in consternation, feeling her muscles stiffen at the thought of what he was proposing. The major's face filled her mind, the smell of his cologne flooding her nose. She saw the hurt in Rudi's eyes as she began to stammer an excuse. She stopped herself in mid-sentence and began again.

'I can try. I'll say yes—I would meet you at the usual place?'

His expression changed immediately, though he appeared to offer her a get-out clause too. 'I would like that very much. But you already know that. If it's difficult, you only have to say so.'

'If I'm not at the hotel by midday, there's a problem. Otherwise, I will see you there.' Élodie had to smile at the pleasure she saw in his eyes.

Rudi brushed his hand across her cheek. 'I will wait for you in the lobby, *Liebchen*.'

Her mother looked sceptical when Élodie announced her wish to go to Argentan again but contented herself with a raised eyebrow and a long look, and a reminder that she expected her to be home in time to see to the chickens. Élodie countered with a guileless smile, knowing she had not yet quite been forgiven for her previously broken promise.

This was the third time Élodie had travelled to Argentan since her encounters with the major at the Manoir. The first instance had been a disaster. Rudi had been his usual attentive, considerate self, but she had frozen at his touch and she had wept inwardly at the bewilderment in his eyes. But she had not explained—could not, and would not, reasoning that if he knew the truth, he would no longer want her. The sense of shame that had clouded her judgement rested on a nagging doubt that somehow it had all been her fault, even though logic told her otherwise.

The second occasion had been four weeks later. The major had decreed in the meantime that Rudi could not be spared from his duties, and Élodie was secretly relieved. When she had arrived at the station Rudi was not there, and she had waited for ten minutes before making for the hotel, unsure what to do. The fear that he would not arrive had somehow been cathartic, the thought of losing him beyond consideration. She had heard footsteps behind her, running, and had pivoted and thrown herself into his arms as he was about to tap her on the shoulder. His smile when she released him told her all she needed to know, but still she had struggled—and failed—to share his passion in the dim, shabby room that she now thought of as their own.

A further four weeks had passed. The sky was a washed-out, wintry blue, the fields below a muddy brown, punctured by drab-coloured stalks of rotting stubble. Here and there crows were wandering along awkwardly on their oversized flipper-feet, sometimes cocking their heads in anticipation, or despondently pecking at the soil.

As the train puffed onwards, Élodie allowed herself to be lulled by the regular click-clack of the wheels on the rails, repeating to herself 'He is not the major'. There had been even more grey-clad soldiers on the train when Élodie boarded, but their constant chatter served to divert her sense of foreboding. She started from her introspection as she became aware that she was being watched. Three uniformed Germans on the other side of the carriage had been talking especially noisily throughout the journey, and one, she saw, was staring at her lewdly. When her eyes met his, he winked at her and made some ribald remark to his companions, who all turned to stare, obscene grins on their faces. Loud guffaws followed. Élodie glared at them and returned her attention to the bleak fields that stretched to the horizon.

She tried to ignore them, twisting and untwisting the ends of the bright blue cotton bandana that circled her neck. One of the soldiers leant forward and addressed her in German. She frowned at him and pointedly turned away as one of his companions put a restraining hand on the arm he had reached out in her direction.

As soon as the train began to slow for its arrival in Argentan, she leapt to her feet and stood by the door, wrenching it open the moment the brakes ceased squealing and the train groaned to a hissing halt. To her dismay, there was a long queue at the ticket barrier, where two black-coated men were overseeing a document check being undertaken by uniformed soldiers. Élodie watched from the corner of her eye as the three soldiers from the train bypassed the queue with a nod to their colleagues.

Once her papers had been examined, she hurried out of the station. Her heart sank. There was no sign of Rudi but she was immediately surrounded by the three soldiers, who had obviously waited for her to appear. None of them spoke French so she had no notion of what they were saying, though their meaning was abundantly clear. The one who had winked at her brushed her chin with his hand. She smacked it away angrily and he grabbed her wrist. As he did so, a gloved hand caught his shoulder. Rudi's voice was icy. The soldier let her go and stood to attention.

'*Entschuldigung, Herr Leutnant.*'

Rudi took a note of the soldier's rank and number and sent the three of them on their way after a dressing down that Élodie could decipher only by its tone. He was full of apologies—yet again, the major had detained him, and he had had to go along with the charade in order not to have all his free time cancelled. He suggested that they take a walk before going to the hotel.

They crossed from the station and strolled, hands touching, down to the River Vère. Élodie relaxed both mentally and physically as they spoke of things new and old, of the ducks dabbling in the weeds, of the first day they met. Rudi told her more about his training as a *Bauingenieur*, and how, after the war, he planned to return to engineering and work on the construction of hydroelectric power plants. Élodie was unsure she understood most of what he described, but the enthusiasm with which he expressed it shone out from his eyes, and she loved him all the more for that alone.

They continued along the riverbank until they reached the next bridge, then climbed up to the roadway and crossed. Disorientated by the bend in the river, they checked their bearings, unsure of their way to the hotel and arriving from a different direction. As they approached the Hotel Léopold, Élodie knew her steps had begun to falter, her blithe mood fading. She took a deep breath and forced herself to speed up. She told herself she was being ridiculous and ascended the steps two at a time, aware that she was being very unladylike. Rudi followed her, laughing as he caught up with her at the top.

The same down-at-heel clerk seemed to be on duty perennially, his collar worn and his jacket pockets fraying. He gave the lieutenant a bored smile as he handed over the room key, his eyes raking Élodie with faint amusement, as if indicating he had seen it all before, and so many times, with so many soldiers, so many women.

Instead of climbing the stairs, they took the rackety lift to the third floor, its metal structure juddering and rattling noisily as the ancient machinery whirred and wheezed. Their room was a short walk down the dingy corridor. Rudi turned the key and stood back for her to enter, closing the door behind him. Once inside, he unbuttoned his tunic and, to her astonishment, flung it onto the chair in a heap. His shirt he hung on the back of the chair with little more care. He began to unbutton his trousers, then stopped. Élodie stood motionless, licking her lips nervously, fists clenched across her ribs. Her heart felt fit to burst from her chest as he stepped towards her, putting out one tentative hand as she might herself do towards a stray dog. She flinched as his warm skin touched her own, seeing the complete incomprehension in the face now close to her own.

'*Liebchen?*'

'It's nothing—I'm fine, really I am, just a bit tired.'

Rudi stepped back and stroked her shoulders, frowning as he felt her tremble. She put her head against his chest, drawing in the warm, masculine scent of his skin as she willed herself to want him as he so obviously wanted her.

Try as she might to suppress her feelings, and despite his soothing and tender caresses and whispered words of love, Élodie had a crushing desire to slap him away, punch him even, punish him totally unjustifiably for the loathsome deeds of his senior colleague. With deliberation, she rose on tiptoes to kiss him in the way she had so often done, her hands laced at the back of his head, willing herself to forget her body's cruel betrayal on that second occasion with the major. After a long moment she pushed him away and slowly tugged her dress off over her head. Rudi stroked her hair and followed obediently as she clasped his hand and led him to the bed. He kissed her nose and stood, hands on hips, as she fiddled clumsily with his remaining trouser buttons.

As Rudi's desire increased, she blinked back tears and fought to become one with him, as on that first unforgettable occasion, signally failing to achieve even the slightest satisfaction. When Rudi rolled off her, his breathing deep and languid, he turned her face to his own, questioning again.

'*Liebchen?* Have I hurt you somehow? Tell me, please.'

Élodie shook her head curtly, furious with herself for harming the one valued thing in her life. She pressed her fingers firmly over his lips. 'It's not you, *mon beau*, I promise it's not you.'

'Then?'

She buried her head under his chin and held him tight, offering no explanation. He seemed to accept her silence, and gradually his sense of stillness leached away her own taut reserve. She still couldn't tell him, would never tell him, what the major had done. Rudi deserved better from her, didn't he? She drew her index finger slowly down from his chin to his lower abdomen, then raised herself onto her elbows.

'Suppose we try again?'

His smile was tentative. 'You are sure?'

She nodded, responding to the smouldering shimmer in his blue eyes, brushing away the wayward blond hair that fell across his forehead. It wouldn't yet be perfect again, but with a supreme effort she would at least show him that she cared.

When they were sated, and the careworn lines that had formed on his face recently were softened in repose, she smiled as she fixed in her mind the look of delight in his eyes as she had taken the lead, running her fingers across the soft skin that overlay his firmly muscled torso. She had finally understood too that what Rudi expressed for her was love rather than animal lust. The mental scars inflicted by the major would fade in time, albeit largely forced out by her determination that his behaviour would not ruin her life—or her relationship with the man she had chosen to lay beside.

# CHAPTER SIXTEEN

## *November 1943*

CLÉMENCE SAT BACK IN her chair. She'd finished decoding the message and her face was chillingly grave. Félix could see she was weighing up the words she'd pieced together.

'Well?'

Clémence didn't answer immediately, which was worrying, and when she did, her voice was pensive. 'They think Major Wolff may have important papers in his possession concerning troop movements. They're asking for his office to be searched and for any relevant documents to be photographed.'

Félix groaned. 'Of all people—it would be that *malfrat*. How do they propose we do that?'

Clémence laughed drily. 'Well, I have a miniature camera with me that I learnt to use during training, so it'll have to be me, whether he's a thug or not. And obviously he wouldn't be there when I was.'

'No!' Félix whipped bolt upright. 'It's too dangerous. I won't allow it.'

He was surprised by Clémence's reaction. She narrowed her eyes and gave him a long, cool stare.

'It's not your decision on this one, Félix.'

Before he could protest again, she moved across and knelt in front of him, her hands tight on his thighs. Her voice was soothing. 'Félix, we all have to take risks. You know I do that every time I transmit and receive. One day a detector van will be fractionally too close. I was told before I came here that I'd have to live with that danger, among others, every day. And that if I survived, I'd be one of the lucky ones.'

She silenced him with her fingers against his mouth as he began to speak. 'Please, Félix, discuss it with the others and work out a plan. It needs to happen as soon as possible.'

Félix knew he was beaten but persisted nonetheless. 'Surely you could teach me to use the camera—it can't be that difficult, can it?'

Her eyes shone in amusement. 'Because I can do it?'

'No, I didn't mean that. But—'

Clémence made a face. 'Please, Félix, do as I ask.'

He knew she would recognise the reluctance in his quick nod. 'I'll be back later.' He kissed her absentmindedly, his brain racing. As he cycled to Michel's workshop, an idea came to him. His feet pressed the pedals down firmly as he formulated his thoughts. Yes, that might work.

Michel grinned as the workshop door burst open. He put down the tool he was using to straighten a wayward bicycle spoke and wiped the grease from his hands on a none-too-clean cloth that clearly had not been washed in a long time.

'I wasn't expecting to see you today, Félix.'

Félix set out the situation succinctly. 'But I think I know how it can be done. Élodie's been badgering me to let her help—'

Michel's face darkened. He shook Félix's arm roughly. 'Don't involve her, Félix. Don't put Élodie in unnecessary danger.'

Félix was stunned by the ferocity of Michel's reaction. He looked at his old friend thoughtfully, watching Michel colour up at the scrutiny. 'Michel, *mon gars*, I often wondered. Why haven't you ever told her how you feel?'

The pink creeping up Michel's cheeks turned to red. He wouldn't meet Félix's quizzical gaze, merely shrugged and cleared his throat. 'She can do far better than me, Félix.'

'If only—'. Félix stopped himself from saying more as Michel looked at him curiously. He knew his sister was fond of Michel, but he didn't think her feelings had ever extended to the romantic. He changed the subject. 'I'll call in at Thierry's and ask Yvette if it's OK to meet there around eight. That suit you?'

Thierry gave his vigorous endorsement. He clapped Félix on the back. 'Good thinking. Élodie won't be suspected in the way that one of us might.' He turned to Michel, who had remained stubbornly silent. 'Well, it's a good plan, don't you think?'

Michel glared at Félix. 'I don't think we should ask Élodie. I don't care if she's willing—it's too bloody dangerous.'

Félix pressed the point. 'It'll be dangerous for Clémence too.' This earned him another sour look from Michel.

'True, but she's been trained for all this. Élodie hasn't.'

Thierry held up a hand. '*Ça suffit*! This is getting us nowhere. Élodie's the one to tell us whether she's willing to do it. Félix, you'll ask her and let me know what's decided?'

Félix ignored Michel's baleful scowl. 'I'll let you know to-morrow.'

'I don't understand. Who exactly is she?'

Félix had waited until their parents were safely in bed and out of earshot before sounding out his sister. He knew before he said a word that she would jump at the chance, and he had emphasised the dangers in an effort to make her think sensibly. Otherwise, he knew she would simply agree in her usual appealingly impetuous fashion. He was still determined to tell her only as much as she needed to know, to minimise her participation for her own sake.

'Clémence is here to help us communicate with the Allies.'

Élodie grinned. 'She's some kind of spy?'

Félix was not amused. 'This is serious, Él. It's not a game, and the risks are huge.'

She patted his hand. 'I know. Anything to do with that *saligaud* is a threat. He's a *chien fou*, and that unpredictability makes him all the more dangerous.'

'I'll say it again. You don't have to do this. Michel, for one, is adamant that you shouldn't.' Félix waited, keen to gauge her reaction.

Élodie shrugged. 'Well, it's not his decision. It's mine. I love Michel like a brother, you know that, but he can't tell me what to do. And I know the Manoir better than any of you.' Her grey-green eyes held a defiant challenge, echoed by the set of her mouth.

Félix took both her hands in his. 'Then we're agreed. Let's work out how it can be done.'

Élodie had managed to extract enough information from Félix to satisfy her curiosity—at least for now. Clémence wasn't French, or not entirely, but spoke it well. She'd been here before, gone away, and now was back. And the job they were about to do could be vital to the Allies' knowledge. She checked her surroundings for probably the tenth time. She'd arrived early outside the old barn that Félix had directed her to. It seemed a good, safe place, off the road and away from prying German eyes, and in the right direction for their destination. She'd noticed the heavy padlock on the door—unusual in this neighbourhood, though not sufficiently so to raise enemy suspicions.

The sound of twigs cracking on the track alerted her to Clémence's arrival. Élodie had stationed herself on the leeward side of the old wooden structure on the edge of the trees, and waited until she heard the faint squeal of brakes before peering round the corner of the barn. A slim figure stood confidently astride a large-framed bicycle. The girl wore a headscarf, from which had escaped a few lengths of pale-blonde hair. She was clad in a dark coat and sensible shoes, Élodie was pleased to see as she stepped into open view.

'*Bonjour, madame.* It's warm today for the time of year, don't you think?' It wasn't, as it so happened, but this had been agreed as the code.

When Clémence turned towards her, Élodie was startled by the arrestingly pretty face that smiled back at her. It crossed her mind that Félix would have fallen for her instantly.

'I thought it cool enough to need a coat.' The accent puzzled Élodie. So French, though not quite French—but the answer was what she'd been told to expect.

She held out a hand. '*Enchanté.* I'm Élodie.'

'I think I'd have known that. You look so much like Félix ... except for the colour of your eyes.' Élodie envied the slim, feminine fingers of the cool hand that was extended, and felt embarrassed by the workmanlike squareness of her own, the skin rough from farm work. She felt a frisson of irritation at the personal comment. Just how well did this girl know her brother? She let the comment pass.

'Shall we get going? The Manoir's about ten minutes' ride.'

As they passed under the gatehouse archway, Élodie could feel her pulse quickening. The memory of her last visit resurfaced in a kaleidoscope of flashback images. She motioned that they should turn to the left and stop, aware of Clémence's puzzled stare at her shaking hands as she pushed her bike in among the tall chestnut trees that lined the far side of the drive. She breathed in long and hard, exhaling slowly to regain control. Clémence would have to think whatever she wanted. She looked to left and right, scanning all the visible windows of the house in turn. There was no discernible movement, and though the Delahaye's wheels had left a tell-tale trail on the drive there was no evidence of the vehicle itself, or of its owner.

Once she was satisfied that they were apparently alone she preceded Clémence across the gravel to the front door, praying that it was unlocked. She turned the heavy handle and pushed. To her huge relief, the door yielded. She opened it tentatively, remembering how loudly it had squeaked when she fled from the major's fury after shattering his precious photograph. Once inside, she repeated the process until she heard the latch click shut, waited for a few seconds, assessing the ambient sounds: the old *horloge comtoise* across the hall, ticking obediently to the movements of its decorated pendulum, the hum of an engine somewhere in the garden, the tap-tapping of an insect hurling itself against a window.

Élodie pointed to the stairs and led the way, keeping to the broad patterned runner that overlay the polished oak treads, the carpet held in place by brass hoops and rods. She stopped at the top to listen again, then turned down the corridor to the left, the parquet blocks here too protected by a wide strip of carpeting. She indicated the major's door and reached for the handle, which didn't budge. The door was locked. She frowned.

'That's odd', she whispered. 'It wasn't locked the last time...'

Clémence gave her a questioning look. 'I don't understand. The last time?'

'Oh, I mean, it was a long time ago when my mother made the curtains that you'll see in a minute.' Clémence's puzzlement didn't fade from her face, but *tant pis*. That was all the explanation she was going to get. Élodie tried the door again, pumping the handle softly, but it was firmly locked.

'What do we do now? Félix didn't allow for this.'

By way of an answer, Clémence winked at her and reached into her pocket, withdrawing a bunch of strange-looking keys. 'I was top of the class in training. I can open most locks in a matter of seconds.'

Élodie moved out of the way and watched in admiration as Clémence tried first one key, manipulating it dextrously, and then a second. There was a soft click and Clémence smiled in satisfaction. They slipped into the room and Élodie shut the door behind them, stationing herself beside it. The large desk that Élodie knew had belonged to Mme Lagrange's late husband stood against the wall near the window. She wondered idly how many German soldiers had had to puff up the stairs under orders to carry it here from its former home in the panelled study next to the salon. The desktop had been bare when she was last in the room, she remembered, apart from one folder and a fountain pen. It was now stacked with papers in three neat piles.

She stared at Clémence in alarm as they both heard footsteps in the corridor coming from the direction of the stairs. The distinctive sound of a man's boot-clad feet grew louder. Élodie held her breath until the steps had passed and she heard a door open and close. Damn. She'd hoped the house was empty. At least they remained undiscovered, but the risk factor had risen by some several notches.

Clémence set to work, methodically skimming each sheet before turning it on its face. The first two piles appeared to yield only two sheets of interest. Élodie was intrigued by the tiny camera that her blonde companion extracted from an inside pocket before placing and photographing each sheet with expert precision. Clémence turned the two piles right way up and carefully set them back exactly where she had found them. As she turned over the first sheet of the third pile, her hand caught a brass letter-opener that for no logical reason lay on top of the papers underneath. It clattered to the floor with a metallic clang.

Élodie cocked her head at the sound of a door closing nearby. She hissed softly and signalled to Clémence, who whipped a tape measure from her pocket in exchange for the camera and stepped briskly to the window. As the door handle turned, Élodie's heart began to quiver like a captive bird. The relief at seeing Rudi enter the room loosened her constricted throat and she coughed violently. His baffled frown as he stood in the doorway, his shirtsleeves rolled up, was directed at Clémence. Élodie swiftly took charge.

'Bonjour Lieutenant. What a nice surprise.'

His eyes flicked to Élodie, but his frown remained. 'What are you doing here?' A thousand butterflies fluttered in her stomach at the coolness in his voice.

'Madame Lagrange has asked Maman to make some new curtains, so we're here to measure up for her.'

'And who is this?' He nodded towards Clémence. His expression was completely unreadable and, for the first time, Élodie felt a flicker of apprehension in his presence.

'This is Clémence. She's a friend of my brother.'

Rudi's quizzical, appraising gaze towards the loose sheet of paper on the desk further alarmed her. Thankfully, the letter opener wasn't visible from where he was standing. Clémence, Élodie had to admit, seemed as cool as a cucumber, moving into Rudi's line of vision and giving him a dazzling smile that would surely captivate any man. He nodded politely, eyes narrowed, calculating what? Élodie swallowed and slowed her breathing, feeling unaccountably nervous. She needed to defuse the situation fast.

'Is there a problem, Lieutenant? I was told today would be ideal, as the Major wouldn't be here.'

Rudi snapped his eyes back to Élodie and his expression softened slightly. He shrugged. 'Well, I suppose that if that's what you were told, it must be OK.'

'I don't quite understand, though. Where were you that you heard us in here?'

'My room is next door.'

Élodie felt sick, her mind flashing back to the two lascivious encounters with the Major. What if...? Supposing Rudi had been in his room when... She felt alternately hot and cold, and her head spun.

She felt a hand steady her arm. 'Are you all right? You're deathly pale.'

'Thank you, I'm fine.'

Élodie was aware that Clémence was watching them enquiringly. In a soft, purring voice, she addressed Rudi in her distinctive accented French. 'D'you think you could help us measure the length?' She held out the tape measure. 'You're so much taller than either of us.'

The lieutenant gallantly obliged, returning Clémence's kittenish fluttering of her eyelashes with a long look and an equally devastating smile, much to Élodie's chagrin. But she had to hand it to the girl—she was glacially composed.

Rudi rolled down his shirtsleeves and fastened them, then turned to Élodie. 'Are you finished now?'

Élodie shook her head and pointed to the other window. 'But we're fine for the length, thanks to you.'

Rudi took his cue. 'Then I'll leave you to it.' He checked his watch. 'I have to go out again now, but I think Madame Lagrange is due home so you'll probably see her before you go.' He gave Élodie another searching stare as he passed her but closed the door quietly behind him as he left. The tension in the room diluted fractionally.

'You obviously know the Lieutenant quite well?'

Élodie pouted. 'I suppose I do, yes.' Was it any of this girl's business? She gave herself a mental shake. Of course Clémence was curious. She would have been too, in her shoes. Should she try reassurance? Or just get on with the job? She decided on the latter.

'Has Félix ever said, "Nothing you need worry about"?'

Clémence replied with an enigmatic smile. 'Oh yes. I've heard that one several times.'

Élodie chuckled. 'So you'll know I can't say any more. Come on, let's get it over with and get out of here. I've certainly no wish to try and dupe Madame Lagrange if she arrives.'

She returned to her post at the door as Clémence pocketed the tape and took out the tiny camera again. She was swift but thorough, snapping only those pages on the desk that might be of use. She resumed her examination of the third pile and halfway down gave a quiet whistle of surprise. She gave a satisfied smile. 'Jackpot.' Only the next four pages seemed to be vital, and she took two pictures of each. 'OK, I'm done.' She rearranged the last stack with meticulous care and stepped back with her head on one side to check. She leant forward, moved the pile what seemed to Élodie to be a minute distance and was apparently satisfied. She took a step towards the door, paused and bent to retrieve the letter opener, which she replaced under the top document.

Élodie was in awe of the girl's level-headedness. She eased the door open. No one in sight. Clémence repeated her trick so that the door was locked again and the two girls tiptoed along the corridor, down the stairs and across the hall without challenge. As Élodie grasped the front door handle, she heard a swish of tyres on the gravel. Clémence stood on tiptoe and peeped through the small oriel window to the right.

'It's a beautiful old car, maroon and cream.'

'*Merde*. Madame Lagrange is back.' Élodie looked across to the door that led to the kitchen stairs. Dare they risk it? But if Lisette was there... She knew that Clémence was awaiting her decision. 'There's a door to the outside in the garden room beyond the *salon*. Pray it's not locked, or you'll need all your lock-picking skills again in a hell of a hurry.'

She led the way back across the hall and darted through the room she'd last entered on the day of the insufferable afternoon tea with the Major. In her haste, she skidded on the Audubon rug. A vase of flowers on the low table lurched alarmingly, slopping water. Clémence caught and righted it and straightened the rug as she followed Élodie, who was now halfway across the garden room. At least they were now out of sight of the front door. Élodie heaved a sigh of relief to see the key in the lock, but her hands shook as she struggled to align the stiff mechanism.

'How do we lock it again?'

Élodie made a wry face. 'We don't. We can't. We have to leave the key in it, and we'll have to hope Madame overlooks it or thinks one of the Germans was careless.'

Five minutes later they emerged onto the main road, having bumped their bikes through the dense trees that ran the length of the drive. For once, Élodie was glad she'd followed her instinct when they arrived and insisted they leave the machines out of sight. Today she'd thought ahead. Clémence extended her hand.

'I can't thank you enough for your help.'

Élodie shrugged. 'For France. And Félix, of course. *Au revoir—et bon courage.*'

They each set off in opposite directions. Élodie was sure she now understood Félix's distracted air of late. *Tante mieux pour lui.* He deserved to find someone for himself. Did she mean that? She hoped so.

Élodie rearranged the egg trays on the cramped barn shelving for the fourth time. Rudi was uncustomarily twenty minutes late. What did it signify? She heard a noise outside and dropped one of the empty trays. The door creaked open, and Rudi stepped inside. He stood with his back against the door, arms folded, his expression unfathomable, that tell-tale tic of tension twitching his cheek.

'I—I thought perhaps you weren't coming today.'

He frowned. 'Why?'

'Oh, because—because you're always so punctual.' She risked a small smile.

He raised an eyebrow. 'Élodie, I'm going to ask you one question. And please tell me the truth, that's all I'm seeking.'

Élodie's mouth was dry. She licked her lips nervously. 'What is it?'

'You and your brother's "friend", you weren't measuring for curtains the other day, were you?'

The silence stretched almost to screaming point. Élodie swallowed hard, aware of a buzzing noise in her ears, and looked directly into the normally captivating blue eyes, which today were completely emotionless. 'No.'

To her immense relief his reaction was to smile. 'Élodie, *Liebchen*, I'm not stupid. I can see which way this war is going, and I only want for it to be over. And for us all to survive. But whatever you and that girl are doing—it's unthinkably dangerous. I've told you before that Wolff is ruthless, and he's getting more determined—and more unpredictable—all the time.'

'But why did you seem so suspicious at the time, when you came into his room?'

Rudi's laugh was spontaneous, cynical even to Élodie's ears. 'Because, *Liebchen*, I saw the major go out and watched him lock the door before he left.'

'I never thought...'

'And I watched him unlock the door when he returned.'

Rudi held out both hands. Élodie burrowed her way between them and hung on to him as if silence and her closeness could compensate for what she and Clémence had done.

'Rudi, I can't tell you—'

Rudi interrupted her. 'Don't tell me anything.' He heaved a huge sigh. 'I've already put myself in an impossible situation.' Élodie looked up at him, again uncertain. 'Of my own making, *Liebchen*. What can I say to you? Officially, wearing this uniform, I can't even begin to think about, let alone approve of what you've done—or maybe are still doing, or worse still the possible consequences. But I'll never betray you. I hope you know that. And one day...'

Élodie groaned. 'One day. I don't see how "one day" will ever come for us, *mon beau*. My father will never accept it—I mean, us.'

Rudi held her face between his hands. 'When the day comes, we'll speak to him together. Surely he'll understand, or we can make him see, how we feel about each other?'

Élodie shook her head despairingly. 'You don't get it. He hates all Germans.' She winced as she saw Rudi's jaw tighten. 'I can only tell you he was in the Army in the last war and fought at Verdun. He wouldn't talk about it, not ever. Sometimes I wake in the night and hear him screaming. Maman says it's always the same nightmares. I only discovered recently that he watched as his best friend was blown to pieces in front of him all those years ago, and it seems to have killed part of him too. Ever since, Maman says, it's as if a dark red stain has coloured his whole life. He told me a little bit after Guillaume...'. She couldn't go on, the memories still too raw.

Rudi tipped her chin up. The distant, hard glaze cloaking his eyes tore her to shreds.

'After the Eastern Front, I can understand entirely, *Liebchen*, believe me. But when peace comes, we'll do our best to persuade him.'

Élodie had no answer that she was willing to give. Instead, she chose to cherish the here-and-now. Neither of them could predict what was still to come and besides, most of the possibilities were too hideous even to consider.

# CHAPTER SEVENTEEN

## April 1944

ÉLODIE ADDED ANOTHER SCOOP of feed to the bucket and stood up to rest her back. As she did so, the door opened, and Rudi was silhouetted against the rain-soaked grass of the chicken run. She smiled.

'This is a surprise—it's only Tuesday.'

Something in Rudi's expression alarmed her.

'What's wrong?' Élodie had never seen him look so sombre.

'Where is your brother?'

Rudi remained where he was, rain dripping from his uniform. Élodie moved towards him. 'Rudi, you're frightening me. What is it?' She pulled him into the barn and stood at arm's length so that she could gauge his reaction.

'Does he know someone called Michel Moreau?'

Élodie's stomach knotted. 'Why?'

'You have to understand, I shouldn't be telling you this.' Rudi hesitated, his expression guarded. He looked over his shoulder as if he might have been followed. 'I overheard Major Wolff taking a call from the Gestapo, and they are planning a crackdown on the Resistance. Your brother's name was mentioned, as was that of someone called Michel Moreau.'

'Dear God, no.' Élodie took another step away from him, her mind whirling. 'I don't know where Félix is. He rarely comes home now.'

Rudi was clearly stressed. He pushed his hair back with both hands before speaking.

'You have to warn him somehow. He needs to hide, to go away for a while. Anywhere. He must *not* be here if they come looking for him. You understand that? And you shouldn't know where he's gone, either.'

Élodie nodded. Rudi looked like a guileless boy again, a muscle flexing his cheek as he stood staring at her, worry creasing his brow. How much did he know about Félix's activities? She had never admitted to her presence in the wood the night the bridge was blown up and hated that each of them was keeping the secret from the other, but the gravity of Félix's actions was better left unspoken. Was he putting himself at risk too by coming here? She crossed the space between them. Her voice faltered as she spoke. 'Where does Wolff think you are now? Are you in some kind of danger yourself?'

He hugged her to him. 'Wolff is in Argentan today so he can't possibly know I'm here. But *Liebchen*, I can't bear anything that would hurt you, so you must find your brother right now. Wolff is becoming totally obsessive and I've no idea what he's planning next, or how soon.'

Élodie could feel his heart thudding as she laid a hand against his chest. She was sure there was something he wasn't telling her—that the situation was more complicated, but today Félix must come first. She stood on tiptoe and kissed him fiercely, then held his face in her hands for a long moment, fixing his image in her mind for some reason she couldn't quite fathom herself. Things were sliding out of control, and there were no stable boundaries to cling to anymore.

'I thank you with all my heart. But you should go now, and I will find Félix.'

Rudi kissed her forehead. 'I love you, *Liebchen*. I will see you soon, I promise.'

After he'd gone, Élodie robotically picked up the chicken feed. There was almost none left, and she had no idea where or whether—or how—she could source more. She slipped out of the barn, scattered the grain into the run and set off up the path to the house. She stopped halfway with a strange feeling that someone was watching her. She looked back and, as on a previous occasion, thought she saw movement behind the hedge across the lane. Well, she had no time to investigate now.

Her mother was out, she remembered, so she grabbed a raincoat and headed for the bottom field to find her father. She called out to him from the gate and ran the hundred yards to where he was working, her shoes already covered in mud. His old field coat was drenched, as was the navy-blue cap clamped on his head. 'Papa, do you know where Félix is?'

Henri grunted. 'He told me he had business to attend to.'

'Did he say where?'

Henri shook his head. He leant his hoe against the trailer and took a cigarette and matches from his pocket, cupping his hands against the rain. Élodie stifled her impatience as he slowly lit the cigarette and took a long drag. 'He did mention something about having to see Michel...'

'Who has premises in Flers. Well done, Papa!' Élodie kissed him on the cheek and turned for the gate.

'What's this about?' Henri called as she sprinted away.

'Can't stop, Papa.'

Élodie clambered onto her bicycle and sped off. As usual, the side roads were deserted as if life hung suspended. The rain spattered down from the overhanging trees and a fine spray of water from the cycle's wheels soaked her shoes, turning the clinging clods of mud from the field into filthy brown streams. The gloomy weather echoed Élodie's mood. On the outskirts of Flers, a little under half an hour later, she stopped to get her bearings. If she remembered correctly, she needed to fork right beside the station and take a left turn somewhere.

The town looked as grey and forbidding as the sky, the rain still bucketing down from leaden low clouds, soaking everything in pulsating gusts. The roads were strangely quiet for midweek but at the station there was a swirl of activity, with uniformed soldiers checking passengers, and what looked like at least three Gestapo officers supervising. Élodie sped on, keeping her eyes on the road ahead and searching for anything recognisable. She blinked and shook her head as the dripping water clouded her vision. A rush of relief flooded through her as she spied a small café on a corner to her left. The faded red paintwork bore a picture of an ashtray and two cigarette butts, and she could hear again Félix's laughter when he'd told her how its name, *Les deux mégots*, parodied that of its famous near namesake in fashionable Saint-Germain des Prés in Paris.

Turning into the side road, she spied a run-down workshop with peeling black paint, exactly as Félix had described. The front door was locked so she rang the bell. At first there was no sound from inside. She was now wet through and shivering as she looked up and down the road while she waited. Perhaps unsurprisingly, there was no one in sight. She rang the bell again and heard Michel's normally soft voice say testily, 'Alright, alright, I'm coming. Keep your hair on.' He looked surprised when he opened the door but recovered himself, checked up and down the street and pulled her inside with her bicycle. He kissed her on both cheeks.

'Good to see you, Élodie.'

'No, it isn't actually—or it won't be.' Élodie cast an eye over the workshop, which she'd never visited before. It was piled high with car parts, engine blocks, bicycle spares and all manner of other junk. Tools of every description lay higgledy-piggledy on a solid wooden bench whose grooved surface was testament to its age, and there was a strong reek of motor oil.

He frowned. 'Oh?'

'Is Félix here?'

'No, he's....' He tailed off.

'Michel, it's urgent. Where is he?'

'He's with Clémence. Ah, but you met her recently, didn't you?'

Élodie couldn't hide her impatience. 'Yes, yes, of course I did—so how long will he be?'

Michel ran a hand across his forehead, leaving a black greasy smear. 'I really don't know. Why don't we start with why you're here?'

'I have it on good authority that the Gestapo is planning a round-up of *Résistance* suspects, and that you and Félix are on the list.'

Michel's face paled. '*Putain!*'

'Whether or not you're involved, you and Félix have to disappear.' Élodie watched his face carefully. He picked up a wrench and fiddled with the setting. Élodie sighed. Michel, bless him, was always the child who couldn't lie, with his open, honest face and long-lashed eyes.

'Who told you this?'

Élodie shook her head. 'Can't tell you.'

'I suppose it was that German who dragged you away from the shooting in Argentan last year?'

So, it had been Michel she'd seen. Was the whole village in Argentan that Wednesday?

'Well?'

'Michel, it's not what you think. It's complicated. And anyway, that's something else altogether.'

He gave her a sceptical look.

She drew in a deep breath. 'Do you believe I would ever do *anything*, anything at all that could harm Félix?'

'No. No of course I don't.'

'Then you must hurry. Find him now, and go somewhere the Gestapo will never think of. I suppose Thierry's in this too?'

Michel hesitated, then nodded.

'His name doesn't seem to have come up, but I'll go and warn him, or Yvette if he's not at the forge. And I'll do anything at all to help. Get someone to tell me what you need. I can send clothes, food....'

Michel put a hand on her shoulder. 'I'll go now. I've locked the door at the front. We'll go through the back alley. Tell Thierry we'll see him this evening, as planned.'

Outside, more metallic junk was piled under a sagging carport, which at least seemed to be holding its own against the rain. They made their way down the cramped passageway into a broader road that was similarly deserted. Michel stopped and indicated the shortest route to Thierry's house. Élodie gave him a peck on the cheek, waiting till he slipped into another alley across the road before setting off.

Outside the forge, a large car with German insignia was idling, its driver looking bored. Élodie spotted Thierry half-hidden in the shadow below the overhanging roof. He was holding a conversation with a uniformed officer, shaking his head and pointing at another German vehicle, some kind of truck, parked under cover but away from his glowing furnace. She pulled her bike off the road and wheeled it into the bushes. Her clothing was saturated by the dripping foliage as she stood well back, but in a position to observe what was going on. She was relieved when the officer clicked his heels and returned to his car.

Élodie waited until the vehicle was out of sight. She ran into the forge, wondering for the umpteenth time how Thierry could function in the stifling heat. He was leaning over, hands on hips, surveying the damaged wing of the German truck. He turned towards her as she greeted him, his frown replaced by a wide smile.

'Élodie, *ma belle*, it seems such a long time since we saw you last.'

She summarised quickly what Rudi had told her and explained that Michel had gone to warn Félix. 'I understand he's with Clémence. Would you know why?'

Posing the question didn't produce the hoped-for clarification from the famously taciturn Thierry, who merely rubbed his chin thoughtfully as she spoke.

'I offered to come here to warn you. Michel said to tell you they'll see you this evening as planned.'

Thierry grunted. 'Should be safe enough tonight. The Boche aren't expecting their precious truck back for two days, so I'm hoping they'll keep their distance till then.'

Élodie wasn't so sure. 'If Félix and Michel are coming here, I presume you're planning something dangerous?' She knew Thierry was unlikely to confirm this. She was right.

'Steer clear of what you don't need to know, *chérie.*'

His smile was warm, but his furrowed brows told her he was troubled by something, nonetheless. She turned at the sound from the road of heavy vehicles approaching. Thierry pulled her away from the entrance into the dimness beyond as two German tanks rolled past.

'Better you should go and not be seen here.' Thierry stared along the rain-soaked road. 'Are you on foot?'

'No, I have my bike hidden along there.' She indicated the thick bushes on the left. She cocked her head and listened. The only sound was from the coals crackling in the furnace. 'I'll go straight home. But Thierry—you will see that no harm comes to them, Félix and Michel?'

Thierry's smile had been replaced by a look of grim determination. 'I'll certainly do my best, *chérie*.' He held up a hand to her as she trotted away.

Élodie looked back as she rode off. Thierry was already bending over the damaged truck once more, his thumbs hooked through the straps on his leather apron.

# Chapter Eighteen

## April 1944

FéLIX TAPPED AT THE door with the usual double-knock when he and Michel arrived that evening. It was not yet fully dark, so they had left Mme Tailler's drapery in Flers via a series of minor alleyways and unfrequented side streets, which Michel as always appeared to know like the back of his hand. Félix had asked him once how he had gained his encyclopaedic knowledge of the local geography. Michel had replied that it was a combination of necessity for his work, and a misspent youth. Félix knew the latter to be mostly untrue, for they had spent their formative years as inseparable friends, as they were still.

Yvette directed them to the kitchen, where Thierry was sitting by the range basking in its impressive heat output. Once she had promised to bring them beer, she shooed them into the next room where a fire of oak and chestnut logs had been lit, its vivid orange-red flames dancing as they licked greedily at the sides of the chimney.

Thierry explained, once they were settled, that he had been contacted, via intermediary contact as usual, by the Argentan group, which had been forced to lie low since the successful train derailment. It was hoped their inactivity would lull the Germans into thinking they had disbanded or fled, but a request had now been received from London to destroy a vital armaments factory, whose workers had been forced into the production of equipment to boost flagging German military supplies. Despite small-scale acts of sabotage in which minor adjustments had been made to machine calibration or substandard materials smuggled onto the production line, the factory was running at almost full capacity most of the time.

Thierry had been told, he said, that the Argentan group had the necessary explosives to put the factory out of action for quite some time, but it was essential that the lights within and outside the buildings go down first. Félix and Michel exchanged questioning looks whilst Thierry detailed the crucial role they'd been asked to play and emphasised its importance to the whole operation.

It had been established that the factory's electricity supply was fed via a substation, which would have to be destroyed, or at least damaged irreparably by disrupting the wiring, so that the factory could be blown up under the cover of total darkness. Once this had been done, and to avoid possible interception of direct contact with the other group, Clémence would need to transmit an instant message to London. This would be relayed onwards to the Argentan team to confirm the action had been successful and that the lighting had not routinely been extinguished in anticipation of an Allied air raid.

Félix sat back and groaned at the prospect. 'You're probably our best shot at dealing with wiring, Michel. What d'you think?'

Michel looked dubious. 'I'm no expert on electricity, that's for sure. I can certainly set enough *plastique* to send the whole thing sky high, though it'd be a hell of a show.' He turned to

Thierry. 'Why not take out the factory from the air, out of interest?'

Thierry's laugh was scornful. 'Too much risk of missing their target, apparently, even with so-called precision bombing.'

Félix was studying the leaping flames in the hearth unseeingly, aware that something was worrying him. What exactly had Thierry said about Clémence? His head shot up as the implications sunk in.

'Are you saying Clémence has to be with us when we carry out this job?'

Thierry gave him a long, hard look. 'Sorry, Félix, there's no place for emotions in this, so yes, we need her to be there.'

'And when is it planned for?'

'Three days' time, when there's a new moon.'

'So me, Michel and Clémence.'

'No, me too. I'll be driving.'

Michel opened his mouth to speak but shut it again when he saw Thierry's warning glare. Félix, however, was undeterred.

'No way, Thierry. Your leg's not up to it.'

The ensuing argument grew so heated that Yvette rushed in from the kitchen, from which an enticing aroma followed her hurried steps.

'*Mon Dieu*, you lot could be heard in the middle of Flers! What on earth is the problem?'

When Félix explained that he was suggesting Guy should be asked to drive again, Yvette scrunched up her face, her back to Thierry, and emitted a huge sigh. She went to her husband's chair and crouched beside him.

'Thierry, *mon chou*, you know they're right, don't you?'

Thierry blustered and swore but Yvette continued to hold his gaze, one eyebrow raised. When he finally petered into silence, she stood stiffly from her cramped position and stroked his hair.

'I'm sorry, *mon amour*—I know how much this means to you, but you can't be pig-headed over something that's obviously so important, whatever it is. I know as well as you do that you couldn't possibly run if the need arose, and you know that inability would endanger your friends too.'

Thierry looked utterly miserable but finally capitulated.

Yvette turned to the others. 'I also understand that the Boche have begun asking too many questions and may be planning a round-up of those they suspect of being *Résistants?*'

Félix could only smile broadly as he confirmed her suppositions. She didn't miss a trick, Yvette.

'Then can I suggest that from tomorrow you and Michel stay here with us for a few days?'

Michel had remained silent until now. 'Under the noses of the Boche?'

Yvette's answer was unflinching. 'Exactly so. Why would they suspect Thierry, who has become so useful by repairing their vehicles?'

Predictably, Michel's answer was guarded. 'You may be right. But that means the danger's increased for you if they do come snooping.'

Félix stifled a chuckle. For all his friend's compassionate nature, he liked to make his own decisions.

'We'll face that possibility as and when it arises.' Yvette paused, evidently considering the practicalities. 'Félix, can I help by going to the pharmacy to talk to Guy?'

Félix shook his head adamantly. 'Thanks, but no. They'll mostly be looking for me around the farm. I'll go and see Guy and hope to avoid my sister while I'm there.' Yvette looked understandably confused by this remark, but he ploughed on. 'I also need to warn Clémence, and I'll do that first thing tomorrow. Meantime, I'll go home and grab a few things and head for the barn tonight. Michel, you'll join me there?'

'Food first, before you go.' Yvette's statement brooked no argument. Félix and Michel followed Thierry into the kitchen, sharing a jaundiced smile as the thick-set man hobbled along indefatigably in front of them.

Michel took Félix to Flers the following morning. For the sake of expediency, he had driven them both to the farm on his motorbike the night before, where Félix collected a bagful of clothes and other belongings, patiently deflecting Élodie's multiple questions. Yvette had insisted on packing up the wherewithal for breakfast, so they had arrived at the barn with two well-loaded saddlebags. Félix had been glad to relinquish his pillion seat after a hazardous journey via one of Michel's usual tortuous routes.

The plan was for Michel to return Félix to the forge after his visit to Clémence. Félix would then collect his bicycle, which had been safely stashed at the back of Thierry's workspace, and pick his moment to arrive at the pharmacy in search of Guy.

The two men arrived well ahead of the drapery shop's opening time. Michel parked in the side alley and stayed with the bike. Félix knocked tentatively on the rear door and stepped back as he heard light footsteps tip-tapping towards him from the direction of the kitchen. The door was opened by Mme Tailler, who was already dressed for work. She ushered him in and pointed to the kitchen before he could even mention Clémence. She replied to his thanks with an understanding smile and slipped into the shop, closing the intervening door behind her.

Félix was amused to find Clémence dunking her *tartine beurrée* into her coffee. It hadn't taken her long to adapt to the French habit, despite her apparent initial distaste. She wiped her mouth with a buttery hand and kissed him generously, tasting appetisingly of plum jam. Félix licked his lips appreciatively.

'Mmm. That's a delicious morning greeting.'

'Would you like some? I know Madame Tailler won't mind.'

Félix declined. 'I've already eaten, and besides, I can't stop long.'

Clémence listened carefully as he spoke, nodding every so often to show her understanding. When he had finished, she put down the slice of bread she had been clutching and wiped her hands.

'OK. That's all fine. And I can be of more help, too.'

Félix was apprehensive at her eager response. 'You need only send the message, *chérie*.'

'But you don't understand. I was trained in sabotage, including learning about wiring circuits and how to scramble them. And I have dark clothes—and a gun, don't forget.'

Despite Félix's protests, she followed him down the hallway and out into the alleyway. Michel listened as she repeated her offer of help. Félix was relieved to see that he too looked unconvinced.

'You don't need to put yourself in any more danger than necessary. I'm sure Félix has told you the same.'

Clémence airily dismissed their misgivings and said she would be ready at whatever time they came for her two nights later. With that, she gave them both a winning smile and disappeared back into the building. Michel raised his eyes heavenwards as Félix held up his hands in defeat.

\*\*\*

By the time Félix reached Ste-Honorine, the village was busy but at least there were no Germans in sight. He sat out of sight for a while under an awning across the road from the pharmacy, watching the comings and goings. To his satisfaction, when the door swung open for the fourth time, his sister emerged and set off without deliberation in the direction of the Mairie.

When he was satisfied that she was likely to be gone for at least a short time, he crossed the road and entered the shop. To his annoyance, Mme Leroy emerged from the far corner and marched up to the counter, acknowledging him with a curt nod. He hung back while she complained endlessly about her rheumatism, her inability to sleep, and several other ailments. Guy listened patiently, making several suggestions—none of which seemed to interest her until she finally accepted and paid for a bottle of liniment.

The two men shook hands as she bustled out.

Guy correctly anticipated that Félix was there for a reason. Félix began by updating him on Thierry's progress. This was received with a broad smile.

'I'm thinking you'll be needing my help again?'

Before Félix could explain further, the door opened behind him.

'Ah, good timing. Hélène's back.'

Félix cursed under his breath as Guy asked her to mind the shop for a few minutes. To his surprise, his sister greeted him coolly but made no further comment, though her displeasure was evident in the cold glare she cast in his direction. He presumed Guy and she had had words after their last encounter.

Guy led him into the room in which he had patched up Thierry's wound, and ensured the door was closed. He readily agreed to Félix's request but voiced his dismay when he heard that Clémence would have to accompany them.

'I don't like the thought of a woman being involved. Is there no way we could rush back to her afterwards so that she can send her message?'

Félix shook his head. He was uneasy at divulging any details, but he owed it to Guy to put him in the picture. 'I don't like it either, Guy, but at least the transmission will be the final task.

She'll have to go and find a high point where she can get a signal though. She—'

A faint noise outside the door aroused his suspicions. He sprang forward and wrenched at the handle. As the passageway came into view, he saw a flash of skirt hem as a shadow passed across the door into the shop. He pushed the door to and made a quick decision: there seemed no point in antagonising the situation. He could, after all, have been mistaken. Perhaps Hélène had merely been fetching something for a customer from the shelves behind the door.

He felt somehow foolish when he turned and saw Guy standing open-mouthed. 'Sorry about that, but you'll know we can't be too careful.'

Guy suggested quietly that he would cycle to the forge two nights later as dusk fell. The two men shook hands again and Félix left via the shop. Hélène was apparently busy tidying a drawer. There were no customers to be seen. She didn't look up when he said goodbye, nor did she make any comment, perhaps because Guy had followed close behind Félix and was now studying his wife with a thoughtful frown on his face.

Félix checked the area in both directions before he left the shelter of the recessed shop doorway. There were still no uniformed soldiers to be seen. He ran back across the road and collected his bike from outside the ironmongery, but, as he did so, Lisette emerged from the dim interior and grabbed his arm.

'Félix, I've been waiting for you since I saw you go into the pharmacy. I need to talk to you.'

The urgency in her voice stopped him from dismissing her with the excuse that he was in a hurry. Lisette seemed uncharacteristically nervous and bird-like, checking all around constantly and fluttering her hands. He pulled a cap from his pocket and pulled it down over his brow. He followed her into the square and on behind the church, where he spied

Père Bernard heading for the presbytery, his stiff white collar visible even at a distance.

'What's so important, Lisette?'

Lisette was fiddling with a lock of her hair, still flustered, a high spot of pink colouring both cheeks.

'You have some kind of operation planned imminently?'

He nodded. He hated giving either of the Martin siblings any more information than was necessary regarding anything in which they didn't have to be involved.

'*Pour l'amour de Dieu*, Félix!' Lisette shook his arm angrily.

He shrugged. It seemed to be his misfortune to encounter bad-tempered women this morning—apart from Clémence, of course. And the always delightful Mme Tailler.

Lisette had adopted a petulant expression. 'I've a good mind not to tell you anything.'

'I'm sorry, Lisette. I'm sure you have the best of intentions.'

'I've always had the best of intentions where you're concerned. You just don't seem to appreciate it.' Her retort was snappy, and she shoved her hands into her pockets angrily.

'Please, Lisette, I'm sorry. I appreciate your efforts, I really do.'

He hoped his smile would placate her. It seemed to have the desired effect.

'Well, when I was at work yesterday, I overheard two of Major Wolff's men saying the major was expecting a coup soon when he arrests the English spy who's been working as a radio operator.'

For a moment, Félix couldn't speak. His heart was thudding in his chest as fear for Clémence filled him.

'Did they say anything else?'

'No, they walked away and obviously I couldn't follow them.'

'Thank you, Lisette. I'm genuinely grateful.'

'I was sure you would be.' The sarcasm in her voice wasn't lost on him.

He wasn't sure that giving her a peck on the cheek was a wise move, but he did so anyway. The sparkle in her eyes and her inviting smile confirmed that it was not.

'You're lucky that it's my day off and I could come looking for you.'

He wasn't quick enough to avoid the arms that encircled him as she pressed herself against him.

'I hope you'll come to your senses one day, *mon chéri*.'

He hastily prised her away and repeated his thanks. She gave him a look he couldn't interpret, tossed her hair and walked away, her hips swaying provocatively as she disappeared round the corner of the church. He stood indecisively, his eyes fixed on a broken stone protruding from the wall of the building, trying to weigh up the odds. Could they do as Guy suggested and involve Clémence only after the event? Should he insist they abandon the operation? But that would have a knock-on effect on the important task of attacking the factory. He kicked his bike wheel in frustration, instantly ashamed of himself for his childishness. He would have to discuss the situation with Michel and Thierry and devise a suitable strategy.

Even Michel could not regret their agreement to move into the house that adjoined the forge, Félix knew, as he patted his stomach after another of Yvette's splendid meals. They were to share the room that had once been allocated to the child the couple had long hoped for, but which had never arrived. This had not rocked their devotion to one another, and Yvette seemed pleased, as they stowed their few belongings, that the room was for once being put to use.

Félix insisted on helping to clear up and wash the dishes but was then directed to join the others in front of the log fire while Yvette did some mending in the kitchen.

There had been no opportunity earlier to share Lisette's warning, but the atmosphere in the room grew sober as Félix told them what she had overheard. The flames sank low as the discussion continued. Yvette slipped into the room to offer them more beer, tutting as the last log slipped and sputtered in the grate. Thierry followed her pointing finger and added two more, poking at the ash to freshen the blaze.

He blew a kiss to her. 'What would we do without you, *mon chou*?'

'Freeze to death most likely.' With a fond smile, she threw over her shoulder the tea towel she was holding and went to fetch the beer.

In the end, it was decided that the operation would go ahead, but to a strict plan. Thierry would get a message to Argentan to alert them to the threat in advance. Guy's only involvement would be to drive and stay on watch by the main road. Once the operation had been accomplished Félix would wait while Clémence sent her message from higher ground. After Michel and Guy picked them up in the truck, they would all return to the forge together. As long as they remained alert, there seemed no reason why anything should go wrong.

# CHAPTER NINETEEN

## April 1944

THE THREE FIGURES STOOD among the soaring trees that lined the road opposite the substation. All were dressed in dark clothes. The two men each wore a cap that covered half of their face, and Clémence had pulled on a black balaclava that hid her blonde hair, which tonight was gracefully twisted into a pleat that brushed the nape of her neck. To their surprise there was no guard stationed outside the high wire fence that enclosed their target. Presumably it was considered that the fortification of the installation, such as it was, obviated the need for any permanent patrol.

Michel heaved the bulging bag off his shoulders and knelt to sort through the contents. The large padlock on the substation gate was clearly visible and the fence was constructed from heavy-gauge wire. Félix rejected the bolt-cutters Michel held up to him and retrieved a substantial pair of wire-cutters from his own jacket pocket.

They had arrived at the spot fifteen minutes earlier, leaving Guy a quarter of a mile away at the junction with the main road. There had been no traffic of any variety on the side road, unless, as Félix had remarked, you counted the vixen and two tiny fox cubs that had padded past a few minutes ago. He touched Michel's arm, put on his thick gloves, held up the wire cutters and sprinted across the road. He made his way along the side fence of the substation, conscious of the strong humming emanating from within the concrete housing. He was hampered by the profusion of brambles that had self-rooted in the overgrown grass, stumbling several times, and soon realised it would be impossible to enter the site from the rear as they had intended. He surveyed the overgrown foliage that had already penetrated the sturdy back fence. Thick briers and blackthorn had woven themselves rapaciously into an impenetrable barrier. He replaced his cap, which had been torn off by a tall thornbush, and set to work as far back from the road as was possible, cutting the wire from the ground upwards. It seemed unthinkable that a relay station of this nature had been so neglected. Could the Germans possibly not have realised that it fed the armaments factory?

Félix paused in his methodical snipping after about ten minutes, the muscles in his forearms already aching from the strain. He'd been amazed by the force he'd had to exert to breach the wire. He sat back on his haunches, removed his cap, and dragged his sleeve across his sweat-damp forehead. As he did so he heard a sharp whistle. He looked across the road and saw Michel signalling to him. At the same time, he became conscious of the sound of a vehicle somewhere nearby. He quickly plaited the ends of enough strands of the wire to hide his endeavours, fought his way back to the road and joined the others in the shelter of the trees.

Almost immediately the soft glare of shielded headlights approached from their left, and a German Kübelwagen screeched to a halt outside the substation. Its four occupants tumbled out and made a cursory examination of the padlock and front fencing. Félix could neither hear nor understand their muted conversation. He noticed Clémence creeping closer to the road. Despite his concern, there was insufficient cover where he stood for him to risk moving in her direction. She remained hidden behind a thick stand of tall bushes, frowning in concentration, her head cocked.

Three of the soldiers got back into the truck. The fourth remained where he was, a rifle slung over his shoulder. One of his companions shouted something at him above the engine noise and he waved a hand in acknowledgement. Félix and Michel ducked as the vehicle did a clumsy three-point turn, its lights raking the forest, and shot off in the direction from which it had come, towards Argentan.

Michel swore inaudibly under his breath, shrugged and bent stealthily to the bag at his feet, extracting a sheath knife. The soldier looked relaxed, clearly unaware of their presence. He fished a cigarette out of his breast pocket as he patrolled the perimeter. There was a click and a bright flash as he dipped his head to the lighter he held in his right hand. He reached the corner of the fence and executed a smart turn, now facing away from them.

Before either of them could react, there was a sudden swift movement to their right. Michel caught Félix's arm as the slight female figure darted like a passing shadow across the road. A glint from the knife in her hand caught the moonlight as she slid behind the soldier. Within seconds there was a muffled gurgling sound as the blade sliced his throat cleanly. He dropped like a stone. Clémence stepped back and mechanically wiped the blood from the weapon on the long grass.

For a second, Félix was rooted to the spot, hardly believing what he had just witnessed. She motioned for them to join her as she closed the blade and pushed the knife back in her pocket. He caught her shoulder as he reached her, feeling it shuddering under his hand.

Clémence spoke quickly. 'We have very little time. They said they'd be back within half an hour. We'll have to forget any idea of disrupting the wiring, which was a longshot anyway.' She turned to Michel. 'You have the *plastique*?'

Michel could only grunt in reply, obviously as shocked as Félix but clearly impressed by her swift action. The two men dragged the heavy corpse to the far side of the road and forty yards back into the wood. There was no time to attempt further concealment. He followed Michel, who had retrieved the explosives. The three of them wrestled their way to the cut in the fencing, the brambles artfully dragging at their heels.

Félix put a restraining hand on Clémence's wrist as she bent to worm her way through the gap. She paused, pulling the balaclava away from her face.

'Félix, how much do you know about using explosives?'

'Not a lot.'

'Exactly. Let me help Michel. It'll be much quicker that way.'

He stood aside unwillingly as she squeezed through the gap followed by Michel. He watched as the two dark figures conferred and pointed to left and right. They worked methodically and quickly, but still the minutes ticked by. Félix checked his watch constantly, his eyes intermittently scanning the road. Finally, he saw Michel pull the detonators from his pocket and hand several to Clémence. Within seconds the two nodded to each other and made for the fence.

Félix looked at his watch for the umpteenth time and frowned. The operation had taken fifteen minutes. Thank God they had opted for one-hour delay switches to give them time to be well clear. Clémence ran to retrieve her radio case from the spot where she had hidden it in dense undergrowth.

'D'you want me to stay here on watch?' Michel looked worried.

Félix ran a hand through his hair, listening for any sound of the Germans returning. He shook his head. 'Better you go for Guy. At least that way you'll be back by the time we're finished.'

Michel looked doubtful. He squeezed Félix's shoulder. '*Alors, à très vite—et bon courage, mon pote.*'

He set off at a brisk trot and was lost to view by the time Clémence re-emerged. The terrain rose only marginally in any direction, but Clémence had done a reconnaissance trip the previous day and had managed to get a signal a few hundred yards to the left of the substation along a wide track that led into beech woods. They kept up an even pace until she came to an abrupt halt in a clearing where the woodcutters had recently been at work. Lengths of felled timber were stacked on one side, exuding a nutty, moss-scented odour. Félix saw that the earthen roadway continued upwards on the opposite side of the clearing. It was obviously a well-used forestry route.

It took Clémence a frustrating fifteen minutes to set up, make contact, transmit her message and receive acknowledgement. She dismantled the equipment and packed it into the case while Félix retrieved the aerial wire that she had earlier directed him to position as high on a suitable tree as possible.

They made their way back down to the substation, hearing no evidence of the German patrol returning. Félix heaved a sigh of relief when they crossed again to their arrival point, where the trees stood thick and dense, hugging the verge along the entire length of the road. He had half-expected Guy and Michel to be waiting for them with the truck and risked a quick flick of his torch to check his watch. Half an hour in total since Michel had left them. That didn't make sense. What could have hindered them? With a growing sense of unease, he pulled Clémence back into the deeper shadow.

They picked up the steady drone of a vehicle engine at the same time and permitted themselves a shared smile. Their lift home, at last. As Thierry's truck approached at speed, its contours unmistakeable thanks to the fuel tanks on the roof, another vehicle came into view behind it. The Kübelwagen horn blared like a foghorn in the night, veered out dangerously and overtook, careering towards them frighteningly fast.

Félix grabbed the radio case from Clémence's grip and hurled it into the shrubbery before she could object. He pointed across to the forest track. The German vehicle slowed when it spotted them.

'Run!'

They hurtled up the dusty path with Félix leading the way. He heard the Kübelwagen accelerate on the roadway below. When they reached the cleared area, he felt Clémence tug at his hand. He looked over his shoulder and saw she was pointing to a narrower path he hadn't spotted earlier. He also saw the German vehicle now very close behind them. He cupped his hand against her ear.

'We have to keep going. It's our only chance.'

Advantageously, their progress was unimpeded, but Félix heard an ominous squeal of brakes behind them, followed by several separate loud shouts of 'Halt!'. He felt as though his heart would explode through his chest wall and drew huge mouthfuls of air into his lungs as he thundered uphill. He could hear Clémence's swift footfall behind him and her sharp intakes of breath, but he knew if he turned to check on her, even for a second, he would slow them both down.

Félix heard the loud crack of a shot and registered with relief that the bullet had missed him. He turned to Clémence, who was still on her feet. As he reached for her hand, she gave a soft, sighing moan and crumpled onto the damp grass at the foot of a tall tree. His brain went completely numb. He could hear running footsteps approaching from beyond the bend in the track, but he knelt and took her in his arms regardless. This couldn't be happening. Not now. Not after everything they'd been through. Her hand was across her chest, and blood began seeping out between her slim fingers.

His eyes darted to the pale elfin face. Her forehead was creased in pain. Her eyelids fluttered and the soft blue eyes that had come to obsess him looked up, trying to focus.

'Félix, *ma poche*.' Her fingers hovered over her right thigh.

Félix had no idea what she meant, but his scrabbling hand felt a small object in the pocket of her dark flannel trousers. He held up the tiny metal tin in front of her face. She nodded and with great effort pointed a hovering finger at him. '*Pour toi*, Félix—just in case. You have to bite—hide it...' He hoped there would be time later to investigate and shoved it quickly into the double pocket in his shirt.

'*Embrasse-moi une fois*, Félix, *je te supplie*—kiss me, before it's too late.' Her voice was barely a whisper as her quivering fingers reached out to his jacket.

Félix bent and covered her lips with his own, kissing her softly. For a few joyful seconds there was a response, before her chest shook and her head dropped back. She coughed convulsively, blood streaming from her mouth, until her breathing melted into silence. He hugged her tight, vaguely aware of grey uniforms surrounding him.

He screamed in despair, though already it was too late. 'If there's a God, don't let this happen. Don't take her now.'

A firm hand wrenched his shoulder, its owner speaking bad French with a strong German accent. 'That bitch of an English spy is beyond God's help now. And so are you.'

Félix heard a high, wild laugh that could only have come from the depths of his soul. He looked up at the grey-clad figure that loomed over him. 'There's no more you can do to her now. And I don't give a fuck what you do to me.'

Félix winced as a heavy boot connected with his thigh muscles. He laid Clémence carefully on the verge, then, propelled by fury and anguish, leapt up. He launched a well-aimed punch that caught the soldier who'd spoken squarely on the jaw, knocking him to the ground where he landed with a heavy thump. Félix registered the ominous click of several guns being readied to shoot, but what did it matter? They'd already taken Clémence from him.

A voice he'd heard before snapped out an order in German, and then said in clear, practised French, 'They want him alive'. Before he could establish who was issuing the commands, there was a blinding pain behind his left ear and his vision was clouded by a shower of sparks. His knees buckled, and the world turned black.

Félix came to in the back of the fast-moving vehicle, with a uniformed soldier on either side of him and a splitting headache. He peered to left and right groggily, uncertain of their direction or destination. As buildings began to line the roadsides, he recognised the outskirts of Saint-Lô, which could mean only one thing: he was on his way to Gestapo headquarters. He swallowed hard as the last things he remembered floated into his mind—Clémence, lifeless beside him on the grass, her silky blonde hair fanned out like the first time they had made love; the troop of grey-clad soldiers enclosing him; and a blinding pain behind his left ear, as evidenced by his woefully throbbing head.

The truck swept to a halt some minutes later and he was dragged from the car unceremoniously. His arms were firmly locked and supported by his none-too-genial escorts, which was probably as well, Félix considered, as he doubted whether he was capable of taking his own weight at present.

They entered a harshly lit hallway. One of his guards gave a peremptory knock on a door to his right. There was an answering '*Herein!*' The door was opened, and he was pushed roughly to a chair in front of an imposing wooden desk.

The occupant of the chair behind it looked up appraisingly as he was dumped opposite and hauled up straight. Félix tried to focus on the face of what he assumed was to be his inquisitor. The man looked to be not much older than himself, perhaps in his early thirties. His close-cropped dark hair was already beginning to recede, and Félix noted, despite his blurred vision, a fine white scar that followed the man's jawline from the right ear to the side of his mouth. Pale-grey eyes watched him closely from below thin, arching brows. The man touched the SS insignia on his high collar before picking up what looked like an expensive fountain pen in burgundy red with gold trimmings. He spoke at last, his voice clipped, precise, cultured.

'Name?'

'Feldmarschal Rommel.'

The officer's eyes narrowed. He pursed his lips as he laid his pen down meticulously on the paper on which he had been about to write.

Félix heard movement and saw a hand beginning to swing towards him. The officer gave a sharp shake of his head. Before he could speak, another voice from further behind broke in, the one he'd recognised when he was arrested. Who *was* it?

'His name is Félix Duchamp, *Herr Kriminalkommisar*.'

He tried to swivel in his chair and received a rough shove. His head was jerked back towards the desk.

The officer directed his reply over Félix's shoulder. 'Thank you, Major Wolff. You may go now.'

So that was who it was. That *putain de connard* who'd been dogging his footsteps for months. He heard heels click and a door close, and the officer picked up his pen and addressed Félix again.

'We have established that you are Félix Duchamp, and that you are an active member of the *Résistance*. Please tell me the names of the other members in your group.'

Félix knew that he had to try and hold out for as long as he could bear to, without letting slip any incriminating information. 'I have nothing to say.'

The officer sighed. 'I can assure you it will be far better for you if you cooperate. The alternative will be distasteful to me and painfully unpleasant for you.' The slow-blinking eyes betrayed no emotion whatsoever.

Félix shifted in his seat. '*Rien à dire*, and that will continue to be my answer.'

A flicker of annoyance clouded the officer's face. 'We shall see.'

The interrogation continued for two hours. The same questions were repeated unremittingly, over and over. Posed politely, barked into his ear, explained with indisputable reason; whichever tactic, his answer remained the same. His throat was sore, his voice becoming hoarse. He repeated to himself endlessly the same phrase: forty-eight hours. He must hold out for forty-eight hours, to give his comrades time to erase all remaining traces of their activities and disappear if need be.

The officer's patience finally snapped. 'So be it.' He addressed the guards on either side of Félix. 'Take him downstairs and I will join you in a few minutes. In the meantime, prepare him so that he is ready when I arrive.'

Félix gritted his teeth as he was dragged to his feet. He had no idea what awaited him, only that 'painfully unpleasant' doubtless didn't even begin to describe it. He was marched along a corridor that led from the rear of the room, down a flight of bare stone steps and into a room that contained two chairs, a plain scrubbed wooden table and in one corner a large drum-shaped container, which stood beside a long, low china sink, from which snaked a length of hose. The concrete floor sloped down to a drain in front of the metal tub, which appeared to be slightly above waist level in height. He arched his shoulders as the handcuffs tethering his arms behind his back were removed. One of the guards motioned for him to undress, pointing to a peg on which hung a shapeless one-piece garment. Félix stripped to his underpants and passed his clothes to the guard, who pointed at his crotch and continued to hold out a hand. He removed his final piece of clothing with bad grace, handing over the underwear and with it the remnants of his dignity. He suppressed the urge to punch the guard, who was eyeing him with a smirk on his face, grabbed the coverall, which was made of some rough brown fabric, and stepped into it. He winced as he shrugged it over his shoulders, the depth to the crotch having clearly been intended for someone of extremely short stature. He was repulsed when he noted the stain marks that peppered the cloth, doubtless evidence of the sufferings of a previous wearer. The guard gave a hearty laugh, amused by his discomfiture, and pointed to the nearest chair. His clothes and shoes were flung aside and the guard crushed Félix's bare feet into the concrete floor with the heel of his boot as he crossed to the door to await the officer's arrival.

Other than a large tin box at the far end of the table, the contents of which Félix chose not to dwell on, the white-tiled windowless room was stark beneath the one bright, unshaded light that hung from the ceiling. And cold. Félix's feet were already beginning to turn numb from contact with the chill of the rough concrete, and he wriggled his bruised toes in an effort to maintain circulation. Forty-eight hours, he told himself.

He reckoned it was another ten minutes before the officer appeared, by which time he had lost almost all feeling in his feet and was beginning to shiver. The officer picked up the second chair and sat so close that his knees were almost touching Félix's own. He cleared his throat and held a palm out to one of the guards, who handed over the clipboard and pen.

'Let us begin again.' The voice was patient but intimidating.

Félix tried to muster his fading strength. After another fifteen minutes, the officer screwed the cap onto his pen and placed it on the table with the still bare sheet of paper clipped to the board.

'Very well. I have given you every chance to cooperate.' He motioned to the guards. 'Proceed.'

Félix was hauled across to the tank, which he now saw was full of water. One of the soldiers picked up from the sink a bucket that Félix hadn't noticed and tipped its contents into the tank, stepping back smartly as the ice blocks splashed water onto the floor when they hit the surface. The guard looked in the officer's direction, but Félix was unable to see the wordless response. His head was grabbed from behind by the hair and plunged downwards. He had time only to take one deep breath before his face sank below the surface, and he scrabbled at the rough edges of the tank to steady himself. Very soon he felt as if his lungs would burst, and he struggled like a wild thing to free himself. He felt a second strong pair of hands press hard on his neck and a few bubbles of air escaped upwards from his nose as he was held down firmly.

He was suddenly jerked backwards. He gasped for breath, his chest heaving, as his face emerged from the water. He was turned to face the officer.

'Is once enough?' The smile was resigned, the eyebrows questioning.

Félix coughed and spluttered, then drew in a deep breath. *'Rien à dire.'*

After the fifth dunking, Félix was shivering uncontrollably. The officer sat watching dispassionately, one smartly booted leg resting on the other knee and his arms crossed. He might as well have been watching a game of sport with no preference for the winner, Félix thought. He indicated that the guards should repeat the exercise. Félix was now so weak and cold that he could hardly drag in a breath before his head hit the water. As the slowly melting ice rushed past his eyes, he thought again of Clémence. It seemed as if she were smiling up at him from the depths of the tank, her blonde hair floating in the turbulence, her blue eyes sparkling. Wouldn't it be easier to give in? To succumb now without the growing risk of betraying his friends? The burning in his chest was agonising, and he could feel his weight sagging into the grip of his captors. Before he could open his mouth and inhale the water that pressed in on all sides, Élodie's soft face appeared. Her recent words filled his ears. 'You know I couldn't bear it if anything happened to you?' He pressed his lips together, gathered his remaining strength and kicked his right foot back. Even though it was unshod, it connected with a shin, eliciting a loud expletive. The pressure on his shoulders loosened and he shot upwards, fighting for air as soon as his face left the water. Despite the ringing in his ears, he could hear the high-pitched whooping sounds he was making as he dragged air into his lungs. He let go of the rim of the tank and collapsed onto the floor, gasping and jerking.

He watched as the officer rose, a disgusted look replacing his impassive stare. 'That's enough for now. We'll begin again later.' He turned on his heel and was gone.

The guard Félix had kicked aimed a retaliatory blow with the toe of his boot. It connected with his unbruised thigh, though the flesh was so cold that it produced only a dull ache. The other soldier dipped the bucket into the water and threw the contents over the lower half of the coverall, which until that point had been relatively dry. Félix was manhandled along a corridor and thrown into a small, dark room that contained a concrete shelf and an empty bucket. He recoiled at the smell of sweat and human excrement, but the guard had already slammed the door shut, the key grating in the heavy lock as if from afar. He crawled to the shelf, heaving himself up and away from whatever he had seen scuttling across the floor, and sank into oblivion.

Soon afterwards, however, he was awakened by the sound of the door being unlocked. One of the two guards entered and hurled a bundle onto the floor. In halting French, he told Félix to change back into his own clothes, adding that the officer did not intend for him to die before he'd told them what they wanted to know.

Grateful for the dry garments, Félix clambered laboriously off the bed, fumbling with the two buttons that fastened the sodden German garment. He dried himself as best he could with his shirt, and dragged on his jumper, jacket and trousers. He extracted the little metal tin during the process, pushing it deep into his trouser pocket. Where his underpants had disappeared to was anyone's guess. The clothes had been wrapped in a blanket, in which he cocooned himself as he climbed back onto the hard shelf. The windowless cell was at least draught-free and felt reasonably warm, in stark contrast to the sub-zero conditions of the water chamber in the interrogation room. As he drifted off into a restless sleep, he felt the sensation returning to his aching limbs, degree by throbbing degree.

When he was woken by the clanging of the lock and the door swinging open, he had no idea whether it was day or night. The only light came from the corridor and the powerful torch held by the guard, who set a tray on the floor and retreated without comment. Félix inched his way along the shelf and examined the two items on the tray, which was itself dimly visible in the chink of light that filtered under the door.

He picked up the tin cup and sniffed the contents. Whatever it was, it didn't smell like coffee, but the liquid was warm and his throat was so parched that he wouldn't have cared what it was as he sipped it cautiously. There was also a tin bowl containing what might be some variety of thin soup, with a few unidentifiable lumps floating in it. It smelt vaguely savoury. His fingers searched the tray but found no spoon, so he picked up the bowl and drank from it, gagging at the rank taste of the few scraps of what he took to be tough meat.

He dropped the bowl onto the tray and sat back against the wall, his head swimming and his stomach on fire. The dizziness engendered by sitting up made him bilious, and he swallowed frantically to keep down the meagre nourishment he'd consumed.

His bodily responses were soon sidelined when the door swung open again and two guards motioned for him to get up. His shoes had not been returned to him and he trod gingerly on the rough flooring until two pairs of arms seized him and propelled him back to the white-tiled room. The officer from the night before was already seated at a table, alongside a colleague of apparently similar rank, but entirely different appearance.

The second man lacked the slim, elegant stature of Félix's original interrogator, his jacket bulging ominously at the seams round his blocky build. His bull neck strained at the restrictive collar of his uniform, a roll of flesh escaping as he turned his head to examine their prisoner. His steel-grey hair, cut *en brosse*, sat deep on his brow and his square jaw offset a wide-lipped mouth below a fastidiously clipped moustache. He turned to his colleague and asked a question in rapid-fire German that eluded Félix's meagre knowledge. The original officer gave a curt nod, his eyes never leaving Félix's as the guards pushed him towards the remaining chair to sit facing his interrogators. He had a sinking feeling that the worst was indisputably yet to come.

The two officers took it in turns to ask the same questions that he'd refused to answer earlier. The more refined officer remained cool, aloof almost, and merely continued to stare at Félix as he replied '*Rien à dire*', no matter how the questions were worded. After twenty minutes, his coarse colleague's colour was rising. Each time Félix refused to cooperate, he slammed his fist on the table. At the half-hour point, he leant across and slapped Félix's face hard on both sides with the back of a squat hand. Despite knowing the situation could only deteriorate still further, Félix held his ground.

After an hour, the slaps were abandoned. A well-aimed punch smashed into Félix's face. He yelled at the pain that exploded in his head and put a hand to his nose, feeling the warm blood spurt down his mouth and chin. The original officer rose hurriedly, a look of disgust skewing his striking features. He shook his head at Félix.

'You will cooperate eventually. I advise that you do so sooner rather than later.' He gave a curt nod to his colleague, who was distracted as he massaged his sore knuckles, and hurried out of the room.

The remaining officer rubbed his moustache thoughtfully. 'So, we change tactics now. We are wasting much time.'

Félix flicked his eyes to the metal box as the German pulled it towards him. He couldn't see what was inside because the lid obscured the contents, and the officer took his time making his selection. He closed the box and pushed it aside, placing an implement that closely resembled a police truncheon on the table. He gestured for the two guards who had been standing some way behind Félix to station themselves either side of him, then lifted his bulk slowly from the chair. In a few short paces he stood menacingly above Félix.

'I give you one last chance. Tell me the names of your *Résistance* colleagues and I shall have no need to hurt you further.'

Félix drew in a painful breath. '*Rien à dire.*'

The officer gave an instruction to one of the guards, who forced Félix's right hand flat onto the table, palm down. His wrist was firmly restrained by the soldier as the officer snatched the stick and wielded it with expert precision. There was a sickening thwack as the weapon connected with his outstretched fingers. Félix yelled from the bottom of his lungs as a wave of nausea swept over him. He forced himself to concentrate and opened his eyes; the officer's face loomed six inches from his own. A thread of spittle hung from the corner of the perfectly trimmed moustache.

'The seriousness of your situation doesn't seem to have registered. You and your colleagues have caused an inconvenience to the Reich's armaments production locally. It will be temporary, no doubt, but the culprits will regret their actions. I suggest you see sense and start giving some answers.' Félix stared back unblinkingly and shook his head, gagging at the odour of garlic. The caustic thought stole into his addled brain that the man had probably been enjoying dinner in a fine restaurant in Saint-Lô with his French mistress while Clémence lay dying in his arms in the back of beyond.

The officer stood upright and leant back against the table. His voice was calm and conversational as he began again, a smile appearing as he spoke. 'Tell me about your sister.'

Félix surged forward until a restraining arm caught him by the throat, half-choking him. He waited till the pressure was released, giving himself time to control his anger. 'My sister has no involvement in anything I may have done.'

'And your brother-in-law?' Félix was caught off-balance. Which sister was he referring to? He had assumed Élodie. And why was he being asked about Guy? Surely he was long gone before Félix's own arrest? Or was he receiving similar treatment somewhere else in this unspeakable netherworld?

'I have no idea what you're talking about.' He was vaguely aware of the stick swinging down again, his left hand having replaced his right on the table. This time he blacked out completely.

By the end of the day he had been hauled back to the interrogation room four times, on each occasion receiving further beatings. To his intense relief, he was finally reprieved when a terrified-looking young soldier burst in and handed over a message. The officer appeared to blaspheme vociferously before instructing the guards to return Félix to his unlit cell, where he lay for a while half-senseless, his arms still manacled behind his back. He had no idea what was going on above ground, but he prayed for a few hours' respite.

He soon grew cold, then remembered the blanket he had pushed out of sight under the ledge that morning in the hope that it would be overlooked. He inched forward and could see an uneven heap against the wall. A ridiculous frisson of triumph surged through him. He shuffled himself down and whimpered at the excruciating pain in his inept hands as he fell to the floor and tried to fumble behind him. He manoeuvred himself to his knees, reached back for the cloth and managed to stand. He made a clumsy attempt to shake the rough fabric, hampered by the handcuffs but revolted by the thought of the unspecified creatures that might have crawled into its lingering warmth when he had abandoned it earlier. He shuddered as he enveloped himself with a mammoth effort in its scratchy folds.

He was awoken sometime later by raised voices outside his cell. Suddenly the door swung open with a clatter and Lieutenant Hoffmann walked in. He instructed the guard to turn on the light and gestured for the door to be closed behind him. He stopped dead as Félix gazed at him impassively.

'*Lieber Gott*—what have they done to you?'

'What does it look like? And why are you here?' Félix didn't want to believe the slowly dawning implication. 'Don't tell me you're part of this disgusting set-up?'

The German's tone was incensed. 'Don't be ridiculous—of course I'm not.'

'So why are you here now?'

'The major was summoned to give a progress report on the search for your colleagues. He needed back-up and ordered me to accompany him. And I don't have much time. I wanted to check on you, to see that you were—'

'Still alive?' Félix didn't attempt to hide his sarcasm.

'If you insist on putting it that way, then yes.' Before Félix could vent his own fury, the lieutenant bent low over him and spoke quickly. 'They have caught no one else. Yet. They will keep you here for forty-eight hours, and then...' He grimaced. 'If there is any way I can influence where they send you, I will do so, though I hold out little hope.'

Félix knew full well he might not be sent anywhere further than wherever they shot—or, rather, executed—noncompliant prisoners. Could he trust this man standing over him? How many options did he have, though? He made a swift decision. 'There is one thing you can do for me.'

'Yes? Tell me.'

The lieutenant's blond-lashed eyes widened in horror as Félix asked him to slip under his tongue, against his cheek, the suicide pill he'd found earlier in the tiny tin. Initially, the officer refused point blank. Félix reflected later that it was likely only the need for speed that had shortened the ensuing argument, which encompassed Élodie never forgiving either of them, and a refusal to be party to Félix deliberately sacrificing himself. Finally, a combination of the time factor and Félix's assertion that the alternatives would all be far worse for him persuaded the lieutenant to acquiesce. He placed the capsule without comment, then laid a hand on Félix's shoulder.

'I am no longer a religious man, but I will pray for you just the same.' With that, he strode to the door, summoned the guard, and was gone without looking back. The light was extinguished and the room returned to darkness.

Some hours later, Félix was aware of the low, booming growl of heavy aircraft somewhere close overhead. He hoped with his entire being that they were Allied planes. It crossed his groggy mind that if the building were hit and he didn't survive, at least he had managed to hold out for twenty-four hours. An ironic thought occurred to him: he'd have no need of the capsule under his tongue should he be buried under a mountain of rubble. He groaned, rolled over, and settled himself uncomfortably to await his fate.

# CHAPTER TWENTY

## April–May 1944

THIERRY TURNED TO MICHEL and shook his head. 'This place is a *putain de bastille*—totally impregnable. Unless they move him and we can find out when, and where to, there's no chance of springing him. Or unless our message got through.'

Michel swore under his breath. 'A bloody fortress is right! Who was it suggested we might have a chance?'

Thierry scowled. 'Lisette. *Quelle imbécile!*' He tipped his head to one side as a faint, deep rumbling noise began to the north. The two moved back into the shadows and waited. Thierry sniffed and wrinkled his nose. The side alley stank of stale piss. A few minutes later, he punched his fist in the air and grinned at his companion.

'Do you hear what I hear now?'

'Yes, I think—yes! How long?'

Thierry shrugged his shoulders and listened again. 'Not more than a few minutes, I'd guess. We need to move our arses. Assuming they're heading this way, I hope to hell they've marked their target well.'

The two men retreated down the side street in search of shelter. Michel tugged at Thierry's sleeve and indicated a solid archway on the right, between buildings across the road. The drone of aero engines grew more distinct, and the sound of shouting echoed from the main street. A loud whistling from above was followed by three enormous thuds. The dark buildings they'd been surveying exploded into an incandescent blaze with an ear-shattering roar as the ground shook beneath them.

'Ouf! Bravo to the RAF.' Thierry grinned at Michel, who gave a thumbs-up. When several further loud explosions echoed along the street as more bombs dropped, Michel's face grew solemn. Thierry shrugged. 'Can't be helped, *mon pote*. There have been plenty of civilian deaths already, and these won't be the last. But, *quand même*, God help whoever lives—or lived—in those buildings.'

The two men watched as the heavy planes banked in turn and headed for home, thundering unchallenged overhead with their night's work done. Emerging vigilantly from the archway, Thierry checked further up the side street, which was eerily quiet against the background din of falling masonry and spine-chilling human screams. The truck was still there, faintly visible, and as he raised a hand Serge chanced a quick flick of the dimmed lights. Thierry acknowledged with a wave, pointed to the ruined building, and held up his fingers to indicate ten minutes. The lights flickered again.

'It's now or never. Let's go. Be warned, we might walk straight into...'

Before he could finish, Michel grabbed his arm and started to move. They ran down the road to the side door they'd been checking earlier. It now hung open at a drunken angle. Pushing their way through the gap, they entered a corridor that clearly led to the front of the building. About fifteen yards away the ceiling had collapsed and blocked the passageway. The air was full of choking dust. On the wall, a large picture of

Adolf Hitler hung at a forty-five-degree angle. Michel dragged it off the wall and flung it to the floor. To their right lay a flight of stairs to the lower level, damaged but intact.

Thierry raised his eyes and whispered, 'God is with us tonight, that's for sure.'

They descended slowly, Thierry first. His movements were almost silent, despite his bulk. At the foot of the stairs a pillar had collapsed onto a uniformed German soldier whose head was crushed and covered in congealing blood. Thierry raised his eyebrows questioningly as Michel bent and felt for a pulse, shook his head and grimaced.

They began to creep along a poorly lit corridor. The unmistakeable sound of a door opening in a passageway to their left, barely thirty feet in front of them, brought them to a sharp halt.

Thierry whispered, 'Follow my lead.' He began to move at speed, the limp from his injured leg still apparent. Michel sped up in unison.

Suddenly Thierry bellowed, 'Is anyone here? Anyone here?'

Another German, clearly a guard, his hand hovering over his pistol, staggered out of the dim passage. His uniform was covered in cement dust and his mottled face was chalk-white with shock.

Thierry didn't hesitate. 'Quick, quick, we've been sent to help.'

The German's hooded eyes registered complete incomprehension. Thierry summoned up the few words of German he'd learnt.

'*Schnell, schnell.*' He jerked his thumb up to the ceiling, then thrust both hands downwards. 'Collapse. Imminent. *Verstehen?*'

The German nodded uncertainly.

'How many prisoners? *Gefangene?*' He held up one finger, then two, then three.

The guard indicated his understanding. '*Zwei*—two.'

Thierry urged him on. 'We have to get them out. *Schnell*. OK?'

Still looking unsure, the guard led them down the corridor and stopped in front of a solid door. Thierry presumed it was secured and mimicked an unlocking gesture. The German hesitated, but the noise of falling debris somewhere behind them seemed to panic him. He shuffled a bunch of keys twice before he located the right one. Once the lock was released, Michel put his shoulder to the thick metal and looked inside. A man lay on a wooden bench against the wall, barely lifting his head towards the sudden wedge of half-light that slanted across his face. Thierry raised his eyebrows, but Michel shook his head almost imperceptibly.

He turned back to the guard. 'And the other?'

'We take?' he said in halting French, indicating the prone figure.

'Yes, but you said two. The second one?' He pointed to the unlocked room, indicating one, and held up a second finger. 'The other prisoner?'

The German pointed to the next room but didn't move. Thierry tapped his watch. At the sound of pandemonium from the floor above the man sprang into action, shuffling the keys yet again though with agonising slowness. He turned the key in the lock, and as Michel pushed open the door Thierry rushed past him. He swore involuntarily, hardly recognising Félix whose face was bloodied and puffy almost beyond recognition.

Thierry crossed the small room, followed by the guard, and realised Michel could now see the state of his lifelong friend. Félix, battered and bruised, was trying to prop himself up on one elbow. With an animal sound Michel leapt forward. The guard's hand scrabbled for his pistol as a strong forearm tightened around his neck. In one swift movement Michel relieved the soldier of his sidearm and jerked his jaw with a snap. The soldier grunted and collapsed in a heap. Thierry

turned in astonishment as the normally equable Michel pointed the pistol at the guard's head, teeth gritted, his expression
a contortion of fury and hatred.

Thierry had to act promptly. 'No, my friend. Too much
noise. There may be more guards.' Michel looked across at
Félix. Thierry shook his arm roughly. 'Michel, *no*. I understand. But we are leaving, and right now.'

Thierry knelt beside Félix, whose swollen, pain-filled eyes
were barely open. 'You recognise us, right?

Félix nodded and tried to sit up. 'I... Thierry. Thank God. I
didn't...'

'Shush.' Thierry put a finger to Félix's bruised lips. 'Stay
quiet now.'

He looked down as Félix's swollen fingers scrabbled at his
sleeve. With great effort, Félix pointed at his mouth.

'Out.'

'What?'

'Out, out.' He lifted his tongue slowly to his bottom lip.

Thierry glanced at Michel, who shrugged, anxiety clouding
his face. He inserted his finger into Félix's mouth, checking
the inside of his cheeks, then searched under his tongue. As
he made contact with the capsule, Félix's eyelids flickered.

'*Putain*! Where the hell did you get this?' He extracted the
rubber-covered pill carefully.

Félix tried to answer, his brows furrowed with the effort.
'Cl..., Cl....'

Thierry bent to listen. 'Clémence?'

'Yes.'

'Is she here somewhere?'

Félix tried to shake his head. His words came out in a sob.
'No, thank God. At least she was spared this.'

Thierry knew what this must mean. He looked down at the
deadly capsule he'd been about to hurl across the room but
thought better of it. Instead, he took a matchbox from his
pocket and inserted it for later consideration.

He raised his brows at Michel and indicated the guard. 'Alive?'

Michel placed two fingers on the soldier's neck and gave a sanguine smile. 'He won't trouble us.' He tucked the guard's pistol into his waistband. He took the bunch of keys from the German's belt, hoping that they included one that would release Félix's handcuffs.

The two of them lifted Félix with coordinated precision. He moaned quietly, his breath shuddering in irregular wheezes. Thierry checked the corridor, which remained empty, and hoisted Félix over his shoulder.

As they passed the other cell, Michel took a peek. The man was motionless, either asleep or unconscious.

'What about him?'

Thierry shook his head. 'We don't have time and we can't take the risk. I've no idea who he is but the door's open. If he comes to, he might make it by himself, or someone may find him.'

Michel wiped his hand across his mouth uncertainly, then indicated his agreement.

They made their way back to the stairs as fast and quietly as conditions allowed, Michel checking behind them all the way. As Thierry started to climb with his burden, Félix cried out at the jerking motion. Thierry felt the heavy, semi-conscious head move as Michel calmed the figure that hung down his broad back, and was grateful for the quiet reassuring words he heard behind him.

'It's Michel, Félix. Not long now. Stay quiet, *mon pote*.'

Thierry stopped for breath halfway up and then continued to climb. The ground-floor corridor was in semi-darkness now, the overhead light fizzing on and off spasmodically. There was an acrid stench of burning electrical components, and the sound of steadily dripping water nearby. Thierry grunted. 'Let's get out of here *vite*.'

Michel stuck his head out of the sagging exit door. The only noise was still on the main road, where sirens wailed. A fire engine shot past the end of the side street, bells clanging, and flashlights wove a pattern across the front of the building.

He ducked back inside. 'All clear. Do you want me to take him?'

Thierry grunted and held Félix's legs securely against his chest. 'Nope. Let's go.'

They set off up the street, keeping to the darkest shadows. Michel walked backwards, alert for any movement behind them, but they reached the truck without incident. Serge had already unhooked the tarpaulin at the back. He leapt onto the cargo bed and shifted heavy crates and boxes, grabbed two blankets and laid them flat against the truck's cabin. Michel took off his jacket and folded it for a pillow, then jumped up alongside Serge to take Félix from Thierry. Between them they covered him with another blanket and rearranged the crates to keep his limp form stable and hidden. Finally, they replaced the tonneau cover, clipping the connectors at the sides and checking there was plenty of airflow. Once satisfied, the three of them climbed into the cab.

'Where to?' Serge asked.

Thierry replied. 'The old water mill on the road to Flers. Michel has it all set up.' He exhaled emphatically. '*Merde*, I can hardly believe it, but we've done it. We've got him.'

In the dim light of the cabin, Michel's eyes glistened. Thierry bumped his fist reassuringly on Michel's thigh. 'I'll fetch Guy to take a look at him in the morning. He'll be OK, my friend, I'm sure of it.'

Michel gave him a sharp look. '*Guy*! You're sure about that?

Thierry tipped his head almost imperceptibly in Serge's direction. 'Sure as I can be—and he's still a safer bet than that old fool Leblanc.'

As they had expected, there was no traffic on the road. A waxing moon hung low in the clear night sky as the truck hurtled away from Saint-Lô. Michel had chosen a circuitous, ill-frequented route and directed Serge, who was driving like a maniac to put as much distance as possible between themselves and the Gestapo. He had agreed with Thierry in advance to keep their destination vague until the last minute, neither of them entirely trusting Serge, despite knowing he would be aggrieved at his exclusion from the big decisions. Other than the necessary directions, the three men settled into a contemplative silence.

Félix slipped in and out of consciousness all night. He was dimly aware that he was no longer in that pitch-dark hell, and thought he saw Michel sitting watching him from across the room. Or was he delusional? Conversation was quite beyond him, he knew, but for the first time in two days he felt moderately warm under a heavy covering of blankets and glad that he also had something on which to rest his head.

As the dawn light began to penetrate the small upper room at the mill, he stirred and blinked. Where the hell was he? He coughed as he heaved himself up with a huge, agonising effort and stared at the small window in the opposite wall.

'Félix! *Dieu merci*.'

The voice was Michel's. He hadn't been hallucinating after all. He struggled to sit up, but Michel sprang to his side, encouraging him to lie down again.

'Stay still, my friend. Thierry will have gone for Guy by now. He'll put you right.'

Félix's head was spinning, and he felt abominably sick. He lay back and the nausea lessened a little.

'Michel, I...'

'*Chut*, Félix. Save your strength.' Michel patted his arm. A few minutes later he jumped up and went to the window.

'Thierry's truck's coming down the lane. And he has Guy with him.' He returned to the hastily constructed bed and crouched on the rough floor, whose wooden planks still bore signs of dusty, age-old flour in the crevices between them. Félix reached out a misshapen hand, which was supported in the comforting hold of his old friend's palm.

Thierry's customary whistle echoed on the stairs as he and Guy pounded up from the entrance. As the two of them entered the room Félix registered the look of shock on Guy's face. His brother-in-law's normal professional manner seemed to have deserted him—a reaction, Félix presumed, to his appearance following his treatment at the hands of the Gestapo.

Guy quickly recovered his composure and was by Félix's side in half a dozen swift steps. He had with him a large medical bag, which he opened and set on the floor.

'Félix, I'm so sorry about all this. I don't know how I'll ever make it up to you, but I'll start right now.'

He had no idea what his brother-in-law was talking about, but Thierry's sharp glance at Michel, lips tight and eyebrows lowered, told Félix that despite his befuddled state there was something he wasn't understanding. Whatever it was, it would have to wait for later—at present it was hard enough simply to survive.

Guy lifted first one, then the other swollen, bruised hand. Félix cried out as each finger was manipulated by the pharmacist, and bit his lip to counteract the raw surge of pain. He noticed Thierry restraining Michel, who was standing with his arms raised to chest height, his fists clenched.

When Guy spoke, his voice was trembling with controlled rage. 'I think they've broken every finger, Félix, those utter bastards. I'm going to strap them for support, but the dressings will need changing regularly as the swelling lessens. I'll do that myself every day, and later I'll splint them.'

Félix nodded weakly. Christ, why did even moving his head hurt like hell? He couldn't suppress the groans that escaped him as Guy efficiently examined the rest of him from top to toe, occasionally shaking his head. When he finished, he stood up and gave Félix a reassuring smile.

'I don't think anything else is broken. I'm mainly worried about the sounds in your chest. Tell me, what the devil did they do to you?'

'For starters, repeatedly held my head underwater till I was certain I'd choke to death.'

Michel cursed aloud and thumped the wall. Félix's attempt at a sardonic smile was distorted by the painful bruises on his face, and he was racked by another coughing fit as he raised his head and shoulders. Guy supported him with one hand and plumped the two coats that were serving as a pillow before lowering him back onto their lumpy support. He turned to Thierry.

'I don't want him lying flat—he might choke on the mucus if he does have a chest infection. If only I could get some of that wonder drug that I've read about, some new antibiotic called penicillin—but I know I can't. I do have a small stock of sulphonamides that should help though, so if one of you could come back with me, I'll give them to you. He needs to start on them right away.'

Thierry volunteered. 'I'll drive you back right now, Guy. Michel, you'll stay with Félix?'

'But of course.' Michel's features were screwed into a scowl. 'If I could get hold of whoever did this...'

'Console yourself that whoever it was may well be under several tons of brick and concrete thanks to the RAF.' Thierry's smile was ugly but softened immediately as he laid a hand on Félix's shoulder. 'We'll get you on the mend soon, *mon camarade*. After what he did for my leg, Guy here's proved he's a better bet than that old scoundrel Leblanc ever was.'

Michel moved a chair close to Félix and sat down heavily with an angry grunt as the other two men left. The sound of the old truck outside was soon lost and Félix longed only for untroubled slumber. He knew he couldn't want for a better companion than Michel, the man of few words who'd repeatedly proved his abiding friendship. His eyelids felt heavy. Thank God he could relax at last. His mind began to drift, but as sleep held out its arms to claim him Michel sprang from his chair, knocking it over in his haste and returning Félix to full alertness.

'Michel? What's up?'

His friend's tense voice came from the direction of the small window. 'I heard something. *Merde*—someone's out there.'

Félix swivelled his neck as far as the pain would allow and kept his voice low. 'Anything to be seen?'

Michel shook his head and reached into his jacket pocket, pulling out the German pistol he had liberated the night before. He headed for the half-closed door, positioning himself behind it as one of the stairs creaked. Félix watched his friend double-check that the gun was loaded and that the bed was not directly in line with the door. Michel flashed a taut smile and motioned for him to stay still. For some seconds there was silence, broken only by what sounded like a mouse scurrying across the floor above them. Another stair tread squeaked, close by, and Michel levelled the gun at approximately head height. He grabbed the worn metal handle, yanked the door fully open from behind and Félix saw Rudi Hoffmann, his own gun drawn, framed in the doorway. As Michel moved, Félix shouted as loudly as he was able.

'No, Michel—*arrête!*'

Michel's attention was distracted for only an instant, but it was long enough for the Lieutenant to grab the hand pointing the pistol at his face and force it upwards. The sound of the shot was jarring in the confined space, and splinters of wood and plaster fell from the ceiling.

Michel was the first to speak. 'Félix, what the fuck—why did you interfere?'

Félix looked towards the Lieutenant. 'He's one of the good ones as best I can judge. D'you not know who he is?'

Michel looked the German up and down, his eyes fierce. 'Oh, sure I do. I saw him in Argentan the day Julien was executed.' He glared at Félix, his expression unforgiving, his tone contemptuous as he spat out his words. 'He was with your sister. What's more, there's no such thing as a good German in my experience.'

Félix's exasperated sigh caused a further paroxysm of coughing to consume him. He watched helplessly as Rudi faced Michel. He saw the lieutenant's gaze drop to the Luger that Michel held, aimed unwaveringly at his grey-clad torso.

'Liberated from a certain German guard in St-Lô last night, I presume?'

Michel's glare hardened. 'And what if it was?'

He raised the gun threateningly as the lieutenant turned away with a pained expression and ran a hand across his brow. With slow deliberation, Rudi holstered his pistol and pointed towards the makeshift bed. 'I wish, please, to speak with your friend.'

Michel gave a curt nod, but the Luger tracked Rudi across the narrow room.

Félix wiped his mouth with the back of his bandaged hand and observed the specks of blood dislodged by his coughing spasm. Somehow, he couldn't give a damn. A vision of Clémence flooded his head, her blue eyes closing, the life pumping from her in spilt blood, her sensual scent filling his nose.

Rudi stood towering over Félix for a few seconds, then dropped to his haunches. 'I am so glad to see you again. I thought I may never do so. That capsule...'

Félix was disconcerted by the apparent concern in the German's eyes. After recent events, he wanted to hate them all.

Every one of them in that abhorrent uniform. But he couldn't. 'Safely removed by my friends.'

Michel interrupted him. 'How did you find us?'

The lieutenant sought to reassure them. 'I saw the truck leaving as I was passing the track that leads here. Don't worry—I have left my machine hidden from the road. I would say you are quite safe. At least for now.'

'And my sister?'

Rudi's face tightened as he refocused on Félix and saw the extent of the blackened swelling of his swaddled hands. 'Élodie will not be at home today. I am on my way to the farm to suggest strongly that, shall we say, she disappears for a while. And before you ask, yes, I'm sure your parents will be questioned, but Élodie has already sworn they know nothing of their children's activities. That is correct?'

Félix closed his eyes and his chest rattled painfully as he exhaled. 'Yes—that is, they know nothing.' What a *foutue désastre* this had all become. For him. For his friends. Now for his sister and his parents. He groaned.

The lieutenant straightened up. 'But now I must go. Until you can do so yourself, I will look after your sister, I promise.' He frowned at Michel's derisory snort from behind him and held out a hand to Félix. 'I hope that on one not too distant day we shall meet again, perhaps, as I would wish it, even as friends.' After a few seconds' silence, he spoke again. 'However far in the future that may prove to be, I hope this bloody war will spare us both.'

Félix regarded the outstretched arm for a long moment and then, for the first time in their acquaintance, extended his own bandaged hand. The German held it with care, a warm smile lighting his face and bolstering Félix's recently altered opinion. At last, he knew and understood what—with that unfathomable female instinct—his sister had recognised so soon: that this good-looking, caring young man's misfortune was to have been ordered into an enemy uniform.

'May God go with you, Lieutenant.' He eased down, exhausted, as Rudi backed away, turned and left with a nod to Michel, who stared at him stony-faced, his eyes still alight with hostility.

Michel waited till he heard the outer door close downstairs. 'I think you've lost your damned reason, *mon pote*.' His caustic tone was not lost on Félix, who answered only once his friend was again seated beside him.

'He risked his own safety for me—I need you to know that.' Michel lifted his chin, gesturing for Félix to continue. 'I don't know how much longer I could have held out in that hellhole, but that *brave type* sneaked downstairs and by some fatuous excuse talked his way in to see me. I almost had to force him to put that capsule into my mouth.'

'*Putain*! At least Thierry will now understand how you achieved that when you were trussed up like a chicken with your arms behind your back. And now you'll tell me he wasn't joining in the effort to murder you?' Michel's hands were shaking, from pent-up anger, Félix assumed.

'No, he wasn't—in fact, you couldn't be more wrong. He didn't want to do it even though I begged him to, kept telling me Élodie would never forgive him...' He was undeterred by Michel's contemptuous reaction, which mostly took the form of muttering profanities to himself. 'Michel, we're never going to see eye to eye on this. For a long time, I thought—well, never mind what. The whole bloody world seems to have gone crazy now.'

Michel cocked his head and went to the window to check. 'Thierry's back already. Must have got that stuff Guy promised for you.'

# CHAPTER TWENTY-ONE

## *May 1944*

ÉLODIE LOOKED UP FROM scattering the meagre helping of chicken food as the sound of an approaching engine grew louder. A motorbike came into view on the lane, revealing the rider to be Rudi, head down and driving far too fast along the narrow gap between the bocage hedgerows. He skidded to a halt, sending a shower of grass and mud into the run, the chickens scattering, uttering alarm calls as they ran. Élodie didn't move but watched him closely, assessing his expression.

'*Liebchen.*' His uniform was covered in fine dirt from the road, as was his face, which he wiped distractedly with a gloved hand.

He looked so serious that she was suddenly afraid. This had to be something to do with Félix. She took a deep breath. 'Just tell me. Whatever you've come to say, say it.'

Rudi bent and kissed her forehead. 'I'm sorry, I didn't mean to alarm you. Your brother...' Élodie flinched, covering her mouth with a clenched fist.

He continued without pausing for breath. 'Don't worry, he's alive. The RAF bombed the Gestapo headquarters in Saint-Lô last night, and when a check was made on the prisoners in the basement, Félix was missing. They've found no sign of him.'

'Then how do you know he's alive?'

'Trust me, I do. But for his sake and yours, I'm telling you nothing more at present.'

Élodie opened her mouth, a torrent of questions flooding her brain, but he held up a hand to silence her. 'I don't have any details, but a German guard was found in his cell, his neck broken, so they suspect that his Resistance colleagues were on hand and got him out.'

Élodie allowed herself a small smile. Rudi looked over his shoulder, clearly ill at ease, and spoke again. 'I can't stay, but I wanted you to know. And to tell you that you need to disappear, at least for today, because they'll come looking for him—and with vengeance on their minds.'

'But my parents... I can't leave them to deal with all this!'

Rudi shook his head. 'I don't know for certain what will happen, but they will be questioned. When they are they need to make it obvious they don't know anything. I hope that will be enough.'

Élodie interrupted him. 'Well, they don't know anything. Papa has had strong suspicions, but that's all.'

'Tell your parents Félix is free, as far as you know, and make an excuse—any excuse—to be somewhere else today.'

Élodie nodded, still unsure. 'You don't think the Gestapo have...'

'No, I have it on good authority that it was a huge surprise to them that he's simply disappeared. He wasn't—I'm not sure he could have walked out of his own accord, which is why I think they suspect that he's been taken somewhere safe by others. That and the dead guard.' Rudi grimaced and avoided looking at her directly.

Suddenly he shrugged, sighed, and stroked her cheek. She knew it was unfair, but she remained statue-like and unresponsive.

'I have to go.'

'Wait.' Élodie shivered as a cold chill settled on her. A piece of this puzzle was missing. She caught his arm and shook it. 'Why did Félix get caught? Did they know he'd be there? Did someone betray him?'

Rudi looked uncomfortable. 'I don't have an answer for you. But it was said that certain information had been received.'

'From whom?'

'I've no idea.'

'But you could find out. I know you could.' Élodie wasn't going to let it go at that. 'Could it have been Lisette?' She was surprised by the taut squeaky sound of her own voice as she asked the question. And deep down she hated the unfairness of her suspicion, and logically knew she should dismiss it—Lisette had been the fiercest of her brother's admirers for as long as she could remember.

'Who? That girl who works in the kitchen at the Manoir? No, I'm sure not. She's never been present when such matters have been discussed.'

'Then who? Rudi, I have to know.'

'Because?'

'I have my reasons. Will you do it?'

She could see the reluctance behind Rudi's half-smile. She took his face in her hands and kissed him impatiently. 'Please? Please say you'll find out for me?'

Rudi threw up his hands in defeat. 'OK, I promise I'll do my best. I'll see you again as soon as I can. And please, *Liebchen*, do as I ask—at least for today.' He straddled the motorcycle, revved the throttle, and at last she nodded in agreement. She was rewarded with a quick, bleak smile and he was gone.

She watched as he checked in both directions, and the machine shot off in the direction of the Manoir, the sweet, heavy smell of petrol lingering in his wake. A flash of movement caught her attention as she turned away. She scoured the side of the barn where she'd caught sight of whatever it was, her senses alert for any anomaly. Relief flooded through her as Michel, looking decidedly dishevelled, stood up from the shrubbery and stretched his legs. He ambled towards her, a self-conscious smile spreading. Élodie flew at him and hugged him with relief, seeing the grin replaced by a look of astonishment.

She let him go and took a step back, a sudden thought crossing her mind. 'How long have you been hiding there?'

Michel hopped from one foot to the other. 'Well, I—er, I'd just arrived when your grey-clad friend turned up.'

Élodie stopped herself from issuing a crisp retort. Félix was her prime consideration right now. 'Michel, please say you know where Félix is.'

The smile returned to Michel's face. 'Yes, I do. And he's OK. Well, he's not exactly OK but we have him safe. But, like I heard the lieutenant telling you, you can't know where.'

His self-conscious expression returned as she reached up to hug him again. Her voice from the depths of his thick woollen pullover was muffled. 'Thank you for whatever you've done.'

She let him go once more, still absorbing his initial comment. 'What d'you mean, he's not OK? And what about Clémence?'

Michel cleared his throat. 'Clémence didn't make it, I'm afraid.'

'Oh no—*quelle tragédie!*' Élodie was appalled. 'How? What happened?'

Michel shook his head. 'She was shot before Félix was arrested. Félix being Félix, he'd stopped to help her.'

Élodie looked in the direction of the departed motorbike.

'Don't worry. Your lieutenant didn't take any part in it.'

Élodie ignored the dry comment. She clutched her hands and breathed deeply to regain her composure. Félix could so easily have been shot too. And poor, beautiful Clémence.

What a pointless waste of life. Her eyes watched Michel un-comprehendingly as he continued.

'So, Félix was taken away and interrogated. I assume what's-his-name told you that the RAF half-flattened the Gestapo headquarters in Saint-Lô last night?'

Élodie stared at him. 'But how did they know to do that? And surely Félix could have been killed in the process?'

'We had to take that chance, Él. We confirmed the location of the building to London and were told the RAF would be happy to target it as a priority. It would have proved impossible otherwise. We were about to give up on trying to get him out of there when we heard the planes approaching. The RAF did a grand job that coincidentally cut off the main building from the basement. We got Félix out while the Boche were busy in the front offices trying to put out the fire.'

Élodie smiled in spite of her fretfulness. That was the most she'd heard Michel say since he was a *petit gars*. He was still shy, even as an adult—or with her, at least.

She realised he was checking to see that he still had her full attention. 'We took him to safety, and before you try and insist, I still won't say where.' Élodie tutted. Unusually, a flicker of irritation crossed Michel's face. 'It's best that way, better to keep you out of it all.' She pursed her lips, but for once he was resolute in her presence. 'I fetched Guy first thing this morning...'

'*Guy?*' Élodie couldn't hide her surprise.

'Yes, Guy. He—well, no matter, Guy's checked him over and patched him up, and says that with time he'll pretty much be fine again.' His long lashes blinked as Élodie absorbed his words. Mixed emotions of utter relief and, equally, horror at whatever had been done to Félix swirled through her. The harsh, laughing yaffle of a nearby woodpecker refocused her mind, and she watched as the shapely olive bird rose from the grass and disappeared with its signature looping flight.

'When can I see him? If Guy can, why not me?'

Michel shook his head. 'Not for now. I'm sorry. Suppose I come by every day to tell you how he's doing?'

Élodie made a face, knowing she was being ungracious, then patted his arm in gratitude. 'Yes, please—and give him my love. If there's anything I can do, you'll tell me?'

'Of course. That goes without saying.'

'Rudi—the lieutenant', she corrected herself, 'says I should make myself scarce today. I don't want to leave Maman and Papa to cope when they come looking for Félix, but I don't want to cause further problems either.' She reached up to give Michel a peck on the cheek and found herself enveloped in an impulsive, clumsy bear-hug. When he relaxed his grip, she saw that he was blushing. She laughed involuntarily and stroked his cheek with the back of her hand, seeing the redness spread up his face as she did so.

'I'll see you tomorrow, Michel, and thanks again.'

Michel turned up his coat collar and diffidently kissed the top of her head. '*À demain*, oh, and Élodie, I hate to agree with him but the lieutenant's right—make sure you're not here when the Boche come calling.'

Once he had disappeared beyond the barn, doubtless following one of his own convoluted routes, she hurried back to the house, despite the temptation to try and follow him. She was relieved to see her father arriving for a late breakfast as she reached the door. They went in together and Élodie called out to her mother, who gave an answering 'Coucou' from the kitchen. She asked her parents to sit at the table, aware, as she joined them, of the pair exchanging anxious looks.

'Maman, Papa, please don't ask any questions, because I can't answer them. But Félix is safe and out of harm's way.'

Her father's reply was predictably grouchy. 'Do you really know that—and how do you know?'

She reached across and squeezed his hand. 'Papa, no questions means no questions. I can't even tell you who told me, only that the source is entirely reliable.' She told them the little she could share and explained without conviction that it had been suggested she disappear for the day. She could hardly bear to meet her mother's perceptive gaze, but when she did so she saw only love and understanding radiating from her face.

'Maman, you realise the Germans will come looking for Félix today?'

Her mother shrugged and her father swore beneath his breath.

'Go, *ma chérie*. Your father and I will cope. After all, we know nothing, do we?' Her smile was wry as she stood up to give her daughter a hug. Élodie reached out a hand to her father. To her surprise, he rose too and embraced her in turn, his stubbled cheek rough on her face.

With tears in her eyes, Élodie grabbed a coat. 'I'll come back in time to see to the chickens later. I hope...' She was silenced by her mother, who pushed her briskly towards the hallway.

'Be careful, child. You go. We shall be fine.'

Élodie crossed the farmyard with her bicycle, heaved it over the wall, hopped over herself and made her way towards the forest. As she trudged uphill, the machine unwieldy on the long, uneven grass, a suffocating sense of loneliness enfolded her like a shroud. She shivered despite the relative warmth of the morning, wondering how her family had come to this: her brother arrested by the Gestapo and subsequently snatched from their hands, now lying injured and sheltered by his friends, all of them in danger; her parents awaiting the arrival of God knows who to interrogate them; and she herself, escaping like a disloyal coward. When she reached the trees, she pushed the cycle out of sight from below and sat in the shadow beneath two hefty overhanging oaks, wishing she'd thought to grab something to eat and drink before she set off. She settled as comfortably as was possible, laying her coat on last autumn's fallen leaves that were now bedding into the soil beneath.

Within half an hour she felt her eyelids closing and blinked furiously to try and remain awake, her attention never wavering from the entrance to the house below. Almost immediately, the unmistakeable rumble of a powerful car's engine floated upwards, carried clearly on the gusting breeze. Now fully focused, all her senses strained to analyse the scenario unfolding below her. When the vehicle appeared from under the trees, bouncing down the farm's rutted drive, she could see the fluttering pennants on either wing. It was surely Major Wolff's car? She dropped to her haunches and inched towards to the edge of the trees. The driver got out and opened the rear door. Yes, unmistakeably the major. Was that good or bad news? She hoped her mother would be more restrained than during her two previous encounters with the man.

After what could only have been a bare ten minutes, the major reappeared, saying something inaudible over his shoulder. He shook his head and got back into the car, which started immediately and was soon out of sight, despite the necessity for caution as it negotiated the uneven, tree-lined track. Élodie sat up again, briefly distracted by two young squirrels that had been playing in circles, their rust-red coats jewel bright against the dank forest floor. They fled into the leafy shadows, startled by her sudden movement.

She fidgeted for a further half an hour, constantly checking the unchanging scene at the farm. Was that, could that have been it—only a brief visit from the major? It seemed unlikely, but was there any point in sitting there all day waiting to see what transpired, when she couldn't influence the outcome anyway? Her mind had been revolving around where Michel, and doubtless Thierry, had stashed Félix. Could she risk taking a back road to the village to ask Guy, or might the Germans be watching the pharmacy because another member of her family lived there? She sighed at her own indecision, listlessly snapping the twigs that littered the ground due to the recent storms, and conscious that the earth was sufficiently wet for the moisture to have already penetrated her coat and begun to encroach on her dungarees. She stood and wriggled the damp garment away from her skin, snatched up the coat and righted her bicycle, which had slid down beside the tree against which she'd leant it.

She paused, trying to make up her mind where to go. How about the barn where she'd met Clémence for their eventful trip to the Manoir? The young agent's dazzling smile was still imprinted on her brain as she remembered Clémence's courage and coolness under pressure. All for what? A heap of life-endangering messages sent to the Allies in London, which may or may not have helped change the balance of the war, and some deftly taken photos from the major's office whose acquisition had put them both in jeopardy. And that beautiful girl was now dead. Élodie gripped the handlebars as she began to bump the machine along the root-encrusted woodland path, boiling with exasperation at her inability to influence events in this damned never-ending war.

Élodie chose not to follow the deer path that led to the road which passed the Manoir, and turned right through the clearing where she had found Félix on the night of his encounter with Rudi. She eventually emerged onto a wide forest track used by the woodsmen and made her way to the barn via a snaking set of twists and turns. It occurred to her that, paradoxically, even Michel would be proud of her navigational skills today.

She came to a halt where the trees thinned, listening acutely for any trace of human sounds. There were none. And the barn, she was disappointed to see, was firmly padlocked as usual. The sun had disappeared and drops of rain began to spatter on the canopy of leaves above her. She draped the now mud-plastered coat around her shoulders and double-checked the outside of the building to no avail. There was no sign that anyone had been here recently. She had no Plan B. Even if she deemed it worth the risk of trying to speak to Guy, would he give her any more information than Michel had? She doubted it and, besides, in her present mood the likelihood of encountering her sister at the same time was more than she could bear.

She cycled aimlessly for a couple of hours along small, unfrequented lanes, stopping in the next village where she knew the owner of the *épicerie*. She made an excuse for having no money and, with a promise to return the next day to make payment, picked up a bottle of local cider, two apples and a small hunk of cheese. The rain had stopped almost as soon as it had begun and her clothing was only slightly damp by the time she stopped by the river, well downstream from where Félix fished near the bridge. The simple food revived her, and she was glad to feel warmth surge through her veins. She glugged the cider straight from the bottle, wiping the drips from her chin when she'd satisfied her thirst.

At half-past four, impatience overcame her. She'd returned to her vantage point above the farm, where she had dozed in the afternoon sun, oblivious to the scamperings of small creatures on the forest floor and birds in the tree canopy above. She sat up, yawned and stretched. In the distance she spotted her father in the field nearest the house, guiding the horse-drawn muck spreader. Fuel for the tractor was almost impossible to source, she knew, and her mother worried constantly as the only alternative, hard manual labour, had taken its toll on his health during the previous winter. And now there was no Félix to help. Well, she could—and would—take his place for as long as necessary.

She jumped up and set off down the hill, cursing each time the handlebars hopped out of her hands when the wheels hit a bump. By the time she'd reached the farmyard, her mother was visible in the vegetable garden. She looked up and smiled, wiping her forehead on her sleeve as her daughter called to her. Élodie rushed over and hugged her mother, despite her protests that she was muddy from harvesting potatoes.

'Did they come today, Maman? Are you unharmed? Papa too?'

Rose threw up her hands, laughing as she did so. 'Too many questions, *ma fille*, as always!' She pointed towards the shed. 'Fetch that box of potatoes and I'll bring these other vegetables. We should go into the house.'

Élodie did as she was told, hurrying indoors, anxious to know that her parents hadn't suffered at the hands of the Gestapo. She'd grabbed the last of the cider from the cycle basket on her way, and took a long swig. She tore off a lump of baguette that still lay in a basket on the table and stuffed it into her mouth, half-choking as she saw her mother's disapproving expression.

She swallowed and coughed as the dry bread caught in her throat. A further mouthful of the cider helped her to regain her breath. 'Maman, *please*. What happened today? I saw the major this morning, but he wasn't here for long.'

'If you'd allow me to get a word in, I'll tell you.' Her mother's tone was patient as she pulled out one of the chairs and motioned for Élodie to sit. She joined her daughter at the table after washing her hands methodically, ignoring Élodie's fidgety finger-tapping.

'As you say, the major arrived this morning. I got the impression he was pleased you weren't here.' Her eyes searched her daughter's face, Élodie supposed for some comment, but, when no response was forthcoming, she resumed. 'He was, of course, looking for Félix. Surprisingly, he seemed to believe that we knew nothing. Unsurprisingly, your father was totally uncooperative, but the major merely warned us to expect a visit from the Gestapo, whose methods, he said, would be more direct than his own. And he left. Just like that.'

'And then?'

'Your father didn't want to leave me alone here, so he went and tinkered with the tractor in the barn. Sure enough, about an hour later, two most unpleasant men in leather coats arrived. They asked a lot of questions that they kept repeating, and they made various threats...'

'Please tell me they didn't hurt either of you, Maman.' Élodie cradled her mother's hands in her own, her anxiety rising.

Rose shook her head. 'Indeed they did not. I don't know why. But I doubt if we've seen the last of them.'

'Did they ask where I was? It didn't cause problems that I wasn't here?'

Her mother shrugged. 'I said you were staying with a friend in Argentan and that I didn't have the address. I'm not sure they believed me but eventually they seemed to tire of repeating themselves and left. We shall simply have to be alert for their next visit.' She made a face. 'I'm sure they'll be back—it's just a question of when.'

# CHAPTER TWENTY-TWO

## *May 1944*

RUDI RETURNED EARLY THE following morning. He shook his head regretfully as she flew at him, a question forming on her lips.

'I'm sorry, *Liebchen*, I haven't any answers for you. And if the major knows anything he's hiding it well.'

Élodie nodded slowly. The major. The germ of an idea began to form in her mind. Rudi was turning his cap in his hands, and she sensed from his agitation that he was in a hurry. There was no point in trying to press him further. If the major was being tight-lipped, he wasn't the kind to bow to pressure from a subordinate. But there were other means of persuasion with such a man.

'I can see you need to leave. But thank you for trying.'

She kissed him quickly as he began to apologise again, reassuring him before sending him on his way. He set off down the path to the road, the bike spitting up shards of compacted earth. He waved once when he reached the junction and was gone in a roar of acceleration. Élodie stared after him for several minutes, formulating her plan. She shuddered at the thought of what she must do, heaved a sigh and returned to her chores.

Élodie arrived at the Manoir shortly before midday. There was no sign of Mme Lagrange's Delahaye. It was market day in Flers, so she crossed her fingers that her calculations were correct and that was where Madame had gone. The major, however, was a different matter. HJHHis presence was uncertain, and she had no idea of her next move if he wasn't here. She stood astride her bike in the shrubbery and waited, alert to any movement.

After twenty minutes watching birds dart in and out of the trees, their melodious song irritating her today with its repetitiveness, her patience was rewarded when the front door opened and Major Wolff emerged, cigar in hand. He stood on the wide stone step at the top, smoking. He looked as pleased with himself as a cat who'd got the cream. Élodie's heart skipped a beat as she screwed up her courage, left her bicycle resting against the nearest tree and smoothed down her blue dress before emerging onto the gravel drive. The major's eyes instantly flicked towards her and narrowed as she walked confidently towards him.

So far, so good. He didn't speak until she stopped at the bottom of the steps. His tone was honeyed, which momentarily unsettled her. Had he known she would come? His question suggested not.

'Well, if it isn't Mamselle Duchamp. Why are you here?'

Feeling at a disadvantage while he towered over her, she ascended the steps and stood beside him outside the open front door. Before she could speak, and making no move towards her, he cocked his head to one side and tucked his thumbs confidently into his belt.

'Don't tell me. Let me guess. It concerns your missing brother, yes?'

Élodie wanted to smack the conceited smile off his face. Knowing that would prove self-defeating, she took a small step, closing the space between them, and waited to see if he would move away. He did not.

'*Alors*, major, I thought we could make a fair exchange.'

She saw the interest flare in his watchful eyes and pressed home her advantage. Seduction had never been her forte. She normally left that to the likes of Lisette, with her carefully waved hair and her fashionable high heels. But she had looked and listened over the years. She reached out with her right hand, laid it on the perfectly fitting field-grey jacket and slithered her fingers up the fabric. The top button was already undone. The major didn't move a muscle until she had unfastened the third, then, with tiger-like speed, caught her hand in his own and held it so forcefully that she gasped. He bent his head to within inches of her face.

'You'd better be clear about your intentions here, young woman.'

Despite the threat in his voice, she conjured up a provocative smile, lowering her eyelashes before looking upwards to meet the unblinking glint of his sharp-eyed scrutiny.

She fought to keep her voice soft and level. 'Are you interested in doing business, major?'

He stared at her without any change in his expression for so long that her nerve began to fail, then gave a peremptory nod. 'I will hear what you propose, yes. Come.'

He turned away and marched into the house. She re-examined the drive, serene and silent apart from the birds, before crossing the threshold into the dim light of the hall. On the table under the window, she noticed an exquisite arrangement of sweet-smelling blooms that had been artfully arranged in a huge glass vase, as if life were normal—as if there were no strife tearing half the world apart outside. Scurrying to keep pace with his long stride, she walked wordlessly alongside him up the stairs and down the corridor to his room. He held open the door for her, followed her inside and kicked it shut behind him. He spun her round to face him and crossed his arms, his tone still sceptical.

'Well? What is it you want from me?'

Élodie knew intuitively that directness was the only approach with this man.

'I want a piece of information that I'm sure you can give me. In exchange you may do whatever you want with me, and I will make it an occasion to remember.'

She watched him closely. The smouldering heat that filled his eyes, that suffused his whole face—although momentary—was clear to see. It was not the look of love that lit Rudi's face but something deeply carnal. At that moment a chilling lucidity sealed her determination. She'd hooked him, just as Félix would carefully lure a trout.

His voice was thick, despite clearing his throat. 'Why should I trust you?'

'Because, major, for one thing I am here, and for another I have given you my word.'

He considered this, his expression remaining suspicious. 'Go on.'

'I want to know who betrayed my brother to the Gestapo.'

The major laughed once, a short, hard, triumphant bark.

'Then I surely have the better half of the bargain. But you are quite certain you want to know? What is your best guess?'

Now he was playing cat and mouse. His teasing smile froze her. 'If I had any real idea, major, I wouldn't be here.'

'Well, suppose you keep your half of the bargain first, and then I will tell you.'

She surprised herself with her own boldness. 'No, that is not how it will be. First you will tell me, then I will do whatever you ask.'

'Very well. After all, you will have realised you have no means of escape.'

Élodie was all too aware of this but lifted her chin and faced him down. His answer, when it came, shocked her so profoundly that for a full minute she was speechless. She queried it just once, her voice beseeching, hoping for a different name. She watched him closely. 'It cannot be so.'

'Oh, but it is. And on that you have *my* word.'

Almost nothing could be worse than what she had been told a moment earlier. 'So be it, major. Now tell me what you want.'

As he conveyed his lewd wishes, Élodie felt her flesh grow cold. She fought an urge to scream, numbly took off her clothes and stood in front of him while his eyes roamed her figure. She stepped closer and unfastened his uniform button by button, first his jacket, then his breeches. She waited while he removed his boots, and submitted to his fantasy. She did not allow him to kiss her, jerking her head away each time he tried. But she had learnt how to please a man and her hands moved dextrously in the hope of curtailing the experience. His physique was thankfully still tight and trim, his muscles firm under her fingers. She noted with surprise that his overpowering cologne was missing. No forewarning he might wish to impress anyone today, she supposed.

She had no idea how much time passed before he was done with her. As she sat up, he stroked her hair but didn't try to restrain her. He lay back, hands behind his head, watching her retrieve her clothes.

'What a waste.'

Had she heard him right? 'What are you saying?'

'You are such a prize, and we could have shared so much all this time.'

If she had learnt any lesson in the recent past, it was not to rise impetuously to the bait. She therefore resisted the urge to antagonise him now, simply awaiting his next words.

'And now it will be too late.'

She frowned, unsure of his meaning.

'I'm under no illusions, Élodie. This war is almost lost. The Allies are advancing daily and soon we shall be gone—or dead.'

She swallowed the desire to say she wished the Allies had arrived sooner. Something made her glance at the chest of drawers beside the door. The picture of his wife and sons was no longer there. She looked back at the major, who had followed her gaze and now gave her an unfathomable half-smile.

'I shall not forget you, just the same.'

'Nor I you, major, believe me.'

She crossed to the door and looked back at him one last time.

'*Adieu, Herr Major.*'

As she closed the heavy front door, a huge parliament of rooks roosting in the tops of the tall trees across the drive laughed raucously in unison.

She struck out for Ste-Honorine, head down, pedalling strenuously. 'Life is full of surprises', he had said, 'some of them far from pleasant'. Angry tears stung her eyes as she rode towards the village. They were not for herself. She had made her pact with the devil and would now have to live with it, but the major's revelation was something else. His words still echoed in her ears. 'Your sister was so concerned about that precious husband of hers that she sang like a canary.'

The pharmacy door crashed on its hinges when she stormed in. Guy looked up in surprise. Élodie offered no preamble.

'Is Hélène here?'

Guy looked troubled.

'Élodie—I, she...'

'I've no time for niceties, Guy. Is my sister here or not?'

'Well, yes, she is, but she is busy upstairs with Lucie.'

'I need to see her. To speak to her. Now.'

He made only a feeble attempt to stop her as she lifted the counter flap and passed through. She made for the door at the back of the shop, but Guy caught her arm and blocked her way.

'Élodie, please.'

She shook her head obstinately. 'This is something I have to do, Guy.'

He stood aside and let her pass. She raced up the stairs two at a time. Lucie appeared on the landing, squealing with pleasure. Élodie picked her up and hugged her.

'Let me take you down to your Papa for a few minutes, *mon biquet*. I have to speak to your maman.'

As she turned towards the stairs, Helen appeared from the kitchen.

'Élodie, what—'

'Just you wait there, Hélène. I have things to say to you.'

Élodie didn't miss the fleeting look of fear that mired her sister's normally confident features. She was relieved to see that Guy had just served a customer who was leaving the shop. She handed over a protesting Lucie to her father.

'Look after her for a few minutes, please, Guy. I shan't be long.'

He began to say something but thought better of it and nodded mutely. Élodie hesitated at the foot of the stairs, corralling her anger, then hurtled up to look for Hélène, who had disappeared. She headed correctly for the kitchen. Her sister stood defensively by the cooker, a pan in her hands, her froideur regained.

'What makes you think you have the right to invade my home so rudely?'

'You know very well why I'm here, you traitor.'

If there was any vestige of shame in Hélène's expression, it was short-lived. Her voice was sharp, accusatory.

'You really don't understand, do you?'

How Élodie stopped herself from gripping her sister by the shoulders and shaking the piety out of her, she would never know.

'Oh, I certainly understand what you did. What I want to know is why. Why did you do it?'

Hélène's tone was petulant now. 'Because I have a husband and child.'

'And that made it right to betray your own brother to the Gestapo? The bloody Gestapo! Do you have any idea what they've done to him?'

'It was the major, not the Gestapo. And I didn't know he would be there.'

'He—Félix?' Élodie gripped the back of one of the chairs ranged perfectly under the table, forcing herself to keep her distance. 'What, exactly, are you saying?'

Hélène at last looked away, a wave of what Élodie hoped was at least discomfort clouding her eyes.

'They knew there was an English radio operator in the area working with the *Résistance*.' She stopped, presumably to gauge Élodie's reaction.

'And?'

Hélène glared at her. 'So, I told them what I overheard.'

'Overheard? When?'

'When Félix came to see Guy. I'd warned him before not to involve Guy. And besides, the actions of the *Résistance* have led to the deaths of many innocent French people.'

Hélène's defensive stance was not lost on Élodie.

'Including, almost, that of your brother.'

Élodie saw her sister's knuckles whiten as they gripped the pan tighter.

'I thought—I thought she would be alone. What's happened to him?' The words came out in such a whisper that Élodie strained to hear.

'*Putain*! At last you ask. What has happened to him is that he has been tortured in some rat-trap in Saint-Lô, and it's only thanks to the *Résistance*, which you seem so keen to despise, that he's been rescued.'

'There's no need for profanity, Élodie.'

Her sister's sanctimonious tone finally snapped the last shreds of her self-control.

'My God, there's no talking to you. You should be ashamed of yourself, yet you stand there complaining about profanity.' She moved slowly towards her sister. 'I sincerely hope you suffer for what you've done. A brave young woman is dead because of you.'

Hélène regarded her as if she were a specimen in a glass jar, like those Élodie had seen in museums in her schooldays. 'Tell me, how did you find out it was me?'

The question hung in the air. For a second, Élodie considered telling her sister exactly how she had found out, but she had already decreed that her self-debasement, the depths to which she had stooped, would be locked away permanently in a closed vault in her memory.

'You'll never know that. But I can tell you it cost me dearly. And as far as I'm concerned, you no longer exist.'

Hélène's expression remained set, like a sour-faced stone mask. She disclosed no emotion, made no attempt to absolve herself, even failed to express any sorrow for her brother, Élodie later realised. She would never fathom the woman who stood before her, who had been raised by the same mother, who was born of the same flesh and blood.

'*Adieu*, Hélène.' This was the second time she'd used that word today, that final goodbye. She shook her head and, with an infuriated sigh, turned her back on her sister and clattered down the stairs. In the pharmacy, she was relieved to find that

Guy was busy serving a customer. Lucie was sitting on a low stool, playing house with some empty boxes. Élodie picked her up, hugged her tenderly, kissed her warm, soft forehead and set her down again.

'*Au revoir, ma petite.*' Lucie's outstretched arms tore at her heartstrings, but she couldn't stay in this place. 'I'm sorry, *chérie*, I have to go.'

She squeezed Guy's arm as she lifted the counter flap. His uncomfortable smile told Élodie that he knew the unwholesome truth. Well, he too would have to live with that knowledge. Poor Guy. He had tried to help and had unwittingly led Félix into a trap. She apportioned no blame to him. He was far too principled a man to have gone along with such treachery.

'*Au revoir*, Guy.'

The shop door swung closed behind her and she picked up her bike, which she had flung to the ground when she arrived a bare fifteen minutes earlier.

# CHAPTER TWENTY-THREE

## May 1944

MICHEL WAS LATER THAN usual, but Élodie knew he would appear and had busied herself tidying the barn, which certainly needed it. He arrived at the gallop, tripping over the stool she'd pushed aside a few moments before he burst through the door. Élodie was suddenly overcome with relief. Dear, dependable Michel.

'I'm so sorry I'm late, Él.'

She noticed he'd adopted Félix's pet name for her. She kissed him on both cheeks and waved away his apologies.

'No matter. I'm so pleased to see you. How's Félix, and when can I see him?'

Michel laughed, his eyes bright with amusement. 'Always the same questions. He's getting better, growing stronger by the day. And I'll confirm with Thierry, but I think tomorrow I could take you to him.'

Élodie clapped her hands, then grew serious. 'Michel, there's something I need to ask you.'

'Oh?' He looked wary.

'Do you know how it happened? How Félix was captured, and Clémence...' She couldn't bear to think about the girl whose life had been sacrificed through her own sister's actions.

Michel indicated the hay bales and pushed her down gently onto the nearest, lowering himself to sit beside her.

'Should we not just accept that it was grossly bad luck?'

Élodie shook her head vehemently. 'You know something, I can see that. Michel, tell me. Please.'

Michel looked so uncomfortable that she briefly regretted her insistence. He stared at the floor, kicking at the loose hay. When he began to speak, she was glad she had persisted.

'We—Thierry and me—we think it has to have been Guy.'

'Why?' Élodie gave nothing away. She wanted to know more, to understand what had occurred on that terrible day.

'Because, when we'd completed our operation, Félix went with Clémence to send her message, and I left to fetch Guy. We got held up evading two Boche patrols, but when we were finally on our way back for them the Germans caught up with the truck.' He broke off, his voice choked with emotion. 'Rather than stopping us, they stormed straight past and went after the others. There was nothing we could do, Él. So what other conclusion is there?'

The injustice of this assumption was too much. Élodie took Michel's hands.

'Look at me, Michel. You're both wrong, you and Thierry—but you deserve to know the truth.'

She summarised her visit to the pharmacy, leaving out all reference to what had gone before.

'*Hélène?* It was definitely Hélène?'

She nodded and felt his hands tighten on her own. He frowned suddenly.

'How did you find out?'

'I won't tell you now, and I won't ever tell you. But you can believe me—regrettably it's the truth and she's admitted it.'

There was a brief, awkward silence.

'I suppose, Él, you have to accept she felt she had no choice.'

'No!' Élodie held up a hand to silence him. 'This is Félix's life we're talking about. And she knew that. She could have maintained all along that she didn't know anything.'

'She's not like you, Él.' His smile was soft as he ran his thumb across her chin.

'Thank God for that. Let's leave it there. I'm sure you'll want to tell Thierry, but maybe it can stay between the three of us?'

'And Félix?'

Élodie passed a weary hand across her brow. 'I don't know. Certainly not yet. Has he asked questions?'

'No. For now, he seems to think it was some awful twist of fate.'

'Then let him think that.' She stood, brushed the strands of hay off her dungarees and stared down at Michel's bowed head. He looked like a lost, defeated soul. She laid a hand on his tousled hair, her voice tender. 'I only hope it was all worth it, Michel.'

Michel gave her a subdued smile, his shoulders sagging with fatigue. 'That was Félix's first question as soon he was thinking straight. Those *salauds barbares* told him our strike was a pointless waste of effort because full production would resume within a couple of days. In fact, our inside source has confirmed those machines won't be rolling again for at least a couple of months, if ever.'

He put his hands on his knees, pushed himself to his feet with a weary sigh and took his leave, with a promise to return the following morning. Élodie was glad Félix had come to his own conclusions, and she had no intention of telling him otherwise unless it became unavoidable.

Élodie was up early the next day and completed all she had to do in record time. Every small noise distracted her as she collected the eggs and fed the chickens. Up at the house, she looked out of the door or a window so often that her mother begged her to stay still.

'I'm sorry, Maman', was her only repeated and lame apology.

At ten, her heart leapt at the sound of a motor close by. The long-limbed figure of Michel appeared seconds later, crossing the yard. She rushed out to meet him, bombarding him with questions. Had he come to take her to Félix? Was he in good spirits? Would he know she was coming?

Michel threw up his hands in self-defence. 'Yes, yes, and yes, Élodie. I've parked my motorbike down in the lane. Can you come now?'

Élodie turned and saw her mother watching from the kitchen doorway. Rose raised a hand to Michel, who returned her greeting but remained stationary when Élodie whispered 'Wait here'. She had no wish to compromise her parents' ignorance of their son's whereabouts lest the Germans return with further questions, or worse.

She ran indoors and grabbed a jacket. It might be chilly on the back of the bike. 'I'm going out for a while with Michel, Maman.'

'I take it you're not going to tell me where?'

Élodie tacitly blessed her mother's common sense. She knew when not to probe for information that would not be forthcoming.

'No, Maman, but I'll tell you more as soon as I can.'

'You'll be home for your meal at midday?'

'I'm not sure how far we're going, but I'll try.'

Her mother smiled. 'I'll ask no more questions. Tell that boy to be careful with you. I assume that was his motorbike I heard in the lane?'

Élodie laughed. Her mother missed nothing. '*Oui*, Maman. I'll tell him what you say.'

She re-joined Michel, sneaking her arm through his, but kept her own counsel as they set off down the path. Although she knew all the lanes near the farm well, it was quite impossible to follow Michel's sudden turns to left and right. Indeed, she would have sworn they passed the same broken farm gate twice, but the noise of the engine made conversation impossible. She had linked her arms around his waist, feeling the warmth of the sun on his back as she pressed her cheek against the sturdy flannel fabric of his blue shirt.

The bike slowed, at her reckoning, after about twenty minutes and bumped down a rutted lane. When it came to a halt, Élodie surveyed her surroundings. The building in front of her was obviously an old mill, but not one she recognised. Michel grinned at her evident puzzlement. She opened her mouth to ask where they were, but he had anticipated her inquisitiveness and tapped his nose.

'OK, I get it. No questions.'

Michel proffered his arm and led her into the mill. Thierry had just reached the bottom of a flight of perilous-looking wooden stairs as they entered. He greeted her warmly.

She looked at Michel and then up the stairs. He nodded and addressed Thierry, a restraining hand resting on her arm. 'Félix is awake?'

'Yes, and eager to see his sister. Go on up, Élodie. I'll bring us all some coffee, courtesy of Yvette.'

She crossed the bare room past the exposed stone mill wheel, its hefty curves chipped and moss-green with age. Michel followed. He stopped her at the foot of the steps. 'Él, be warned—he still doesn't yet look like the Félix you know.'

Despite the butterflies that fluttered in her stomach, she smiled as positively as she could. 'I'll be fine, thanks. Give me a couple of minutes alone with him, will you?'

At the head of the stairs, she pushed open the old, panelled door, its brown paint long faded. In a chair under the small window, Félix sat wrapped in a grey blanket. Élodie's hand flew to her mouth when she saw his two blackened eye sockets and swollen nose. His smile was tender but resigned as he looked across at her and shrugged. She went to his side and put her arms round him diffidently, afraid of hurting him.

'You've no idea how I've missed you, *mon frère*.'

'Or how glad I am to see you again, Él.'

She fetched the stool she had spied by the makeshift bed and placed it alongside his chair. She couldn't understand why it seemed to be such an effort for him to struggle out of his cocoon. She offered a helping hand but paused when he made a face. And then she saw his hands. She stifled an involuntary cry as she took in the bandages covering the splints Guy had placed on his fingers. He reached out a white bear paw and brushed away the tears that had sprung to her eyes.

She forced a smile. 'I'm OK, Félix. Just tell me what they did to you.'

He sucked in his cheeks, his eyes looking away. 'You know—'

'About Clémence?' Félix winced as she mentioned the name. 'Michel told me. And I'm so very sorry. I only met her once, but I liked her. She was brave. And beautiful. And I think that you loved her.'

She could see that Félix was struggling. She sat quietly by his side, one hand across his chest, as slowly and painfully he recounted the horrors of the twenty-four hours he'd spent in the hands of the Gestapo. Her jaw clenched so hard as she listened that it began to ache. She massaged it with her free hand and, as his voice faltered, providentially there was noise from the stairs and the others appeared from below, each carrying two bowls of coffee. Élodie took one for herself, which she set on the floor, and another for Félix. She held it up to him, intending to help him drink, but he waved one swaddled hand and laughed.

'Bandages make good insulation, Él. Thanks, but I've learnt to manage things for myself.'

The four of them sat and consumed the hot liquid, their conversation inconsequential for Félix's sake. After half an hour Élodie could see the strain on her brother's face, which had turned deathly pale, his forehead beaded with sweat. She patted Michel's arm.

'I don't want to tire him. Could you take me home?'

Félix gave his sister an indulgent smile. 'You never make me tired, Él. Well, almost never. But right now, I am pretty exhausted.'

'I'll come again. Soon.' She kissed his forehead and hugged him again. 'Stay safe, Félix.'

'I told you I wasn't planning to make my exit yet, Él. I'm doing my best to stick to that promise.'

When they reached the farmyard, Michel halted the bike alongside the old tractor that now stood by the water trough. Élodie dismounted.

'That'll be Papa home for his meal. You'd be welcome to join us.'

Michel declined the offer. 'I don't think so. I don't want to be put on the spot about Félix and his whereabouts.'

Élodie chuckled. 'You're just frightened of Papa, that's all.'

Michel's answering smile was sheepish. 'You're not wrong there. But thanks for asking. I'll come and update you tomorrow and take you back to Félix in a few days. He is getting stronger every day, you know.'

Élodie stared at the old stone wall of the farmhouse, her gaze coming to rest on the window of Félix's empty room before she replied. 'In all honesty, I think I'm glad I haven't seen him till now.'

'Not as glad as I am.' Michel was still sitting on the bike but leaned forward as she reached out and squeezed his shoulder. 'He'll be OK, Él. We have to give him time, that's all.'

Élodie inclined her head towards the kitchen. 'I can at least tell them I've seen him?'

'As long as you don't say where he is, then of course.'

'You are joking? You took more diversions than there are months in the year, and I was totally lost before we even got there.'

Michel looked pleased with himself. 'Let's keep it that way, eh?' With that, he revved the engine, took a wide turn to avoid the cat, which was padding purposefully out of the shade by the barn, and with a roar from the exhaust disappeared down the main drive towards the Flers road.

# Chapter Twenty-Four

## August 1944

Who on earth was making such a racket banging on the door at this hour of the morning? Élodie finished rubbing herself dry, flung on her work clothes and clattered down the stairs. Before she reached the door her mother appeared from the scullery, frowning at the disturbance as the knocking continued. Élodie spread her hands wide and shook her head before pouncing at the doorknob and yanking it savagely. Michel, gasping for breath, almost fell into her arms as the door opened.

'You've heard?'

'Michel! You're making enough noise to wake the dead. Heard what?'

'The Boche. They're leaving.'

He gave her a huge grin, wiped his sweat-plastered forehead, and lifted her into the air. When he set her down again, Élodie hugged him tight before turning to her mother and embracing her in turn. Her instant joy was suddenly replaced by a sobering realisation.

'When you say "leaving", Michel, what exactly do you mean?'

She saw the shine leave his eyes, and his smile faded. 'I mean a whole stream of German vehicles has passed what's left of Flers heading like scalded cats in the direction of Argentan.'

'If it's true and they're all going, Félix can come home at last.' Élodie squeezed her mother's hands. 'But, Maman, I must go out for a bit.'

'Oh?' Her mother's puzzled look took in both Élodie and Michel. He fingered the cap in his hands and said nothing, staring at Élodie with a knowing look that unsettled her, his open, honest face reflecting some inner unrest. No time to deal with this now, and she could certainly not give her mother any explanation.

'I won't be long, but there's something I need to do.'

She gave her mother a swift kiss, patted Michel on the arm, and rode off as fast as she could pedal.

Before she even reached the gateway to the Manoir, four military vehicles came down the drive at speed, gravel spinning away from their speeding wheels. Behind them, she recognised the Major's staff car, its pennants fluttering from either front wing. She came to a halt and dropped her bike onto the verge. An officer she didn't recognise was sitting beside the driver. When the car pulled alongside her, she saw that Major Wolff was in the back with another man. The vehicle slowed to turn left, and she was now able to see that the third passenger was Rudi. She was filled with a mixture of relief and despair, aware of a pulse racing in her temple as she watched the convoy.

The car screeched to a halt twenty yards down the road, its red brake lights blazing bright despite the morning sunshine. She took a step back as the rear door opened and the Major emerged. He strode towards her, his expression unreadable. The ice-blue eyes were sober, straying neither to left nor right.

'So, here you are yet again, Mamselle.'

Élodie longed to wipe the resigned smile from his face. 'Meaning?'

'You have come to gloat? Or, more likely,' he glanced over his shoulder, 'to bid a final *adieu* to the Lieutenant?'

So, it was true. They were retreating. So much to celebrate, to be free at last of this man who now stood in front of her—this man in whose presence she still felt agitated, even knowing she would likely never set eyes on him again. She had tried innumerable times to rationalise the overpowering sensations he aroused in her: he exuded an inexplicable aura of animal magnetism—repellent to her rather than attractive, but it was a moth-to-the-flame pull that was as strong as it was terrifying. She resisted the urge to clutch at her tightening stomach muscles, her hands automatically dropping to her abdomen, and stood firm as he took one more step.

'You are my one regret here, you know.' His voice was calm, gentle almost.

Hers was the opposite, she knew, both accusatory and hostile. 'How so?' Why did he not simply leave, and leave her alone?

'I have told you before. We could have been perfect lovers, if only you had been as willing as you were when you wanted something from me.' He hesitated. 'Maybe I was partly at fault after all. If I would have taken things more slowly...'

His eyes never left Élodie's face, seeming to seek some reassurance, a response to satisfy his wounded pride. This time, remembering how unpredictably he exploded into anger, she chose not to react and instead turned her head towards the Manoir, registering the dust motes that still swirled and danced above the driveway from the rush of the departing vehicles. A sudden exclamation from the Major recaptured her attention and she scanned his face as his expression changed.

'There's something different about you today.' He took a step back and his penetrating gaze dropped to her clasped hands. 'Are you pregnant? *Verdammt, du dummes Mädchen!*'

Élodie was stunned by his words. She knew whatever he was saying wasn't complimentary, but as for his implication... 'No, no of course not.' She'd been sure her monthly cycle was affected by all the recent turmoil. The alternative had not even crossed her mind.

'Don't lie to me, Élodie.' He reached out and held her chin in a gloved hand. 'I have two fine sons, as you recently so kindly reminded me. I could tell immediately each time my wife was expecting.'

'I'm hardly likely to forget your wife and children.' She knew she should not provoke him but, somehow, in that moment, it was irresistible. 'And if I had "responded" as you put it, you would have left them for me? I think not.'

The major laughed. The sound was harsh, low, unsettling. 'Don't push me too far.' He paused and gave her a calculating look. 'Does he know?'

'Does who know what?' Élodie was afraid now. Afraid of what this man, with his seemingly endless power, might do next.

'Don't take me for a fool.' The major's next icy words chilled her to the marrow. 'Perhaps I may sow a seed in the Lieutenant's mind. Maybe you get the pun?'

Élodie stood her ground. 'So far as I know, there are none to sow.'

The major was still watching her. What *was* the emotion that shone in his eyes? It now looked like a glint of amusement. She stared in mute disbelief as the ghost of a smile hovered briefly on his lips before he delivered his parting shot.

'But then again, it may not be his at all.'

Rendered rigid with shock by those ten small words, she peered past him towards the car at the sound of a door slamming. Rudi had emerged and was half-visible directly behind the major, standing by the vehicle with hands on hips. A frown creased his forehead as he took a pace and removed his cap. Élodie smiled involuntarily as the endearing comma of blond hair fell across his brow. The major had let her go as he swivelled to pinpoint the source of the noise. He held up an admonitory hand.

'You can get back in the car, Lieutenant. We are leaving.'

The major turned back to Élodie and gave her a long, hard look. Did she now see a glimpse of regret, a flash of humanity, or was she imagining it?

Rudi stepped crisply into her line of vision. He pressed his mouth to his glove and turned his palm to her. She observed the expression of contempt on the face of the outrider who sat astride his motorcycle six feet from the car. *Tant pis*. At least she had made it to the Manoir in time.

The major gave her one last sweeping scan from head to toe, as if imprinting her on his mind. Then, with an almost imperceptible, meditative headshake, he turned and walked away. The instant he got into the car, she heard the clunk of gears and the motorcade pulled away, two grey caps visible side by side through the rear window. Neither of the back-seat passengers turned his head as the car accelerated in a cloud of desiccated mud. A huge sigh escaped her lips as she bent to retrieve her discarded bicycle, her fingers strangely steady as she righted it, but a pummelling surge of horror and emptiness hit her as she stood alone in the road. She stared after the car till it disappeared over the brow of the hill.

Élodie sat nursing her coffee bowl two days later, willing herself to drink the unappetising liquid but overcome by a strong feeling of nausea. The major's last words swirled in her brain. This was the third day she had rejected her breakfast. Today, as she had pushed her plate away and fled from the kitchen with a hand over her mouth, her father had challenged her.

'Don't waste good food, my girl, when others have none. Besides, if you're going to help me today, you need the nourishment.'

She'd also heard his comment to her mother as she ran up the stairs.

'What's wrong with the girl? Is she ill or something?'

Once the queasiness had passed, she had come downstairs again, dressed for work. Her mother had watched without comment as she put on her jacket, and she had avoided eye contact. As she'd concentrated on pulling on her boots, her mother had spoken at last.

'Papa is in the bottom field. He said you should join him there.'

Élodie had buttoned her jacket, looking towards the open air, praying for no awkward questions. 'Thank you, Maman. I'll see you later.'

'Élodie!'

She had paused on the threshold at her mother's commanding tone. 'Oui, Maman?'

'Is there anything you want to tell me?'

'Non, Maman.'

After all, she thought as she re-ran the scene in her mind, willing herself to keep down the coffee, there was nothing she knew for sure herself—yet. And nothing she therefore needed to share.

She had returned to the house after two hours helping her father turn the hay. The kitchen door was open wide, and the birdsong was achingly sweet in the warm morning sunshine that flooded in, striking the corner of the table where she sat engrossed in her thoughts.

She strained to hear another noise that diverted her attention. Was it...? Yes, it was a motor and it sounded like Thierry's truck. She scrambled to her feet and called to her mother, who had come into the scullery from the vegetable garden. The two women hurried into the yard as the truck came into view. Thierry beeped the horn in greeting. Sitting beside him was Félix, who leant out of the side window as they came to a stop. When he clambered out, Élodie stood back. This visit was for their mother, who had not seen Félix since early June. Rose opened her arms to her son, but her eyes darted in instant dismay to his disfigured hands. He gathered her into a firm hug to forestall too many questions.

Thierry stayed only briefly, pleading a plethora of tasks that awaited his attention, though Élodie sensed his discomfiture. She knew he would consider this a family event at which he was an intruder—for all his tough exterior, she knew that a soft heart beat within that bulky torso. She accompanied him into the brightness of the yard, speaking only when they reached the truck.

'Has Félix asked any more questions about what happened that night?'

Thierry shook his head. 'Not really. He started to ask Michel something one day but, when Clémence's name was mentioned, he clammed up and dropped the subject.'

Élodie gazed towards the house. 'Maybe it's better that way.'

Thierry opened the cab door and climbed into the truck. 'I'd say yes, certainly for the time being.'

'And, Thierry...' He paused with the door half shut. 'Thanks for all you and Yvette have done—are doing—for him.'

'*De rien, ma belle*. I'll come back for him in an hour.'

He slammed the truck into gear, gave her a wink and a gap-toothed grin, and drove off with another toot of the horn.

In the kitchen, their mother was fussing over Félix, who was tolerating it all with easy-going acceptance.

'Ah, Élodie. I was just telling Félix that when you were visiting him yesterday, Hélène was here.'

'Oh?' Élodie stiffened. She tried to stem the fierceness in her voice and clenched her fists in her pockets.

'Yes, and she was so worried about Félix. She—'

This was too much. Élodie slapped both hands on the table. *'Elle est tellement hypocrite!'*

She shouted so harshly that her mother flopped down on the nearest chair with a thump. Félix leant across the table and smacked her hand, drawing in a sharp breath as he made contact.

'Élodie, *arrête!*'

Félix never used her full name unless he was truly annoyed with her. She rounded on him. 'If you only knew.'

'Knew what?' Her mother's voice was unaccustomedly cold. 'Don't say anything you might regret, my girl. And don't make any false accusations against your sister.'

The warning was clear. Élodie took a deep breath, then another.

'Maman—*et toi*, Félix—you have no idea what Hélène has done.' She jutted her chin out and sat down at the table level with her mother and brother. In the ensuing silence, the tension was as taut as a tripwire.

Félix continued to stare at her, his eyes sparkling with anger. She watched as his facial expression altered, the fury replaced by dawning doubt. She turned to their mother, who looked as if all the stuffing had been knocked out of her, her face pale, her eyes full of grief.

Élodie knew she had backed herself into a corner from which there was no way out but to present them with the facts. She shuffled her chair closer to her mother's.

'I'm so very sorry, Maman, but the truth will come out one day, so you may as well know it now. I—'

They both turned to Félix as he interrupted. 'Does this concern me and Clémence?'

Élodie nodded, her mind and her stomach in turmoil.

Félix leant back with a sigh and closed his eyes. 'Go on, then. Get it over with.'

Élodie hardly recognised her own shaky voice. 'It was Hélène who betrayed Clémence to the Germans and, by extension, you *mon frère*.'

'Could someone please explain to me who this girl is that you're talking about?'

'She was an English radio operator sent to work with the *Résistance*, Maman.' Élodie caught Félix's eye. 'Well, half-French actually.'

'I still don't understand.'

'I think you do, Maman. At least, you'd half-guessed. You've asked me countless times what Félix was up to, but he—we—didn't want you to know anything that could compromise you or Papa.'

Félix had obviously been thinking it through. 'Who told you it was Hélène, Él?'

'You don't need to know how I found out, but I knew it must be true.' She stole a quick look at her mother, who was sitting bolt upright following every word. 'I went to the pharmacy and confronted her, and she admitted it.'

'*Putain!*'

Félix apologised promptly for swearing in their mother's presence. They watched her push herself up from the table, her shoulders sagging in acknowledgement.

'I think I've heard enough for one day. I have your father's dinner to prepare.'

'Maman, I—'

'Enough, Él.'

Élodie heeded Félix's rebuke. She knew he was right. There was nothing more to say, even though her sister's duplicity was still burning a hole in her gut.

Her offer of help was refused, their mother turning her back on them as she walked wearily to the stove. Félix steered his sister towards the door.

'Let's take a walk round the yard. I could certainly do with the exercise.'

Outside, Élodie realised how extensive her brother's injuries must have been. His pace was slow and hesitant, though he was neither limping nor in obvious pain as far as she could see, apart from his hands. He bent to stroke the cat when it rushed up to him, meowing with pleasure at his return, but stood with difficulty, wincing again as he did so.

'What hurts, *mon ours?*'

Félix's laugh was cynical. 'What doesn't hurt might be a better question.'

Élodie tucked her arm through his and fell into step with him as they resumed their circular trajectory.

'I didn't mean to hurt Maman, you know that?'

'I do. But how *did* you find, out, Él? Through your German friend, I suppose?'

Élodie's heart skipped a beat, a vision of the major blocking rational thought. She brushed it away, knowing Félix was instead referring to Rudi. Should she just say yes? Somehow, she couldn't bring herself to lie to him, not even for expedience. She stopped and turned to face him.

'Félix, I can't tell you. It's something I'll have to live with, that I'll never share with anybody. But I can promise you that what I've told you is the beastly, awful truth. And I feel ashamed to call her my sister.'

He gathered her into that comforting brotherly hug that promised all would be right with the world and held her close until she felt the coiled spring of her mind slowly unwinding.

# CHAPTER TWENTY-FIVE

## August 1944

ÉLODIE SURVEYED THE EARLY morning sky and was mesmerised by a stunning vista. A pearlescent blue shone behind a lattice of lilac-grey cloud, which leached into a broad band of oyster hue. Where sky met earth, a glowing blush peach brushed the horizon. She stopped to marvel at Nature's beauty, still enduring despite the carnage that warring mankind continued to wreak below.

She'd wandered out into the lane beyond the henhouse, her fingers rippling the long unmown grass as she walked. The chickens were fed, the air was fresh, and it was such a beautiful morning that she wanted to linger before returning to the house and the highs and lows engendered by her father's reports on the latest Allied advances and retreats. Nevertheless, they were very near now and the sound of artillery was frighteningly loud, but so far today there was a lull. Someone at the bar in the village, which Henri had taken to frequenting each evening to gather the latest news, swore he had seen soldiers—he couldn't say whether British or American—on the outskirts of Ste-Honorine only yesterday.

When she was a hundred yards down the narrow, dusty road she heard the now familiar barrage of gunfire begin. She sighed and began to retrace her steps. She was startled by the sound of a rasping wheeze, followed by a moan, from the dense greenery that bounded the hedgerow. As she stopped to locate the source, she spied a khaki-clad leg. Its owner was obviously prone and certainly unmoving.

'Bonjour... 'Ello. *Qui est là?*'

Her heart was pitter-pattering in her chest as a figure rose slowly from the undergrowth onto one elbow. She thought the greenish-brown battledress signalled a British uniform and tried to summon up the small amount of English she had absorbed at school, wishing she'd paid more attention.

'You are who, *Monsieur?*'

The pale, solemn face, half-covered in dried blood, split into a smile. Its owner coughed and Élodie was alarmed to see him wipe away fresh blood from his mouth. He replied in French, albeit comically accented, '*Bonjour, Mamselle. Je m'appelle Richard.*'

Élodie ventured closer and shook his outstretched hand. She judged him to be older than her, the same age as Félix or perhaps Rudi. He had an open, appealing face with a crooked, previously broken nose. '*Enchanté, Monsieur Richard. Et moi, je m'appelle Élodie.* You can rise?'

He nodded. 'Think so.' He grimaced as he struggled to get up. Élodie went to his aid, registering his sinewy build as she heaved his arm across her shoulders to support him.

'You come. Yes? I live here.' She pointed towards the farmhouse, hidden from view by the curve beyond the hen run. He nodded but stumbled as he tried to put his left foot to the ground. Élodie noticed the ragged tear in his trouser leg, edged worryingly in dark, congealed blood. The two made their way achingly slowly up the path. The soldier exhaled with relief when they reached the farm buildings and grunted with pain as Élodie helped him rest against the water tank in the yard. She indicated that he should stay there and ran indoors.

Her father swivelled round from his usual seat at the table as she arrived breathlessly in the kitchen. 'Papa, I need your help. There is a wounded Tommy outside, well, he's from the Allies anyway. I found him near the henhouse. Where's Maman?'

Henri stared past her through the kitchen window, though the soldier was out of sight from that angle. 'Your mother's out collecting vegetables. I'll help the soldier. You fetch your mother.'

By the time Élodie and her mother reached the kitchen, the young man was sitting beside Henri at the table, his face now drained of all colour, his breathing laboured. Her mother took quick stock of the situation.

'We need to get him out of sight. And quickly, just in case. Henri, you take one side, I'll take the other. Élodie, you go ahead and fetch some towels and put them on Félix's bed, then bring me some warm water, a cloth and the disinfectant you'll find in the larder.'

Élodie remembered the last time she'd gone looking for antiseptic, to attend to Félix's head wound. Her parents still knew nothing of that incident, dismissed by Félix as a triviality when his mother questioned the darkly bruised but closed gash on his forehead the next day.

By the time she'd gathered everything together and reached the first floor again, her father had been dismissed. He met her at the head of the stairs and shrugged. 'Surplus to require- ments' was his only growled comment as he stomped off to finish his coffee in the kitchen. Élodie stifled her amusement.

The two women propped up the wounded soldier with sev- eral pillows and Rose cut open his trouser leg with her sewing scissors, struggling with the stiff khaki drill fabric despite the sharpness of the blades. She grunted when she saw the extent of the injury, but light pressure and movement of the leg elicited only a few gasps and no loud cries. She looked up at her daughter.

'I don't think there are any broken bones. I'll do what I can, but this needs stitches.'

To Élodie's astonishment, this was conveyed to the young man in slow but apparently perfect English. She then recalled that, in her dressmaking days, her mother had had as a client at least one high-society Englishwoman, who had spent her summers sea-bathing at Deauville and had later kept in touch, even claiming to have met Flaubert on the famous *planches* in 1924.

She hesitated for a few seconds, surveying the angry-looking wound. 'Maman, do you think... What about Guy? I could ask him to help—I know he can do stitches because Hélène's boasted about it more than once.'

Her mother frowned. The soldier was twisting in discomfort as he tried to make himself more comfortable, looking from one to the other of them as he sought to follow the discussion. Rose patted his hand. 'Guy is a member of the family. And a pharmacist.' She turned to Élodie. 'Yes, that's a good idea *chérie*. Go and see if he's free to make a visit.'

Élodie headed for the door and listened in admiration as her mother asked the soldier when he'd last eaten. One day she too would learn more English. She'd understood most of what was being said, but as for producing a full sentence herself... Out of the question!

Guy was alone when she reached the pharmacy, apart from Madame Leroy who was complaining that she needed something for her nerves. Élodie gave her brother-in-law a sympathetic smile from behind the solid, black-clad back of his customer and busied herself looking at the now meagre range of products on the stack of shelves to her right. It took ten minutes for Guy to find something the woman hadn't already tried, patiently replacing each item as she rejected it with a dismissive wave of her hand. How did he remain so good humoured? Finally, Madame accepted a made-up potion of some kind and hmphed at Guy's words of advice. She gave Élodie a sour look as she swept past her and crashed the door shut as she exited.

Élodie raised her eyebrows. Guy adopted his professional smile in return, though with a distinct reserve. 'Bonjour, Élodie, I was wondering when we might see you again. What can I do for you?'

Élodie had no quarrel with Guy and was only thankful Hélène was not in sight. She double-checked that she hadn't missed anyone lurking in a shadowy corner, and explained the problem.

Guy listened attentively, then looked at his watch. 'How urgent is it? I'll be closing for lunch in an hour.'

'That should be fine. But Maman says at least one wound will definitely need stitching.'

'Hmm—seems I've missed my vocation.'

Élodie had no idea what Guy meant and he didn't offer to enlighten her, but she left with his assurance that he'd be there within an hour and a half and would bring all the necessary equipment. He was such a dear man. She couldn't help thinking he deserved better than her sister for a wife, but she made a mental note not to say that in her mother's hearing.

When she arrived home, there was no sign of her father. She could hear voices in Félix's room, where she found their unexpected visitor was sitting up in bed being fed soup. He already looked better, a healthier pink shade now suffusing his cheeks. She reassured them both that Guy would be on his way shortly and offered to take over the feeding duties. Her mother seemed pleased, handing her the bowl and spoon and adjusting her crumpled apron as she got up.

'I'll go down and start preparing the midday meal, so I'll be on hand when Guy arrives.'

Left alone with the stranger, Élodie promptly felt tongue-tied with shyness, especially now he was alert and attentive and smiling broadly. She moved close enough to offer him a spoonful of soup with the least likelihood of spilling it, and wrinkled her nose unthinkingly at the smell of sweat and unwashed human that was now evident in the warm environs of the house.

The soldier responded with an apologetic smile, again practising his respectable French skills as he explained. 'I'm afraid we haven't had a chance to do our ablutions for, well, probably three days now.' He ran a hand over his rough-haired chin. 'Or shave, for that matter.'

'No, it's for me to apologise, that was rude of me.' Élodie spoke slowly. She wanted to kick herself for embarrassing him. 'Either Maman or Guy, my brother-in-law the pharmacist, will help you with all that later, I'm sure.'

Richard winked at her. 'You're not offering, then?'

Élodie knew she was blushing and looked down at the counterpane. This was ridiculous—after all, she had a brother of about the same age, so it wasn't as if men's bodies were a mystery to her. Especially not after... She closed her mind to all thoughts of Rudi, or for that matter the major, calmed herself and looked Richard straight in the face. 'No, not even for a representative of our liberators, which I know you'll soon be.'

Richard sighed deeply. 'I wish, Élodie, that were already the case. I have to admit it's proving a harder task than we originally hoped. But there is progress and I'm confident that we're winning, if slowly.'

'But at what cost to the people of Normandy—and to the Allied troops too? Please, I don't mean to sound ungrateful, but they're saying almost seventy per cent of Flers has already been destroyed and the fighting's not over. And that's only the one local town I know of.' Élodie offered another spoonful of soup as he opened his mouth to reply.

She decided there was nothing further either of them could usefully add, and the only sound to break the ensuing amicable silence was the scraping of the spoon round the bowl.

Guy's arrival was heralded by Blaireau barking madly from his favourite vantage point. He had been lying draped across the kitchen threshold and rose laboriously to challenge the newcomer. Élodie watched from the bedroom window as Guy, unused to domestic pets of any kind, called a greeting but kept his distance. She knew that the old dog would be in his element, still able to score a victory despite his advancing age. His still-bushy tail wagged as her mother came into view, caught him by the collar and remonstrated with him affectionately.

Élodie went out onto the landing as Guy trotted up the stairs. She led him into Félix's room. Both men accepted her offer of coffee, and on her return with a loaded tray she was astonished to hear her brother-in-law holding a conversation in fluent English.

Guy chuckled. 'Don't look so surprised, Élodie. Have you forgotten that my grandmother is English?'

How she envied him and her mother. To slip from one language into another—as Rudi did too, between German and French—was a skill she longed to possess. She had so far learnt a few dozen German words, but that was all. Well, so be it. Maybe one day, but for now there was too much else to do. She saw from the corner of her eye that Richard was watching her closely, a pensive smile on his face. Perhaps he would teach her some new words in English while he was here.

In the meantime, Guy had concluded his examination and confirmed that there were no broken bones as far as he could tell. He had cleaned and dressed the leg injury, explaining to each of them in turn, in French for Élodie, that it was most likely a bullet had shredded muscle fibres in Richard's thigh before exiting cleanly, apart from the ragged exit wound and the bleeding, without doing further damage. He was unsure as to the cause of the head injury, but this too had now been attended to. The bloody cough he attributed to a chest infection the soldier had probably contracted from lying exposed to the elements. Élodie sat and listened as he and Richard finished their coffee, unable to follow all of what was being said but understanding that it concerned the Allies' progress to date since their arrival in France in early June.

# CHAPTER TWENTY-SIX

## August 1944

AFTER FOUR DAYS OF the antibiotics provided by Guy plus his regular visits to check on his patient, Richard's colour had returned to normal. His recovery had been aided not a little by rest and good country food, for which he never-endingly expressed his appreciation.

Élodie knocked on the door as usual to deliver his breakfast. She set down the tray, plumped the pillows behind the soldier and was surprised to hear Blaireau barking excitedly. On her way to the window to check the cause, she saw that her mother had laid out on the bedroom chair some old but serviceable clothes of Félix's. It had already been planned that Richard would get up and be helped downstairs to eat with the family at lunchtime. She gauged that the trousers would be too short for their tall guest, but at least he would have something to wear until his uniform was fully dry and mended following her mother's sterling efforts to rid the fabric of mud and blood.

No one was evident in the yard, and she had to lean out perilously far before she could spot a khaki-uniformed soldier with two light-gold chevrons on his sleeve hovering in the doorway. She called to him to wait and ran downstairs, pulling the bedroom door almost closed behind her as a precaution.

The fresh-faced young man pulled off his forage cap and stuffed it into a pocket when she appeared, plastering back his wayward sandy hair from his freckled face with his free hand.

'Good morning, miss.' He gave Élodie a cheeky smile, exposing a chipped upper tooth as he did so.

'*Bonjour, monsieur. Je peux vous aider?*'

His face fell. 'I'm sorry, miss, I don't speak French.'

Élodie heard footsteps behind her, and her mother joined her at the door, wiping floury hands on her apron.

The young man began again. '*Bonjour, madame.* That's all my French, I'm afraid. I'm looking for a mate of mine.'

'And he would be...?'

The soldier's grin returned, and his shoulders relaxed. Her Maman had that effect on most men, Élodie had noticed, with the exception of a certain German major.

'He'd be Richard Brooks, my Lieutenant, ma'am.'

Élodie glanced at her mother, whose expression remained benign but gave away nothing.

'And is he lost, young man?'

The corporal laughed. 'You could say that I suppose. Our tank took a hit in the battle near here earlier this week and we ain't seen him since.' He took the cap from his pocket and began twisting it between his fingers. 'I'm hoping he ain't copped it. I got permission to come back and look for him today.'

Élodie could see from her puzzled frown that even her mother didn't entirely comprehend. At that moment a voice floated down from above.

'I'd know that voice anywhere. What the devil's led you here, Chalky?'

She looked up and saw Richard leaning on the windowsill, clad in Félix's old blue shirt that hung free from his shoulders. He clearly hadn't had time to tackle the buttons.

'May he come up, Madame Duchamp?'

The two women stepped back to allow the corporal indoors. Blaireau was now sitting watchfully in the kitchen doorway. Before Élodie could warn him, Corporal White strode over and held out a hand to the dog, who promptly allowed himself to be stroked and fussed over.

'I've a dog at home much like him. Your lad's a lovely old feller.'

Élodie beckoned him to follow her up the stairs. Her mother had preceded them, and when they reached the bedroom Richard had been helped into the too-short trousers and had buttoned up the shirt, albeit unevenly.

The corporal beamed, taking in the clean if simple room. 'Blimey, you've landed on yer feet, Sir. Looks like you're leading the life of Riley. Took me a long time to find you—must've knocked on fifty doors!'

The two women looked at each other, Élodie completely lost and even her mother struggling with the vernacular. A three-way conversation followed, during which Chalky was able to explain that his unit had been obliged to move on without their lieutenant after the battle, because they couldn't locate him. The corporal had apparently today 'borrowed' a pedal-bike—Richard's eyebrows rose sceptically at this point in the exchange—and proposed to return on the following day with transport to take the lieutenant to the nearest field hospital, which it transpired had been set up in the grounds of the Manoir. Élodie wondered how Madame Lagrange was faring with her new guests.

Élodie looked up as Richard came down the stairs for breakfast. He was limping heavily on his injured leg but otherwise much restored. He was still clad in Félix's old clothes for now, a clear two-inch gap visible between the trousers and the top of his socks. It had been decided that he should not don his cleaned and repaired uniform until Chalky was due later. They had all agreed with Henri's declaration the previous evening that there was no point in throwing caution to the wind too soon.

Richard ate with gusto, expressing his gratitude for the care the family had given him. As the old hall clock struck seven-thirty, Henri grunted and heaved himself up from the table. He shook Richard's hand in formal fashion and wished him well for the onward Allied advance, and with a gruff nod to the two women put on his boots and left for the fields.

The ensuing good-natured silence was broken when Richard looked from Rose to Élodie and back.

'You know, madame, your daughter reminds me of my wife. She has the same spirited nature. I have a picture of her somewhere I'd like to show you.'

Rose gave a small gasp and delved into the drawer beneath the tabletop. 'Thank goodness you said that. I found this in your breast pocket and put it away safely while I was cleaning your uniform.' Richard took the dog-eared photo from her, and Élodie didn't miss his affectionate smile as he ran his finger over the matt image.

'*Je peux?*' She held out a hand and Richard handed over the sepia picture. A vivacious young woman with dark wavy hair smiled up at her. She laughed as she handed it back. 'She's very pretty, but her hair is a great improvement on mine.'

Richard grinned. 'She'd just had it done when this was taken. Believe me, it looks quite different after a windy walk along the cliffs at home.'

Élodie excused herself to go and let out the hens. 'I'll be back before you leave, and anyway, I'll hear the corporal if he arrives.'

When she returned to the house, her mother was busy in the kitchen and Richard had disappeared to his room. Within a few minutes she heard the loud roar of an engine on the drive and reached the door as the Jeep that Chalky had managed to scrounge made a tight and noisy turn in the yard, much to the disgust of the cat, which shot away with a loud yowl.

Chalky gave her a shamefaced grin. 'Sorry about the cat, miss. Didn't see it at first.'

'No harm done. *Entrez.*'

She beckoned him in. He followed obediently, snatching his cap off his sandy hair as he entered the house. The kettle was singing on the stove and her mother turned to offer him coffee, apologising for the foul brew they had never grown used to drinking.

''Scuse me a minute, ma'am. I quite forgot.' Chalky rushed out and returned brandishing a packet of genuine coffee.

Élodie watched in amusement as her mother clapped her hands with pleasure. She took the welcome donation and stroked the packet reverently. 'Where on earth did you get this?'

Chalky's grin spread from ear to ear. 'I won it off a Yank playing cards, ma'am. Thought you might like it, somehow.'

Richard joined them a few minutes later, sniffing appreciatively as the aroma reached his nostrils. Chalky jumped up and saluted the officer, now in uniform once more. 'Blimey, Sir, wish I could get someone to smarten up my togs like that!'

Élodie was stumped by the English argot. Her mother was beaming, so she guessed she had understood.

As soon as they had finished their coffee, Chalky began to fidget. 'I'm sorry, Sir, but I think we'd best make a move. I was told to come straight here and take you to the field hospital right away.'

Richard slapped him on the back, laughing heartily. He turned to Élodie and her mother, his expression now solemn. 'I don't have words, certainly not in French, to thank you enough for all you've done for me. One day I hope to come back when the world's at peace again, and bring my wife to meet you.'

Richard shook hands politely with Élodie's mother, then bent impulsively to kiss her cheek. Élodie pivoted towards Chalky as a sudden thought struck her.

'I don't suppose you're going to Flers after you've taken your lieutenant to the field hospital at the Manoir?'

Chalky's puzzled frown lifted as Richard began to translate for her. 'I am indeed, miss.'

'And it's true that the town was liberated yesterday at last?'

Chalky nodded, then grimaced. 'It was, miss, but it's a helluva mess.'

Élodie felt fear contracting her gut. 'Maman, I'm worried about Michel. May I go, if I'm allowed to ride in the truck, to see if I can find him?'

'But of course, chérie.' Rose turned to the two soldiers. 'May she come with you?'

The two men spoke in unison, Chalky in English, Richard in French. 'With pleasure, madame.'

Élodie sat between the two men in the Jeep as it bumped its way along the lanes. They chatted about their unit's progress, Richard haltingly passing on the gist of the conversation to Élodie, though she presumed she was hearing the censored version. When the Jeep turned into the drive at the Manoir, Élodie was astonished to see the lawn covered in large tents, between which scurried both nurses and men in uniform. There was no sign of Madame Lagrange. She clambered out of the truck after Richard, who held open his arms. Shyness overcame her again at the intimacy of receiving and returning an affectionate hug. Richard repeated his intention to return to Normandy one day, his thanks unreserved. Élodie climbed back into the Jeep, swallowing the lump in her throat. Yet another goodbye. The two men disappeared into the Manoir and Élodie sat watching the activity until Chalky returned.

'Doc's seeing him now, miss. Next stop Flers.'

Élodie wrinkled her brow at his English. The short journey passed mostly in silence, but when the outskirts of the town came into view Élodie cried out in dismay. Chalky stopped the Jeep. He patted her hand and spoke slowly.

'I'm so sorry, miss. It must be quite a shock to see it.'

Élodie stared at him, her eyes lacking focus. 'I—I had no idea it would be this bad.'

Chalky gave her hand a squeeze. 'I think I heard you mention someone called Michel. Is that who you're looking for?'

She nodded uncertainly, though had at least understood that his question concerned Michel.

'Just tell me which way, miss. I'll try and take you there.'

Chalky drove expertly, swerving to avoid the debris that littered the streets, most rendered unrecognisable by the recent bombardment. The majority of the buildings were in ruins, or at least semi-ruins, some still smouldering or wreathed in clouds of choking smoke. Élodie looked distractedly to left and right, seeking any undamaged landmarks. She tapped Chalky's arm as she caught sight of an undamaged Cinzano advertisement high on a wall that was still standing, its colours incongruously bright amidst the desolation.

The brakes squealed as Chalky slowed. Élodie pointed to the left. At the next junction, she caught her breath as she spotted the remains of the *Deux mégots* café. One side of its awning rested forlornly on two tables that were topped by chunks of fallen masonry. A man, presumably the owner, was incongruously sweeping the pavement between the chairs and tables. Élodie leant across and shouted to Chalky to stop. The vehicle came to a halt bridging the narrow side road. Élodie could hardly bear to look to her left. Most of the buildings that were visible had been reduced to rubble. About halfway down, the dusty black frontage of Michel's workshop was still standing, though the upper floor of the building had only half of one wall intact. She slid from her seat and held onto the side of the Jeep.

'It's down there.' She pointed.

'Oh, wait, miss. Before you go...'

Chalky fished under the dashboard and handed her a small flat package. She stared in wonderment at the nylon stockings, and he grinned from ear to ear when she planted an enthusiastic kiss on each of his cheeks. She had only ever seen a picture of nylons in an American fashion magazine that Agnès had been sent by an aunt after their unveiling at the 1939 World's Fair in New York.

'*Merci beaucoup*! They are my only... *non*, my first. But where...?'

Chalky looked delighted at the success of his gift, but slightly embarrassed as he stuttered that they too had been won when playing poker with an American soldier. His broad grin returned. 'But I hope you enjoy wearing them, miss.'

Élodie hugged them to her chest. 'I keep them. Maybe for my wedding.'

Chalky looked abashed. 'Gosh, miss, I'd love to think you would.'

He insisted on staying until she had investigated Michel's workshop. She refused his offer to accompany her, shaking her head and patting his hand. She had to pick her way gingerly between the ruins. Sombre residents were dejectedly gathering what was left of their belongings from the shops and houses. She had to look away from one group, a mother trying in vain to comfort her small son who was sobbing for his teddy-bear while his father, hands raw, scrabbled frantically among the rubble for his child's toy.

The instant she reached the workshop door it gave a loud shudder and burst open. Michel emerged, almost unrecognisable, his hair grey with plaster dust. A huge, blood-stained gash adorned his forehead. She ran to him and held him close, all words unnecessary. She felt his cheek on her hair and leaned back to look at him properly.

His words were soothing. 'Él, I'm fine. Honestly. I'm so glad to see you, but what the hell are you doing in Flers?'

Élodie sighed with relief. 'Looking for you, of course.'

She suddenly remembered that Chalky had said he'd wait. Michel followed her gaze as she turned to wave to him. The corporal gave her a cheeky grin and a smart salute, revved the engine and reversed away.

Michel looked completely confused. 'Who was that? And what on earth are you holding?'

'It's a long story. I'll explain later. For now, tell me how things are here. Have your tools survived? Can you take them somewhere safe? Can I help?'

Michel shook his head, a broad smile creasing the dust on his cheeks. 'More questions, Él—you're always full of questions.'

She stuck out her bottom lip and frowned. 'I was only—'

He interrupted her by ruffling her curls. 'Trying to help. I know. And I thank you for that. And if you mean it, I'd be truly grateful.'

Michel had already set up two wooden crates in the cramped and overflowing workroom. He had begun to fill them and explained to Élodie what should go in each. For the next hour they worked quickly. When a third crate had been found and filled, the grimy workbench was at last empty.

Élodie groaned as she straightened up and wiped her forehead, realising too late that her hands were black with oil and grease. Michel took a none-too-clean handkerchief from his pocket and wiped off the worst of the dirt.

She pointed at the overflowing crates. 'What'll you do with this lot?'

'For now, and because the door still locks, I'll leave them here. Thierry's coming over later with his truck and will store them at the forge for me. Meantime, I'd guess you need a lift home?'

She agreed gratefully. Michel led her out the back way. He explained that his motorbike had by mere chance been at the old mill when the worst of the battle had taken place. He'd been spending every night on watch over Félix, so the machine had been spared a pounding as the artillery on both sides had shelled Flers remorselessly.

Élodie was solemn as she took her leave of Michel in the farmyard. 'I hope the end of all this is at last in sight. But it's at such a price. D'you think I could visit Félix again tomorrow?'

'Not only that, but within a few days we're planning to move him to Thierry's place.'

Élodie frowned. 'Why not here, at home with us?'

'Soon enough, Él. But the Boche aren't by any means gone yet. We're told there are areas not far from here where the losses and gains are ebbing and flowing all the time. We've kept him safe for two months now and I'm not jeopardising that. And no one's going to be looking for him at the forge. You'll just have to contain your soul in patience, Él.' Michel upped the engine revs. 'However foreign that idea is to you.'

Before Élodie could protest, he adroitly backed the bike and circled behind her, heading for the main road at a lick, one hand raised and waving as he went.

Élodie stood for a few minutes with her arms folded as the sound of the motorbike faded. It was soon replaced by the long slow stroke of a tractor growing closer. She turned towards the house. Perhaps she could help her mother prepare the meal for which her father was heading home.

# CHAPTER TWENTY-SEVEN

## *August 1944*

'*PUTAIN. COLLABORATRICE!*'

The yell startled Élodie from her reverie. She was collecting the last eggs of the day and the hens pecked rhythmically around her feet. At the gate slouched Lucien Martin, his insolent asymmetric smile irritating her as it always had. She hadn't seen him for some time. How tall he had grown, already lean and muscled from farm work at the age of fourteen.

'*Va t'en*! Get lost before I tell your mother what you've been saying.'

Lucien gave a derisory snort, then grinned, showing uneven, crooked teeth. 'Nothing she ain't said already. And not only a whore but a Kraut whore.'

He turned to run as Élodie took a step towards him. She took small satisfaction from his curse when the well-aimed, precious egg broke in his lank hair and dripped down his neck. He turned and made a rude gesture before lumbering off with his usual uncoordinated gait.

She ushered the hens into the coop, secured it for the night and took the overgrown path back to the farmhouse, shaken by Lucien's insults but savouring the whistling cries of the swifts swooping acrobatically over the tank in the yard, gathering insects from the air with an audible snap. She sighed. The Germans had gone; soon the swifts would follow. The birds would return. But Rudi? She prayed that he would live through whatever battles remained, assuming he had not been captured, or... She gave herself a mental shake. She would not allow herself to consider the alternative.

On that drowsy late August evening, the somnolent heat of the day finally relinquishing its stifling hold, her mother stood in the farm doorway. The smell of herbs drifted out into the yard. Élodie baulked at the smell of food and noted the older woman's pensive gaze as she held out a hand to take the egg basket. From indoors her father's voice rumbled out.

'Are we ever going to eat, woman?'

The two women exchanged a solicitous smile and Élodie felt her mother's arm enfold her waist as they entered the house.

The following morning was even more oppressive. The air held the electric smell of a threatening storm as Élodie set off for the henhouse, the early sun warming her skin. The cat followed, soon losing interest and making for the barn door, from whose shelter it could watch the swifts swooping soundlessly from the sky to take insects rising from the rusty water tank.

At the end of the path the door of the coop rested awkwardly, half-open, the top hinge snapped. Two of the birds lay in the run with their heads at an unnatural angle, their limbs rigid. Most of their feathers had been wrenched out and covered the dusty run like fallen blossom. Élodie fell to her knees, tears plopping onto their once-downy breasts, now bruised violet. She gathered the lifeless bodies into her basket. Checking quickly to see there was no further damage she turned away, the eggs forgotten.

As she crossed the yard a pickup truck careered through the farm gate, driven by Serge. Beside him was Lucien, and on the open back of the vehicle a middle-aged man she'd never seen before sat with a shotgun across his knees. Three women were huddled together on the rough planks of the flatbed.

Serge jumped out. 'Get in, whore.' He tore the basket from Élodie's arm and tossed it aside.

'What the... *Non!*'

Before she could protest further Lucien grabbed her other arm. She was thrown onto the rough planks and her hands were tied tightly with twine. The two men jumped back into the vehicle as Rose appeared from the house.

'What are you doing?'

Élodie could hear the challenge in her mother's voice matched by fear.

'Your whore of a daughter is getting her just deserts, madame, for *collaboration horizontale*.' Serge jerked the van into gear and drove off, the tyres spraying dry mud at the farm gate.

Rose leant against the water tank, her breath catching in her throat. She yanked off her apron and ran to find Henri in the lower field.

Élodie peered at the other women. One she vaguely recognised, the second was a stranger. The third, she was startled to see, was Mathilde from the boulangerie, who was trying to catch her breath between uncontrollable sobs, her helplessness making her appear even younger. Suddenly Élodie remembered Mme Martin's salacious comments. But still, Mathilde was so young—she couldn't be more than eighteen even now. Surely she hadn't had a German lover?

In the tree-lined square, normally full only on market day, a restless crowd had gathered, jostling and shouting as the truck arrived, the atmosphere tense and ugly. The oldest of the four women was the first to be hauled roughly off the truck. She struggled and cursed as her hands were untied and she was lugged, lashing out and kicking, towards a kitchen chair set incongruously outside the Mairie, whose newly painted doors and shutters were firmly closed. The *Tricolore* above the entrance, restored with pride when the hated swastika-emblazoned flag of the Third Reich had been torn down and burnt, hung limply on the flagpole in the breathless warmth. The stranger, whom Élodie had taken on closer inspection to be around forty, despite her coal-black hair, was bundled onto the seat as the watchers jeered. Serge reached into the vehicle, pulling out a pair of sheep clippers. The woman fought and spat, scratching at his arms like a cornered alley cat and drawing blood.

'It'll go the worse for you if you struggle, bitch.' Serge wiped his bloodstained arm across her face and twisted a handful of her long lustreless hair till she shrieked. He began to hack. When all that remained was uneven stubble, his brother smeared her shorn head with glutinous pig slurry, with which he drew a swastika on her forehead. She choked and wailed as Lucien added feathers to the stinking brew, patting them on while jigging to a tune in his own head and whooping wildly. She was thrown back into the truck, skinning her knees as she landed.

The two other girls offered little resistance, Mathilde bowing her head passively as tears coursed down her cheeks, the other staring at Serge with unconcealed hatred. Élodie was last. Serge dragged her off the truck and across to the shearing-chair. He came to a halt as a snarling, lion-like roar

rose over the yells of the onlookers, who parted in surprise as
Henri Duchamp grappled them to left and right and hurled
himself at his daughter's captor. Serge sidestepped but the
farmer, strong and agile from years of handling beasts in the
field, turned and caught him with an uppercut that smacked
his teeth together. As he reeled, the man from the back of
the truck smashed the butt of the shotgun into Henri's leg,
triggering a loud, sickening crack. In the few seconds before
he fell a chorus of gasps broke the shocked silence.

Serge stood over him, massaging his jaw where the blow had
hit. 'Don't interfere, old man. It's none of your business.'

'Not my business, you *fils de pute*—that's my *daughter*!'

'It's your daughter who's the whore, and now she's paying
the penalty for sleeping with the Boche.'

Henri lunged for Serge's legs, tearing at the worn fabric of
his trousers. 'Not Élodie, you are mistaken.'

Serge kicked himself free, grinding Henri's outstretched
left hand into the dirt as it smacked onto the ground. 'I'm
making no mistake, Monsieur.' He inclined his head and gave
a mocking laugh. 'Just ask Lucien.'

Lucien chortled and, buoyed by his brother's presence, spat
in Henri's direction. He cackled again. 'I seen them more than
once, her and that Kraut.'

Serge turned back to Élodie. He gripped her face between
thumb and fingers, turning it left and right as the skin blenched
beneath his grip. 'To think you were once considered quite a
catch. Before you let yourself be shagged by a bloody German.'
He grabbed the front of her dress, ripping the buttons from
their shanks and exposing her breasts. 'And once I longed for
those to be mine.'

'Yours? *Yours*? In your dreams, you vile *enflure*. I'd sooner
ten minutes with him than a lifetime with you.' Élodie's voice
was low, her eyes on her father who lay gasping with pain. He
stared back at her with a look she couldn't fathom, his gaze
dropping to her exposed belly, which as yet remained rela-

tively smooth and flat. She cringed at the slow comprehension that began to fill his tormented face.

Serge snatched at her jaw and shook it roughly, took the Gauloise from the corner of his mouth and held it close to her skin, hot and pungent, before changing his mind and taking another deep drag. 'You're not even worth wasting a fag-end on.'

She lunged and sank her teeth into his hand, drawing blood.

'*Merde!*' Serge balled his fist for a long moment then let it drop, settling instead for a string of obscenities.

Élodie's hair joined the lifeless heap, now a mix of black, blonde and brunette, tangled and forlorn. Her mother elbowed through the crowd and fought to push Serge aside.

'Non, Maman, non.' Élodie was insistent. 'Take care of Papa.' She clutched at her faded blue dress whose ragged shreds flapped brazenly in the breeze, and looked out across the crowd. These were neighbours, local shopkeepers, old family friends. Friends—what a joke. Hateful hypocrites. Some looked uncomfortable as she caught their eye, others turned away, a few smirked or faced her with undisguised disgust. Some muttered. Not one moved a muscle to help. She was dumped back on the truck alongside the others, their faces sullen and haunted, their gaze remote.

The vehicle made a slow circuit of the village to its limits east and west. Its honking horn drew out the residents to gawp as they passed. Hands reached up and grabbed at their garments, the tearing of fabric muffled by the occasional terrifying thump of fists on the truck's sides. Stones and rubbish were hurled, and dogs barked and yelped, chasing the truck as it progressed amidst a cacophony of insults, curses and lewdness. Élodie was dazed. How could they? And the menacing women, louder in their spiteful condemnation than the men: were they really all guilt-free?

Finally, the truck turned back into the square. The crowd had drifted away and the chair had vanished. A lone, bent figure, dressed in black, stood outside the church. Mamselle Bonnaire, the elderly schoolteacher, raised a wavering hand to Élodie and crossed herself before pulling at the heavy door and vanishing into the cool interior.

As the four women slid from the vehicle Lucien grabbed their shoes. They exchanged no words, scarcely glancing at one another. Young Mathilde continued to weep, though silently now. Each slunk away, cowed, humiliated, subject to her own torments. When the truck passed Élodie, Serge wound down the window. 'Your Hun boyfriend wouldn't think so much of you now, darling.'

'*Va te faire foutre*, you creep.'

Serge, whose arm hung loosely from the cab window, banged the truck door with an open hand as he threw his head back and guffawed at her earthiness.

She walked the two miles home past hedges heavy in their full-summer green, the fields dotted with tired old horses and the odd tractor, all harvesting the last of the sweet-smelling grain or beginning to plough for the next crop. Halfway to the farm she came across her shoes in a ditch. She slipped them on eagerly, her feet rubbed half-raw by the hot surface of the rough road. Fingering her bare head, she wept quietly for the loss of ... what exactly, she asked herself? Her pride? Her lover? Her ruined country? She was only glad that Félix was still with Thierry and Yvette, because he would surely have killed Serge for what he had done.

Élodie found her mother at home, pacing the kitchen. As soon she caught sight of her daughter she threw open her arms and the two women embraced. Élodie clung to her mother like a distraught toddler, finally releasing all the pent-up trauma in uncontrollable sobs. Her mother rocked her to and fro, hushing her lovingly.

'Where's Papa?' The words came out in hoarse gulps.

'His leg is badly broken. They've taken him to the hospital in Flers. Thank God, it's still standing—or most of it.'

Élodie hung her head. 'Maman, it's all my fault. If only....'

'No time for regrets, my child. But I think the consequences are only just beginning, are they not?'

'What can I say, Maman?'

'You can tell me in a minute how it all came about.'

Élodie let her mother guide her to the kitchen table and sit her down. She surrendered impassively to her old role as child, watching the woman who had raised her and registering incongruously that she was still, despite the deepening lines of age and the traumas of war etching her face, a strikingly handsome woman. Rose fetched a wet cloth and began to cleanse the stinking filth from her daughter's face and head, ignoring the residue that had transferred to her own clothes. When she was satisfied that the job was done, she dried Élodie's bristly skull with soft wipes of a towel, before mechanically pushing back the strands of her own greying hair that had escaped from the bun at the nape of her neck.

Rose spoke first. 'I knew there was someone...' She paused with a bitter laugh. 'I thought it might be Serge. He was always soft on you.'

Élodie smacked the table with her fist. 'Don't even speak his name, Maman. That pig may have had his own ideas, but he was never for me.' The horror was giving way to a deep rage now. She touched her shorn head absently and continued. 'His name is Rudi and yes, he is German. We never meant for it to happen—it just did. I first met him when he and that abominable Major Wolff came to the market. He offered to fetch the eggs from the farm after the Major came and demanded them—you'll remember that awful day. We would meet down by the coop, so you never saw him. And gradually ... he's a wonderful man, a gentle... I think you would love him too, Maman.' She smiled through the tears that stained her face. 'We didn't ask to be born in different countries.' She stuck her chin out defiantly. 'And we didn't ask for a war.'

Rose pursed her lips. 'But this baby is definitely his? This Rudi's, I mean?'

Élodie looked down at her shaking hands in her lap. 'Why would you even ask, Maman?'

'Because there's something... It's a mother's instinct. There's something you're not saying.'

Élodie was silent for a full minute. 'Are you sure you want to know? Absolutely sure?'

'Yes, my child, I do. I know that something is preying on your mind, and heavy burdens are best shared.'

'Well, that same Major—the one who came here several times—'

'That arrogant man whose eyes were full of lust every time he looked at you?'

'Maman!'

Rose permitted herself a half-smile. 'You think I wasn't once your age? That I don't recognise a man who is obsessed with a certain girl? The kind who becomes infatuated with what he can't rightfully have?'

'I didn't mean...'

Rose tapped her daughter's hand. 'Did he do something to you, that major? Tell me. What was it he did?'

Élodie could hear her mother's repressed fury but could also sense her sympathy. How she longed to be free of the secret. Longed for it to be shared. Who better than her mother? She began slowly. Her words then flowed like a torrent from a burst dam. 'You know that sometimes I took the eggs to the Manoir?'

'I thought you always did.'

'Well, now you know that Rudi often came here instead. But one day', she cleared her throat, forcing herself to continue. 'One day when I went to the Manoir the only person there was the Major, who must have seen me arrive. He was polite at first, but then he said he knew about me and Rudi, and that it was "*verboten*", so unless I did what he wanted he would make sure Rudi was punished. And he also made threats against Félix.' She looked up. Her mother was listening assiduously but clearly taking care to display no emotion. She took her daughter's hands in her own and squeezed them supportively.

'Go on.'

'I argued, of course, but he, he became insistent and finally I couldn't stop him.'

'You're telling me he raped you?' Although it was a question, Rose was not asking but making a statement. Relief flooded through Élodie.

'Effectively, yes, Maman.' Tears ran down her face and dripped onto her torn, filth-spattered frock.

Rose shook her head. 'I'm not sure I understand. When was this?'

Élodie snuffled through her tears. 'It couldn't have been worse timing. The first time was two days after I ... after Rudi and I....' She resolved to spare her mother that in fact there had been two occasions on which she'd had to succumb to Wolff at the Manoir. Bad enough that she had to live with it herself. 'And then again, the day after Félix was rescued from Saint-Lô, though that was my fault. So how do I know for certain whose baby I'm carrying? It will haunt me forever.'

'Your fault? Would you care to explain?'

Élodie shook her head vehemently. 'Let it go, Maman. Just accept that it happened, I beg you.'

Rose gave an exasperated sigh. 'Very well. But this is no time for speculation, my child. It is what it is, and the future is all that matters now. But the one thing I still don't understand is how Serge got to know about your German, and how Lucien seems to have got himself involved too?'

Élodie shrugged. 'Oh, you know that boy Lucien, into everyone's business. Rudi and I were always careful when we met. Once, maybe twice, when he was here, I thought I saw Lucien in the lane. Perhaps—I hope—it was only his twisted, juvenile suspicions he fed to Serge.'

Rose gave a huge sigh. 'Well, I could see you were happy then. I'd hear you humming as you went to the henhouse. I'd see a faraway look when we were at table, and you would be smiling.'

Élodie's eyes were swollen from crying, and her lips were dry.

'What does Papa know?'

Rose shook her head. 'Nothing ... until today.' She raised a hand to hush her daughter. 'Leave your father to me. He's not easy, but he's a good man and he loves you dearly. He'll come round. Eventually.'

'But those people in the town, such hypocrites. They all served the Germans in their shops, the bars, and now....'

Rose gave a clipped smile. 'They'll tell you, *chérie*, that they had no option. But that you did.'

For a moment, Élodie was shocked by her mother's plain speaking. Was that true? 'I suppose maybe I did. And you, Maman, what do you say?'

Rose shrugged. 'Life is what it is. We often can't choose how we spend it. And it will go on, as it always has. Thirty years on a farm has taught me that.' There was a long pause, then, as her mother sat down, Élodie saw that she was staring at the table with a faraway look, wrestling with something within herself.

'Is there something else you want to say, Maman?'

Rose's put her head on one side, her mouth firm. 'Yes. Yes, I'm going to tell you something that I've never told a soul, that has remained between me and your father for all these years.'

Élodie's heart fluttered as her mother continued.

'I'm only doing so for your sake, so that you can look ahead and see that your life won't end here. You will soon have a child to raise—a responsibility that will never leave you.' At this she smiled and brushed a hand across Élodie's belly.

'You know that I was very young when I met your father?'

'But you were already well known as a seamstress.'

Rose held up her hand again. 'True, but I'd been working since I was fourteen, or twelve to be truthful, on and off. I knew Henri was the man for me soon after I met him. In those days he was a kind man, with a fine sense of humour, always joking.'

Élodie frowned at this vision of her father as her mother continued.

'Very like your brother in fact. Félix is without a shadow of doubt his father's son, though he'd hate to hear me say so now. Well, anyway, *la Grande Guerre* began in 1914 and your father was called up. We'd already talked of marriage, and when it was confirmed he would be leaving to fight, and might never come back... All wars are the same, you know—passions run so high. When your father came home on his first leave, I had to tell him I was pregnant. He insisted we be married as soon as it could be arranged, preferably right away. Père Auguste was here at the church in those days—still here to christen you when the time came, of course.'

Élodie swallowed her astonishment and willed her mother to continue.

'We thanked the stars that Père Auguste was the soul of tact and kindness. Our wedding was hushed and hasty and soon your father was gone again. When he came home after Verdun, after his friend Léon was killed in front of him, he was never the same again. Oh, he did his work on the farm and was an attentive husband still, but I don't think I've ever heard him joke again. And when Yves caught Spanish Flu and died, something died in both of us too. You know that he—our firstborn—wasn't even four years of age?'

Élodie stroked her mother's arm and nodded. 'Oh Maman, I don't think we ever realised how hard it was for you both.'

'We never intended you to. We agreed that if we had further children, and we were blessed with three, we would do all we could to keep you safe in the world.' Rose gave a wry smile. 'And then another war arrived and every one of you has suffered.'

Élodie made a face. 'And now Rudi is gone and I may never see him again, Félix is scarred for life—well, physically for certain—and Hélène, I hope I never see her again.'

Rose shook her head. 'I do hope you will make your peace with your sister. She already has a daughter, and what she did, she did to protect her family. I'd hope you—.'

'Don't even suggest that I'd betray Félix for someone else.'

'Not even Rudi?'

There was a long pause before Élodie spoke. 'No, Maman, I'm not sure even for him. Rudi is the man I hoped to spend my life with, maybe even will, one day, but Félix is my brother. Félix has been there for me since, well, since my first memories. So, forever.'

Rose sighed. 'I know all that, my child. But you and he have a special bond that's never existed for Hélène, with you or him. She was defending the most important people in her life—that's how you have to see it. And one day, Félix will find someone for himself too.'

Élodie traced the pattern of the smooth, faded wood under her fingers. This table, the chair she sat on, the farm, her parents—they'd formed the backbone of her life. And yet it was true: Hélène had never been part of that to her. Hélène had always wanted different things, had aspirations that had led her onto a different path. And Guy was an honourable man, a kind man who had tried to help Félix. If it hadn't been for the war and Major Wolff, who knew how different it might have been?

She looked up and met her mother's eyes. 'I can only promise I will try, Maman.'

'That'll do for now, *chérie*. Maybe you'll understand her better when you're a mother yourself.'

'*Qui sait?*' Élodie couldn't, wasn't prepared to even consider that yet.

The two women lapsed into silence, each in her own world, contemplating the past, trying to imagine the future. With growing certainty, Élodie vowed to herself that, whatever that future held, self-pity wouldn't feature. The Duchamp women were legendarily forged of stern stuff, and she vowed to take her place among them. She watched her mother's eyes lighting on the everyday objects that filled their home and could see the older woman already absorbing all the horrors of the day with a fortitude that had long ago settled deep in her soul.

From somewhere outside, the short, sharp screams of the swifts could be heard. Élodie knew that sound was transitory. She had already seen the swallows beginning to gather on the telegraph wires, a sure sign that all the migratory birds would soon be flying south.

For a week, Élodie refused to leave the farm. She and her mother ate from the dwindling stores in the larder, supplemented by their home-grown produce. With her father in hospital and Félix still in hiding, it was all the two women could do to achieve even the minimum necessary in the fields. Élodie had long ago ensured she was skilled on the tractor, though there was too little fuel left to run it regularly. Her mother took over caring for the hens, or such as were left after their depletion following Major Wolff's earlier requisition, milked the three cows and her goats, and did more than her fair share of the farm work.

On the following Monday, Élodie came downstairs into an eerily hushed kitchen to find her mother sitting at the table, head in hands, with a half-empty bowl of coffee in front of her.

'Maman?' Élodie flew to her side.

'Don't look so worried, *chérie*.' Her mother smiled reassuringly. 'I was wishing I had some bread that I could coat with jam to hide the taste of this disgusting *soi-disant "café"*.'

Élodie was flooded with shame. She had let self-pity blind her. In a self-conscious reflex, she ran a hand over her head where the hair was beginning to show again, dark against the paleness of her skin. She dashed back upstairs and grabbed a small cotton square, folded it to cover her head, and with the loose ends formed a knot at the back of her neck.

When Élodie re-entered the kitchen, her mother was washing up. Oblivious to the cloth dripping water down her apron, she turned and looked questioningly at the headscarf.

'I'm going to the boulangerie, Maman, to get you some bread.'

She hurtled out of the house to forestall any objection and set off for the village. The queue they had grown accustomed to during the occupation had ceased to exist.

Someone must have recently oiled the sturdy bakery door, which no longer issued an ominous creaking sound as it was opened.

'Bonjour, Madame. No Mathilde today?'

The baker's wife did not return her greeting, a sour expression appearing when Élodie asked for a loaf.

'Mathilde no longer works here, Mamselle Duchamp, and I have no bread to sell you.'

Élodie was nonplussed. 'But Madame, the shop is full of bread.'

'We don't serve collaborators here, Mamselle. If your mother wants bread, she is welcome to come in herself, but there is none for you.'

With that, she turned her back to the counter and began rearranging the tumbling golden loaves on the shelves, their sweet, yeasty smell making Élodie's stomach rumble.

Despite recent events, Élodie was stunned. She could hit back, but what was the point? This woman who, until recently, had served the Germans without demur had now done a complete about-face. She put the coins back in her pocket with a shaky hand and walked out of the shop with her head lowered, unwilling to make eye contact with the two other villagers she could see approaching the shop. She rode home, oblivious to the fulsome glory of late summer, the dusty green roadside vegetation swaying rhythmically as it marked her passage. She had never felt so alone in her life.

With harvest-time imminent, Élodie had no idea how they would cope. When Michel arrived on one of his regular visits, she greeted him wearily. She saw the look of alarm on his face as he took in her pallor, and pulled her sleeves down over her ever thinner arms.

She took both his hands in her own and swallowed her pride. 'Michel, I want to ask for your help with something. Say no if you can't...'

'Ask me for anything, Él.'

She felt his grip tighten as he smiled at her, and he touched his forehead to hers as he moved closer.

'Maman and I have to get the harvest in soon, and with Papa in hospital...'

'I'll be here. When do you need me?'

'Next week, I think. I hate to ask...'

'Don't be ridiculous, Él. I'll do whatever you need. And I'm sure I can get several more pairs of hands to help too. You're not to worry a moment longer. Tell your maman not to worry either.'

Élodie swallowed hard, stifling the urge to weep with relief.

Michel tipped up her chin with his forefinger, his features screwed up in puzzlement. 'Why didn't you say something sooner?' He gave a wry smile. 'No, don't answer that—too proud to ask, I'll bet.'

# Chapter Twenty-Eight

## May 1947

Summer gave way to autumn, then winter. Peace, in name at least, returned to Europe in May 1945, and a full year and three more seasons passed.

One Thursday in the late spring of 1947, Rose was in the kitchen preparing supper as usual. A knock at the door surprised her: there were few callers at the farm these days. She put down her paring knife, wiped her hands on her apron and automatically tidied wisps of hair as she went through the hall. Outside stood a tall young man. Fair-haired, he had a long thin scar down his neck and a fading black eye. She took in his old but well-kept clothes, the fraying haversack on his back, the nervous twitch in his left cheek.

'Yes?' she asked.

'Bonjour Madame,' he began in accented French, from the east of France if she was correct. 'Is Élodie at home?'

Rose felt her stomach lurch. 'Who are you?'

'My name is Rudi Hoffmann. I...' He faltered as Rose reached for the door jamb to steady herself. The heady scent from the purple wisteria smothering the doorway brought her to her senses.

'She's not here. She's gone. Do you understand?'

He flinched, swallowed hard and spoke again. 'You have the same grey-green eyes, madame—you must be Élodie's mother. Madame Duchamp, I've come a long way to see her.'

'Do you know what they did to her—my own countrymen, because of you?'

He shook his head, eyeing the fallen petals on the doorstep and tensing visibly. He wiped a dusty toecap on his trouser leg.

'They dragged her to the market square, shaved her head and worse, then shamed her before the whole village.'

He drew in a sharp breath. 'But she is alive?'

'Yes.'

'Thank God, madame.' Rudi persisted, his voice quiet but firm. 'Please, will you tell me where I can find her?'

'Why have you never written? Why have you waited so long?'

He looked genuinely bemused. 'I wrote at least half a dozen times, madame. Finally I have come to look for her. I had to know she had survived, even though she never replied. I wanted to know she hadn't forgotten...'

From somewhere beyond them the sound of an engine grew louder.

'It's my husband. You must go.' Rose backed indoors.

'May I not meet him, madame?'

Would men never learn? 'They broke my husband's leg when he tried to defend our daughter. Crippled him. What do you think?'

Rudi drew in a sharp breath and grimaced. 'I'm sorry. I understand. But ...'

'Come back tomorrow afternoon ... earlier. Soon after three o'clock. I will talk to you then.' It would give her time to think.

He nodded, set off without looking back and was soon invisible behind the evergreen hedge. A rusty, battered orange Renault tractor swung into the yard a couple of minutes later. Henri clambered down, limped into the house and dropped a skinned rabbit onto the table.

'Who was that in the lane?'

Rose picked up the rabbit before she replied, clicking her tongue at the bloodstain it had left on the scrubbed wood. 'He was looking for work.'

'Oh? Someone local? Only I was sure I'd seen his face before.'

Rose was non-committal, reaching for the worn wooden chopping board.

'What did you tell him?'

As she began to joint the rabbit, Rose regarded her husband of thirty-odd years. 'I said we couldn't help him.' The scent of freshly gathered herbs drifted from the heavy pan on the stove top as she began to stir. 'You'll need to feed the pigs and get cleaned up soon or we'll never eat supper.'

# Chapter Twenty-Nine

## May 1947

FÉLIX AND MICHEL ARRIVED soon after six-thirty, as they had promised. When Élodie opened the door to her shabby flat, there was something different in Félix's smile. Contentment? Happiness even?

From behind her, Vevette roared past like a miniature traction engine and threw herself into her uncle's arms as he stooped to scoop her up. She squealed with delight as he held her high above his head, then held out her arms to Michel, who deftly caught her in mid-air as Félix passed her over. She tucked her head of unruly blonde curls into his neck and kissed his cheek repeatedly.

Félix chuckled. 'We all know who her favourite is!'

Élodie served a simple supper for the three of them, as she often did nowadays. Vevette had eaten earlier but insisted on claiming Michel's lap as her perch while he ate his own food, despite her mother's protestations that she should play with her doll or her beloved *nounours* and leave him in peace.

After they'd finished, Félix gathered up the plates. 'Sorry to leave so soon, but I have to meet someone.'

'Oh?' Élodie looked up optimistically, but no further explanation was forthcoming. Some things didn't change. The expression on Félix's face told her that further probing would get her nowhere. He took the plates over to the sink and returned to drop a kiss on her head and ruffle her hair before he left.

'I'll see you both tomorrow. Michel, I have to help Papa on the farm in the morning but I'll be back with you by early afternoon.'

Élodie turned to Michel as the door shut behind her brother. 'Well?'

Michel laughed. 'Well what?'

'Who is she? Anyone I know?'

As Michel continued to tease her, Élodie threw a napkin at him.

'It *is* a girl he's gone to see, isn't it?

Michel finally gave in. 'Yes. Thank God, at last. And yes, you know her. Long blonde hair, long legs. Lives locally—always has done.'

Élodie raised an eyebrow at the description, unusually perceptive for Michel, then frowned, struggling for an answer. 'Not Mireille Brodeur at last, surely?'

'*Non*. She was swept up by a Yank during the Liberation. He sent her the fare and she's followed him to America. Somewhere by a lake in Minnesota apparently. But you're close.'

Élodie shook her head in frustration.

Michel was solemn now. 'It's someone who reminds him, I'm sure, of Clémence.'

Élodie groaned. 'Such a waste of a young life. I only met her once, but she was brave—and beautiful.'

'Well, she died in Félix's arms, as you know. It's taken him so long to come to terms with that—that and the fact that he blames himself entirely for her death. He still feels if we'd heeded the warning better and abandoned the mission... And there have been days when I thought he'd never recover.'

'Me too. And it was never his fault, we all know that. So, who *is* this mysterious girl?'

Michel hesitated before replying. 'Mireille's sister, Mathilde.'

Élodie almost dropped her cup. She could scarcely believe what she was hearing. '*What*! But she must be ten years younger than Félix!'

'Just so. But I think he sees in her a vulnerability that he loved in Clémence behind her calm and competent exterior.'

'And those eyes, of course.'

'What?' Michel blinked in confusion.

'Surely you must have noticed? Mathilde has those same startling blue eyes that Clémence had.'

Michel shuffled his feet. 'Can't say I have. She and her sister were just the Brodeur girls to me.'

Élodie shook her head, amused by his indifference, loving his easy-going, practical nature. 'You're so funny sometimes, Michel. Wait while I put Vevette to bed, and we can talk some more.'

Vevette was reluctant to surrender her place on Michel's lap, but after extracting a promise that he would read her a bedtime story, she took her mother's hand and trotted off beside her.

Half an hour later, Élodie turned from the stove as Michel emerged from the cramped bedroom that she shared with her daughter. She handed him a cup of coffee and indicated the two old but comfortable chairs he had sourced for her from a client of his.

'As long as Félix is happy at last, I don't care who it is. And Mathilde is a lovely girl. She deserves some happiness too.'

Michel agreed. 'What you probably don't know if you haven't seen her for a while is how grown up she's become since ... since that terrible day when Serge and his fellow thugs did what they did when...' He left the sentence unfinished.

Élodie understood how reluctant he was to raise the memory of old wounds. 'It's in the past now, Michel. I can never forget what they did to me, to Mathilde and the others, and worst of all in some ways what they did to Papa. But we all have to be thankful the war is over and we're alive. And we have to say we're the lucky ones, despite the scars, physical or mental.'

She put down her cup to try and hide the tremors that were shaking her, the legacy of the memories she worked so hard to suppress on a daily basis. Michel reached out and took her hands in his.

'You're an inspiration, Élodie, and I love you for showing us the way back to some kind of normality. But I want you to know, too, that it wasn't only Félix who threatened to kill Serge for what he did. It was only your mother persuading us both that we would make matters worse for you in the long run that stopped either one of us.'

Élodie looked across at the man who had stood beside her brother through the worst days of their lives. In the long-lashed eyes that once were so gentle, she saw the reflection of a hard-won strength born of unwelcome experience. And something else: a look she'd last seen in Rudi's eyes the first time he visited the farm. She felt a rush of surprise. Suddenly it was as if she were seeing him for the first time, and, she realised, as more than her brother's friend.

'I don't know what I'd do without you.' Michel's normal slow, lopsided smile spread into a broad grin, and she realised she'd spoken out loud. She hoped her smile was apologetic as she tried to extract her hands from his, but he tightened his grip with evident deliberation.

'Élodie, there's something I need to say.'

# CHAPTER THIRTY

## May 1947

AFTER A NIGHT OF torrential rain, a watery sun appeared and began to dry the yard with its gathering warmth. Henri came in for breakfast as Rose returned from the morning egg collection. He took the basket from her.

'Élodie's coming home for the weekend, isn't she?'

Rose hesitated. 'I don't know. She may be busy—and might have to work on Saturday.'

'Oh?' Henri frowned. 'The child is growing fast, like the calves in the fields. I wanted to see her. To see them both.'

Rose made coffee and laid the table. She smiled to herself at the conversion in Henri's behaviour towards Élodie from the moment he'd set eyes on his new granddaughter. She sliced bread and fetched butter from the larder. Henri had his back to her as he manoeuvred himself into a sitting position.

'Have any letters come for Élodie since she went to work in Argentan?' She tilted her head, awaiting his response, which was a long time coming.

'Why do you ask?'

'That means yes. What did you do with them?'

'Why do you ask?' Henri growled.

'Because I want to know. She has a right to her own life.'

'They had a German postmark. I threw them away.'

'Unopened?'

'Yes, of course unopened. Élodie doesn't need any more complications in her life than she already has. Rose, why are you asking now?' He paused and caught her arm as she put his coffee on the table. 'Does this have anything to do with that man who came here yesterday? The one I told you I was sure I'd seen before?'

Rose crossed to the stove. Men forgot love so quickly.

'He's the father of your grandchild, Henri.'

Henri thumped the table with both hands and ate in silence. Downing the last of his coffee, he rose as ably as his lame leg would allow. He hesitated in the doorway.

'He'd better not come back, Rose, or he'll have me to deal with ... and I'm not inclined to fantasies, even if you are.'

Henri returned soon after noon. He took his usual chair at the kitchen table, swinging his infirm leg into place with the aid of both hands. Lunchtime was strained, the only sound the scrape of cutlery on crockery. Rose busied herself as Henri pushed his plate away, rose and hobbled to the support of the door frame, where he leaned down to pull on his field boots.

'What time will you be in this evening?'

'Questions, more questions. Why are you so full of questions today, woman? The usual time.'

Rose cleared up, then went down the well-trodden path to check on the chickens. Her spirits were lifted by the bank of cowslips in bloom, their tiny yellow heads lit by the sun. A flash of movement in the nearest field brought her to a stop, and for several minutes she watched two hares performing their annual boxing ritual. They sprang off their back legs, their front feet flailing, tufts of hair floating away as they scrapped relentlessly.

Back in the farmhouse she resumed her chores, sweeping the kitchen flagstones to the somnolent rhythm of the hall clock. At five past three there was a light tap on the half-open door. Rudi stood on the step, dressed in the same clothes as before, his black eye beginning to fade to mustard yellow. Wordlessly, Rose motioned for him to follow and went into the kitchen, where she could keep an eye on the farmyard.

'So, young man', she began. 'Would you like some coffee?'

Rudi thanked her.

'How is Élodie? You said she isn't here now?'

'She's worked in Argentan for some time, since... The people there don't know her.'

'Where does she work? What work does she do?'

'She works in a hotel.'

A half-smile lit Rudi's face. 'It wouldn't be the Hotel Léopold by any chance?'

Rose raised her brows. 'Yes. You know it?'

The pink flush that suffused his cheeks confirmed her suspicions before he answered. 'You don't need to say another word.'

He met her eyes directly and shrugged.

Rose gave a wry smile. 'So much for visits to her old school-friend Agnès. Did you meet a girl called Agnès?'

'Pardon, madame? I'm sorry, I don't understand.'

'No matter.' She got to her feet and rummaged in the dresser, taking out a scrap of paper and a pencil. She returned to the table with the coffee, sat and wrote something and pushed the note across to Rudi. Before he could reach for it, she withdrew it slightly.

'This is her address. But there is something you should know first. Of course, you may already know.' She looked up enquiringly, but his face wore a confused expression.

'In March 1945, Élodie gave birth to a daughter.' She opened the table drawer and extracted a small, well-thumbed photograph from its deepest recesses.

'A child? *My* child?' An incredulous smile softened his gaunt face and Rose noted him blinking as he cradled the image. He ran his finger shakily over the picture and rubbed the dampness from his cheeks.

Rose swallowed hard as her own throat constricted.

'*Mein Gott*, it is like looking at my sister, but with Élodie's eyes—your eyes, madame. Grey-green?'

Rose nodded. 'But she has your fair hair. You say you have a sister?'

'A twin sister. She lived with my parents in Dresden but moved to be with my grandparents in Alsace after her husband went to the war. He had joined the Nazi party...'

'But you did not?'

'Never. My brother-in-law and I disagreed totally. He's not a bad fellow, but he was a party faithful for a long time and still it stands between us.'

'And what about your parents? They survived?'

Rudi's eyes took on a distant look. The mood changed instantly, the tic returning to his cheek. 'In February 1944 the British bombers arrived. The devastation had to be seen to be believed—first the bombs, then the firestorm. My father was killed outright. My mother survived until last month, but her wounds were so bad, her brain so injured ... it was a relief when she died. My sister and family still live in Alsace on my grandparents' farm, and she came to help when she could, but it's a long way to Dresden and she has a small child of her own to look after.'

He paused, apparently seeking a reaction, but Rose ensured her face gave nothing away. 'That's why I couldn't come back sooner and wrote instead.' He was struggling for self-control, arms crossed, fists clenched. He gave a huge sigh and laid his palms flat on the table.

Rose reached across and touched his hands hesitantly. 'I can only tell you she didn't see your letters.' Rudi looked nonplussed. She held up a hand. 'The war has ruined so many lives. But you have returned, and maybe...'

'Ruined lives, yes. But Félix's too, your son Félix. May I ask?'

Rose was nonplussed. 'You knew Félix?'

'Yes, we met several times.' He looked up questioningly. 'How is he?'

'He's doing well at last, thank God, despite what those evil men did to him.'

Rudi bit his lip. He struggled to find his words. 'It was unforgiveable. I cannot myself forgive what my countrymen did....'

'Men—and women—do terrible things in wartime.'

'And now?'

'Now Félix spends half his week on the farm, and half his week running a garage in Argentan with his friend Michel. He adores his niece and spends as much time with her as he can.'

Rudi nodded. 'That's good.' He shifted in his chair. 'And there was a girl who worked for Madame at the Manoir. Lisette?'

'Lisette? Well, she eventually snared a Tommy. The English were at the Manoir after the Germans left, and there was apparently a sergeant who was full of himself, or so Madame Lagrange tells me. Predictably, Lisette fell for his charms. So that's one member of that family out of the way. And, you know, Élodie and Félix have many friends of their own age. They all know the part Lisette's brothers played in what happened. Those terrible events. I have to say, their parents were so kind when we were first married, but they never taught their children self-discipline. Allowed them to run wild. So it was no real surprise where their behaviour led them.'

Rudi's next question was hesitant. 'Terrible events? When your husband was injured? And Élodie?'

Rose didn't reply immediately. Should she tell him the whole story? He had the right to know, surely? 'Well, after the Allies fought their way through Normandy in 1944, Serge, two of his *copains* and Lucien rounded up four women who were rumoured to have been involved with German soldiers. They...'

She saw that Rudi's face was contorted, his fisted fingers bone-white.

'They threw them all in a truck, took them into Ste-Honorine and shaved their heads.' She looked up again as Rudi gasped. She struggled to keep her voice neutral. 'Then they covered them in pig swill and feathers and drove them all round the village, where they were spat at, screamed at in foul language and totally humiliated.'

Rudi was shaking visibly. 'Was she, was Élodie...'

'Already pregnant? Yes. But no harm came to the baby. Henri—my husband—tried to intervene during the shearing outside the *Mairie*, and one of Serge's thugs, a real *vaurien*, broke his leg with a gun butt.'

'*Gott im Himmel*! I'm so very sorry, Madame.'

'You've no reason to apologise. It was a damned Frenchman who was to blame when all's said and done.'

Rudi sighed and rubbed his eyes with his fists. 'But if I'd left her alone...'

Rose could see exactly why her daughter had fallen for this man. 'You're forgetting Élodie in this equation.' She smiled across at him. 'She always had a mind of her own, and if she'd taken the decision that you were the one, neither I nor her father—nor even her beloved brother Félix—could have changed her mind.'

She gave Rudi a bitter smile. 'But of course, Serge in particular has paid the price for his actions. There's always a price to pay if you survive. He still lives on the farm. No one in these parts wants to know him now, and I can see him fifty years hence, an ever more reclusive bachelor, only leaving the house for church on Sundays. As for the youngest one, Lucien, he's madder than ever.'

Rudi made a face before Rose spoke again. 'Now let me ask you a question.'

'Anything, madame, I'll answer if I can.'

'That major.' She watched Rudi as she spoke. 'The one who came here twice. What happened to him?'

Rudi frowned. 'Major Wolff? He died during the battle at Falaise. I think the Allies called it the closing of the Falaise Pocket.'

Rose saw that he was pressing his fists against the end of the table as he spoke, looking at his hands rather than at her.

'But you know he died?'

Rudi nodded. 'Oh yes, madame, for sure. He was shot in the back of the head.' He raised his head and his jaw tightened as he looked at Rose with a level gaze. 'I told you yesterday that I knew Élodie was special from the minute I met her. It was Wolff who gave the order about "no inessential liaisons". He wasn't—forgive my frankness, madame—he wasn't only referring to sex when he said that.'

'I imagine not. There was plenty of evidence of that going on with every French whore and more women besides.' Rudi's eyebrows shot up. Rose was surprised when he gave the first real smile she'd seen from him.

'I know now where your daughter gets it from—she is so like you. She is...'

Rose smiled back. 'Forthright is probably the word you're looking for.'

He repeated the word and nodded. 'Yes, that seems right.'

Rose tried to piece together what he had told her. 'But Wolff, did Élodie ... did you know...?' Her voice faltered. It was not her place to divulge the secret she and her daughter had kept so well, if he was still unaware.

Rudi balled his fists. 'I know what he did to her, yes, I presume that's what you mean?' His eyes never left Rose's. 'But it wasn't Élodie who told me. Oh, twice I am sure she tried to. I realised something was very wrong when she was reluctant to ... to lie with me. I'm sorry. It is hard to say these things to her mother.'

'You think I wasn't her age once?' Her laugh was brief, tender. 'No matter. Carry on.'

'In some ways I regret stopping her. But I didn't want there to be any barrier between us while we were parted by the *verdammten Krieg*.' There was silence until he pressed on. 'In the event, Élodie didn't have to tell me, because Wolff did so himself.'

Rose's mouth became a tight line. Rudi smoothed his hair and looked away, as if deliberating how best to continue.

'As the Allies advanced and we began the retreat towards Falaise, Wolff took great delight in telling me... At first he lied, saying she had thrown herself at him. I knew she had not, and I don't know how I didn't strike him, but we were surrounded by our troops—and of course I was expendable. He taunted me, saying he hoped I had enjoyed her as much as he had. He was disgusting. I believe he thought he meant something to her.' He picked up his cup with shaking hands and took a mouthful of coffee.

Rose frowned. 'But were you involved in the attack by the Allies?'

'Eventually, of course. But Wolff was long dead by then.' He put the cup back on the saucer, and concentrated on pushing the saucer to and fro as he spoke. 'Madame, I had sniper training at some point.' He looked up and held Rose's gaze across the table.

Rose raised a hand. 'I don't want you to tell me anything more. You have said all you need to. Men like that don't deserve to walk this Earth. It is between you, your conscience and God, though I query my own faith increasingly these days. But I will thank you on Élodie's behalf for ending what she suffered at his hands.'

Rudi visibly relaxed a little at last. The stillness between them was punctuated only by the regular ticking of the hall clock. He touched the photo again where it lay on the table and sighed.

'But you have spoken to Élodie, Madame? She knows I'm here?'

Rose shook her head. 'I've prepared the way. I've told her father she may not be home for the weekend.'

'But...'

He was silenced by Rose's firm tone. 'It is better this way. Maybe one day we will meet as a family, God willing, but for now ... can you get to Argentan? The train from Flers is running again.'

'Then yes, madame.'

'I will telephone Élodie when you leave. She has lodgings with a woman who looks after Vevette—Geneviève—during the day.'

Rudi was staring unblinkingly at the photograph. He appeared reluctant to look away from the picture and though he was smiling, his eyes were moist again. 'That's my sister's name. Our maternal grandmother was French.'

Rose nodded. 'At last I understand. We've no one called Geneviève in our family, but Élodie was insistent that she be called Geneviève Rose—Rose is my name. I'm glad to know why.'

Rudi looked back at her at last. 'For tomorrow, you don't think it would be a good surprise if...'

Rose was adamant. 'No, I do not. I think it would be a huge shock. Too much for her. I will explain everything when I ring her later.'

He appeared to accept that. Afternoon sunlight flooded the kitchen as he told Rose of his first meeting with Élodie. He laughed at a memory. 'We had been told not to enter into any "inessential liaisons" with the locals, as I explained. But the moment I saw Élodie, I knew that wouldn't be so. Those eyes, her directness. After all the death and misery I'd experienced, she was so full of life. I had to get to know her.'

Rose smiled warmly at his description. 'She was born with a rebellious spirit—but also a joy in life.'

The hall clock chimed the quarter hour.

'It's quarter past four.' Rose's voice rose in agitation. 'I think you should go. Please.'

Rudi stood and pocketed Élodie's address.

'I can't thank you enough, madame.'

'There'll be plenty of time for that, I hope. Now you must go.'

Rudi touched the photo tentatively. Rose picked it up and closed his hand over it. 'You will love her. Oh, and the train goes on the half-hour, every two hours. She gets home from work generally soon after four.'

'I shall catch the first that will arrive by that time.'

She went with him to the door. His gaze dropped to the egg basket. She smiled. 'My job now. Tell me, before you go, how did you get the black eye?'

Rudi shrugged. 'Most of your countrymen don't welcome a German these days.'

Rose sat back down at the table after he left. She couldn't wait to share Rudi's reaction to his daughter's photo. 'Just like his sister', he'd said. All in good time, she reasoned, but the doubt had at last been quashed. She got up and crossed the hall as the clock struck the half-hour. She picked up the receiver and gave the operator an Argentan number. As Élodie came to the phone, Rose heard the slow rumbling of the ancient tractor. No matter. Rudi would be well clear of the lane by now and Henri always took his time putting the tractor in the barn.

'Hello, Maman. I'll see you tomorrow.' Élodie sounded happy.

'Hello, *chérie*, but wait, I have news ... good news.'

'Oh Maman, at last some good news for you, I hope. And I have something to tell you too. Something important.'

'Oh?' Rose was suddenly apprehensive.

'I can't wait until tomorrow. Michel has asked me to marry him.'

'*What?*'

'Be glad for me, Maman. He's such a good man, and he loves Vevette as if she were his own.'

'But when, how—and what about your Rudi, Vevette's father?' Rose was dumbstruck. To think that Élodie was now faced with making a choice between two good men. What an unbearable irony.

'Maman, I fell in love—we fell in love—and part of me will always love Rudi. But I know with all my heart he'd have come back if he could. It's been so long now that I simply have to assume the worst. And I don't want to be lonely all my life. Most of all, Vevette needs a father—and she adores Michel. And Maman, in my way so do I.'

Rose closed her eyes and tightened her grip on the receiver. She'd heard that defiant tone in her daughter's voice. 'Yes, of course, but...'

Suddenly Henri was yelling. The cat was probably in his way again.

When the shotgun roared, Rose dropped the receiver.

'Maman, what was that? Maman?'

The question went unanswered. Rose couldn't speak. For a few moments, she stood rooted, her heart pounding like a trip-hammer. She forced herself across the room, holding on to the wall as she made for the door.

In the yard Rudi lay on his back, unmoving, his sightless eyes open, a huge hole rent in his jumper by the gun blast. Blood pooled beneath him, seeping darkly across the yard. Rose stared at Henri, who still held the shotgun.

'My God, Henri, what have you done? What in God's name have you done?' Rose stood trembling, aghast. This stranger, her husband: how had she so misjudged the depth of his bitterness?

'I told you not to encourage him.'

'Did you even talk to him?'

'No. He started to say something in that German way and that was enough. Five years more of them was enough.'

'But where was he?'

'Coming up the path from the henhouse as I drove in.'

Rose covered her face with both hands. The foolish boy. Why? Why had he let sentiment triumph over haste?

Henri laid the shotgun on the trailer coupled to the tractor.

'Why, Henri—what possessed you to do such a thing?' This was a living nightmare. Incomprehensible. This, when they had survived the entire war under the crushing oppression of occupation and the trauma imposed on the whole family. And they were all alive in spite of everything. 'It was, after all, a damned Frenchman who crippled you.'

'And a damned German who started it. Élodie's been through enough because of him. She's living a new life. Just when people here are settling down again, the last thing we need is any more reminders.'

'A new life on her own, telling lies that she's a war widow. What sort of life is that?'

'Better than with a bloody German. I've kept hoping that lovesick idiot friend of Félix would take her on.'

For a moment Rose remembered the abandoned telephone call. What would—what *could* she tell her daughter? Certainly not the truth. Not now, not ever. She put a hand to her brow as if to push all thoughts from her mind for the present. With a huge effort, she kept her voice steady, baulking at his description. 'I assume you mean Michel? If so, it would seem your wish is about to be granted.'

'Oh?' Henri looked at her for a long moment, then at the lifeless figure on the packed earth of the yard. 'Well, that's good. Now there's no competition.'

Rose grasped the old water trough, hardly able to believe what she was hearing. She grimaced as the sharp metal corner pierced her palm.

She watched as Henri hobbled across the yard and pulled himself into the tractor seat. He backed the trailer short of the lifeless figure, got down and hauled the dead weight up onto the wooden slats.

Rose grabbed his arm, her nails whitening the skin. 'What now?'

Henri looked away to the line of trees on the skyline that stood, ramrod straight, like soldiers at attention. His jaw was set in a stubborn jut. 'There's enough dead Germans under the fields out there.' He shook off her hand. 'One more won't matter.' He bent again for the rucksack, which lay beyond the pooled blood.

Rose pounced on the bag and swung it out of his reach. 'You'll leave that with me—you'll not bury the last trace of that poor boy.'

Henri shook his head, heaved himself back onto the throbbing machine and set off through the gate, the body jerking as the trailer bounced over the ruts.

Rose couldn't watch any more. She turned to survey the bloodstained yard and bent to retrieve the small square picture that was eddying towards the drain, retching as she did so at the coppery smell of warm blood. The smiling face of her infant granddaughter beamed up at her. Rose wiped the back of the photo on her apron and choked back a half-sigh, half-sob, utterly dazed in her grief. Would men never learn?

As she moved mechanically to the outside tap with a bucket to sluice the yard clean, she heard an unmistakable piping shriek. The swifts were back. Looking up, she saw four small brown bodies cleaving the clear air with their backswept wings, swooping and whirling as if seeking to outdo one another. Like damn humans really, Rose told herself as she bent numbly to her task.

In the silent farmhouse, as the sun dropped towards the horizon, the shadow of the dangling phone cord tracked across the wall until all trace of it was erased.

# Acknowledgements

For inspiration, my initial thanks must go to historian Antony Beevor, whose 2009 article on the treatment of Frenchwoman by their fellow countrymen after Liberation in 1944 gave me the germ of an idea that eventually became a feature element of *An Inessential Liaison*. These events form a complicated and fascinating topic. None of us can say with certainty what our reaction would have been—or indeed would be—to an occupying force, and the novel's heroine, Élodie, is herself surprised by her own reactions.

I additionally consulted many other books, documents and images during the writing process. These are too numerous to mention by name, but I would like to thank the staff at Tangmere Military Aviation Museum, near Chichester, for generously answering my questions during a visit there in 2021. Formerly the site of RAF Tangmere during the Second World War, this was the departure point for many SOE agents dropped clandestinely into France.

On a personal level, I owe a huge debt of gratitude to the group of female friends made during my translation studies, who have encouraged and supported me throughout both my subsequent writing marathon and the book's completion. In particular, I would like to thank Eve Anderson and Caroline Cronin, who acted as my alpha readers, steadfastly absorbing and commenting on chapters and chunks as the story progressed. For cheering me on from the sidelines, I am also grateful to (in alphabetical order) Penny Morris, Ann Patrick and Joan Sandford. Friends forever, my musketeers! Other friends such as Marianne Herrington and artist Julie Weir, who have offered a patient listening ear to progress reports, are also important to mention and thank.

For design advice on the front cover, I would like to thank Emily Blaxill. I am aware that I had strong ideas on how the cover should look, but Emily's help is gratefully acknowledged.

Last but not least, I thank my husband Andrew for his support at all times throughout both my studies and my many absent hours spent either staring at my computer screen or writing distractedly. I have broken it gently that a second book is in the offing...

And to you, my readers, I would like to add that I hope you have enjoyed *An Inessential Liaison*, and that you will wish to follow the story into that of the next generation, when Élodie's daughter is at the Sorbonne in the late 1960s.

## Sources

Beevor, A. (2009) 'An ugly carnival', *Guardian*, 5 June [Online].                    Available                    at: https://www.theguardian.com/lifeand-style/2009/jun/05/women-victims-d-day-landings-second-world-war.

Beevor, A. (2010) *D-Day: The Battle for Normandy*. London: Penguin Books.

# About the Author

In 2021 I took it into my head to do an MA in Novel Writing by distance learning, having completed an MA in Translation (French to English) earlier that year. *An Inessential Liaison*, the idea for which has been brewing for a few years now, is my first full-length novel. Another linked novel is to follow, whose events will be set during the French student revolt of 1968.

For my first dissertation I chose to translate into English a section of *Aux frontières de l'espoir* (Paris: Éditions Le Manuscrit, 2006), an autobiographical account of the exploits of Georges Loinger, a French-born Jew who helped hundreds of Jewish children escape to Switzerland during the Second World War. When this was published, in 2006, he had already reached the impressive age of 96. His death in December 2018 occurred when I had not long begun my Master's studies and was seeking a suitable text. With the 75th anniversary of D-Day in 2019 on the horizon, his inspiring memoirs seemed entirely apposite. For this endeavour and during my novel-writing studies I had to undertake in-depth research, which I found both fascinating and absorbing.

I have tried to ensure that no factual errors or inconsistencies have crept into *An Inessential Liaison*. As one small example, I narrowly avoided Félix smoking *Disque Bleu* as his cigarette of choice: careful checking confirmed the brand was not marketed until 1954. Such pitfalls are ever lurking to ensnare the writer of historical fiction, to the inevitable glee of the eagle-eyed reader who spots them!

As my day job, I have worked for many years as a freelance editor on a wide range of subjects. I am a member of the Society of Authors, the Alliance of Independent Authors, Jericho Writers and the Institute of Translators and Interpreters.

All of this matters not a jot to our dog, a far-too-clever wire-haired Hungarian Vizsla who has no hesitation in letting me know when writing inspiration must be cast aside for a while because it's walk time ...

I can be found on the following websites: https://www.frances-talbot.co.uk or https://www.hoppingharebooks.com

Or via social media as below.

 amazon.co.uk/

https://twitter.com/FrancesTalbot5

facebook.com/frances.talbot.33

instagram.com/frances.talbot.33/

linkedin.com/in/frances-talbot-11b9a554/

Printed in Great Britain
by Amazon

23561832R00199